From the Kiwi Kingdom Series

UNDER THE BLOWHOLES SPRAY

By

Rosemary Thomas

Titles previously published which are included in this book

RETURN of the KIWI KINGDOM

— Previously The Kiwi Kingdom.

- First Edition December 2010, by Dorrance Publishing
- Second Edition August 2013, by the Author
- Third Edition -.2018 by the Author

KEONI'S Kingdom

— Previously Rise of the Kiwi Kingdom.

-First Edition September 2013, by the Author.

Kupe Kiwi's Kingdom

— First Edition September 2013, by the Author.

Also, by Rosemary Thomas — The Islands

The Kiwi Kingdom is also on Facebook.

Information on release of titles in the Kiwi Kingdom series can be found on this page. This page also promotes the groups which care for Kiwis and other animals in the real Kiwi Kingdom in New Zealand.

Acknowledgements

Information about places, the species, distribution and the lives of Kiwi and other animals integrated into the story was obtained from the following sources:

http://en.wikipedia.org/wiki/Kiwi

http://www.nzhuntinginfo.com/game/tahr

http://www.nzhuntinginfo.com/game/chamois

http://www.wildaboutnz.co.nz/index/weasels

http://www.gorgeouscreatures.co.nz/NZ+Possum +Fur/Possum+History.html

Marshall Cavendish Animal world: Hedgehogs and Tenrecs 1993

http://trulyvictorian.com/history/1855.html

http://trulyvictorian.com/history/1869.html

www.premierclothing.com/shop/c/31-maid-uniforms-

http://www.victorianlondon.org/cassells

The Incredible Kiwi, a Wild South Book by Neville Peat

Road Atlas of New Zealand, Paul Hamlyn., 1975

Hema Maps, New Zealand handy Atlas, Rob Boegheim, 2010

The stories within this book and all the characters in them are pure fiction. Any similarities to events or people are a coincidence.

Titles in this Book

Keoni's Kingdom

Return of The Kiwi Kingdom

Kupe Kiwi's Kingdom

KEONI'S

KINGDOM

CHAPTER ONE

KAILEE'S LEGACY

Kamoku Kiwi gazed out on the ruffled waters of Lake Kaniere. In the darkness he could feel the approach of the coming storm. Threatening clouds now hid the starry sky.

As Kamoku waited for his mate kailee to deliver their latest child; he thought about their family. Their eldest son, Kamoku who bore his name, now lived at Punakaiki. Their other children were now scattered to other Kiwi communities, to have children of their own; except for Kaimi who lived nearby on the southern shore of Lake Kaniere. She was too young yet to mate and breed. *We still have time to have more children.* Kamoku thought as he made his way back to the burrow.

Kailee Kiwi was exhausted as she prepared to bring this child into the world. She had secretly hoped it would be her last child; but her knowledge that Kamoku wanted more children, made her wish seem very remote. *This egg seems larger and harder than usual* she thought. With a large grunt and all of her strength, Kailee finally expelled it. Her last act as a mother was to cocoon the egg with her body, as her spirit winged its way to join her ancestors.

Kamoku's call as he entered the burrow was met with silence. *She must be asleep* he thought with a smile; but when he found his mate's limp body entwined with the egg, he gazed at it with disbelief. With mounting grief that his mate was now beyond him and in fear of a now lonely future, Kamoku went to claw the egg from Kailee's embrace. He wanted to destroy it, for he also blamed the egg for the loss of his mate, but when he felt the still warm protective shell harbouring the new life within, Kamoku gently pushed the egg closer to his mate. Flashes of lightning penetrated the burrow and thunder rumbled overhead.

"You keep her company" Kamoku said to the egg, before turning to leave the burrow for he didn't want to stay now Kailee was gone.

Ignoring the breaking storm, Kuri Kiwi hurried through the forest. She knew her neighbour Kailee was due to deliver her egg at any time. Coming to Kailee's burrow, Kuri stopped in her tracks as she was confronted by the sight of Kamoku stumbling away from the burrow, his face full of grief. Swiftly she entered the burrow and searched the passages untill she came across Kailee's body still entwined with the egg. Kuri's maternal instinct took over as she ran over to the egg. It was still warm. Using her bill, she gently eased the egg onto her feet and sheltered it under her front feathers, before shuffling off to her own burrow; a big smile on her face.

I wonder what Kale will think of this? She thought.   For over six years now Kuri and her mate Kale had been together, with no sign of a family. They had settled into a comfortable companionship together, both of them accepting that there would be no children.

 Kale was listening to the storm's fury outside and hoping that Kuri was safe with Kailee, when he heard a rustle and shuffling at the entrance to their burrow. Wondering who it might be Kale went to investigate. He was not prepared for the sight of his mate, who was very bedraggled but with a triumphant beam on her face, the unmistakeable shape of a kiwi egg lay at her feet. At first Kale could only look at Kuri with astonishment, before he found his voice.

"Weren't you going to see Kailee?" Kale asked, not waiting for a reply.

The egg Kuri held required an explanation.   "I didn't know you were expecting a chick.

"I wasn't!" Kuri replied, as she gave herself a good shake to disperse some of the water from her dense grey feathery coat.   As she shuffled over to Kale, Kuri's triumph was replaced by anxiety, as she saw a frown cloud Kale's usually placid face

"I rescued it. Please can I keep it!" she pleaded.   "When I reached Kailee's burrow, I saw Kamoku leave. I could see he was grieving. I went in and found Kailee's body with the egg.   Please!" Kuri implored Kale, "This is Kailee's last child.   Can't we give it a chance?"

Kale's first instinct was to react as Kamoku did.   He wanted to send the egg back to Kailee.   He didn't want to bring up someone else's child.

"Did he see you?" Kale asked doubtfully.

"No, I'm sure he didn't.   Please! We don't have any of our own children."

Kale had never seen Kuri so vibrant or passionate.   He gazed at the egg. Judging by its size, it probably was a girl.   With a small glint in his eye, Kale agreed. "Alright then, on the condition we try making a brother for her."

"Oh, thank you!" Kuri's rapture was complete.   She gave Kale a cuddle, which was difficult with the egg lying between them.

When Kamoku's grief and had subsided, he felt a pang of guilt.   Kailee had tried so hard to protect the child – her last legacy for him.   It then occurred to Kamoku that he should try to save it.   *Kaimi might be able to help incubate the egg.* He thought as he went back to sit on it, only to find it had disappeared.

3

Shrugging Kamoku returned outside. *Maybe some animal has taken it to eat. They will need some luck.* He thought grimly. After Kamoku took a last look at Kailee and the tunnels that had been home for him and his family for so long he set off, for he couldn't stay here now that Kailee's spirit was beyond him. He would visit their children, he decided as he made his way through the cool wet forest

Some stars could be seen as the storm clouds cleared away amongst the Southern Alps. Lightning flashes lit up the snow-capped peaks towards the east. Thunder could still be heard rumbling in the distance.

Kaimi was feeding near the lake shore after the previous night's storm. The downpour had fetched some tasty worms closer to the surface. She heard some footsteps coming through the trees and turned to see her father's familiar form approaching.

Dad, how is Mum? Has she delivered her egg yet?"   She was looking forward to meeting her new sister or brother.

He nodded gravely. Kaimi knew immediately that something was wrong.

"What has happened?" she asked, looking into his sad eyes.

"Mum delivered the egg, but her spirit had left her when I found her." Kamoku's voice broke. Kaimi was silent as her spirit felt the emptiness left behind, now her mother had gone.

"What about the egg? Is it being kept warm?" Kaimi asked anxiously. Before Kaimi had left the family burrow to join the other young kiwis in the community who were too young to breed, Kailee had given her advice on how to look after her own egg when her time came.

Kamoku hung his head and shuffled awkwardly. "It's gone!"

"What do you mean, it's gone?" Kaimi asked in disbelief.

"I was so upset when I found your mother, I tucked it near her and left." He said sheepishly. "When I went back to sit on it, it had gone. I expect some animal has eaten it." Kamoku sighed. The guilt of not caring for his last child was beginning to weigh heavily on his mind.

"Is there any sign it was eaten?" Kaimi asked. "Was there any shell lying around?"

"No, I didn't see anything." Kamoku replied shrugging.

"I'm off to see your brothers and sisters.   Would you like to come with me?" Kamoku asked hopefully.

4

At her father's words, both grief and anger washed over her.   He had abandoned his child! Her sister or brother!   Then she felt a glimmer of hope.   If there was no sign of the egg, maybe someone was looking after it.

"Thanks for asking me dad, but I'm happy here." Kaimi said firmly. "Perhaps when I'm older?"

Kamoku nodded sadly.   He had hoped for some company on his long journey.   Kaimi gave him a quick hug. "Take care and look after yourself."

She then watched until he disappeared into the depths of the forest. Instinct told Kaimi that she should go to the family burrow, but it was bed time and she was tired.   She resolved to go tonight.

When she reached her parents burrow, Kaimi found her instincts had been right.   A number of kiwis were gathered at the entrance.   Someone was calling "Kailee! Are you there?"

"Excuse me" Kaimi said as she pushed through the crowd. "What is happening here?"

"Who are you?" someone asked.

"I am Kaimi, Kamoku and Kailee's daughter."

"We heard Kamoku has left. We knew Kailee was due to deliver, we want to know what has happened."

Drawing herself up with as much dignity as her small body would allow, Kaimi faced the crowd. "I have some sad news for you. After her delivery, Mum's spirit left her.   Dad came to give me the news and has gone to visit the rest of our family."

"Will he be coming back?"

"I don't know, but to respect our mother, this burrow is to stay empty when our family is away."

At this news, the crowd dispersed, except for Kuri, who had joined the crowd after Kale had relieved her from sitting on the egg.

"There's a crowd at Kamoku's burrow. You had better see what is happening." Kale had warned Kuri when he came in.

"Would you like some company while you visit your mother?" Kuri asked.

Kaimi was going to refuse, but after seeing the kindness in Kuri's eyes, changed her mind. "Yes please."

Kuri let Kaimi lead the way as she tentatively made her way to where her mother still lay. Her body curled up to protect something.

"Oh Mum!" Kaimi wailed when she saw her mother.

Kuri took Kaimi into her arms and held her as she cried out her grief.

"What are we going to do?" Kaimi asked when she had recovered her composure. "We can't just leave mum here like this."

"You can bury her here or take her outside and cover her." Kuri suggested.

"I will bury her here." Kaimi decided.

Together Kuri and Kaimi dug a hollow and gently placed Kailee into it. Afterwards Kuri led Kaimi into the forest for some sphagnum moss, bringing back bundles to lie along the tunnel where Kailee now rested. Gazing at the tunnel where her mother lay, Kaimi was pensive.

"We may never know what happened."

"You are talking about the egg?"

"Yes."

Kuri was silent for a moment. Then very quietly she spoke. "Your mother didn't die in vain."

Kaimi looked at Kuri with astonishment. "You mean it is being cared for?" Kuri nodded.

"Oh 'thank you!" Kaimi gave Kuri a hug.

"Are you going to stay here or return to the southern shore? Kuri asked.

"I think I will stay for a while. It isn't often we get a burrow to ourselves!"

Kuri laughed. "Yes, enjoy it while you can. Our burrow will be extra busy in a moon or so when our child is due." She confided.

"That means you will have two eggs to hatch!" Kaimi was concerned. "Can I help? After all, it is my sister or brother you are caring for."

"I will talk to Kale." Kuri promised.

As she left Kaimi's burrow and made her way to her own burrow, Kuri could feel she was being watched.

"She will be alright." Kuri said aloud to all the eyes and ears hidden in the forest.

She took a quick feed on the way home for Kale would want a feed too when she returned. Kale was glad to see Kuri return to relieve him. He wasn't used to being confined like this.

"You were gone for a while, what happened? Kale asked.

"Kamoku and Kailee's daughter Kaimi came up from the southern shore to see Kailee. I helped Kaimi bury her mother. She is staying on at the burrow for now." Kuri then looked at Kale with a little smile. "We will be extra busy from the next moon." Kale looked at Kuri with surprise.

Kuri gave a little nod. "Yes, our own egg will be due then!"

As Kale started to look alarmed at the prospect of looking after two eggs, Kuri intervened.

"Kaimi knows her mother's egg is being cared for. She wants to help."

Kale didn't need any persuading this time. He nodded his agreement. "It's only right that she helps with her brother or sister."

A routine was quickly established where Kaimi took her turn to sit on the egg when Kuri or Kale wanted a break. A month later she saw Kuri deliver her own egg. Kaimi noticed how much thinner the shell was and became worried whether her brother or sister could escape their shell.

One dark moonless night they heard movement and tapping as the chick attempted to break out of the shell. Not waiting, Kaimi attempted to break the shell with her bill, but had no success.

Using her claw Kaimi picked up a sharp stone she had kept, just in case and banged the shell as hard as she could. After a couple of blows, a crack began to form. The chick saw the crack and began to tap furiously until the shell finally broke. Kaimi helped to open the remaining shell and could hardly believe her eyes. Her new brother looked just like their mother! He had a determined look in his eyes that showed he would be a leader one day.

"What would you like to call him?" Kuri asked softly

"He will be Keoni." Kaimi replied, "Welcome to your world my brother."

Keoni was feeling confused. There were two females looking at him. Which one was his mother? He looked at Kuri's bigger frame and kind eyes and decided she must be Mum. Keoni looked at Kuri with his already wise eyes to imprint her on his mind before closing his eyes for a well-earned sleep.

As Keoni began his new life, on the other side of the world in rural Surrey, fourteen-year-old Emily was also beginning her new life. As she stood in front of her mirror, Emily's heart sank at the sight of her new uniform; for she was to be sent to the Manor house to assist the nanny to care for Lord Applebee's children.

Was it only a week ago? Emily thought of when she had come home from a ramble in the nearby bluebell woodland to find the housekeeper waiting for her with tears in her eyes.

"Miss Emily, there is a lilac dress on your bed. Will you please change and join your mother in the drawing room?"

Quickly Emily ran upstairs to change. She knew something serious was happening. When Emily came downstairs, her mother was dressed in black, sitting looking bleakly at the garden.

The news that her father had died brought much change and upheaval in the following days. Emily missed her father's return from London for the weekends, his presence invigorating the usually quiet household. However, he had left many debts to be paid, leaving Emily's mother penniless. Her mother had to make a visit to the local manor house to visit her sister-in-law Lady Amelia.

"Is there anything you can do to help us?" she pleaded. "I don't know how I am going to live and look after Emily too."

"Emily is fourteen, now isn't she?" Lady Amelia asked thoughtfully. When Emily's mother nodded, she added "I'm in need of an assistant for the nanny."

"Thank you." Emily's mother replied with relief.

It was arranged that Emily would be given one day off per week to see her mother, who had found a room in the village where she was able to keep herself with dressmaking.

With the nanny's permission Emily would amuse the children by drawing and painting pictures of the animals and flowers they saw when they were taken for their daily walks. She also showed the older girls how to embroider their dresses, which impressed their friends when they came to visit. Her new life was so different to her carefree and sheltered upbringing where she had a private tutor, the remainder of her days spent sewing, painting, reading and exploring the nearby woodlands.

CHAPTER TWO

KEONI'S HOME

Keoni stepped out of Kale's burrow with wonder at the sights, sounds and smells of the forest. Ferns sprouted all around him. The trunks of Pongees soared up to spread their fronds to make a lacy green roof over him. The call of a morepork owl echoed through the trees. *What animal is that?* Keoni wondered. He revelled in the earthy damp smell of the forest. The sweet fragrance of Wisteria wafted by him as it trailed down a nearby tree.

"Hurry up" Kale grumbled when he saw Keoni lingering by the burrow. "We haven't got all night!" He was keen to get off for his own feed.

Suddenly Keoni felt movement under his foot. Keoni lifted his foot up and looked down perplexed.

"What's the matter?" Kale asked.

"I felt something under my foot!"

"That is your meal. Put your bill in and pull it out."

Keoni quickly did as he was told and to his delight found and retrieved his first worm. Kaimi followed behind them as Kale led the way through the forest, tapping the floor with his bill to feel the vibrations of any worms moving nearby. Keoni soon became aware they were being watched.

"There is someone watching us!" He said, instinctively turning to Kaimi for support. Kale noticed Keoni's rush to Kaimi. *"I wonder if he knows"* Kale thought as he stopped and came back to support the two younger kiwis. He too had felt the eyes watching, but had ignored them.

"It's alright Keoni." Kaimi reassured him. "It's only our neighbours, curious to see what you look like."

"But, why don't they come out and say Hello?" With a firm tone that surprised everyone watching, Keoni called out loudly. "If you are there, Come Out"!

Suddenly they were surrounded on all sides by kiwis, all eager for a look at Kailee's legacy. When the neighbours eventually left them alone to continue their feed, many comments were ringing in Keoni's ears.

"He's so like his mother!"

"He is going to be bigger than his father!"

"Will he take over the family burrow now?"

Keoni had been puzzled why Kale had been distant and impatient. Suddenly he knew. Kale and Kuri weren't his parents, but where were they? Keoni looked at Kaimi with puzzled eyes.

"Where are Mum and Dad?" he asked.

"I will show you later." She replied with a heavy heart. Kaimi had hoped she would not have to discuss their mother's death so soon.

"I want to go now!" Keoni demanded. To him it suddenly seemed urgent.

"You take him." Kale said to Kaimi with a smile, happy his child-minding duties would end for now.

As Kaimi led Keoni through the dense forest, he stopped her.

"Kaimi, what happened to Mum and Dad?"

Kaimi gave a sigh as she stopped. "I'm sorry Keoni, Mum died when you were born. She is buried in the family burrow. We have brothers and sisters in other communities. Dad has gone to tell them." Keoni knew there was something she hadn't told him.

"Dad didn't stay to look after me?"

Kaimi hung her head. How could she tell him without hurting his feelings?

"Dad was so upset when he found Mum had died that he left your egg with mum. Kuri came to see Mum and saw Dad leave. When she found your egg, she took it home to look after."

"So, Dad didn't want me." Keoni's voice was flat, trying to disguise the hurt he felt.

"After he got over the shock, dad did go back for you, but your egg had gone." Kaimi replied with a little smile. "He thought some animal had taken your egg to eat."

"He doesn't know I'm here?"

"Not yet," Kaimi replied with a little laugh, "but he will do. I'm expecting him to come back for me some day."

"He doesn't want to live here anymore?"

"No. Now that Mum's gone, he is starting a new life."

They continued their journey to the burrow in silence, but there was something that bothered Keoni.

He had also noticed the egg that Kuri and Kale were incubating was quite thin and fragile.

"Kaimi, if dad left me, I would have died too!"

Kaimi had been dreading this question, but managed to stay calm as she replied.

"Mum's body was still keeping you warm, so you were quite safe when Kuri found you."

Young as he was, Keoni was now aware how lucky he was to be alive. He resolved to make the most of this life he had been given.

Kaimi stopped at a thick bush with multi-coloured leaves. (Humans know it as Pepper Tree) She pulled a low branch back to reveal the entrance to a burrow.

"Welcome to our family home." Kaimi said as she led the way in, but stopped abruptly as they heard a scratching noise ahead.

"Who's there? What are you doing in my home?" Keoni called out loudly.

The scratching stopped and the sound of shuffling quickly faded as the intruder escaped from another entrance. Keoni followed Kaimi into the unfamiliar tunnels, but he felt a strange sense of coming home, and let out a happy sigh. Kaimi heard the sigh.

"What's wrong?"

"Nothing's wrong. I feel I've come home."

Keoni's reply brought a smile to her face, but turned to tears when they reached the tunnel where their mother lay. The sphagnum moss was in disarray, the soil had been dug to reveal their mother, still curled up to protect the new life she had produced.

"What were they doing? Why can't they leave her in peace?" Kaimi wailed.

Keoni's instinct told him the intruder was trying to move their mother in order to take over the burrow, but kept quiet about his fears. Instead he started to recover his mother, saying a silent goodbye to her as he worked. Afterwards Keoni was thoughtful as he looked at the tunnel where their mother lay.

"We need to find a way to protect mum. Can you show me the rest of the burrow? Keoni asked, as an idea was forming in his mind. Kaimi led him through the dark tunnels till finally she stopped.

"This is where we came in."

Keoni walked back down the last tunnel and faced a wall.

"Does anyone live this side of us?"

"No." Kaimi was puzzled. "There is a stream that way."

"Good!" Keoni replied and started digging.

"What are you doing?" Kaimi asked.

"I'm building some new tunnels for my new home. The only way to protect Mum is to completely block up the one she is in."

With a smile Kaimi started to help him, moving the loose soil to its new home. At the end of a long and tiring night there was no sign of the tunnel where their mother lay, but two new ones. The first tunnel was a cosy space where Keoni intended to sleep. At the end Keoni had gouged deep claw shaped marks into the wall, filling them with moss. The second tunnel led to the bank of the nearby stream; the entrance hid by a bush.

"Welcome to my Kingdom." Keoni said to Kaimi when they were finished.

In the early morning light Keoni and Kaimi made their way down to the lake shore, feeding as they went. They knew they were watched, but ignored the watching eyes, taking a paddle in the placid waters of the eastern bay. (Known to humans as Hans Bay) As they paddled Keoni gazed at the islands in the bay and the hills and mountains around the lake. He wondered what kind of animals lived there. Sometime soon he would go and explore.

"Don't go out of your depth and watch out for the eels!" Kaimi warned him as she spotted Keoni making attempts to swim. "They have sharp teeth that can bite off your claws! I should go back to Kale's burrow in case they want a break from sitting on the egg." She added with a yawn.

"I will come with you." Keoni said as they made their way back. "I want to thank Kuri." At Kaimi's enquiring look he added "Without her I wouldn't be here."

Kaimi nodded and smiled. For one so young, Keoni was so wise. She knew then Keoni was no ordinary child and was so glad she had saved him. At Kale's burrow they found him to be in a bad mood.

"Where were you last night? You are supposed to be helping us!" Kale snarled.

Before Kaimi could apologise, Keoni intervened.

"Leave her alone!" Keoni shouted at him. "Kaimi is "helping", not taking over your duties!"

Kale was surprised at the ferocity of Keoni's response and had the grace to look ashamed. Keoni then went over to Kuri and gave her a cuddle.

"Thank you for saving me."

"No." Kuri shook her head. "It is Kaimi you should thank." At Keoni's enquiring look, "She cracked open the egg so you could get out."

"Then I need to thank you both." giving Kaimi a cuddle too.

Keoni looked at the egg tucked firmly under Kuri's large frame and turned to Kale.

"Please try to look after your daughter!" Then he stomped off to his burrow for a well-earned sleep, leaving the astonished kiwis behind him.

As Keoni walked away, Kale and Kuri looked at each other.

"It's a Girl!" Kuri tried not to be excited, given that Kale had wanted a boy. "What will we call her?" she asked.

Kale was thoughtful. Even though he was disappointed he wouldn't have a son to carry on his name, he knew Kuri was happy.

"We will call her Kaimani." Kale decided. "It means Diamond. Kaimani will be our diamond."

Keoni and Kaimi woke one damp and gloomy evening. She had been sharing his burrow while she was helping Kuri and Kale hatch their egg. When Kaimi set out for Kuri's burrow Keoni decided to come too. She looked at him puzzled, as he didn't usually bother to come, then she realised why he wanted to come.

"Kaimani is due to be hatched, isn't she?"

Keoni nodded with a smile.

"How did you know?"

Keoni shrugged. "I can't say how, I just know she will be here when we get there."

In Kale's burrow they found Kuri alone with Kaimani. Keoni looked with delight at the little kiwi as she snuggled at her mother's feet and peered from under her mother's feathers with bright little eyes.

13

Was I really that small? Keoni thought as he gazed at her fluffy grey form. He smiled as their eyes met. Kaimani gave a happy sigh and followed Keoni's every move for the remainder of their visit.

"I think she is attached to you!" Kuri observed with amusement.

"I don't mind." Keoni's tone was light, but his mind was in turmoil. When Keoni and Kaimani's eyes met, they formed a bond that Lasted their lifetimes, but images flashed in his mind that told him he would have to risk his life to protect her.

As Keoni was settling into his new home, Emily was settling into hers. She shared a small room with the nanny next to the nursery where the children slept. Between their beds stood a small dresser which held a drawer each for their clothes and belongings. On top stood their candle, for when they had to attend to the children at night, which was often.

The youngest child was teething and needed to be comforted as well as having regular feeds by the wet nurse. The older children also needed to be nursed through the childhood illnesses as they swept through the community.

Each morning the fires in the nursery had to be lit before the children rose for the day. After the children had been woken and helped to dress, Emily would fetch their meals from the kitchen before serving the children their breakfast. Nanny and Emily then took turns to join the other servants to have their own breakfast in the large kitchen. This was usually a silent meal apart from greetings to new arrivals at the table. Many of the servants worked long days, starting their day early in the morning and finishing late in the evening, with little spare time left of their own.

After breakfast the children would be taken for a walk or delivered to the stables for their riding lessons before the tutor arrived to give the older children their lessons. After lunch the children were supervised in activities such as painting or needlework before they were allowed to play a game, a favourite part of the day for the children. After the children were served their tea, they were given their baths before being tucked into bed for a bedtime story. Cleaning and tidying of the nursery were also part of Emily's duties throughout the day Emily and the nanny would then take turns to have their dinner before retiring for the night. They considered themselves lucky to be sleeping in a warm room next to the nursery and not have to join the other servants in the attic which was both cramped and cold, especially in winter.

CHAPTER THREE

KEONI MEETS ORION OWL

The night sky was covered in heavy cloud, and the smell of rain filled the air as Keoni was out feeding. Kaimi had returned to the southern shore of the lake to be near her friends. Kaimani was looking after herself now and chose to go with her.

Come and visit us soon." Kaimi implored him. "I don't like you being alone here with the adults."

"I will" he promised, "But I want to meet some of the animals that live here."

"Why?" Kaimi was puzzled.

"They are part of our world too. I want to make friends with them."

In the forest all was quiet except for some squawking and fluttering in the tree above him. Keoni knew there was a family of owls up there. Kaimi had told him about them. He had seen the parents flying in and out to feed the three chicks in the hollow, formed high in the branches. Keoni stood back and looked up to see what the fuss was about.

With an extra loud screech, a small brown and white feathered owlette tumbled down. Vainly trying to flap its wings and grab hold of the mossy tree trunk as it fell; landing with a loud thump on the thick layer of leaf litter on the forest floor. Keoni looked with interest at this owl from the tree tops. He hadn't seen one on the ground before. Keoni waited patiently for the owl to recover, as he lay prone with his wings spread out wide, his chest heaving as he tried to regain his breath. Above in the tree there was a tentative call as the owl's sister Olivia called down to him.

"Orion! Are you alright?"

Keoni looked up to see two owlettes looking down at them anxiously.

"Now look what you've done!" she added in exasperation to her brother Ogilvie, who was starting to look ashamed.

"I didn't mean to!" he wailed.

Orion put his head up and started to look around. As he gathered his wings he froze, for there in front of him stood one of the creatures he had seen, combing the forest floor for worms. It had a long bill, much longer than his beak and had long claws. They were longer than his too!

15

"Hello" the creature said. "I'm Keoni. Are you alright?"

Very carefully Orion stood up and stretched his wings. They were still covered in white fluffy down, so he wasn't able to fly yet. He then stretched out each foot, opening and closing his claws. They worked too. By this time Olivia was screaming at him.

"Orion, Talk to us!"

With a sigh Orion looked up.

"Calm down, I'm alright."

"Can you get back up?

Orion looked at the tree trunk doubtfully. "I don't know. I may have to stay down here untill I can fly." Orion then looked at Keoni. He saw kindness in his eyes. This creature's eyes at least were smaller than his!

"Hello Keoni, I'm Orion. What sort of creature are you?"

"I'm a Kiwi. I'm a bird like you, only my wings are too small so we live on the ground."

At that moment, Orion spotted a moth flutter out of reach above his head. "I wish I could fly." He sighed.

"It will be another week or two before I can chase it."

Keoni quickly stepped forward and with a snap trapped the moth in his bill. Slowly and carefully he brought the moth to Orion's beak. Just as carefully Orion enclosed the moth with his beak. Orion answered Keoni's smile with his own.

"Thank you." He said.

"Are there any more for us?" Ogilvie was now Jealous. They would have to wait untill mum or dad came back, which could be some time. Orion tried climbing back up the tree trunk, but it was too tall. He didn't have the strength to cling on and climb too. After several attempts he gave up.

"I'm staying down here untill I can fly." Orion called up to Olivia.

"Take care." She replied as heavy drops of rain began to fall.

"You can shelter with me." Keoni said making sure Orion was able to keep up as they made their way through the forest. When they reached the pepper tree both Keoni and Orion were quite wet.

Orion was quite happy to follow when Keoni ducked under the bush to shelter from the rain. As they shook themselves dry Keoni saw that Orion had spotted the opening into the ground and smiled.

"Welcome to my home."

As the rain drops started to penetrate the pepper tree Keoni led Orion into the tunnels. When Orion's eyes had adjusted to the gloom he was fascinated by this new world. Down a short tunnel Orion saw a claw mark on the wall.

"Who made this?" he asked, feeling the power of the symbol.

"I did." Keoni replied quietly. "This is where I sleep."

Orion nodded. Suddenly he felt very humble as he felt his new friend would become a power in his world and for generations to come.

"Are you still hungry?" Keoni asked after he had shown Orion the tunnels.

"I am, a little bit." Orion admitted, but didn't want to complain.

"Good, I'm hungry too. Come on; let's see what we can find." Then lead Orion back to the surface. As Orion followed, he spotted a beetle scuttling down the tunnel. Quickly he pounced on it. Keoni turned around to see his new friend happily munching.

"You like beetles too?" Keoni asked. Orion nodded. "We get plenty of those, especially when it rains."

"I'm going to enjoy it here." Orion managed to say as he finished the beetle.

Back at the hollow Olivia and Ogilvie were being questioned by their mother Odette who was alarmed to find Orion had completely disappeared.

"Where's Orion?" she asked.

"He's gone." Ogilvie answered miserably and shuffled nervously, hoping Olivia wouldn't dob him in for being too rough as he and Orion played, resulting in Orion falling out.

"What do you mean, he's gone?" Odette's anxiety was mounting.

"He fell out."

Odette looked down at the ground surrounding the tree. There was no sign of Orion.

"What happened to him?"

"Orion tried to climb back up but couldn't. He met one of those creatures with long beaks and went off with him."

"Do you mean one of the Kiwis?" Odette was still anxious. "How big was the Kiwi?"

"He was about the same size as Orion only he had longer claws!" Ogilvie added with wide eyes.

"His name is Keoni." Olivia added.

"We can only hope Orion can get enough to eat." Odette said with concern.

"Don't worry mum," Olivia added, "Keoni caught a big moth and gave it to him."

Odette was astonished. "The Kiwi fed him?" Olivia nodded.

"Mum," Ogilvie interrupted, "Where's our dinner? I'm starving."

Absently Odette passed them the mice she had caught, her mind on the young kiwi that had helped their son. During the ages that owls and kiwis had shared this land, there had never been any communication between them. She had seen the young kiwi that had chosen to live here among the adults and now he was looking after Orion. She decided to meet him.

In the tunnels Orion found so many beetles, he decided to leave some for his next feed. With his hunger satisfied he happily followed Keoni outside. At the entrance Keoni stopped.

"When we get outside you may feel that we are being watched. It is only the adults in our kiwi community. If they want to speak to us, they will come out."

By now it had stopped raining. All the leaves on the plants and the moss trailing down from the trees glistened with raindrops. As they walked Orion grew to love all the different kinds of ferns and pongees that he had missed from his view in the tree top.

It would be easy to hide amongst them he thought as he spotted insects he had never seen before sheltering under the leaves. He also could see the birds eyeing him with suspicion from the trees. Orion watched Keoni pull out a worm and hold it up with his claw.

"Have you eaten worms before?" Keoni asked.

"No, but I will try anything once." Orion replied, knowing he was being tested.

Gently he closed his beak over the slippery creature to hold it, and then sucked it into his mouth quickly before swallowing it with a large gulp.

"What do you think of them?" Keoni asked in the following silence.

"I think I will keep to my moths and beetles!" Orion replied with a smile. Suddenly out of the corner of his eye he saw movement in the bushes. Quickly he pounced and caught a mouse. He resisted the impulse to swallow it and held it out to Keoni who had a big grin on his face as he knew what was coming.

"No," Keoni said, before Orion could ask, "I haven't eaten mice before, and I will give it a try!"

Solemnly Orion held out the mouse. Keoni grabbed it with his bill, tossed it in the air and opened his bill as wide as he could and hoped it would slide straight down. But the fur seemed to catch in his throat and he nearly choked! Trying to stay calm he extended his neck, eventually the mouse moved down past his throat and he could look at Orion again, this time with a big smile.

"I think I will keep to my worms!" Keoni declared with some relief. They both were happy to eat their own food after that contest.

Keoni then showed Orion some of his favourite places. They sneaked down to the stream by his burrow, to watch and listen to the water as it flowed past them, being careful not to wake the pukekos who were asleep in the bulrushes nearby. A visit was made to a large fallen tree, covered in lichen and moss. Keoni started to probe the fragile bark with his bill and to Orion's amazement brought out a large beetle.

"Have you room for another one?" Keoni asked.

"You can put it back. I'm full!" Orion declared. "We know where it is if I get hungry."

Keoni carefully put the bewildered beetle back in its spot before taking Orion to a cave he had found. On the ceiling were glow worms, their blue lights twinkling in the dark space.

"What are they?" Orion asked. His parents hadn't told him about these creatures!

"They are glow worms." Keoni replied. "Hello Gabrielle." He added quietly.

On hearing her name, Gabrielle turned on all the lights along her silky thread, to illuminate the cave and her friends, who looked like a bunch of white silky streamers swaying from the ceiling. Orion noticed some of them had insects trapped in their threads.

"Hello Keoni," Gabrielle replied. "Who have you brought to see us?" she asked.

This is Orion owl." Keoni introduced him to them. "He fell out of his tree and is staying with me untill he can fly."

"We sometimes have owls share the cave with us. You are welcome to stay with us if you ever need somewhere to live." Gabrielle offered to Orion.

"Thank you." Orion was touched. He hadn't expected such kindness from creatures he hadn't met before. "We will come to see you again."

"Please do. We like to have visitors." Gabrielle said before turning off the lights along her tail to join her friends. As Keoni and Orion left the cave they took a final look at the soft blue lights on the ceiling before making their way through the forest.

"Are you able to see the lake from your tree?" Keoni asked.

"What is a lake?" Orion asked with a yawn. It would be daylight soon and after such an eventful night, he was starting to get tired. Normally he would be asleep by now.

"It will be our last stop," Keoni replied "before we go to bed."

As they walked through the forest, Orion was amazed to see birds he had never seen before, beginning to move through the trees, and to hear their calls.

"Here is the lake." Keoni said as he parted some flax.

Orion stood next to Keoni on the soft grey gravel beach. Before him lay a large area of water that rippled in the early morning breeze. It was surrounded by forest and in the distance hills and mountains rose, their tops hidden by clouds.

"Would you like a paddle?" Keoni asked.

Orion was wary of the dark waters that lay before him and watched with astonishment as Keoni wadded into the water and splashed about.

"Come on!" Keoni encouraged him with a grin. "The water isn't as cold today."

Very cautiously Orion approached the water and put a claw in. It was wet and cold! He tried a paddle but quickly returned to the shore, finding a log to climb and sit on while Keoni played in the shallows. While he was waiting, Orion noticed some of his downy feathers were loose and started to preen.

"Have you tried to fly yet?" Keoni asked when he joined Orion.

"No, I'm not sure I will be able to untill all these downy feathers have gone."

As Orion spoke a pair of ducks glided in to land to land on the lake in front of them. The noise of a bird's alarm call startled them and they quickly took to flight again.

"Did you see how they landed and took off?" Keoni asked with excitement.

Orion nodded and stood up on the log, spreading his wings and starting to flap them. His wings still felt very heavy with the extra down on them.

"Come on." Keoni encouraged him as he started running down the beach.

Orion launched himself off the log as he flapped his wings and was elated to feel the wind lift him into the air briefly and glided down onto the beach in front of Keoni, nearly landing on his face, remembering to put his feet out at the last moment.

"You did it!" Keoni shouted as he ran up to Orion with a big grin which was answered by his own.

"Yes, but I need lots of practice though."

"We will come down every night." Keoni promised. Orion nodded his agreement and they happily returned to the forest for a well-earned sleep.

In the forest of the bay an owl had been watching the pair with much interest. *Who was the owl who had obviously left their nest too early? She thought. Their parents would be worried about them; and who was the young Kiwi who was helping him? Tonight, she would find out!"*

Keoni was thankful he had Orion for company when he slept that day. He kept waking up from strange dreams – dreams of a tall creature that terrified him. The creature was dark and very tall. The creature's body was bare except for black very long "fur" on its head. It wore a strange garment that swished about the body as the creature moved and wore a cover of kiwi feathers on its back. This creature was chasing him!

As Keoni and Orion left the burrow that night they could hear owls calling to each other.

"That's interesting." Orion commented as they wandered through the ferns.

"What's interesting?" Keoni asked.

"One of the owls is calling mum to see if she has lost anyone." Orion replied.

"She must have seen us on the beach." Keoni said with a grin. Orion nodded his agreement.

Before going to the lake Keoni took Orion down to the stream by his burrow to look for the large green frog he had wanted to meet, but it wasn't to be seen.

They meandered down to the lake shore, feeding as they went.

When Keoni went into the water for his paddle, Orion sat on the log preening. More of the downy feathers were loose and his wings were feeling lighter. He was flapping his wings as he prepared to try flying again when he saw a familiar form flying down to him.

"Mum!" Orion called as Odette glided in to land next to him. She had a mouse in her beak.

"You can give that to Olivia or Ogilvie." Orion told her. "I've already eaten.

"Are you sure?" Odette asked. She was happy though that he was able to feed himself. Orion nodded.

Keoni had seen Odette fly in and guessed it would be Orion's mother. He came over to join them.

"Mum, this is Keoni. I have been staying with him after I fell out of our tree." Orion said as he introduced them.

"Hello Keoni. Thank you for looking after Orion. Kiwis and owls don't usually mix with each other so I am interested to know why you are doing it." Odette said curiously.

Keoni thought for a moment then surprised her by asking her a question.

"When you listen to the "voices" around the lake, what do you hear?"

Odette listened to the sounds of the night. An owl was calling its mate. A pair of ducks quacked noisily as they greeted a visitor.

A frog could be heard croaking in the nearby stream. The steady clicking of a bat sounded overhead as it searched for food, and a Kiwi could be heard challenging an intruder near their burrow.

"I hear all different animals." Odette replied puzzled.

"Yes." Keoni said with a smile. "All the different animals here are part of our kingdom too. I want to meet and make friends with them all to make a community we all can be part of."

"What sort of community would it be?" Odette was intrigued.

"We would still live the same, but we would respect and look out for each other and make sure no-one was ever harmed. We could have social gatherings for all the animals at the lake to make friends."

Odette saw the enthusiasm in Keoni's eyes and knew this young kiwi was starting something that would change their lives! Every night while Orion was practicing his flying and gliding along the beach, Odette would visit. She also brought her friends along with her to meet Keoni and to hear about his plans for the community. Soon all the owls around the lake and the valleys beyond it knew about Keoni Kiwi and the new community he was bringing to them.

As Keoni was making new friends, Emily had also made a new friend. On fine days the nanny would allow Emily to take the older children to the stable where their father or Jimmy the groom was waiting to give them riding lessons on their ponies. Jimmy looked after the horses in the stables and helped in the fields on the manor farm. Jimmy had grown up on a small farm with his family untill he was ten years old when his mother became ill and passed away from consumption (tuberculosis). His father was unable to look after his young family which were then parted.

The three younger children, Harriett who was six; Annabelle eighteen months and three years old Edward were sent to an orphanage where they were adopted by a couple with no children. Jimmy's father encouraged him to go with him to Wales where there was promise of regular work in the coal mines. Jimmy preferred to work in the outdoors and remained behind to seek work and shelter as best as he could. For several years, a bed in the hayloft and a meal at the end of the day were exchanged for help on local farms. Eventually Jimmy found a secure position on Lord Applebee's estate after he was recommended by a friend that Jimmy had worked for.

At first Jimmy and Emily only exchanged a smile when they met before they gained the courage to greet each other. They had to be so careful when they spoke or smiled that their feelings didn't show in case one of the children told the adults.

CHAPTER FOUR

THE NEW LEADER

The new moon had appeared as Keoni foraged in the forest. He sensed the approach of a bird and looked up to see Orion silently weaving his way through the trees to land in the tree next to him. During Orion's time with Keoni he had become expert at flying under the forest canopy, to the envy of Olivia and Ogilvie whose flying skills were yet to match his.

"Hello Orion" Keoni called softly. "How is your family?"

Before Orion could reply, a scream filled the air and the sound of a fleeing animal was coming towards them. A bedraggled and terrified pukeko Keoni recognised as his friend Pio rushed past them, followed closely by Kuma, one of the adult kiwis.

"Stop!" Keoni shouted as he stepped between them. "Why are you chasing the Pukeko?"

Kuma could hardly believe his eyes. Barring his way stood the young kiwi Keoni. Keoni's eyes pierced his own, his voice filled with anger. Keoni's claw was raised ready to strike. Kuma grudgingly admired the courage of the young kiwi who dared to challenge him, showing no fear in the face of a much larger opponent.

"Why are you chasing the Pukeko?" Keoni asked again as Kuma hesitated.

"It was in my territory!" Kuma spluttered.

"The Pukekos don't harm us or take our food. If you can't make friends with them, leave them alone!"

"What nonsense is this?" Kuma tried to dismiss Keoni's demand.

"This area is their home too. They are entitled to be here." Keoni replied. "If you can't or won't make friends then leave them alone." Keoni repeated firmly.

Kuma was angry. This young kiwi was telling him what he could do! He lifted his claw to strike Keoni when a voice from the bushes rang out.

"Stop, leave him be!"

Keoni and Kuma turned towards the voice and found themselves surrounded by a large group of kiwis. Keoni saw Kale and Kuri amongst them and knew he was among friends.

"Keoni is right." Kale spoke up. "We should be respecting the animals that live with us." His words were followed by murmured agreement from the others.

Kuma knew he was defeated and turned to slink away. Keoni had stopped him from taking over Kamoku's burrow and now Keoni had stopped him from protecting his territory. Kuma vowed he would get his revenge!

"Thank you for helping me." Keoni said to the crowd as they watched Kuma depart. He knew he had made an enemy and would have to watch out for him.

"We've been looking for another leader since Kamoku left." Kale said with a smile. "We like the way you have been helping and protecting the animals here. Will you be our next leader?" Keoni looked around at the smiling faces and nodded.

"I will if you want me to. I will check that Pio Pukeko is alright and then we will have to make sure Kuma abides by the new kingdom rules."

"What if he won't?" someone asked.

"He will be expelled." Keoni declared. There were nods of agreement from the group.

After Keoni left the group and headed towards the stream, Kale turned to the others with a smile. "We have chosen well."

"I hope there aren't too many rules in this new kingdom." A kiwi commented anxiously.

"There won't be." Kale reassured him. "To respect, help and not harm others is reasonable to comply with, isn't it?" Kale asked the crowd in front of him. He was happy to see the nods and smiles from the group as they waited for Keoni to return.

At the bulrushes Keoni found Piri Pukeko looking out anxiously.

"Hello Piri" Keoni said. "I saw Kuma chasing Pio. Is he alright?"

"Thank you for stopping him." Piri replied, looking behind him at the stream. "Pio is upset, but I think he will recover when he has calmed down."

Keoni walked down the bank to see around the bulrushes. At the sight of a kiwi form Pio squawked and rushed out to the opposite bank, trembling violently.

"Pio, it's me Keoni. It's alright." Keoni reassured him.

"But what if Kuma comes after me again?"

"He won't bother you ever again, I can promise you that!" Keoni said firmly. Pio looked at him puzzled.

"How can you do that?"

"The kiwi community here have just made me their leader. When I have seen you, I will be going to Kuma to ask him to comply with the new kingdom rule, to not harm others. If he won't comply, he will be expelled and won't be allowed to live here anymore."

With a relieved sigh Pio slipped back into the stream. Watching him glide through the water Keoni commented.

"When I've dealt with Kuma, you can show me how to swim!" To this Pio smiled for the first time.

"I will be here, and be careful!" he called after Keoni as he returned to the kiwis.

"Pio Pukeko will be alright." Keoni reassured the group. "Where is Kuma?" he asked.

Kale saw the determination in Keoni's eyes and led the way, with the group following Keoni. Kale pulled some ferns aside from a log revealing the entrance to a burrow.

"Kuma are you there?" Keoni called.

"Who wants me?" Kuma's voice came from behind them.

As Keoni turned around, instinct told him to step aside. As Keoni faced him, Kuma's claw swiped and just missed Keoni's head.

The kiwis in the group quickly pounced and overpowered him.

"As the new leader here, I want to speak to you." Keoni replied as calmly as he could. Kuma faced him in sullen silence. "The new rules here include respecting and not harming other animals. Will you abide by them?" Kuma remained silent.

"If you won't, you will be expelled from the area around the lake."

"You will live to regret this!" Kuma hissed at Keoni as he shook himself free and stomped off into the forest. Keoni then addressed the crowd.

"Thank you for your support. With your help, we are now able to make a new beginning in our lives and the animals that live with us."

"You have spoken about a social gathering to meet all the animals," Kale asked. "When and where will we have it?" Keoni thought for a moment.

"We will meet on the shore of the bay at the next full moon at dusk, so both day and night animals can come." After the crowd had dispersed, Keoni looked up at Orion.

"Have you been over to the western shore yet?" He asked.

"Not yet." Orion shook his head. "I will come and visit you though when you go."

"I will listen for your call." Keoni replied.

"I must tell everyone about the meeting." Orion said as he prepared to leave.

Keoni returned to see Pio who was waiting for him on the bank.

"Can you bring your claw back like this?" Pio asked as he brought his claw forward then swept it back under his body. Keoni tried it and nearly fell over. Once he had mastered it, he practiced on the other leg.

"Now you are ready for the water." Pio said as he slipped in to the stream. Keoni followed him and nearly sank.

"Start paddling." Pio encouraged him as he saw Keoni start to panic.

As Keoni tried the strokes he had practiced, he was delighted to find he didn't sink and he was able to move himself through the water. Pio swam with Keoni as he practiced swimming downstream and back up to the bulrushes. Finally, Keoni headed for the bank and shook himself dry.

"Thank you, Pio, I really enjoyed it."

"You will be able to join me now when I'm swimming." Pio replied with a grin.

During the following evenings and mornings, he joined Pio for a swim, gaining strength and speed as they had races up and down the stream untill even Pio started to complain.

"You will be able to swim better than the ducks soon!"

Keoni knew he would soon be ready to start his journey to the western shore.

As Keoni was adjusting to his new role, in Surrey Emily was continuing to adjust to her new role as an assistant to the nanny, starting with her clothes.

In her old life she wore fine crinoline gowns in pretty florals or finely embroidered satins for special occasions. Emily left them all behind the day she left home, when her mother gave Emily a black cotton gown to wear, its plainness relieved only with a white collar and cuffs and a frilly white apron and cap for her head.

"This will be your uniform." Her mother told her.

"What other dresses will I need?" Emily asked, her heart sinking at the future that now lay before her.

"You have been provided with a warmer petticoat and cape for winter. You won't need your other gowns." She did not tell Emily that all of her other gowns were to be sold.

"Is there anything else of my possessions that I can take?" Emily asked. "What about my books, paints and embroidery?"

Emily's mother sighed and brought out a small trunk.

"Whatever you take, it must fit into here. You will be given one drawer for your possessions. Now do it quickly, for you will be collected in an hour."

The precious things Emily could not live without, her pencils paints and embroidery found their way into her trunk as she said goodbye to her old life.

She also missed her lessons with her tutor who had introduced her to faraway places such as Italy Greece and Egypt in her history lessons, encouraging Emily to visit them when she came of age. Now she was lucky when she was allowed to supervise Lord Applebee's children as they did their homework. Her chances of travel now seemed very remote.

The one thing Emily missed most of all, the freedom to walk and explore in the woods never returned. On the days Emily was allowed to visit her mother she chose to walk than have a ride in the horse and buggy. It was the only time Emily had, to be herself again - to remember the life she had and to dream of what life could be.

CHAPTER FIVE

KEONI'S VISIT

The kiwis weren't the only animals to notice Keoni's friendship with Orion Owl and Pio Pukeko. A young eel called Elijah had seen Keoni, Orion and Odette on the beach. He had heard of the plans Keoni had for the kingdom when he spoke to Odette. Elijah had tried to approach Keoni several times when Keoni was splashing in the water, but Keoni had always retreated to the safely of the beach when he came near.

Elijah had found the stream one day when he heard the Pukekos calling to each other. Knowing that they lived by water he decided to investigate. Quietly he slithered across the gravel beach, and through the flax to the damp mossy bush where the stream lay before him; The Pukekos foraged nearby. Slipping into the water he felt the current drawing him under the ground. He allowed the water to carry him in to the dark space, to emerge from under a rock in the bay.

"It is strange," he thought *"that I haven't noticed it before."*

Diving under the rock, Elijah swam against the current and returned to explore the stream, which was so different to the wide-open spaces of the lake. He revelled in the cosy spaces of the narrow shallow channel and admired the ferns and bushes hanging over its banks along with the shady canopy the trees and pongees spread overhead. When he heard Keoni and Pio's voices in the stream, he went to see what they were doing. Elijah was envious as He watched them race each other.

He would have loved to join in too, but didn't want to scare them away. Elijah was fascinated to hear of Keoni's plans to visit the western side of the lake and of his plan to have a meeting of all the animals in the bay. He would have to tell the elders, but would they listen or be interested in joining in?

Keoni was making his way back to his burrow in the dim pre-dawn light when he was confronted by a tall fierce looking creature. It was the creature from his dreams! With a scream he turned and ran for the lake as fast as his legs would carry him, the creature in fast pursuit. Keoni crashed through the flax at the water's edge and started to swim across the bay, barely noticing that he nearly trod on Elijah who was leisurely swimming along the water's edge. Startled, Elijah wondered what Keoni was doing, rushing to swim out so far into the bay in such a hurry and decided to find out. Elijah soon caught up with Keoni and was about to ask Keoni what he was doing when he saw the Maori hunter appear at the water's edge.

The hunter had a spear in his hand that he started to aim at Keoni. Elijah knew what the hunter was doing. So many eels had been taken by the hunter's spear.

Quickly he ducked under the water and grabbed Keoni's claw in his mouth, pulling him under the water and swimming as fast as he could towards the western shore. Keoni barely had time to take a breath as he felt himself being dragged and towed under the water.

He felt and saw the spear brush past his feathers to land harmlessly on the floor of the bay. Soon Keoni needed some air and tried to wriggle out of Elijah's grip. Elijah immediately let him go. Keoni popped up on the surface, gasping for air, his new friend by his side. They both looked over to the eastern shore. The hunter was still standing on the shore, scanning the water. Luckily, Keoni was now well out of reach of any more spears the hunter might have.

"I'm Keoni, thank you for saving me."

"I'm Elijah. You should be safe for now." The eel replied. "I must go and warn my community the hunter is here." Elijah then turned to disappear towards the deep area of the lake beyond the islands.

Muru the Maori hunter had made the journey from his Pa in the next valley at Arahura. This lake was a good place to catch some eels for a meal. The rowi (southern Brown kiwis) on the western shore were also prized for their feathers, woven into warm cloaks. It was also a favourite place to find Pounamu, the treasured greenstone they made into weapons and jewellery to wear.

He had intended to visit a rocky creek running into the lake to see if the last rain had brought any Pounamu down, only to cross the path of a young roa (Great spotted kiwi). Its feathers were finer and denser than the rowi on the other side of the lake. It would make a fine cloak for his daughter who was betrothed to the chief's son.

To Muru's disappointment, he knew his spear had missed the kiwi as he watched the kiwi emerge from under the water to swim strongly to the other side. *"Where there are young ones, there must be adults."* He thought with a smile and decided to organise a hunting party.

Deep orange light spread over the horizon, lighting the darkness of the early morning sky as Keoni visited Piri in the bulrushes. He saw Piri bring his head up at his approach.

"Hello Piri." Keoni said softly. "I'm going over to visit the western side of the lake on my way to see Kaimi. We will be back before we have a meeting of all the animals at the next full moon." Piri frowned at this news.

"Beware of the kiwis over there!" he warned.

"Why?" Keoni asked. "I've been warned about the eels, but no-one mentioned them."

"The kiwis over there are a different species to you. Years ago, there was a big fight over territory. They have been separated from your kiwis ever since."

"Where does their territory start?" Keoni wanted to know.

"It is from the other side of our bay to the south end of the lake." Piri advised him. After saying goodbye Keoni made his way through the forest. The day animals were now waking.

"Hello Keoni, where are you going?" Paranui pigeon asked.

"I'm visiting the west side of the lake." Keoni replied.

"I will come to visit you." Paranui promised.

"Please do!" Keoni replied. If he was going into hostile territory, he would like the support of seeing a friendly face.

When he came to the western side of the bay Keoni knew he was now out of his territory.

He made a temporary burrow under some logs, after deciding to wait untill the evening before continuing his journey into unknown territory.

Clouds hid the late evening sky as Keoni fossicked around the logs he had been sleeping under.

He detected movement in the log and started digging untill he pulled out a HuHu grub. Keoni enjoyed them as a change from worms and started digging for some more. He felt someone watching him, but couldn't see them in the dense bush. Keoni pulled out several more and was about to devour them when a young voice came from the bushes.

"Is there any left for me?"

"Come and join me." Keoni invited him.

Out of the bushes stepped a young male rowi kiwi, similar in age to Keoni. His body covered in long glossy brown feathers; his dark brown eyes twinkled at Keoni.

"Hello I'm Kahui."

"I'm Keoni." He replied as they fed.

"You look so different to me." Kahui was curious, "Where are you from?"

"I live here too," Keoni told him, "on the other side of the bay."

Kahui looked at Keoni with surprise. He hadn't been told of a different species living so close to them. He had just been told it was not safe to go to the east side of the lake.

"Our ancestors had a big fight a long time ago, and we've been separate ever since."

"Maybe we can change that or at least be friends?" Kahui was tentative.

"I hope so." Keoni smiled. "I'm the leader of our group. I came over to meet the animals here and invite them to a social gathering we are having at the bay at the next full moon."

Kahui stared at Keoni with wide eyes "You are their leader?" Keoni nodded.

"You must be good at fighting!"

Keoni shook his head at these challenging words.

"In my kingdom fighting is discouraged." Keoni responded. At Kahui's astonished look he continued. "Our Kiwis have to respect, help and not harm kiwis and other animals."

"What happened to your leader?" Kahui asked. I haven't heard of one our age before."

"My father was our leader. He left when my mother died."

"He made you the next leader?"

"No, the adult kiwis asked me to lead them."

There must be something very special about this kiwi, Kahui thought *if he has been made a leader before he has proved himself.*

"I have proved myself." Keoni said, reading Kahui's thoughts.

Kahui also knew he would have to try to protect him. If the leader here knew Keoni was a leader, he would destroy him! Kahui told Keoni about his life here as they walked.

"We have strict rules on where we feed and where we walk. If you stay near the shore you should be safe. Don't call out loudly or the adults will think you are challenging them!" Kahui looked around nervously as he spoke. "I think we are being watched!" Keoni nodded his agreement.

"They've been watching us since we first met. My group watch me all the time. I'm used to it now and just ignore them. Your kiwis will come out if they want to talk to us."

Keoni could hear a fast-flowing river nearly. He spotted the lake through the bushes and gasped.

"What's wrong?" Kahui asked anxiously.

"Nothing's wrong." Keoni replied. "This is the first time I've seen how big the lake is."

When they came to the river, the water flowed swiftly from the lake into a rough narrow channel, dense bushes and ferns lined its banks. Keoni thought about swimming out into the lake, but saw the long sleek shapes of eels nearby and thought better of it. Kahui saw Keoni study the water intently.

"What are you doing?" he asked.

"I was thinking of swimming the lake to avoid the river, but I can see eels here. I'm not going to risk my claws untill I've talked to them."

"You are able to swim?" Keoni nodded "And, you talk to other animals?"

"Yes." Keoni replied with a smile. "Owls, Tuis, Pigeons and Pukekos are among the birds I have made friends with so far. How do you cross this river?

"There is a large tree over it, but...." Kahui hesitated pensively.

"Your kiwis will stop me?" Keoni finished for him. Kahui nodded miserably.

"I will see you on the other side." Keoni whispered to him.

Just then Keoni felt rather than saw a large kiwi step out of the bushes. Swiftly Keoni launches himself into the dark water, letting the current carry him downstream; steadily paddling across to the other bank as he went. Keoni heard the kiwi call loudly behind him and knew there would be trouble later. As Keoni passed under the tree, several kiwis on it watched him swim by.

"He's a strong swimmer." commented one.

"He looks like he's enjoying it!" commented another.

Keoni was in fact elated, enjoying the ride as he was swept down the river. He knew though he would have to get out soon. The cold water was penetrating his thick fur, cooling his body. Grasping a fern trailing in the water, Keoni hauled himself up onto the bank and hid under a nearby bush which grew next to a path that led to the lake. He heard kiwi voices approaching from the distance and quickly darted across the path to climb the steep wooded hillside overlooking the river. From the ridge he could see and hear the group of kiwis as they passed by.

"Make sure you catch him. I don't want him left loose here." Their leader ordered the group.

"You don't believe what Kahui told you?"

"Even if it is true, we aren't changing how we live now!"

"What are you going to do with Kahui?

"He will have to be eliminated!" was the chilling reply.

Keoni knew he had to try and find Kahui and rescue him, but how? Above him in the tree sat an owl silently watching Keoni and the group below. In the distance he could hear Orion calling him, but he couldn't answer him without revealing himself. He looked up at the owl.

"Owl, I am Keoni." Keoni spoke as softly as he could, "That is my friend Orion calling me. Can you call him to me? I need help." The owl nodded and called so loudly that the owls on the eastern side of the lake also heard it and responded to his calls. Orion Landed in the tree above Keoni, followed shortly after by the other owls that had come to help.

"Hello Orion and thank you all for coming." Keoni greeted them.

"I've met a young brown Kiwi called Kahui, but his kiwis are going to kill him because he met me! I need to find him and help him escape."

"I think we saw him." An owl said. "A young one is being taken towards the river."

Kahui was frightened. After Keoni slipped into the river the leader and his followers surrounded him and asked him questions about Keoni, which he answered as well as he could. Why did he come and were there any more kiwis with him they wanted to know? From the stony expression on the leader's face when Kahui told him Keoni came in friendship, Kahui knew that the leader didn't believe him. Now he was being hustled towards the river and he was worried what they were going to do to him.

34

Suddenly a large flock of owls came charging out of the darkness and bombed the group, making the kiwis cower in fright. They had never experienced anything like this before.

"RUN KAHUI, RUN!" Keoni yelled from the ridge.

Kahui didn't need to be told twice. He ran towards Keoni's voice as quickly as his legs could carry him while the owls kept the kiwis at bay.

"I'm here!" Keoni called, to encourage Kahui as he climbed the bank.

"Are you alright?" Keoni asked as Kahui scrambled up to him. Kahui nodded.

"Is the mountain part of your kiwis' territory?" Keoni asked.

"No." Kahui replied and smiled. He hadn't thought of going there!

Orion led the way through the forest with Keoni and Kahui behind him. Olivia and Ogilvie followed them to make sure they weren't tackled from behind. They came to a stream and started following it uphill. When they came to a small clearing, Keoni could see the mountain looming in front of them. It no longer looked the friendly and easy to climb place he had seen from the distant shore.

Barring their path stood a large male kiwi

While Keoni was developing his friendship with Kahui, in Surrey Emily's friendship with Jimmy was developing too. They had to keep their relationship secret in case they were parted or dismissed in disgrace as their employer Lord Applebee and Lady Amelia had to give their permission for Jimmy and Emily to marry.

Both Jimmy and Emily knew that they could never marry while they lived and worked at the manor and had to bide their time untill an opportunity came their way.

CHAPTER SIX

THE RESCUE

Kaga Kiwi had lived on the mountain nearly all of his life. His father had been the leader of the brown kiwis who had lived peacefully with the grey kiwis for generations, before his father had been deposed and killed. The brown and grey kiwis now lived completely separate lives, most of them completely unaware of the others existence. Kaga as a young child had been allowed to live as long as he stayed on the mountain and didn't interfere with the group's affairs. His mother and a group loyal to his father had escaped to the mountain with him.

Kaga had lost hope that any change would come untill now, but with the loud calling and gathering of the owls and the calling of a kiwi child (only heard in extreme danger) he knew that change had finally come. He followed his instinct to come down from the mountain with words of advice to take care ringing in his ears.

Kaga heard the sound of running kiwis coming his way and decided to wait for them. To his delight, into the clearing a young owl led two young kiwis, one brown, the other grey; followed by two more young owls. The leading owl swooped on him, but Kaga did not flinch. Keoni looked at the kiwi and saw he had kind eyes and was smiling at them. Orion turned around and was about to "ruffle" the kiwi's feathers when Keoni intervened.

"Orion, I will speak to him."

Orion retreated to a nearby tree with Olivia and Ogilvie.

"I am Kaga." The kiwi introduced himself. "My children, what brings you here?"

"I am Keoni and this is Kahui." Keoni replied. "We seek shelter."

"You are safe with me." Kaga reassured them. "I will take you to my home on the mountain."

Keoni turned to Orion Olivia and Ogilvie. "Thank you for your help."

"I will visit you tomorrow." Orion promised Keoni before he led the way back down the stream to the lake. There he called to the owls to stop their bombardment of the kiwis. They disappeared into the night as swiftly as they had come.

As the leader and his supporters attempted to get up, they were surrounded by an anxious crowd who wanted some answers. Who was the grey kiwi that Kahui had brought with him, and why did he send the owls to attack their leader? Was he trying to take over their area?

A kiwi that had seen Keoni and Kahui's meeting and followed them, spoke up.

"The grey kiwi is called Keoni. He is the leader of his group on the other side of the lake. He came over to meet the animals here and invite them to a meeting at the next full moon."

"He came in friendship?"

"Yes."

"Then why did he send the owls to attack our leader?"

"Our leader was going to kill Kahui for bringing Keoni here. Keoni sent the owls to rescue him."

"Where are they now?"

"They are safe."

"Not for long!" said the leader.

"You are not worthy to lead us." The kiwi said boldly. The crowd agreed with this. "You and your supporters are to live in the next valley."

"You can't make us go."

"If you don't, we will send you for a swim, as you have done to too many of our kiwis here."

The leader knew he was defeated and bowed his head as the crowd parted to allow him to leave. In the silence after they left came a question.

"Who is to lead us now?"

"Our true leader Kaga lives on the mountain. We only have to ask him."

As Keoni and Kahui followed Kaga up the mountain side, Keoni was glad he had a guide. He would have become lost or fallen on the now slippery slopes as rain now drenched them. Hours seem to pass as they climbed higher and higher untill Kaga stopped with a grin.

"Are you ready for a feed?"

Keoni nodded and made straight for a fallen log with Kahui close behind. Between them they found some huhu grubs. A worm under Kahui's foot was winkled out too.

"Are you going to have some?" they offered Kaga.

With an even bigger grin, Kaga came to join them. *These kiwis would fit in well here*. He thought, but he doubted that they would stay. He then led them to one of his burrows, lying under a protected rock. It was a cosy space that the three of them squeezed into together.

"Is this how you usually live?" Keoni asked. Kaga and Kahui looked at Keoni with surprise at this question.

"How do you usually live?" Kaga wanted to know.

"We build long tunnels with more than one entrance." Keoni replied as he shuffled to make himself more comfortable.

While the rain pelted down outside, they talked about their lives. Kaga told them about the life he had as a young child when both grey and brown kiwis lived together and the upheaval that came when they were separated.

He spoke about the fun he had on the mountain, having many adventures as he and his friends found all the safe places to climb and learnt the "moods" of the mountain when the weather could suddenly change, and they had to make places to quickly seek shelter

Kahui told them about the strict upbringing he had, having to learn the places that he could travel shelter and feed. He was taught to have play fights with his friends as training for when they grew up and have to challenge for their own territory and to have a mate. The threat hanging over them that they would be thrown in the river if they disobeyed. He voiced his amazement that Keoni had swum in it and survived and made Keoni promise that he would show him how to swim.

Keoni told them of how his mother died when his egg was delivered and that her neighbour Kuri and his sister Kaimi had brought him into the world after his father had left. His decision to make the family burrow his own place, and choosing to live among adult kiwis when young kiwis were sent to live separately at the southern end of the lake. His friendship with Orion and all the other animals, which had led to him becoming the leader of his group. As darkness changed to light, they heard a pigeon call nearby. Keoni moved to leave the burrow.

"Where are you going?' Kaga asked. "It is sleep time."

"I can hear one of my friends calling me." Keoni replied as he slipped outside and called softly "Paranui, I'm here."

The flutter of wings heralded the arrival of Paranui Pigeon. Keoni was aware of movement behind him and knew that Kaga and Kahui had come to see his friend.

"Hello Keoni." Paranui greeted him. I hear you have had an eventful visit here."

"Yes," Keoni replied with a grin "but I have made some friends here." He turned around to introduce Kaga and Kahui to him.

"Paranui meet Kaga and Kahui."

"Hello Paranui." Kahui said shyly. "Do you know any pigeons on this side of the lake?'

"Yes." Paranui replied. "We are all friends and visit each other often."

Just then a rustle in the bushes brought a mountain kiwi with some news for Kaga.

"Kaga, some kiwis from the bay have come and want to talk to you."

"Give them some shelter and tell them I will see them after my sleep." Kaga ordered him. Paranui watched the kiwi leave before giving him some news.

"We saw some kiwis walking to the next valley."

Kaga frowned. "The one where humans live?" he asked. Paranui nodded.

"They won't last long there," Kaga commented "unless they move further north."

"Why, what will happen to them?" Keoni asked.

"The humans kill and eat kiwi." Kaga told him.

"They also kill and eat pigeons!" Paranui added despairingly.

"Even the eels are caught and eaten too." Kahui advised him.

"We need a warning system so you can run away and hide." Keoni was thoughtful. "When do humans come?" he asked. "Are they night or day animals?"

"They usually come in the day, but sometimes they come at night with fire sticks that light the forest like daytime." Kaga replied.

"They can make calls like we do, to challenge us to fight them, but we always loose!" Kahui was fearful.

"You have seen them?" Keoni asked. Kahui nodded.

"They are very big and very tall. They have four legs but walk and run on two of them. The other two legs they use to hold the fire sticks and long sharp sticks to hunt us with."

Keoni now knew the creature that hunted him in the bay was a human who would come back to hunt his kiwis again.

"When we meet at the next moon, I will organise all the animals to keep a lookout and warn everyone to run or fly to a safer place. Do they come on the mountain?" Keoni asked Kaga.

"No, they don't." Kaga smiled at Keoni, realising that his home could become a safe haven for all of the kiwis on his side of the lake.

"What about your kiwis?" Kaga asked.

Keoni pushed aside the bush in front of them. For the first time he saw the whole lake with the lake hills and Alps behind them.

"We have our mountain to shelter on too." Keoni said pointing at the mountain that humans named Mount Tuhua.

That morning Keoni took a long time to sleep. The size of his kingdom amazed him. He vowed to get up early to see what lay on the other sides of the mountain. But when he did sleep, his dreams were disturbed by the human he had seen. He tried to return to sleep, but dozed untill the fading light told him it would soon be time to get up. Very carefully and quietly he snuck out of the burrow. He pushed aside the bush to take another look at the lake and noticed how small the islands looked from here. He turned around to look for a path to explore, to find Kaga and Kahui were up too.

"You couldn't sleep?" Kaga asked.

"No." Keoni replied. "I wanted to see the view from the other sides of the mountain before it got dark."

"Come on then." Kaga said with a smile. "We should be in time to see the sunset."

As Kaga led them along the steep mountain slope, a river valley came into view. (Humans call it The Arahura valley)

"That is where the humans come from." Kaga told him. "They live by the sea that surrounds the land we live on."

On the western side of the mountain the ground sloped away to another river valley. Beyond the valley water lay as far as they could see. What the Kiwis could not see though, was a ship sailing along the shore.

"Is that the sea?" Keoni asked in wonder. Kaga nodded, sitting down to enjoy the view as the western sky changed from gold to orange and red hues before it sunk below the ocean.

"Is it like this every night?" Keoni asked.

"Sometimes," Kaga replied with a smile "When it's not raining."

On the south western side of the mountain a small valley separated them from another mountain; its peak was higher than their own. It is known to humans as Mount Graham.

"Have you been on there?" Keoni asked.

"Yes." Kaga replied, "I have explored it, but it is more dangerous than this mountain."

"What is beyond this river valley?" Keoni wanted to know.

"There are rivers and lakes all along this coast." Kaga said before leading them to his burrow. He then went off to see what the bay kiwis wanted from him. Keoni was fossicking on the southern side of the mountain when he heard Orion calling him from the other side of the mountain.

"Orion, I'm here!" he called out as loudly as he could.

Orion swooped in to Keoni's call.

"Hello Keoni, how is your visit going here?"

"It is well." Keoni beamed at Orion. "Kaga took us for a tour round this mountain. Is everything alright at home?" he asked, seeing Orion's anxious expression.

"We've seen humans moving with their fire sticks. They seem to be heading for our side of the lake." Orion couldn't help showing the fear he felt.

"Can you and the other owls warn the birds and all the kiwis to flee to the mountain?" Keoni asked him. With a nod Orion swiftly flew towards the eastern shore. As he flew, he started calling to the other owls. Answering calls could be heard from the eastern shore. Keoni could only hope that they were in time. Orion wasn't the only one to hear Keoni's call. The north westerly breeze carried his call to the southern end of the lake where Kaimi heard it too. *"What is Keoni doing on the mountain?"* Kaimi thought. I will go and see him. As she made her way towards the western shore three young males Kekona, Kahika and Kaipo saw her and asked where she was going.

"We will come too," Kekona said, after she had told them of hearing Keoni's call. "Just to make sure you are safe." They had always been curious about the mountain and the western shore but had been warned not to go there.

While Kaga was meeting with the bay kiwis he noticed with concern the owls were calling again.

"Kaga, will you be our leader?" they asked.

"I will." Kaga agreed. "I hear the owls are calling again. I will see if Keoni knows what is happening."

He quickly returned to Keoni who was anxiously peering over at the eastern shore. Small dots of moving light could be seen on the ridge separating the northern valley from the lake.

"The humans are coming to my Bay!" Keoni said in anguish. "I've sent the owls to warn the animals and our kiwis to shelter on the mountain."

"I will do the same in case they come our way." Kaga replied and ran to warn the bay kiwis.

Kale and Kuri were out feeding when an owl suddenly landed on a branch near them. To their shock it started to talk to them.

"I have a message from Keoni. Humans are coming to hunt you. Tell everyone to quickly hide on the mountain."

Ogilvie disappeared as quickly as he came. He and Olivia had to warn the pigeons and Pukekos too, for they were also hunted by humans. Kale raised his head and screamed as loudly as he could. Kales alarm call froze everyone who heard him, before there was a rush in his direction.

"Why did Kale scream out, what is happening?" everyone wanted to know.

As everyone gathered around, he gave them the news and implored them to run to the mountain.

"Don't be silly!" one scoffed. "They never come here."

"They are coming our way! The owls have seen them." Kale retorted. A passing pigeon stopped briefly.

"Kale is right. The humans are coming here. I have seen them too. Go while you can!" before winging their way to safety.

"What about our eggs?" One of the females asked anxiously.

"You can always make another one." Kale replied as he started to make his way to the mountain.

In the distance they could hear the sound of heavy footsteps and alarm calls as birds were disturbed by the fire sticks. Kale soon found he had a large following as he silently and swiftly led the way up the mountain, ignoring the challenging calls they could hear down below as they huddled high on the mountain.

When dawn came, the sound of human voices could still be heard in the bay and smoke could be seen rising from the beach. Very quietly, Kale and the survivors made temporary burrows to rest in. It was still too dangerous to return home.

Down by the lake shore, Muru the Maori was happy with their nights hunting. They had found a couple of plump Roa and their eggs they had sat on. There was also a nice juicy eel they had spotted as it sidled by the water's edge. He was surprised there weren't more Roa here; maybe this side of the lake didn't have enough food for them.

On the western mountain (known to humans as Conical Hill) Kaga Keoni and Kahui were finally settling after a long night.

Keoni did not feed during the night, but kept a silent vigil, watching and waiting untill Orion returned in the hour before dawn.

"How are they?" Keoni asked anxiously.

"Everyone who followed Kale up the mountain survived." Orion's expression was sorrowful.

"Some stayed behind?"

Orion nodded. "Only a few stayed. The humans haven't left yet. Your kiwis will probably have to sleep on the mountain today."

"Thank you, Orion. I will see you tonight." Before Orion left, Paranui Pigeon also called to see Keoni.

"Thank you for the warning you sent last night. We all escaped along with the pukekos. We are sorry to hear about your kiwis."

"Yes, but we saved most of the animals. That is important for our future." Suddenly Orion saw Keoni's face change. It was full of pain.

"Keoni! What is the matter?'

"It's nothing." Keoni tried to shrug off the vision he had just seen.

"No, it's not nothing, what did you see?" Orion demanded to know.

"I saw some humans bring a ferocious animal with them. It is similar in size to us and can outrun us. It can also chase us down our burrows!"

While Keoni was meeting with Kaga, Emily had been summoned to a meeting with her mistress, Lady Amelia.

"Jimmy the groom has asked for your hand in marriage and wishes to take you to the New Zealand gold rush! How long has your relationship been going on for and who is to assist the nanny with our children?" Lady Amelia asked. She was annoyed that none of her trusted staff had spotted this relationship to warn her. She was also very reluctant to let Emily go as she intended to have her trained as her maid when the children no longer needed her.

"Jimmy and I became friends soon after we met." Emily replied nervously. "We chose not to develop our friendship further while we were committed to your family. Jimmy has just heard that New Zealand is looking for migrants to settle and develop farmland there. He intends to mine for gold so he can buy land for his own farm."

"What about our children?" Lady Amelia asked. "Nanny needs help to care for them."

"The housekeeper told me that Susan from the village had been in recently to ask if there was a position available in the nursery." Emily replied. "If she is interested in caring for children, she should be suitable."

"Very well then," Lady Amelia said with a smile. She made a mental note to get the housekeeper to contact Susan immediately. "I will contact the vicar to arrange your marriage for tomorrow. You can have the morning off tomorrow to pack your belongings and get ready for the ceremony. You are NOT to see the groom now untill you marry."

Emily borrowed a white Muslin gown for their wedding, a garland of Honeysuckle flowers from the garden in her hair. Round her neck was a gold chain with a locket. Inside the locket was a sovereign case with two gold sovereigns Lady Amelia had given her.

"These are from your father." Lady Amelia told her. "Use them wisely."

After a simple ceremony at the village church and a final hug with her Mother, they boarded the stage coach to Dover, waving goodbye to their old life. Emily was happy to leave behind the dowdy black uniform which Susan thankfully took over. Nursery maids, along with other maids in the house had to provide their own uniforms which were very expensive to buy.

Emily's mother had done well in her dressmaking business during Emily's time at the manor. Her wedding gift to Emily was two crinoline dresses and a pretty bonnet which she was overjoyed to now wear.

Emily smiled whenever she remembered their first night together in a cosy room upstairs in an Inn near the ocean; the white cliffs soared behind them. Little did they care for the noise of the locals at the bar downstairs for they were finally free to be together and to live the life that they had dreamed of.

CHAPTER SEVEN

NEW FRIENDS

In the lake, Elijah the eel was full of sorrow. He had just lost his best friend Esi to the humans. In the centre of the bay and well out of reach of the humans' spears, he watched them prepare their breakfast. *"If only I could do something!"* he thought as he retreated to the safety of the lake beyond the islands in the bay.

Below him the lake bed sloped away to the canyon below. At the bottom lay the eels' sanctum, where eels ventured only when they were summoned. Female guardians controlled entry to it. In his sadness, Elijah was drawn to it, ignoring the swishing and swirling tails of older eels he passed as he dived.

Suddenly Elijah felt a sharp nip on his tail. This he also ignored.

"Elijah, what are you doing?" one of the guardians asked, as she swam along-side him.

"I need to be alone." Elijah replied.

"Why did you come here?" the guardian asked, "There are plenty of places to hide near the shore."

"It isn't safe there. Humans have taken Esi!" Elijah's voice broke.

"They have taken your friend?"

"Yes."

"I will come with you." The guardian decided. Together they descended into the cold darkness of the sanctum. A place so deep, daylight does not reach it. Other eels that saw the pairs' descent came to see what was happening. When they heard of Elijah's grief, they surrounded him and cuddled up to him to give him comfort.

With a sigh, Elijah settled on the soft floor and let the peace of this place surround him and sooth his despairing spirit, while the guardian watched from nearby. Eventually Elijah knew it was time to leave and stirred himself from his resting place. When he looked up Erron the eels' male leader and Erena the female Matriarch had joined the guardian and was looking at him with concern.

"Are you feeling better?" Erron asked. "I'm sorry to hear you have lost your friend, but there is little we can do when humans come hunting here."

46

"There may be soon." Elijah replied. "Keoni Kiwi is having a meeting of all the animals in the Eastern Bay at sunset on the next moon."

"Who is Keoni and what is the meeting for?" Erron asked with interest

"He is the leader of the grey kiwis and is starting a new kingdom."

"What sort of kingdom will it be?" Erena wanted to know.

"He told an owl that everyone would live the same, but all the animals were expected to respect and look out for each other and make sure no-one was ever harmed."

"How would he make sure that no-one was harmed?" Erron was doubtful. He and Erena could see they would have to call a meeting of all the eels to see if they would agree to be part of this kingdom. At present the eels did as they pleased, sometimes taking some of the ducklings that came near or had a nibble of any of the adults' feet as they swam. This would have to change.

"Keoni is organising the animals to give a warning when humans come so that everyone can escape."

"I think I may attend this meeting." Erron was thoughtful. *If this kiwi could protect them from the humans, it would be worthwhile living with the restrictions of the kingdom rules.* "We will call a meeting of all the eels. You stay here Elijah as we want you to tell them what you have seen and heard so we can take a vote on whether to join the kingdom."

When Keoni and Kahui awoke a howling gale and driving rain greeted them as they ducked outside for a feed. It didn't take long for the rain had brought more worms to the surface.

"Do you have to go?" Kahui asked. "Why don't you stay here untill the rain clears?"

"I could, but we don't know long it will take to clear. It could be many nights and I don't have that long." Keoni didn't know why, but it suddenly seemed urgent to get on with his journey to see Kaimi and Kaimani.

Kaga led Keoni and Kahui down the mountain slopes towards the southern shore. Keoni was once again grateful for a guide as they slipped and slid down the slopes which were more treacherous now that streams of water poured down the pathways. Suddenly Kahui was swept off his feet by the water and was carried down the slopes towards the lake below.

Frantically he reached out to a bush to stop his fall. He couldn't hold on and kept sliding and tumbling his way down the slope untill he reached flat ground. Kaga and Keoni rushed down to Kahui who was now covered in grey mud.

"I look like you now." Kahui said with a grin, trying to hide the fright he had just had.

"I thought you were in a hurry to get down for that swimming lesson I promised you." Keoni was also was trying to hide the fear that he had nearly lost his new friend.

Kaga shook his head that Kahui and Keoni were able to joke when Kahui had nearly lost his life. There was no beach along this side of the lake and the water was too deep to stand in so Kaga lead them to a shallow stream where they all took a quick dip to remove the grime from their journey down the mountain. While they were in the stream a brown kiwi called Kaino and his two children appeared on the bank.

"Hello Kaga." Kaino greeted him. 'We have some young grey kiwis come into our territory. One of them is a female called Kaimi. She said she heard her brother Keoni on the mountain and wanted to see him."

"Keoni is here with us." Kaga replied with a smile. "Where are they?"

Before Kaino could call Kaimi she appeared through the trees. She had three male kiwis with her.

"Hello Kaimi! Are you coming in for a swim?" Keoni called. "Who are your friends?"

"Keoni, I heard you calling so I came to see what you were doing." Kaimi replied.

"This is Kekona, Kahika and Kaipo. They came to keep me company."

Kekona Kahika and Kaipo gave Kaga Kahui and Keoni a smile and jumped into the water with them. They surrounded Keoni and bombarded him with questions.

"We hear from Kaino that you are the leader of our kiwis, is it true?"

"We've heard you have been rescuing our families. How did you do it?"

"We've heard you are making a kingdom that is famous through the land. What sort of kingdom are you making?"

Kahui gave Keoni a big grin and spoke up before Keoni could reply.

"Yes, it is true that Keoni is the leader of your kiwis. Keoni has been making friends with all the animals. It is his friendship with animals such as owls and pigeons that allowed him to rescue your kiwis. He also rescued me when he came over to visit us, from a bad leader who was going to kill me. That leader has been expelled and the rightful leader has been restored." Kahui grinned up at Kaga.

"In my kingdom all the animals will live the same, but kiwis and other animals are expected to respect, help and not harm others." Keoni added.

"What if someone won't live by your rules?" Kahika asked.

"They will be sent out of the kingdom. I have already expelled Kuma kiwi when he attacked Pio Pukeko without a good reason, also he refused to live by the kingdom rules when I asked him to."

"Does he have dark grey fur?" Kaipo asked with a frown.

"Yes, why do you ask?" Keoni asked.

"I think I saw him following Kaimani."

"Which way did they go?" Keoni asked as he started getting out of the stream. He now knew why he had been anxious to move on from the mountain. Kaimani was in danger!

"She was heading towards the eastern shore. Do you want some help?" Kaipo offered.

"I will take all the help I can get!" Keoni then turned to Kaga. "Thank you for looking after us, but I have to go and find out what has happened to Kaimani."

"I look forward to seeing you at the meeting next month." Kaga replied with a smile.

"We will help." Kekona offered on behalf of Kaimi, Kahika and Kaipo.

Following the lake south, Keoni swiftly led the way to their territory.

"Show me where you last saw them." Keoni asked Kaipo. "How long ago did you see them?" Kaipo thought for a moment before he answered.

"It was about three nights ago when Kaimi heard you on the mountain."

Keoni was in despair at this news for they could be anywhere by now.

Kuma was slowly making his way south. There was no hurry after he had been expelled from his burrow with the lake kiwis. *"It's time I took another mate."* Kuma thought. His first mate had left him for another male. He remembered the younger kiwis of their community lived on the southern shore of the lake. *"I will pick up one from there and take her with me."* As he meandered on the southern shore, he saw a young female. Her grey fur was glossy and her eyes also sparkled in the moonlight.

When Kuma came to approach her, Kaimani looked up with a start. *"Who was this strange adult in their territory?"*

"Who are you and what are you doing here?" Kaimani challenged him. She started to back away as she spoke.

"I'm here for a mate. Come with me!" Kuma commanded her.

"No, I'm too young!" Kaimani protested. "Besides, I will choose my own mate when I'm ready." She added with spirit and began to run towards the eastern side of the lake. *"I must find Keoni he will know what to do."*

Kuma began to follow her. He was glad she was heading towards the eastern shore. There were fewer males around there to protect her, but he would have to stop her before she reached the adults. He increased his speed.

Kaimani was getting desperate! This was the third night she had been evading Kuma Kiwi as he followed her through the forest. He seemed to know the way she was going. *"Was he from their community?"* she wondered. Kaimani was also very hungry. She had been unable to feed properly with Kuma on her trail. She came across the shallow rocky stream and saw the waterfall nearby. (Humans call it Dorothy Falls), Kaimani quickly crossed the stream and hid in the thick bushes nearby. It wasn't long before Kuma's familiar form passed her. She then turned and headed towards the waterfall to climb the steep and slippery slopes beside it.

Kuma had not been fooled for long though. When he realised he could not hear Kaimani in front of him, he turned back. He was about to recross the stream when he saw Keoni and his friends on the other side. Kaimani wasn't with them, so he turned towards the waterfall. Kaipo and Kekona spotted Kuma as he moved upstream.

"Is that him?" Kekona asked. Kaipo nodded.

"Can anyone swim?" Keoni asked

"I can." Kaipo replied.

"Can you come with me?" Keoni asked Kaipo. "I think we might have another swim."

Kaimi eyed the waterfall in the distance. "Please be careful!" she implored them.

"We will wait for you by the waterfall." Kahui told Keoni as they set off after Kuma.

After her long hard struggle up the hillside, Kaimani sat beside the stream and listened to the sounds of the waterfall as it flowed over the cliff top to a narrow rock pool before cascading down the cliff face to the large deep plunge pool below. To her horror she heard movement in the bushes at the top of the cliff. Kaimani tried to hide among the ferns but it was too late, Kuma had spotted her.

"Where do you think you are going?" Kuma snarled.

Kaimani was too tired to argue with him, so she stayed silent. She wanted to jump into the water, but she couldn't swim.

Kuma was tired too. He hadn't expected such a long chase with a hard climb up a cliff at the end of it. Slowly he came towards her. Kaimani cringed as she felt him put a claw on her shoulder.

"Stop!" Keoni yelled. "Leave her alone."

"She is my mate, don't interfere!" Kuma growled.

"I'm not his mate. Let me go!" Kaimani wailed as she tried to wriggle out of Kuma's grip.

"No-one else is going to be your mate either!" Kuma said as his fury got the better of him. He dragged her to the water's edge as Kaimani tried to fight him off by scratching him with her claws. Kuma tried to throw her in, but overbalanced and fell in with her. Keoni and Kaipo saw what was happening and jumped into the stream too.

Kuma was unable to swim and was too busy floundering and trying to keep his head above the water to worry about Kaimani as the stream swept him towards the waterfall. Kaimani gasped for air as she surfaced in the stream. Not knowing what to do, she panicked and started thrashing at the water with her claws as she found herself sinking in the stream.

"We are here Kaimani." Keoni called. She turned her head to find him and Kaipo beside her. "Get on my back." Keoni ordered her, which she gratefully did, as they were swept towards the waterfall. Kuma's scream could be heard as he was swept over the edge.

"Are you ready?" Keoni asked Kaipo as their turn came to ride the waterfall.

"This will make a good story if we survive it!" Kaipo answered with a grin.

Kaimani gripped Keoni extra hard as she saw how high they were and how far they would fall if they were swept over to the bottom of the falls. She also saw Kuma's limp body being swept swiftly over the edge of the rock pool into the cascading falls. She didn't see or hear Kaimi's gasp as Kuma dropped and was tossed around in the cascading water like a rag doll, to disappear into the depths of the plunge pool. Neither did she hear Kaimi's wail as she spotted Keoni Kaimani and Kaipo plunge over the top of the falls. Kaimi and their friends watched and waited, but as the minutes went by there was no sign of them.

With a big splash they plunged into the narrow channel of the rock pool. Kaimani was worried as she could feel them being swept along while they were still under water and was glad when they resurfaced for Keoni to swim strongly to the side of the channel. Kaipo was already waiting for them.

"Do you think we can get out this side?" Kaipo was doubtful, looking at the slippery wall next to them.

"It looks worse on the other side." Keoni answered. Kaipo had to agree. The sheer wall on the opposite side was higher and harder to climb out of.

"You go first Kaimani." Keoni told her. "I will be right behind you."

"What will I hold on to?" Kaimani asked perplexed.

"See the Moss; dig your claws in to get a grip."

Kaimani did as she was asked and was surprised to find that it held. Very slowly they clung and clawed their way out of the waterfall. At last they flung themselves exhausted onto the bank. Meanwhile down on the rocks Kaimi was getting worried.

"Maybe they are injured and need our help? Shouldn't we go and have a look?" She asked.

"If you take someone with you to check where they are," Kahui replied, "The rest of us should start making somewhere to sleep and look for some food for us all."

"I will take Kaimi." Kekona offered.

"I don't fancy the climb up there." Kahika said with a grin looking at the waterfall. "Where do you think is the best place for our shelter?"

As Kahui and Kahika climbed off the rocks to search for a suitable spot, they missed the grey shadow of an eel that had claimed Kuma and was taking his prize to the lake.

As Keoni continued his journey at the lake to search for Kaimani, Emily and Jimmy were beginning their journey to their new life. In the morning they joined the crowd of other settlers at the dock. Emily had to hold tight to her bonnet in the strong sea breeze, which had also whipped up white caps on the choppy water in the English Channel. Emily exchanged smiles with the ladies nearby her who were lined up with their families. She was looking forward to making some friends on this voyage, for during her time at the manor the strict rules in the household didn't encourage friendships among the servants.

Over the next twelve weeks they adjusted to the constant rolling motion and the creaking timbers around them as the ship ploughed through the waves. The small hard bunk in the large cabin was their only space to both sit and sleep on, with only curtains for privacy. They had to stay in the cabin for many long days when the weather was too wet to walk on deck.

During this time Emily made friends with several of the ladies with neighbouring bunks. Katherine and William had been working on his father's farm which would eventually pass to William's brother, so they had decided to try a new life in New Zealand too. Fiona and her husband Angus had been moved off their croft in the Scottish Highlands when the lease ran out. They were heading for Dunedin where there were many jobs available. Caroline and Henry had two young boys and hoped a new life in New Zealand would be better than the life they would have if they stayed in the harsh streets of London.

After wilting from the hot muggy days as they crossed the equator, Emily and Jimmy welcomed the cool change as they rounded the Cape of Good Hope to land in Cape Town. While the ship took on fresh provisions, they marvelled at Table Mountain which towered over the settlement. Emily was fascinated by the mud walled and thatched homes the natives lived in and the colourful costumes and beaded jewellery the ladies wore.

She was amazed at size of the elephants as they grazed the grasslands, the gracefulness of the giraffes as they nibbled on the tall Acacia trees, the nimbleness of the monkeys as they swung through the tree tops and the strangeness of the zebras as they galloped through the bushland. The beautiful large protea flowers had Emily reaching for her sketch pad.

Recreating the scenes she had seen while in South Africa helped Emily to pass the long days as they crossed the Indian Ocean to Fremantle. There the sun blazed under a cloudless blue sky; cream limestone buildings nestled along the golden sandy shore.

53

Emily was delighted to see the beautiful parrots in the trees, calling raucously to one another. As they walked past a patch of bushland yet to be developed, Emily could hardly believe her eyes to see the carpet of wild flowers out in bloom. Jimmy picked a leaf from a gum tree and crushed it. They both loved the eucalyptus smell. When they returned to the ship Emily had several books on Australian birds and plants to find a place for and some seeds from the gum tree in their trunk.

As the ship travelled down the coast to Albany they passed through a storm. The next day large plumes of smoke could be seen in the forest on shore. When they asked a sailor if the fire would be put out, he shook his head.

"Forest fires are common here. Many plants here depend on fire to regrow."

"But how do they do that?" Emily asked. She had never heard of such a thing.

"The Aborigines used fire to catch animals when they came here and the land has adapted to it." The sailor replied before resuming his duties. They weren't encouraged to talk with the passengers unless they needed to.

When they crossed the Great Australian Bight, they saw some whales with their calves. They also saw some large sharks. Emily was glad they didn't have to bathe in these waters. By now they were tired of bathing in a bucket and were looking forward to the day when they could have a bath. At Port Piri the driving rain and cold wind deterred the passengers from any attempt to explore the settlement while fresh provisions were brought on board.

Once the ship entered the Tasman Sea the passengers were asked to stay down in the cabin as it was safer to be below. At night everyone was strapped into their bunks to ensure no-one fell out. During the crossing Emily was feeling unwell. However the sickness she felt wasn't just from the rough motion of the ship, she knew she was expecting their first child.

CHAPTER EIGHT

THE MEETING

There was much rejoicing at the eastern bay when Keoni returned and brought his friends with him. Everyone was grateful to Keoni for saving the community from the humans and Kale and Kuri marvelled at how much Kaimani had grown since she had joined the younger kiwis at the southern shore of the lake.

"Will you be returning to the southern shore?" Kuri wanted to know.

"No mum." Kaimani replied. "I will be staying with Keoni from now on."

"You are his mate?" Kuri was surprised as Kaimani was too young to mate yet.

"No, but I will be when I'm ready." Kaimani replied in a firm tone which allowed no argument.

"Do you think he will live on the southern shore now he has made friends with kiwis his own age?" Kuri wondered.

"I don't think so. He said that there will have to be changes to how our community lives as it is not safe any longer to keep our younger members separate from the adults."

Kuri pondered this news with a frown. Many adults would not welcome this change. They had been content with the present arrangement where the young ones were encouraged to move away from home to their own area as soon as they were independent.

"I expect we will hear all about it at the meeting?" Kuri asked. Kaimani nodded in agreement.

"Mum, are you expecting a baby?" Kaimani asked noticing her mother's wide body.

"Yes, it will be nice to have you nearby." Kuri smiled "I will get you to help me to sit on the egg."

"I will be glad to help, but won't dad be helping you?" Kaimani asked concerned.

"He should, but he didn't like the restriction of egg sitting last time." Kuri said with a sigh.

"I will be having words with him if he doesn't do his share!" Kaimani said firmly.

Life was definitely going to be more interesting with the younger ones around Kuri decided. *It might also be fairer as well.* She was looking forward to the meeting now.

In Keoni's burrow Kahui Kekona Kahika and Kaipo were sitting with Keoni and discussing how they could help him with his kingdom.

"You need a way to keep your kingdom safe." Kekona told Keoni. "Now we are getting kiwis from outside areas coming to the southern shore to feed and find shelter. It will help if you plan to end the separation of our younger kiwis from adults as we need adults on the southern shore to help us to protect the territory and enforce your rules."

"As your allies, Kaga and I can promote the kingdom rules to our kiwis and make sure they are kept." Kahui suggested.

"I can stay on the southern shore and make sure the kingdom rules are kept in that area." Kahika proposed.

"You will need someone to be on the Eastern shore to ensure your rules are kept there too. I can help you there." Kekona said.

"You need a supporter with or near you, so I will help you here." Kaipo added.

"I want to thank you all." Keoni's eyes were bright with emotion. "My kingdom will be much more secure now with your support. The meeting we are having in a few days is only the first of many that we will have, to make sure all is well and that we can catch up with each other."

Dark clouds gathered over the valley as Paranui pigeon sat in the tree that over looked the Arahura River. He knew he shouldn't be here, but the large Cabbage tree was now full of berries to feast on. As he fed, Paranui noticed some Maoris on the river bank. They were searching for small green pebbles to make into the Taonga Pounamu they wore around their necks.

Paranui didn't realise it, but he had been spotted by Muru, one of the men in the group. Standing up and stretching, Muru grabbed his spear and walked away from the group to disappear into the bushland downstream.

Stealthily Muru crept back upstream again, making sure he kept out of sight of Paranui in the Cabbage tree. Suddenly a voice called from the dense foliage of a nearby tree.

"Paranui, fly away!"

Paranui didn't need to be told twice. He launched himself and fled into the forest just as Muru's spear flew through the air.

It just missed Paranui to land in the foliage where he had been sitting. The group laughed at Muru for missing his Kereru.

"You will have to brave the spikes to get your spear back."

"You will have to try fishing for your meal tonight instead."

"Or, you will have to settle for some Kumara for your supper."

Paranui trembled as he recovered from his encounter with the Maori hunter. He jumped as flashes of lightning and thunder rumbled overhead, followed by heavy rain.

"Surely the humans won't stay by the river in this?" Paranui thought. Very carefully and quietly he made his way back through the forest to the tree where he had heard the voice. As Paranui eased himself into the shelter of the dense dark foliage, he met the pigeon who had warned him.

"Hello Paranui," she smiled. It was Pania, a female who lived here.

"Thank you for saving me," he cautiously looked out at the river bank. "Are they still there?"

"No, they left when the storm started."

"Good, I will finish my feed."

Despite the noise of the storm and getting soaked, Paranui and Pania relished their feed of berries, knowing they were safe for now. As Paranui finished his feed, he spotted the green pounamu pebbles the Maoris had left behind on the rocks as they fled the storm. Pania saw Paranui staring at the rocks.

"What are you looking at?" she asked.

"Those green stones sitting on the rocks, I want to take them back to our community." Paranui replied as he flew down to the rocks to pick one up in his beak.

He flew back to the tree they sheltered in, to deposit the stone in a hollow of the branches. The hollow was well out of sight of any humans who might walk by. With Pania's help all the stones were swiftly stored in the tree, just in time as the storm caused the river to flood; the rocks now covered in fast flowing water.

With the rain still falling steadily in the valley, Paranui found some soft twine from a nearby flowering vine. Snipping it off with his beak and with Pania's help wound it firmly around five of the stones, before she secured it around his neck.

"I will be back for the other stones if they like them." Paranui said as he departed.

"Be careful." Pania warned him.

Dusk was fast approaching when Paranui reached the forest at the Eastern bay. Paranui flew to the tree where Orion owl had slept during the day, to find him waking up.

"What is that around your neck?" Orion wanted to know.

"I found them by the river in the next valley."

"You mean the valley where humans live?" Paranui nodded.

"What were you doing there? Don't you know it is very dangerous to be there?" Orion asked incredulously.

"Yes I know it is dangerous, but there are some big berry trees there." Paranui tried to justify the risk he took. Orion shook his head at the danger his friend had put himself in.

"Why did you get these?" Orion asked as he admired the green colours in the stones in the late evening light.

"We need something special for Keoni to wear as our leader." Paranui suggested.

Orion was thoughtful. There was enough for his supporters to wear one too. "Are there any more?" Orion asked.

"Yes, there are another five stones where these came from." Paranui replied. "I will get them tomorrow."

Pania was disappointed when Paranui didn't return that evening, so she was surprised when she was awakened at dawn by his call.

"Hello Pania," he greeted her, "I've come back for the other stones."

Paranui then retrieved some more twine from the vine. After the remaining stones were secure around his neck Paranui pleaded with Pania to come back to the lake with him.

"Please come, you will be safer there!"

Pania was about to refuse when the unmistakable sounds of a human climbing the tree made her freeze in horror. The Maori had heard them in the tree and was trying to trap them.

"Come!" Paranui called as he forced his way out through the canopy of the tree.

The sight of a large brown hand reaching into her refuge was enough. Swiftly Pania followed Paranui into the sky and to a new life at the lake. The hunter set a snare in the tree, but Pania and Paranui never returned.

The day of the meeting came at last. In the late afternoon the trees in the bay were full of Pigeons, Tuis and Fantails, Robins, bellbirds and wax-eyes chatting and squabbling as they claimed the best spots to watch the proceedings. They were joined by the owls and some bats that came to join in when they heard of the gathering. The Pukekos and ducks settled themselves under the trees while they waited for the kiwis to arrive. In the water eels came to swim in increasing numbers, jostling for position near the shore.

The sight of Keoni and Kaimani with his supporters when they emerged from the forest brought a hush to the waiting crowd. His supporters were followed by the eastern bay kiwis and kiwis from the next valley who had heard of the meeting.

They all sat down on the gravel beach of the bay. As they were seated Kaga and his kiwis emerged from the forest of the western bay to join Keoni's kiwis. Kaga came up to stand with Keoni with a big smile on his face.

"I never thought I would live to see this day." Kaga commented with a grin.

"We intend to have many more of them." Keoni replied with a smile before turning to address the crowd.

"Thank you all for coming. Today is a new beginning for us all in the kingdom, the start of a new way of living in our communities." Keoni noticed Erron the eels' male leader and Erena the eels' matriarch coming forward to the edge of the water. "I also extend a big welcome to the lake eels that have come to join us."

"Hello Keoni, I am Erron the leader of our group and this is Erena our matriarch." Erron introduced them. "Elijah has told us of your proposals to respect all animals, to not harm any animals and to help each other. Our community has given careful thought to your rules and we are now happy to join your community.

We are especially interested in how you intend to protect us from the humans when they come to hunt us."

"Hello Erron and Erena. Thank you for joining us and welcome to our kingdom." Keoni replied.

"We propose to protect you by giving you warning when the humans are coming so you can retreat beyond their reach. "On the western and northern side of the lake Kahui or Kaga will alert you (Keoni introduced them as he spoke.) On our side of the lake to the north either Kaipo or I will advise you. On the eastern and southern side Kekona or Kahika will give the alarm. When we want to talk to you, we will come to the water's edge and make a noise. Any eel nearby is to come when they hear the sound."

Keoni walked to the water where he lifted a claw and slapped it down as hard as he could several times, causing the eels to retreat from the sound which rang in their ears.

"Do you think my warning system will work?" Keoni asked Erron and Erena

"It will work well." Erron and Erena replied with a grin, looking at the slightly stunned looks on the eels faces.

Keoni then announced the news that he knew the adults in his community would disagree with.

"Part of the new way of living for kiwis on the eastern side of our lake is that our adults will need to spread out."

"Why?" Kale asked, "What is wrong with our present arrangement?" to murmurings from other adults who didn't like the idea at all.

"In the southern area where all our younger kiwis are gathered, our territory is under pressure from adults from other areas who are trying to take it over." Keoni replied.

"We have three choices to solve the problem," Keoni continued. "One, we allow the outside kiwis to take over, and if we do, how much of our territory do we let them have? Keeping in mind this choice will also put our friends and allies on the western side of the lake at risk. Our second choice is to spread out, to live near our younger members and assist them to defend our territory. Our third choice is to still spread out to be near our younger members, but to welcome outside Kiwis into our kingdom, providing they live by our rules. We cannot expect our younger members to enforce our rules on their own. Those who won't live by our rules will be able to feed and shelter with us while they are passing through to their preferred place."

"Who has to go?" Kale asked sulkily.

"No-one has to go," Keoni insisted, "But if you want to keep this territory, someone needs to volunteer to live at or near the southern end of the lake. I will leave it to you all to decide.

Remember we will be having regular meetings to catch up with each other. Has anyone got anything they want to discuss before we relax and enjoy ourselves?"

"Yes," Orion replied. "Paranui and I have something we want to give to you and your supporters to show the special role that you have in our community."

At that Orion, Paranui and Pania flew down from their perches in the trees. They had the greenstone amulets around their necks. Carefully Pania leaned forward to allow the amulet to slip off her neck before she picked it up and approached Keoni who leaned forward to let her put it over his head. She then retrieved the other amulets from Paranui and Orion to give to Kahui, Kekona Kahika and Kaipo. When this was completed there was a big cheer from the crowd who gathered around to congratulate them all.

A big feast was set out for everyone to share, the party lasting long into the night. The new arrangements worked well, the small community quickly expanded to become much bigger as more Kiwis came to stay and be part of Keoni's Kingdom.

While Keoni's Kiwis were adjusting to their new way of life, Emily and Jimmy were arriving at Hokitika to begin their new life. It was a wet and windy morning as they crossed the treacherous sand bar at the entrance of the Hokitika River. Emily watched the bustle on the wharf, beyond it, timber buildings lined the shore behind the beach, rows of tents nestled near the forest which stretched into the distance of the valley. Low cloud hid the snow-capped mountain range of the Southern Alps beyond. Jimmy frowned when she insisted they look for a hotel to stay the night. He was worried that their money wouldn't last long in a hotel.

"I want one night of comfort before we head for tent city!" she grinned at his frown.

"Alright." He agreed with an answering grin. He was looking forward to some comfort too.

Emily was forever grateful for the welcome they received at the hotel. The owner's wife, Molly on hearing of their journey took them to some comfy chairs for a warm drink while baths were run and a set of clean clothes awaited them.

When Emily came downstairs the next morning to thank Molly, Jimmy had already left to seek a partner to mine with.

When she asked Molly if a bank was nearby, she took Emily to her own trusted bank to deposit the two gold sovereigns Lady Amelia had given her.

After talking to the manager she chose to sell one to open a savings account which would give Emily her own income. The other sovereign was kept safe in the bank vault. When she left the bank Emily had been given a large cash allowance to buy all the items they needed to live untill income from the gold mining came in.

Molly then took Emily to a dressmaker where she ordered one dress, several loose tunics and pairs of trousers, to the consternation of the two ladies.

"Ladies don't wear trousers here!" the dressmaker protested.

"I'm being practical." Emily explained calmly "if I wear dresses at the mine, they will get filthy very quickly." The dressmaker shook her head as she prepared to take Emily's measurements and hoped she wasn't starting a new fashion.

While looking at the downpour outside Emily asked, "Does it rain often here?" Molly exchanged a look with the dressmaker and smiled.

"It can rain for weeks without end! Although in summer it can get quite warm."

"I will need a waterproof cape or coat and hats for both the sun and rain."

You will need some waterproof boots as well. Shoes will rot very quickly at the mine." The dressmaker warned.

After their visit to the dressmaker, Emily asked to see a midwife. Molly took her to a small cottage near the wharf. Isabelle, a migrant from Cornwall who had learnt her knowledge from her mother welcomed them in. Her own children could be heard playing in the next room as it was too wet to play outside. After exchanging stories of their travels, Isabelle examined Emily and was able to confirm that her baby was due in about seven months' time and arranged to see her in a couple of months to see how she was progressing. Emily also decided to come in to deliver the baby at Molly's, much to her delight.

Over lunch at a tearoom, Emily made a list of all the things they needed to start their new life.

"You will need a cart and horse to carry it all." Molly commented.

"Can I hire one?" Emily asked.

"You could, but they are very expensive, especially if you travel out of town." Molly advised. "You would be better investing in your own."

When Jimmy returned to the hotel later in the afternoon, he looked downcast.

"How did you get on?" Emily asked as gently as she could.

"I've found a partner, but I'm not sure we can afford to go with him. He has given me a list of equipment I need to bring, which will take up nearly all our money. There won't be any left for a tent or anything else we need."

"I've taken care of that." Emily said with a smile, leading him out to the stable where a horse called Hector and a laden cart stood waiting. "If you are certain you want to work with your new partner, then go and tell him and get your equipment on your way back. I want to be in our new home before it gets dark!"

With a smile and a new spring in his step Jimmy set off to see his new partner. While she was waiting for Jimmy to return, Emily showed Molly her sketch pads.

"I would like these to be made into books I can keep. Is there a printer nearby I can get them covered properly?"

"Leave them with me, I know someone who will enjoy making them for you." Molly promised "They will make a fine library when they are done."

When they were finally ready to make the journey to the camping spot they had been given, the rain had stopped and the air was full of scents from the nearby forest. They tethered Hector to a sturdy tree and set up their new home under the protection of the forest. Molly had thoughtfully given them some bread and cheese before they left, knowing that they would want a simple meal after unpacking.

At dawn Emily rose to check on Hector who came trotting over, eager for the carrot she held out for him. He didn't seem to mind the fantail that came to land on his back to catch the insects which had settled on him. When Jimmy's new partner Jack arrived they were ready for him with the mining equipment stowed in the cart. He added his equipment to theirs and jumped up on the cart, and directed them to the dirt path through the forest to the mine site at Kaniere where they began their new venture.

CHAPTER NINE

KAMOKU'S RETURN

Keoni was feeding by the southern shore of the lake when he felt someone watching him. He usually ignored this attention, but something made him look up. A large male kiwi was staring at him.

"Hello," Keoni greeted him, "Are you looking for shelter?"

There had been so many kiwis coming through in recent months with the settlement of humans in the next valley, (humans now call the area Kokatahi and Kowhitirangi) that Keoni and Kaimani had gone to the southern shore to help with the new arrivals, now made homeless with the clearing of land for farming. Before the stranger could answer, Kahika called Keoni.

"Keoni, where are you?"

"I'm here." Keoni answered, turning towards Kahika's call as he answered. When he turned back, the stranger had gone.

"I wonder who that was." Keoni thought as he waited for Kahika to come.

As Kamoku melted into the forest; feelings of shock, grief, and shame came back to haunt him. On his travels south word had come through of the rise of a new leader called Keoni at his lake. Keoni had become famous for protecting the animals from humans and had changed how everyone lived.

Kamoku had looked forward to meeting and hopefully giving the interloper a lesson that he was still in charge – the fact that he didn't intend to stay didn't matter. His intentions fell into disarray as he gazed on the face of his beloved Kailee – a young Kailee who was forever beyond him. When the young Kailee answered to Keoni, he then knew that this was the child he had abandoned, but had survived despite him and was making a better leader than he had been!

He had hoped to see Kaimi here, but there was no sign of her. As he made his way north, striding quickly and deep in thought he didn't see the other kiwis, both familiar and new who were now living here. As he passed, there were many whispers from the bushes.

"That's Kamoku! What is he doing here?"

"Has he come back to stay?"

"Is he going to fight Keoni for the kingdom?"

64

"Will he be taking Kaimi with him if he leaves again?'

"Won't he have to fight Kekona to do that?"

Unaware of all the questions being asked, Kamoku stopped at the familiar waterfall, to listen to the soothing sound of the water as it tumbled and flowed down the cliff face. As he crossed the rocky stream, he took care not to step into the water in case an eel was nearby. Even though he had heard that the lake eels were part of the kingdom now, he could not believe that they wouldn't take advantage of a careless claw plunged into the water. Then he heard Kaimi's voice from the other bank.

"Dad, you came back!" Kaimi called. She watched as he very carefully crossed the rocks in the stream.

"You don't have to worry about the Eels now." She reassured him. "They aren't allowed to hurt anyone anymore."

"What if they do hurt someone?" he asked, once he was safely across.

"They will be expelled!" Kaimi was emphatic.

"I can't see that happening!" Kamoku was still doubtful.

"Kuma was expelled when he tried the hurt Pio Pukeko."

"Where is he now?" Kamoku wanted to know. Kuma had been a friend of his.

"He drowned in the waterfall; it is just as well too!" Kaimi said with feeling.

"Why?" Kamoku was intrigued.

"He tried to drown Kaimani after she refused to be his mate, but Keoni saved her." Kaimi added with satisfaction.

"You will see that Keoni and I have made changes to the family Burrow, speaking of Keoni, have you seen him yet?" Kaimi asked her voice was full of pride.

"Not yet." Kamoku lied.

"You will be proud of him." Kaimi was enthusiastic. He has achieved so much. You can't miss him," she added. "He looks just like mum!"

"I don't want to see him!" Kamoku's voice was harsh. "I don't want to be reminded that Kailee is gone." He was blind to her shock at his words. Kaimi could only look at her father in disbelief.

"But we all....."

"I'm tired from travelling." Kamoku cut off her words. "Are you coming with me?"

Kaimi's reply was flat and with finality that Kamoku could not ignore.

"No dad, I'm staying here. I've made my life with Kekona now."

Kamoku nodded and started to move on, realising he had just "lost" his daughter too. As Kamoku disappeared into the forest, Kekona emerged from the shadows to comfort Kaimi who now had tears in her eyes as she watched her father stride out of her life.

"We must make sure this doesn't happen to our children." Kaimi was determined.

"It won't." Kekona promised as he gave her a cuddle.

Kamoku was glad to reach the pepper tree where his old home lay; he was ready for some sleep. As he eased into the entrance he wondered what changes Kaimi and Keoni had made. It didn't take him long to find out. When he reached the place where Kailee had been, he met a smooth blank wall. The tunnels now led Kamoku in a different direction. As he followed the new path he came across a new smaller tunnel with deep claw marks etched into the wall.

Even Kamoku could not ignore the power of the symbol and knew that Keoni had taken over the family burrow. At the tunnel's end lay a thick bush. As he pushed it aside he looked down on the local stream. Knowing the tunnels belonged to Keoni now he slowly made his way back to the pepper tree. Kamoku was wondering whether to press on and leave the lake forever when Kale came by.

"Kamoku, you've come back! You must come in and tell us about your travels."

Kamoku allowed himself to be led into Kale and Kuri's tunnels where their welcome eased some of the anguish his return to the lake had brought to him.

As Keoni was helping displaced kiwis settle into his community, Emily and Jimmy were beginning their new venture at the mine. At first Jack wasn't happy with a woman working there, but after showing him she was as keen as Jimmy was to learn the different jobs in the process, he relented and soon she was enjoying her new role.

When it became obvious that Emily was expecting a child, both Jimmy and Jack tried to stop her from working, but Emily insisted on continuing to work for as long as she could.

"I am healthy and some exercise is good for me." She reasoned, which they could not argue with.

One morning near her due date, she was separating gold from the contents of a pan when she felt a twinge and knew it was time to deliver her baby.

"I'm going into town to see Isabelle and Molly." She said to Jimmy with a smile. "I've started my labour." When she saw Jimmy's look of panic she added, "Don't worry, I have plenty of time."

"I will take you in." Jimmy insisted. When he dropped her off at Molly's he promised to come in to see how she was when he had finished work for the day.

When Jimmy eventually returned late that evening; for he had Emily's jobs to finish as well as his own, Molly met him at the door with a smile.

"Everything has gone well. Come and meet your new son."

Emily was sitting up in the bed with Tommy in her arms.

"Here's Daddy." She said as she handed Tommy to Jimmy to hold.

Jimmy was very nervous as he had never held such a small child before and marvelled at the new life that now belonged to him. Sensing the change in position, Tommy woke up and started to cry for a feed. With some relief he handed Tommy back to Emily.

"Here's Mummy." He said.

"Will you be giving up work at the mine now you have Tommy to look after?" he asked Emily, for if she was, he would have to find a third person to help at the mine. He had managed to do her job as well as his own today, but he couldn't manage it for long.

"No," Emily replied with a smile. "I will take a couple of days off to make sure Tommy is feeding properly, but I will bring him with me."

Jimmy smiled and nodded; relieved they wouldn't have to find a replacement for her. The arrangement had worked out better than he had dared to hope. After a few days Emily returned to the mine, Tommy was content to be carried in the sling she had made. Several months passed in their new routine, when Emily found she needed to see Isabelle again. Isabelle confirmed Emily was expecting again.

67

"You may need to come in earlier for this baby." Isabelle warned "The labour won't be as long as the last one."

"What will I do if the baby comes at home or at work?" Emily asked. Molly gave her instructions on the instruments she would need and what she needed to do if it came. "Keep a little pack with you wherever you go, especially in the later months."

This advice was handy one wet afternoon at the mine when Emily went into labour again, with several strong contractions close together.

"Jimmy!" Emily called urgently as she went to the tent they had put up at the mine. "I need your help here." "Jimmy came running in to see her squatting on the edge of the chair. "The baby is coming; can you get the pack out of my bag?"

He could hardly believe his eyes as the baby's head emerged and quickly rummaged in the bag for the pack Emily asked for. Following her instructions he caught the baby in a blanket and wiped the baby's mouth and nose clear. The baby took a deep breath and began to cry, much to their relief. The baby was quickly wrapped in the blanket and cuddled in Emily's arms.

"What will we call her?" Jimmy asked with a big grin. He hadn't expected to deliver his child, but he was glad he was there for this one, for it would be many years before husbands were welcomed into the delivery room.

"We will call her Alice." Emily decided. Jimmy agreed happily, for Alice was one of his mother's names. "You've earned a rest." He said as he prepared to take the family in to Molly's.

When Jimmy came to take them home, Emily noticed he was very quiet.

"What's the matter?" she asked.

"Jack has left." Jimmy replied. "He has heard there are richer gold fields down in Otago. I've paid him out his share, but I will have to find another partner."

"Do we have to find someone else?" Emily asked. "I know that mining will be slower with just the two of us, but at least all the income will be ours now. We should try it for a little while to see how we manage."

"Do you think you can do it, now you have both the children?" Jimmy was doubtful.

"Of course I do!" Emily was firm. I will carry Alice in a sling and I will set up a safe play area for Tommy where I can keep an eye on him. Everything will be fine" she reassured him, and it was.

CHAPTER TEN

THE NEW ARRIVALS

Freckle Fantail's alarm call woke Orion Owl from his sleep. In the corner of his eye he saw a flash of brown fur as a creature jumped down from the trunk of the tree where Freckle had built her nest.

Swiftly and silently Orion swooped down to grab the creature around its neck. Ogilvie and Odette came to help hold the now fiercely struggling body as it dropped the Fantail egg to hiss and snarl at the owls as they firmly held the creature still.

"Why did you take my egg?" the now furious Fantail demanded as she flew down to peck the creature's head, before carefully picking up her egg to return it to her nest.

By now Keoni and Kaimani had emerged to see what all the fuss was about. Keoni was surprised to find Orion, Ogilvie and Olivia holding down a brown furry creature that he hadn't seen before. He noticed there was a second creature watching from the shadows. Orion saw Keoni emerge and called him over.

"Keoni, thank goodness you are here. This creature tried to take Freckles egg."

Keoni ran over to confront this new creature, wondering where it had come from.

"I am Keoni the leader of the animals in this forest. Who are you and where have you come from?"

Suzie stoat looked up at this strange animal with fear. She and her mate Sandie had come so far on their adventure, but the owls' sharp talons told her it could end at any moment. They had slipped onto the ship from their home territory near Dover to look for food, surviving the long voyage by stealing food from the humans when they could and hunting any mice they could catch. When the humans disembarked at this port, Suzie and Sandie had to leave too, having to run the gauntlet of dogs and cats before they reached the safety of bushland further up the river. As they moved inland they found plenty of berries and birds' eggs to feed on. No animal had challenged them until now.

Suzie was also wondering what sort of animal was in front of her. It's large round feathered body and small head with small eyes and an enormous long bill. This creature stood on long thin legs with long sharp claws which were much longer than hers.

"I'm Suzie Stoat. I come from a land far away. We came onto a ship to find food. The ship brought us here with some humans."

"Will you be able to go home again?" Keoni asked hopefully.

"I don't think so." Suzie was doubtful. "They brought dogs onto the ship when it came here. We had to jump off the ship and swim for our lives to the shore."

"Do you normally eat birds' eggs" Keoni asked with concern.

"Yes," Suzie replied. "Why do you ask?"

"In all the forest around this lake, animals are protected. If you are going to stay here, you will have to find other things to eat."

"We can do that, can't we Sandie?" Suzie called out to her mate. Slowly and carefully a nervous and worried Sandie appeared from behind his tree.

"Yes, we can change what food we eat." Sandie replied. He was prepared to do anything to save his mate.

Keoni nodded to Orion to release Suzie. Slowly and carefully Orion Ogilvie and Olivia released their hold on Suzie, who swiftly joined her mate. Pippa Pukeko who had also been watching the event unfold came forward to join the stoats.

"Hello, I'm Pippa Pukeko." She greeted them. "I will show you where to find food. Have you found any shelter yet?"

"Not yet." Suzie replied shyly. She found it hard to believe that they had been accepted by the local animals and free to live here.

"Do you prefer to live in trees, caves or burrows?" Pippa asked.

"We are happy to stay anywhere that is dry." Suzie replied as Pippa lead them away to meet Tarania Tui and Pania pigeon who then came along to show Sandie and Suzie flowers and berries they could eat. Sandie spotted a beetle and pounced on it.

"Are we allowed to eat these?" he asked.

"Yes." Pippa smiled. "We have plenty of those."

Sandie and Suzie quickly settled into their new home, finding an old hollow tree to live in, but back by Keoni's burrow Orion looked at Keoni with concern.

"If the stoats came here with humans, what other animals will come?"

Keoni nodded. "I'm concerned too. I think there will be many of them" A picture of the ferocious creature came back to his mind, filling him with dread. "We can only hope they will fit in with us."

"What if they won't?"

"We will have to change or make way for them." Keoni sighed bleakly before turning to return to bed. Even though Kaimani cuddled Keoni to give him comfort, it took a long time to sleep again.

In the coming months and years many new animals, both small and large came to the kingdom. Some animals such as Pixie and Porky Possum and Wattle and Wes Weasel stayed to live peacefully and to become part of the kingdom family. Stumpy the stag and Dorrie the Deer chose to live in the hills behind the lake while Thyme and Ted Tahr passed through to their new home in the Alps.

While Keoni and the animals were adjusting to the new arrivals to the kingdom, Emily and Jimmy were adjusting to working with their new family. The changes worked well and during the next three years the gold claim gave them a steady income.

They didn't know how much longer it would last though, as several of their neighbours had already abandoned their mines and moved on

One day the family made a trip into town for some supplies. There were more homes in Hokitika now and tent city had moved further into the forest. As Emily walked down the street she saw a sign which made her pause for a second look.

Wanted!

Workers for Water Supply Project at Lake Kaniere

Good rates of pay

Apply within

The next day they had packed up and were on their way to their new life at Lake Kaniere.

CHAPTER ELEVEN

KEONI'S LEGACY

Dawn was breaking when Orion Owl and Paranui Pigeon flew to find Keoni.

"Keoni!" panic could be heard in Paranui's voice, "Humans are coming. They are cutting the forest and bringing strange animals with them. What will we do?"

Keoni's heart sank when he heard this news, for he knew that to survive, kiwis would soon have to leave this area.

"We all need to shelter on the mountain." Keoni told them. "Paranui, will you go and see Kaga and tell him to take his kiwis to the mountain. Orion, will you tell the Pukekos? I will warn the eels too."

Keoni ran to the water's edge and began to smack the water as hard as he could with his flattened claw. From beyond the islands the long dark shadow of an eel swiftly crossed the bay to surface by Keoni's feet.

"Did you want me?" Erron asked.

"Yes" Keoni replied. "I've come to warn you all to keep away from the shore. Humans are coming. They are cutting the forest and are bringing animals with them. I think they are coming to stay."

"What will you do?" Erron asked.

"We will shelter on the mountain to begin with, but we may have to leave." Keoni's voice was bleak.

"Who will look after the kingdom when you go?" Erron was concerned.

"I will ask Orion."

"He is a good choice."

Keoni gave Erron a final warning before they parted.

"Don't take food or fish from a line dangled into the water!"

"Is that another human trick to catch us?" Erron asked grimly

"Yes."

"We will miss you all"

"It won't be forever." Keoni said with a smile. A vision of a young kiwi suddenly came into his mind.

"It won't?"

"The kingdom will rise again one day."

"We will look forward to it." Erron said realising Keoni was talking about a time well into the future.

Back in the forest, Pio Pukeko ran to Keoni when he heard the news. "We will shelter on the mountain too." Keoni nodded his agreement as Pio ran to collect his family.

Keoni raised his bill and called as loudly as he could. All the kiwis who were settling to sleep came running. When they had all gathered, he addressed the crowd.

"We need to shelter on the mountain today. We may be there for some time as humans are coming. These humans are cutting the forest and are bringing animals with them, so I expect that they have come to stay."

As the kiwis turned to make the journey up the mountain, Kekona, Kahika, Kaipo and Kahui who were visiting for their meeting, came up to Keoni.

"We will have to leave soon won't we?" Kekona asked anxiously realising the change that was coming to their lives. Keoni's bleak look and faint nod confirmed his fears.

"I will head back home and have a talk to Kaga." Kahui said as he looked at Keoni with sadness. Keoni nodded. He knew they would be making plans to leave.

"If you decide to leave, make sure you come back to see us first!" Kahika implored him.

The animals on the mountain took a long time to settle that morning. There were many discussions and plans being made of where they would go if they had to leave.

 Pio Pukeko decided to join his relatives in the next valley south of the lake, (to be known as Kokatahi). Kekona felt this would be a good time to explore the mountains and join the kiwis living in the Alps. Kahika had plans to head south to relatives near Okarito. With luck he would meet up with Kahui and travel with him. He knew Kahui was planning to go to Okarito to his relatives if he had to leave.

Kaipo was planning to head north to the Paparoa range, to an area known to humans as The Three Sisters Mountain. Kale and Kura had decided to visit her family in the north, beyond the Buller Gorge.

"Where are we going to go if we have to leave? Kaimani asked Keoni anxiously.

"We will head north," Keoni reassured her with a smile "and find somewhere nice to settle. I have family near Punakaiki." He didn't tell her he wasn't sure of his welcome there.

Orion flew through the forest wondering what changes he would find. Both the day and night animals had been disturbed as the humans came to set up their camps at Hans Bay and in the west at Sunny Bight. As Orion flew he saw a light flickering in the darkness and decided to investigate.

Orion was surprised to find the light in the forest was from a small fire stick that was sitting in a holder on the forest floor. Sitting on a log near the fire stick was a human. They held a feather in one claw and held a large white sheet in their other claw. Although the human had long claws and more of them than him, Orion was pleased to see the human didn't have any sharp talons. The human was making marks on the sheet with the feather, which they dipped in a pot of black ink. Intrigued, Orion silently flew to the branch above the human to see what they were making. Orion could hardly believe his eyes. A picture of the lake and the mountain in the western bay was appearing on the paper.

Suddenly the human turned around and looked straight at him. He saw fear in the human's eyes as they jumped up and ran away from the log. Orion knew he was safe from this human as they stood some distance away and watched him.

Wanting a closer look at the picture, Orion flew down onto the log and gazed at the page. He was amazed to recognise the islands and some of the trees in the bay. Ripples spread out in the water from a duck's wake as it swam. Billowing clouds swept across the sky above. Looking up at the human, he wondered what other pictures they could make. Quietly, he flew back up to his branch and waited. His patience was rewarded when the human picked up the paper and sat down again to draw. A clump of Flax in the foreground and a log on the pebble beach were added to complete the picture. A new blank page was produced. This time they drew symbols and pictures of animals. Some of the animals he knew, others he had never seen before. Orion was sorry when the human gathered up their paper, feather and ink to retreat to the tent nearby, leaving the forest in darkness.

Jimmy and Emily were happy with their new life at the lake. During the day Emily set up the camp, caring for the children and keeping them safe while Jimmy worked with the timber crew at the eastern bay as they cut trees. The timber from the trees was hauled away for the water duct they were building to bring water to the town.

After Jimmy and the children went to sleep in the tent nearby, Emily sat on the mossy log; her candle flickered and cast shadows in the darkness of the forest as she worked on her drawings.

She didn't hear Orion as he landed on the branch above her, but she could feel his eyes watching her sketch. Turning around Emily found the large brown eyes of a morepork owl staring into hers. She had heard the owls calling, but had never been so close to one.

Emily jumped up in fright, dropping her sketch pad on the ground as she ran several yards away. Slowly she turned to face the intruder. To her surprise the owl remained sitting on the branch. It then flew down onto the log Emily had been sitting on to peer down at the sketch pad. Emily realised to her amazement the owl was more interested in her pictures than her. After taking a good look at the picture she had made of the lake, the owl looked up quizzically at Emily before flying back up to the branch it had been sitting on. Cautiously, Emily picked up her sketch pad and sat down on the log again to finish her sketch.

The next night Orion saw the human had two children with them. The human was pointing to a picture and then the symbol saying words and getting the children to repeat them. Through these lessons, Orion learnt about human language.

One evening it was raining. Orion didn't expect to see the humans out in the wet, but was surprised to see light moving in the forest. He followed the light to find the human holding a canopy (humans call them umbrellas) over their fire stick. The children were following behind. They went into the cave where the glow worms live. Orion followed them in and sat on a rocky ledge above the humans who had sat themselves on some rocks on the floor.

Also in the cave was a big box. The human opened it and brought out some books Orion had not seen before and placed them on a shelf made from pongees.

The human opened a book to show it to the children. It was from a place far away called Africa. Brightly coloured pictures of humans with black skin and coloured costumes along with beautiful flowers and strange animals leapt from the pages. Seeing the books gave Orion an idea, he flew off to find Keoni.

"Keoni are you there?" Orion called as he flew over the slopes of the mountain.

"I'm here." Keoni answered him from under a nearby tree. Orion quickly joined him to feed together. He looked for beetles while Keoni looked for worms.

"I've been watching one of the humans." Orion was enthusiastic. "They make pictures and words on paper to make a book to read."

"How can that help us?" Keoni was puzzled.

"I've been learning their language." Orion replied. "You could make a book about your kingdom."

"But we may be leaving soon!" Keoni protested.

"Yes." Orion agreed. "You need to leave something for the next leader."

"You are right." Keoni acknowledged the wisdom of Orion's idea. "How do we make one?"

"The human has left paper and things to write with, in the cave where Gabrielle lives. Come and have a look at all the books they have left." Intrigued Keoni followed Orion to the cave.

"Hello Gabrielle." Keoni called as they entered the dark cave. A cluster of blue lights shone from the roof. Gabrielle turned on the lights along her silky thread to light the cave.

"Hello Keoni, Hello Orion. Did you bring Keoni to see the books? "

"Yes" Orion answered. "I'm trying to persuade Keoni to make a book about the Kingdom."

"What a wonderful idea!" Gabrielle exclaimed. "We will be happy to give you light while you make one." Gabrielle's friends also turned on their lights to make the cave very bright.

Orion took Keoni over to the pongee shelf and very carefully showed Keoni one of the books Emily had made. Orion couldn't help smiling at the delight on Keoni's face as he was transported to a new world, through the pages of the book.

"Alright, you have convinced me!" Keoni admitted. Let's get started."

Orion opened the box and brought out some paper, the feather and the ink. He found the feather quill harder to grip and to write with than he thought.

The human made it look so easy to do, but with practice he found he could write too.

"What do you want to call your book?" Orion asked. Keoni thought for a minute.

"The Kiwi Kingdom" is the best title I can think of." Orion carefully wrote the title at the top of the page. "What about a picture or symbol on the front.?" Keoni found that easy.

"The claw marks I made on the wall at home should look good. The first two pages inside the cover need to be left for some pouches. I'm not sure what to say next though."

"Pretend you are talking to them." Orion suggested. "They will want to know the history of how your kingdom started, the rules and any codes you want them to know."

During the night they worked on the book untill eventually Keoni called a break.

"I'm getting hungry."

"So am I." Orion replied. Carefully putting the feather and ink back where he found them. The book carefully stored away in the back of the cave where it couldn't be seen.

They went out into the forest together and searched for a feed as they did the first time they met.

"Do you remember the first time we did this?" Orion asked.

"I do!" Keoni replied with a smile.

Suddenly there was a growl and the running of an animal they hadn't seen before running towards them. Keoni knew instantly it was the creature of his dreams and started running for his life. Orion flew into the tree to see what the creature was. He hadn't seen one before either. He was alarmed to see it had a big mouth and lots of sharp teeth and was very swift to run on its four legs. He saw it gaining on Keoni. He didn't wait any longer and swooped down on the animal, his claws outstretched.

Toby the terrier had been brought out to the lake with his new owner Jimmy. His previous master was sailing to Australia and did not want to take him. Toby hated the sand-flies that bit him but did love the children, Tommy and Alice who played with him at his new home. He understood he was on guard when he was put outside at bedtime. Toby heard the noise of two animals coming steadily towards his territory.

With a deep growl he started running towards them. One of the animals opened his wings and flew out of Toby's reach into a tree, but the other creature ran swiftly away. Toby loved to chase and sped after it. Just as he was getting close to it, he felt the winged animal's claws dig deep into his neck. With a yelp Toby ducked his head and rolled into the bushes, making the animal let go.

When he cautiously emerged there was no sign of them. Carefully he made his way back to the family tent and set himself on guard again with a sigh.

Back at the cave Keoni and Orion looked at each other glumly. They knew Keoni had a lucky escape.

"Are you alright?" Orion asked. Keoni nodded.

"I was lucky you were with me though. I'm not sure how much time we have now that that creature is here. It is important I finish the book."

Silently Orion went to fetch the feather and ink while Keoni brought out the book. Quietly they continued their task untill finally they were able to look at each other with a look of triumph.

"We've done it!" Orion smiled. Keoni gave a tired nod in agreement. He looked out of the cave to see daylight.

"Look how late it is. Kaimani will be wondering where I am." Keoni then spoke the words Orion had been dreading. "It isn't safe for us to be here any longer. We will leave tonight."

"I will find Paranui and get him to tell Kaga and Kahui." Orion offered Keoni.

"I was going to go over to say goodbye to them on my way...." As he said it there was a rustle near the cave.

"Who is there?" Keoni challenged.

"It's only us!" Kahui replied as he led Kaga Kekona Kahika and Kaipo into the cave.

 "It isn't safe for us on the western side of the lake now that humans are there. We came over to say goodbye before we leave tonight." Kaga said sadly.

"It isn't safe for us to stay here either. I was going to come over to see you on our way tonight too." Keoni replied.

They all looked at the book in front of Keoni.

"What is that?" Kaga asked

"I'm leaving a book for the next leader. Kahui, Kekona Kahika and Kaipo, I want you to think of a rhyme that only you and your families will know, of where you live so that only a kingdom supporter will be able to tell the next leader where to find you."

"Orion, will you take off my amulet?" Keoni asked as he lowered his head.

Carefully Orion opened the book at the front page where the pouch was waiting then used his claw to lift the twine over Keoni's head before putting the amulet in its place in the book. Keoni then put the book away at the back of the cave.

"I don't know about you, but it is my bed time!" Keoni said with a yawn.

"Yes," Kaga replied with a grin. "Kaimani sent us down to fetch you!"

As they quietly retreated up onto the mountain, they could hear the sounds of the humans beginning their day. Kaga and Kahui were amazed at the large burrows the grey kiwis lived in. There was enough room for all of their kiwis to sleep comfortably there too. He now understood why Keoni found it hard to sleep when he visited his cosy burrow on the mountain.

Kaimani was feeling restless when she woke. Keoni was still sound asleep. All her life she had lived at this lake and now they were leaving. She knew they would never come back again. She wanted to see the lake one more time before they left for their new life. Quietly she eased herself out of their sleeping spot, being careful not to disturb Keoni and tiptoed out of the burrow. Kaga and Kahui were outside feeding as she emerged.

"Is Keoni up yet?" Kahui asked.

"No, he is still asleep." Kaimani replied. "I am going down to see the lake before we leave. I shouldn't be long." Kahui and Kaga nodded. Leaving this lovely place was going to be a wrench for them too.

Making her way through the forest in the late evening light, Kaimani saw Freckle the Fantail was settled in her nest. Paranui and Pania pigeon were quietly sheltering in their tree too. She was very careful to keep well away from the humans' camp, though the humans were being quiet this evening too she noticed. What she didn't know was that the human's Dog, Toby was already following her. He had heard and smelt her from some distance away. Toby had already fed well on the scraps from the humans' dinner, but he was still hungry enough for another snack if he could catch it.

At the water's edge Kaimani's eyes feasted on the scene in front of her. The sky beyond the mountain in the western bay was bathed in gold and pink light from the sunset. Its dark green slopes forever watchful over the lake waters, now calm waiting for the cloak of darkness to descend. She was watching the eel Erron lazily swimming nearby when a growl behind her made her jump. Kaimani glanced around. The dog was about to pounce on her!

With a scream Kaimani dived into the water with Erron, the dog following her into the water. Kaimani thrashed at the dog with her claws as hard as she could. She was relieved when Erron also launched himself at the dog with his razor teeth, making the dog retreat to the beach. Erron smacked his tail on the water before renewing his attack to keep the dog at bay.

Darkness had fallen when Keoni woke. Kaimani and their visitors had already left the burrow. *"They are probably out feeding."* Keoni thought as he made his way outside. Kaga, Kahui, Kahika, Kekona and Kaimi were waiting for him. Kekona and Kaimi were going to travel with the others to the Styx River in the next valley before heading up to the Alps.

"Take care" Keoni said "and have a good life."

"I'm sorry it's over...." Kahui began sadly.

"It's not over." Keoni replied cheerfully, "We are just spreading the kingdom to make an Empire."

"Kaga had to smile at Keoni's optimism as they set out on their journey. He had the longest journey of all, down to Fiordland. He wasn't sure how the kingdom would be received down there either.

Keoni went to find Kaimani, but there was no sign of her. He was starting to feel anxious when he spotted Kaipo feeding nearby and joined him.

"Have you seen Kaimani?" Keoni asked.

"Hasn't she come back from the lake yet?" Kaipo asked "She wanted one last look before she left."

Keoni's anxiety was increasing. He knew something had happened to her.

"I think she is in trouble." Keoni said, taking off down the mountain with Kaipo keeping close to his heels. Racing through the forest, all was quiet untill they came close to the shore. They could hear the sound of growling from the dog. To Keoni and Kaipo's horror they found Kaimani sitting in the water, surrounded by eels who were snapping at the dog every time it tried to enter the water to reach her.

With a deep growl, Keoni and Kaipo launched themselves at the dog, slashing at his back and nose with their claws as he turned around to attack them. Yelping, the dog ran off into the forest.

"Thank you for saving her." Keoni thanked the eels.

"We are glad we could help." Erron replied. "When are you leaving?"

"As soon as I'm sure Kaimani is able to travel." Keoni replied, watching with concern as she shivered after coming out of the water.

"Take care and have a good journey." Erron said in parting.

"We will do, thank you." Keoni replied as they watched the eels melt into the dark waters of the night.

The wind was cold as it blew across the lake. *Autumn is coming.* Keoni thought as he felt the coolness through his feathers.

"Do you want to go back to our burrow to warm up before we leave?" Keoni asked Kaimani.

She nodded and wondered why she couldn't stop shivering. Keoni led the way with Kaipo following, to make sure the dog couldn't get to her easily.

In the shelter of the tunnels they retreated to their sleeping area, Keoni and Kaipo placed themselves either side of Kaimani to comfort and warm her. Eventually the shivering subsided. Suddenly they heard a noise at the entrance under the pepper bush. The dog was coming! Silently Keoni led Kaimani and Kaipo out of the entrance by the stream. Once out, they ran for their lives, quickly crossing the stream where the Pukekos lived and through the forest; not stopping untill they reached the Arahura River. Keoni led them upstream untill he found a shallow stretch to cross. They didn't linger in these waters which were icy cold. Once safely on the other side they were happy to hear a soft call from Kaipo's mate, who with the rest of the group heading for the Paparoa range was waiting for them.

Back at the lake Erron started his descent to the sanctuary. The eels that had come to help him came with him. Soon the sanctuary was full of eels, waiting to hear what Erron had to say.

"I thank everyone who came to help protect Keoni's mate. Tonight Keoni and the kiwis leave us for it is no longer safe for them to stay. Orion owl and his descendants will continue to keep the kingdom rules in our forest while we will continue to protect the lake untill the kingdom returns."

With these words the animals of the lake and forest at Kaniere began their long wait for the future.

CHAPTER TWELVE

NEW CHALLENGES

Emily brushed away the sandfly that nipped at her ankles and drew her skirt closer as she sat on the narrow gravel beach. She watched her children, Tommy and Alice as they splashed in the water's edge of Hans Bay, the sight and sound of timber being felled and hauled away from nearby. As Emily enjoyed the afternoon sun, she thought of how different her life had been and was glad she and Jimmy had made their life here. Soon they would start looking for the farming land that Jimmy had dreamt of.

Suddenly the sound of a galloping horse made her look up. It was one of the crew that Jimmy worked with. He pulled up on the dirt track near to Emily.

"Emily can you get Hector and your cart? There has been an accident!"

"Who is it?" she asked, but he had already galloped off towards Hokitika. Starting to feel anxious, Emily called the children.

"Tommy, Alice, we have to go!"

Heeding the urgency in her voice the children quickly joined her instead of pleading for another five minutes as they usually did. They had seen the horseman speak to their mother and knew something important was happening. Hector greeted Emily with a gentle neigh when she approached with his bridle. He knew there was work to be done.

After loading the children and Toby into the cart they set off down the track. When they reached the scene several of the men were hacking furiously with their axes at a large tree lying on the ground so they could attach ropes to it.

Emily could not see Jimmy among the crew working desperately on the tree and knew he was under it. Mick the foreman saw Emily waiting and watching and came over.

"I'm sorry Emily," he said. "The tree fell the wrong way. Jimmy's leg is stuck under it." She could only nod, feeling numb inside.

"Where is daddy?" Tommy asked interested in the hive of activity in front of them.

"Daddy has been hurt when the tree fell on him. They will get him out soon." She tried to reassure him.

Six horses were attached to the ropes and urged to pull. Emily gathered the children close to her and tried to cover their ears to block out the scream that came as the log was lifted off Jimmy's leg. Mick reached into his pocket and brought out a small whiskey bottle, ordering Jimmy to drink, for first aid kits and pain killing medications had yet to be invented.

When he was feeling more comfortable, Jimmy was lifted onto Emily's cart with some canvas they had made into a stretcher. Carefully she covered him with a blanket she had brought with her. Tommy sat next to his father, silently holding his hand. Toby now subdued, lay next to Tommy with his head on his paws.

"I will be in to see how he is when we have finished." Mick told Emily.

"Thank you." Emily managed to say as she turned the cart around for the long twelve mile trip to town.

Near the Kaniere Township they were met by the Doctor and Molly who had been told of the accident. The reins were taken off Emily and she and the children were transferred to Molly's cart. Emily watched the doctor as he looked under the blanket at Jimmy's leg.

"I won't be able to save it, I'm sorry." The doctor said when he looked at her.

Emily nodded and waited untill their cart had disappeared into the distance at a speedier pace before she allowed her tears to flow.

"Where is daddy going?" Tommy wanted to know as he watched their cart leave.

"The Doctor is looking after him." Molly reassured him.

Some hours later the Doctor brought Jimmy to the hotel. He spoke to Molly.

"How is she?" he asked.

"She is sleeping soundly." Molly replied. "I gave her one of my cocktails as a nightcap. One of the maids is keeping an eye on the children so she won't be disturbed."

"If she wakes up badly give her some of this." The doctor said as he produced a brown bottle of medicine from his pocket.

Jimmy gave Emily a faint smile when she was allowed to see him the next evening. His ashen face told her he wasn't out of danger yet.

"Don't worry about anything....." she started to say.

"Everything will be alright." Jimmy finished for her, before drifting back to sleep.

In the following days as Jimmy made a steady recovery, Emily wondered about their future. The team out at the lake had packed and sent in all of their possessions, except of course the books she had left in the cave, something she didn't think about until many years later when she was too frail to retrieve them.

Emily knew that Jimmy's dream of a farm was unlikely now, so she would have to find a job. The next morning as Emily was having breakfast with Molly an idea came to her.

"I have to find a job soon." Emily broached the subject. "I can embroider, but I'm not sure about my dressmaking skills. I know I can teach though. Do you know of any families who would like a tutor?"

"I'm sure there are plenty of them." Molly said with a big smile, thinking of the many children in the town in need of an education. "I will make some enquiries."

By the next week Emily's career as a tutor was launched and their future was now secure. When Jimmy became mobile after a long convalescence, He was sporting a peg leg and walking stick and used a wheelchair for long distances. It was time now to move to their new home.

"I know your dream of a big farm is out of reach now," Emily said to Jimmy as he looked despairingly out of the hotel window at the passers-by. "What do you think of a home with a small one?" She asked with a little smile. Jimmy looked at that smile and knew she had found something special. Jimmy allowed himself to be led outside to the cart where Hector was waiting patiently. The children and Toby came too. There were many waves and "Hellos" to Emily as the family passed by.

A small distance out of town in bushland stood a gate. Tommy hopped down from the cart to let them through. As they travelled down the long drive they came to an orchard of apple and plum trees planted on both sides. Beyond the orchard was a rambling white house with big verandas set in a large lawn. Fir trees had been planted to protect the house from wet and windy weather. Nearby stood a barn, chickens ran free in the yard. A vegetable patch lay safely behind a tall fence. Two large paddocks lay beyond.

"We could have some sheep and a cow if you want." Emily said at the large grin on Jimmy's face.

"We will have them!" he said giving her a big hug. He had never dreamed they would find a home and a life like this.

Kaimani sat on her egg with a happy smile as darkness reclaimed the Punakaiki coast from the setting sun. The journey to get here seemed like a bad dream now.

They had to overcome the challenges of crossing the many rivers and streams on the way, though the biggest challenge of all were the animals whose territory they had to cross. They learnt to fear the possums with their strong furry limbs and long sharp claws; that were so agile in shinning down trees to challenge them as they passed by.

The biggest danger of all was from other kiwis, which were now prepared to kill anyone they found on their territory. Keoni and his band soon found it was safer to travel at dawn and dusk. At dawn they were able to avoid the night animals that had gone to rest for the day and at dusk they were able to avoid the humans who had retreated to their homes for the evening.

The day finally came when it was time to say goodbye to Kale and Kuri as they ventured further north. Kaimani wondered if she would ever see her parents and her new brother Kaliyah again but managed to smile as she wished them a safe journey.

Kamoku was feeding quietly in the dense forest of the Paparoa Range with his eldest son Kamoku who was nearby.

After he had left Kale and Kuri on his last visit to Lake Kaniere he headed north until he reached his son Kamoku's territory where he was now living. His son had been generous and given him his own territory inside the large territory he controlled. Young Kamoku had been shocked at how much his father had aged since he had last seen him only a few years ago. As Kamoku fed two kiwis appeared through the trees. The first was the unmistakable image of Kailee.

"What are you doing here?" Kamoku demanded. "Why can't you leave me alone?" he added in frustration and despair.

Keoni recognised this was the stranger who had disappeared from his southern shore and wondered why he was being so angry.

Hearing his father's harsh tone, Kamoku came over to see what was happening.

"I'm here," Keoni replied "because Kaimi my sister told me that we have family here. We had to leave our territory when humans moved in and have cut down our shelter.

They brought animals with them that chased us and would have killed us if they could."

"Who are you?" Keoni added. "I remember that you came onto my territory but disappeared before I could talk to you and, why are you hostile to me?"

The two Kamoku's looked at each other in dismay. The son he had not expected to see ever again was here.

"I'm Kamoku." As Keoni's eyes widened he added, "Yes, I'm your father, and this is your eldest brother, Kamoku. You are no doubt wondering why I abandoned you and didn't try to look after you?" Keoni could only nod his agreement.

"When I found Kailee had died after she had delivered your egg, I was full of grief that she was gone from me and I somehow blamed your egg for it. It wasn't till later when I calmed down that I went to retrieve your egg, but it had gone by then."

"Yes," Keoni replied. "I was lucky Kuri had come to see mum and saw you leave; she found my egg and took it home. I was also lucky Kaimi helped me to hatch. I would never have got out on my own."

"Your territory at the lake is still my territory too." Kamoku reminded Keoni. "While I was travelling south I heard another leader called Keoni had taken over. I was going to teach you a lesson, but when I saw your face and saw my Kailee again and you answered to Keoni, I knew who you were and couldn't do it."

"Why did you change the tunnels in our burrow?" Kamoku wanted to know. "There is no sign left that my Kailee is there."

"I had to do it." Keoni said in sorrow. "When Kaimi took me there for the first time someone else was in there. They had dug mum up, which upset Kaimi terribly. I think they were trying to move mum so they could take over the burrow. This way no-one can touch her ever again and the burrow remains ours!"

Kamoku nodded his agreement at the wisdom of this, but the sight of his son was becoming too much for him to bear.

You don't know how much I still miss her and how much it hurts when I see your face! Please go!" Kamoku cried as he turned away. Young Kamoku became angry at seeing his father so upset.

"You are not welcome here. Go back to the valley." Young Kamoku demanded.

Keoni was upset too that his father still rejected him, but he now understood why and accepted that his life now lay apart from his family.

"There are humans in the valley too." Keoni said carefully. "If you can tell us where your territory extends to, we will make sure we don't disturb you again."

After giving Keoni instructions he asked, "You aren't bringing your kingdom here?"

"We will live by my rules of course, but we don't expect anyone else to unless they want to; besides it will be another hundred years before the kingdom rises again."

"When will that be and how do you know that?" Kamoku asked alarmed that this young kiwi seemed to know what the future held.

"That's about three or four of our lifetimes away." Keoni replied. "As for knowing, I just do." He said with conviction as a vision of a young kiwi came back to him. With that Keoni and Kaimani turned away to find their special place where they could begin their life together.

RETURN

OF THE

KIWI

KINGDOM

CHAPTER ONE

KEANU AND KEONA KIWI

Keona Kiwi sighed contently as she lay down to rest with her mate Keanu in their burrow at Punakaiki. They drifted off to sleep to the sound of Nikau Palms rustling in the sea breeze and the waves sweeping in from the Tasman Sea to smack against the Pancake rocks below them.

Their search to find a suitable place to dig their burrow had been long and hard. Ever since Keanu's great grandfather Keoni had come here 100 years ago, pressure had been put on the family to move elsewhere by their relative Kamoku who claimed most of the territory in the area. As soon as Keoni had passed on to the spirit world, Kamoku had sent a member of his community to occupy his burrow. Kaimani was forced to share with their son and his family. The family was surrounded by members of Kamoku's community who had been sent to spy on the family and make sure they never strayed on his territory.

Some years ago, a bulldozer had cleared a track up the hillside to a flat level area, which had since been left to nature and was covered in moss and ferns, with young Nikau palms starting to sprout. The only place available for Keanu and Keona to make their home was in the bank at the back of the flat level area. They had made friends with their neighbour Kahi who was nearby, ignoring the fact that she was there to spy on them and were looking forward to delivering their first egg in a month or so.

Keanu and Keona's sleep was interrupted by the sound and vibration of a heavy vehicle labouring slowly up the track, to stop at the flat area near their burrow. They watched with horror and worry as a human emerged and used a hoist to offload a large load of timber onto the ground in front of their burrow. They both knew that their life here was to end.

"I think some humans are going to live here." Keanu voiced their fears. "We will have to find another place to live."

"Where will we go?" Keona asked, "All the other safe places for us to live here are in Big Kamoku's territory. We know he won't allow us to go there."

"We could try living at Lake Kaniere." Keanu suggested. "My great-grandfather Keoni used to live there before humans came and hunted Kiwi. He said it is a big, beautiful and peaceful place with plenty of food."

"How far away is the lake?" Keona asked. She was anxious to be in her new home before her egg was due to be hatched.

"It will take some time for us to reach it." Keanu was frank.

"We have three big rivers to cross and in between there are big forests and towns where humans live to travel through."

He looked at Keona's expanding body. "If your egg comes before we get there, we will have to manage wherever we are untill our chick is big enough to travel"

After the truck left, their neighbour Kahi came to see what all the noise was about.

"Keona, what are you going to do?" Kahi asked, after seeing all the timber in front of their burrow.

"We are moving south to Lake Kaniere." Keona advised her, and added. "Kamoku should be pleased. Humans have succeeded where he didn't!" Seeing Kahi's raised eyebrows, Keona elaborated.

"Kamoku's side of our family have been trying to force us from here ever since Keanu's great grandfather came years ago.

"But Kaniere is so far away!" Kahi protested, realising she was going to miss this young couple.

"Yes." Keona agreed. "But we will have all the room we need and we can always come back to visit."

"You must try to come back for a visit after you have settled in." Kahi invited them. "If humans keep building here, we may come and join you."

That evening both Keanu and Keona rose early to search for extra food to sustain them on their journey. At sunset they wandered down to the pancake rocks and found a spot to watch the golden glow from the sun spread out over the water as it sunk beneath the waves.

Being high tide, the waves crashed into the rocks, making the ground tremble under their feet and then shot up through the blowholes, soaking them with water.

"I'm going to miss this." Keanu said, feeling sad to be leaving this beautiful place.

"Yes." Keona agreed, "But we will find other things to love at the lake."

Keanu and Keona quietly set off on their journey, however news of their departure had spread through the Kiwi population and calls of "Goodbye" and "Good luck" rang in their ears as they steadily made their way south.

Up steep ponga-clad hills, down fern filled gullies and over creeks spilling onto the black sandy beaches Keanu and Keona walked.

By dawn they had reached a headland overlooking the sea, and after scratching out a temporary burrow, they were ready for sleep. After several more nights of travel, sometimes in starlight, others in driving rain, Keanu and Keona found themselves in suburban Dobson and facing the wide, fast-flowing Grey River.

"This is the first river we have to cross to reach the lake." Keanu said as he led the way upstream.

Keanu and Keona kept to the shadows of human's gardens as much as they could, but had to run the gauntlet of dogs snarling and barking at them as they passed by.

The Kiwis were relieved to find a big metal bridge and were nearly across to the Greymouth side, when out of the shadows a large black cat appeared to bar their path, arching his back, hissing and snarling.

Keanu didn't say a word, but put his head down and launched himself at the cat, his big claws about to descend and rake it. The cat took one look at the claws and turned to flee!

On the south side of the bridge, Keanu and Keona were in the business area of Greymouth, which was well lit and with few places to hide. They crept along alleyways and back streets while listening for the ocean and found their way back to the coast. By morning Keanu and Keona had come to a farm. They made a quick search of the vegetable garden for their supper before the retreated to the safety of a hollow tree in the sheep paddock to sleep, covering themselves with some leaves for extra shelter.

That night under the starlit sky Keanu and Keona continued their journey. In the coastal forest, Owls and Bats watched with interest as they quietly passed by.

At the Taramakau River Keanu and Keona waited for a quiet time to pass over the narrow metal and wooden bridge, as the deep fast-flowing river looked too dangerous to swim across.

On hearing a rustle in the bushes behind them they turned to find a large Possum with claws and teeth barred rushing at them! Possums are well known for killing Kiwis, so united, Keanu and Keona lifted up their claws. In the following battle where both feathers and fur were sent flying, they defeated the Possum, who fled up the nearest tree to lick his wounds.

"Who are you, and why are you in my territory?" the Possum demanded.

"We are Keanu and Keona, and we are passing through to Lake Kaniere."

"What are you doing at the Lake?"

"My great-grandfather used to live there, so we are going there to live.

"That's all right then. Have a good trip and tell Paddy and Pansy Possum that Perry and Prunella say "Hello." At that a smaller female Possum appeared next to Perry giving the Kiwis a smile.

"We shall." Keanu and Keona promised as they carried on towards the Arahura Valley.

Primrose Pigeon was visiting her cousin Polly in a nearby tree and saw the battle between Perry Possum and the Kiwis. She listened with delight to hear the Kiwis were returning to Keanu's family home at Kaniere.

Kiwis were leading members of Lake Kaniere community before they were forced to leave, so long ago. She must go home and tell everyone so they could organise a welcome. After saying goodbye to Polly, Primrose set off towards the lake. Keona saw the bright colours of Primrose's feathers as she left, thinking what a beautiful bird it was and wished she could fly too.

As Keanu and Keona made their way south, the bush-covered ridges above the narrow coastal plain gave plenty of shelter and food as they recovered from their wounds.

At the Arahura Pa, a dog heard and smelt them as Keanu and Keona tried to sneak by. It chased them to the river where both Keanu and Keona were forced into the freezing cold water that came from the mountain snow in the Southern Alps. Taking advantage of the dog's unwillingness to get wet, Keanu and Keona swam across to the other side of the river and the safety of some bulrushes.

"I think we are near the end of our journey now." Keanu said, once he was sure that they weren't being followed. "That was the last river we had to cross. It is time to head inland."

Keona brightened at this news. She was feeling tired after all of their adventure, also she felt she would soon need to nest.

On reaching the scrubland of Blue Spur, they sheltered in the bracken for a rest. Beyond the scrubland lay large boulders, left behind from a gold-mining dredge, as far as the eye could see, with only a narrow winding track through it. (The gold dredge tailings at Blue Spur have now been rehabilitated and are covered in Pine forest.)

"What happened here?" Keona wondered.

"I don't know." Keanu replied. "We can only hope the forest will grow back."

Onward they travelled untill a row of houses brought them to the Lake Kaniere Road. Keanu and Keona were happy to raid the gardens for a feed, before they headed for the safety of the forest. Excitement grew as Keanu and Keona steadily made their way through the dark and damp under the forest canopy towards their new home.

Finally they came into a clearing, and there before them lay the lake, like a mirror set into the landscape; reflecting the sky and the forest around the lake.

"Oh," Keona marvelled at the sight before them. "I will be at home here." Then she spotted the pigeon she had seen at the Taramakau River. "Hello" Keona called out to her. "Weren't you at the bridge while we were there?"

"Yes," the Pigeon replied. "I'm Primrose, and welcome home."

Then Keanu and Keona found they were surrounded by animals saying "Hello" and "Welcome."

Baskets of food were produced, including one full of worms, which Keanu and Keona accepted gratefully. Everyone sat down for the feast as they were introduced.

Owen the Morepork Owl asked Keanu if he knew what his grandparent's names were.

"Yes," Keanu replied. "They were Keoni and Kaimani."

"Excellent!" Owen replied. He thought for a moment before asking, "Would you like to see their old home?"

Keanu was astonished. "Is it still there?"

"Yes." Owen confirmed. "The tunnels are still in good condition. You can have them if you want, unless you prefer to make a new home."

Both Keanu and Keona were delighted that a home was already waiting for them.

"Can you manage to travel some more?" Owen asked after the feast. "Keoni's territory was on the eastern side of the lake." Owen pointed to an area several Kilometres further on and shaded by Mount Tahua from the early morning sun.

"We would like to be in our own home for our sleep time." Keanu replied. They then set off with Owen leading and all their new friends and neighbours followed them.

Keoni's territory lay in an area of thick forest where the branches and tree ferns formed a dark canopy overhead, while ferns of many sorts covered the ground. A creek with mossy banks and bulrushes gently meandered nearby between the trees to the lake. Owen pushed aside a thick bush in the bank to reveal the opening to a long tunnel.

"Welcome Home."

Keanu and Keona wasted no time in exploring their new home. At the end of another tunnel Keanu and Keona saw a claw mark on the wall. They meant to ask Owen Owl if he knew anything about it, but after making themselves at home, forgot about it.

Soon Keona laid a single large egg. Keanu and Keona took turns to look after it untill Kupe was hatched. Now Keanu and Keona's happiness was complete. They finally had a safe place to live and care for their son.

CHAPTER TWO

KUPE KIWI MEETS SAM STOAT

One night Kupe was out looking for something tasty for his meal when he saw a brown furry head looking at him from behind the tree fern. Remembering his father Keanu's warning that there were brown furry animals called Stoats that hunted Kiwi, Kupe turned to flee to the safety of the family burrow.

"Please don't go! I want be friends and play with you." called a little voice.

Kupe turned to face the tree fern and out scampered a young stoat to trot over to Kupe, his coat gleaming in the moonlight.

"Hello, I'm Sam." the Stoat introduced himself. "I don't have any brothers or sister to play with. Will you be my friend and play Chasey with me?"

"I'm Kupe." The little Kiwi replied. "I will be your friend. What is Chasey?"

"It is a game where one animal runs after the other until they touch them somewhere. It is then the turn of the other animal to try and touch them." Sam explained.

"You're first!" Kupe called as he scampered off with Sam in hot pursuit. Squeals and shouting rang through the forest as the Kiwi and the Stoat chased each other in and out of the trees. Keanu came out of the burrow to see why Kupe was making so much noise. He was both afraid and angry to see Kupe being chased by a Stoat!

Keanu rushed over to protect Kupe from the enemy. He was about to slash Sam with his big claws when Kupe stopped him.

"Dad, please stop! Don't hurt him!" Kupe shouted.

Keanu put down his claws, but looked at Sam with suspicion.

"Dad, this is Sam my friend." Kupe introduced him. "We are playing Chasey."

"It is nice you have found a friend to play with, but you have woken all of our neighbours from their sleep." Keanu warned. Looking around, Kupe could see Tania Tui looking from the Kowhai Tree and Fern Fantail was peering over her nest in the Rimu Tree. Paddy and Pansy Possum also were watching from the Rata Tree, Heather Hedgehog was peering out from the leaf litter underneath the nearby Totara Tree and Poppy Pukeko was looking out from the bulrushes by the stream.

"I think it is time you said goodbye." Keanu advised them.

"I will see you again tomorrow. Meet me down by the lake." Sam invited Kupe.

"I will look forward it." Kupe agreed as he waved his new friend goodbye and watched Sam slip away into the darkness of the forest. The next evening, Kupe found Sam waiting for him, curled up under Flax by the water's edge, reading a book.

"Hello Sam, what are you doing?" Kupe asked.

"I'm reading a book from the school library." Sam replied.

In the book were pictures of animals Kupe had not seen before.

"What do you do at school?" Kupe wanted to know.

"They teach us interesting things such as how to tell time, so we won't be late. We also learn to read signs and about all the plants and animals to keep us safe. We play games and have excursions to different places. Best of all, we can make friends." Sam advised him.

"It sounds like fun." Kupe was impressed.

"It is." Sam reassured him. "Ask your parents if you can go."

At that moment, there was a rustle among the flax and Keanu appeared to see who Kupe was talking to.

"Hi Dad," Kupe greeted his father. "Sam was showing me this book he learnt to read at school. Can I go too? They learn many good things there." pleaded Kupe.

Keanu thought for a moment. Kiwis normally learned everything they needed to know at home with their parents. He realised that Sam's mixing with other animals at school had helped Sam to make friends with Kupe, an animal he would normally hunt; so school must be a good place.

"Yes, you can go to school." Keanu agreed. "I will take you along after you have had your sleep. Who teaches the class?" Keanu asked Sam.

"I go to the day class. Mrs Tui teaches us and Mr. Owl teaches the night class." Sam informed him.

The next evening as the sun was setting behind the lake hills; there was much excitement in the Kiwi burrow as Kupe prepared for school by eating a big breakfast of worms and slugs. Finally, he was ready and set off with Keanu and Keona for the big cave by an old Totara Tree, where the school was held.

The path to school was dark and quiet, but at the cave the Glow worms' lights shone bright. They looked like strings of fairy lights, bathing the area with light. At the entrance Owen Owl stood, welcoming the parents and children to the class.

"Hello Keanu and Keona. Are you bringing your child to join us?" Own asked with delight on seeing the Kiwi family here. "Would you like to stay for the first session?"

"Yes please." Keona replied.

One of the parents, Pansy Possum led Kupe to the moss mat in the centre of the floor where other pupils were sitting, then took Keanu and Keona to a log bench at the back where Poppy Pukeko was sitting.

"Is this your first time too?" she asked with a smile. "I have Peony and Pete starting their first class as well."

"Yes," Keona replied. "Kupe met Sam, one of the pupils here and asked to come too."

Owen Owl rang his bell and silence descended on the room as he began the lesson. The first session passed quickly and soon a tired but happy family was ready for home, promising to return for the next class. During the class Kupe made some new friends, including Percy Possum, Danny Duck and Harry Hedgehog, who was excited that he had a newborn sister, Holly to play with. When he arrived home Kupe asked his parents when he was getting a sister to play with.

They looked at each other and smiled.

"It may take a little while, but we will see what we can do." Keanu told him

Kupe became very excited when Keona laid a large white egg, which Keanu and Keona took turns to keep warm. One bright moonlit night the egg hatched and out came the cutest little girl that Kupe could have wished for.

"What will we call her Mum?"

"Her name will be Keely." Keona informed him.

In a couple of days Keely was strong enough to start exploring outside the burrow. Kupe and Keanu walked with her, Keanu showing Keely how to find her food. Keely was so happy when she found her first worm; she pulled extra hard to get the worm from the ground and nearly lost it when the worm slipped from her grasp. Kupe quickly stepped in and held the worm with his bill untill Keely could get hold of it again.

Fern the Fantail was delighted to see the new member of the family and came down from her nest to see her, bouncing around her and chattering to the family.

"Hello Keanu. Is this your new little girl?" Fern asked.

"Yes, this is Keely." Keanu proudly introduced Keely to her.

"I see she is learning to feed herself already." Fern said with wonder.

"Yes. We teach them to look after themselves as soon as we can so they can look after themselves if they need to." Keanu answered with a smile, as Keely found another worm.

"I wish my children could look after themselves so quickly." Fern said with a sigh. "I have another couple of weeks before they start caring for themselves."

The next day Keanu let Kupe take Keely out of the burrow on his own to find their food. They were on the mossy bank by the stream when Keely found some beautiful bright blue toadstools.

"Kupe, look at these! Can we eat them?" she asked. Kupe came over to see what Keely had found.

"I'm not sure," Kupe said after looking at and smelling them. "It's best not to try it until we are sure. We have books on plants at school. I will have a look for you."

"What is school?" Keely wanted to know.

"School is a place where we learn many things and make friends with different animals."

When Kupe came home from school the next morning, he had a book with him. The book had all the fungus plants of New Zealand in it. The children spent so long looking at the book Keona had to remind them that it was bed time.

"Did you find the plant that you were looking for?" Keanu asked as he helped get the children to bed. He had not seen the plant before either.

"Yes, it's a blue toadstool." Kupe told him. "We can't eat it though." Kupe told Keely.

"I don't mind," Keely replied. "It's too nice to eat.

"When can I go to school, Mum?" Keely asked. After seeing the book Kupe had brought home, she wanted to see some more.

"I will take you tonight if you want." Keona offered with a smile, seeing Keely's look of happiness on her face.

That evening the family made the trek to the school, Kupe running ahead to Owen Owl.

"Mr Owl, we've brought my sister Keely." Kupe introduced her as the family came near.

"Would you like to join us at the school Keely?" Owen asked.

"Yes Please." Keely replied and without being asked, went inside with Kupe to join the other pupils.

"We will see you at the end of the session." Owen Owl advised Keanu and Keona.

During the session, Keely made many new friends. Among them she met Holly Hedgehog, Belle the Bat, Daisy Duck, Petunia Possum and Peony Pukeko. After the session the girls decided to have a picnic. After getting permission from their parents, they made their way to the water's edge at the lake, but the strong wind drove them back into the forest.

"Where shall we go?" Holly asked.

"I know just the place!" Keely exclaimed. "Follow me."

She led them to the mossy bank by the stream where the blue toadstools grew, the trees and ferns protecting them from the weather. They had sat down in a circle around the toadstools for their picnic, when they heard a voice by the water.

"Can I join you?"

The girls looked over by the stream. There sat a dark green frog.

"Hello, I'm Fuchsia." She introduced herself.

"Hello Fuchsia. Of course you can join us." Keely replied as the girls moved to make room for her to join them in the circle. The friendship made between the girls that day lasted all of their lifetimes.

CHAPTER THREE

THE KIWIS MEET THE GILMORES

As daylight was breaking over the hills at Lake Kaniere, Kupe and Keely explored and had a snack before bedtime. Suddenly they heard the approach of an animal they didn't know running through the trees.

Kupe found a hollow by the stream to hide in. Keely sheltered in a patch of tall ferns, hoping not to be found. To the Kiwis' dismay, the running slowed and stopped where they had been feeding. Then the sound of loud sniffing could be heard.

Keely risked a peek through the ferns to see a large golden dog, a Labrador, sniffing at the ground where they had been and was coming towards her! Remembering her mother's story of how a dog had tried to attack her, Keely was terrified and curled up in a tight ball, wishing she had spines like her friend Holly Hedgehog instead of feathers for protection.

The sound of footsteps and sniffing came closer and closer until Keely could hear the animal standing over her. Trembling, Keely gave a little growl and stuck a claw out, hoping it would deter the dog.

Fern the Fantail had been watching the Kiwis feed and was alarmed to see the approach of the dog, straight at Keely. With the fury only a protective Fantail can show, Fern launched herself at the dog.

Fern bounced on the Dog's back and head, pecking at the Dog's ears and screaming furiously.

Lady the Labrador was the family pet of the Gilmore family, who lived in Hokitika, escaping to their bach at Lake Kaniere on the weekends and on holidays. This morning Mike Gilmore had woken up early to let Lady have a run through the forest before she settled down for a nap. As Lady ran through the bush, she found a scent she didn't recognise. Slowing down, she saw the ground had been disturbed, then following the scent into the ferns, found a grey and white feathery ball with claws on and it growled at her! She gave a whimper; those claws looked nasty! Also a bird was attacking her and hurting her ears!

Lady didn't know what this creature was, but it was time for help! Lady backed off slightly and gave two loud barks, hoping Mike her owner would come soon.

Mike Gilmore was enjoying his morning walk under the dark quiet canopy of the forest when he heard Lady barking. Lady never barked unless something was wrong.

Mike quickened his pace to find Lady in a patch of ferns standing guard over something. A Fantail was attacking Lady with some force. Had she found some Fantail chicks on the floor?

"Good girl, Lady. What have you found?" Mike asked.

Lady answered with a gentle "Woof" and wagged her tail now that Mike was here.

Fern the Fantail retreated to the Rimu Tree now that a human had arrived but was still scolding the dog furiously from her branch.

Mike had a look at Lady's find and could hardly believe his eyes – it looked like a baby Kiwi. Very gently he picked up the ball of feathers, taking are to keep clear of the claws, which were opening and closing as he lifted her, and nestled her in his arms.

As Mike lifted Keely up he could feel her trembling and could make out the long bill buried in her feather. He saw one little eye open briefly to look into his, then quickly shut again. Mike noticed she wasn't tagged either, which would make her vulnerable to poachers! Mike decided this little Kiwi needed to be checked, so after making a note of where he had found her, he went back to the bach with Lady following close behind him.

After the sounds of footsteps faded away, Kupe very carefully and quietly came out from his hiding place.

"Keely?" he said quietly. No response.

He called louder. The forest remained silent, apart from the chattering of the Fantail as she flitted through the trees. Kupe then screamed out, at the top of his voice, in panic, **"KEELY!"**

Mike heard the call and looked back knowing now for sure that the little Kiwi was not alone and would need to be returned after being checked and tagged.

Keanu and Keona also heard Kupe's call and came running to find Kupe alone and looking round frantically. Kupe told them everything that had happened and what he heard.

"I think humans have taken Keely." Keanu said with alarm. The family immediately started their search for her. It took some time, but the Kiwi family were able to pick up the trail of the man and dog and followed it to the Gilmore bach and hid in the bushes by the garden to see if they could spot Keely.

Mary Gilmore saw Mike and Lady return from their walk. Mike was carrying something very carefully in his arms. Kathryn and James were up having breakfast when their father came in.

"What have you got there, Dad?" James asked.

"It's a Kiwi chick." Mike answered quietly. Breakfast was abandoned as James and Kathryn came to look.

"Mary, have you got a box and something soft to put in it?" Mike asked.

Mary took one look at the bundle of feather and went scurrying out to the shed, coming back with a large cardboard box and some straw from the garden. After Keely was laid gently onto the straw, she felt and smelt the familiar feel and smell of grass. Very slowly Keely lifted her head to look around her. Looking up, Keely saw four human heads looking at her. Keely became frightened.

Where was her family? Will they come for her? Keely curled herself up in a ball. *Maybe if I ignore them, they will go away!* Keely then heard a whimper. She risked a quick peek. Lady the Dog was peering at her. There was a beetle climbing up the box wall. Lady pushed it back again with her paw. Keely snatched the beetle quickly as it dropped next to her.

Keely looked at Lady; she sensed the dog was trying to help her. With a little sigh, Keely settled down to sleep. Lady sat down to keep guard over the box.

"Can we get some worms for the Kiwi?" the children asked.

"That's a good idea." Mary answered. The children went off to the garden to start their hunt, viewed with much interest by the Kiwi family, who were watching from the shadows of the forest bushes.

"Maybe they are feeding Keely?" Kupe asked.

"We hope so." Keanu replied, feeling hungry himself.

"I will go into town and get John." Mike said to Mary as he headed out of the door. John was an old school friend who worked at the Department of Conservation (D.O.C.)

A few hours later Mike returned with John. They also had Dave, who worked for D.O.C. in the Grey Valley, looking after the Kiwi population there. They took a quick look. Keely was still sleeping.

"It's a Great Spotted Kiwi chick." Dave said quietly. "This is an exciting find. Kiwis haven't been in this area for many years."

102

Lady got up for a look and whimpered, which woke up Keely. Keely opened her eyes. The dog was looking at her again and some more humans were there too.

"Where are the worms the children have collected?" Dave asked, seeing that Keely was awake.

James pulled out the container with worms still wriggling in the soil. He then carefully lowered a worm into the box with the Kiwi. Keely knew immediately what this creature was, and it was bigger than the ones in the forest! She quickly grabbed and ate it before the worm could escape in to the nest. Two more worms were happily accepted before Keely felt full. Dave pulled on some thick gloves and carefully lifted Keely out to examine her. The Kiwi Family had been watching carefully to see if they could spot Keely.

"There she is!" Kupe exclaimed as he saw Keely being lifted out of the box.

"How do we get in to help her? Is there a door open?" Keona asked.

The Kiwi family snuck around the bach, looking for a way in. They came to the door to find there was an opening flap in the bottom (for the dog).

"It's nice of them to make a door for us." Keona said with delight.

Keely was placed into a bag to be weighed and then was measured.

"It is a girl and she is about a month old." Dave informed John and Mike. He then held her legs out while John clipped on and ID band and a larger transmitter band. Keely tried to pick the bands off, but they were stuck on. Dave was about to put Keely back into the box when chaos erupted in the room with the arrival of the Kiwi family who came charging through the dog door.

At the sight of so many Kiwis, Lady made a quick retreat out of the room. Keanu spotted Dave was holding Keely and started clawing at his legs.

"What on earth! How did they get in?" Dave asked, immediately lowering Keely down onto the floor. The Kiwi family immediately surrounded Keely.

"Are you alright Keely?" Keona asked.

"What are the bands on your legs?" Kupe asked.

Keanu saw the bands too and remembered when he got his band on. He was about to defend himself from having another check, but it was too late. He felt himself being lifted by a pair of strong hands.

103

Keona struggled as she found herself being plucked off the floor too. Kupe cowered by Keely as both parents were taken away from him and Keely.

John and Dave looked at each other as the family gathered around Keely. Together they quickly picked up the two adult Kiwis.

"Mike, can you get the scanner and run it over this band?" Dave asked as he held out Keanu's leg. After the scanner beeped with Keanu's number, he was put in a bag to be weighed.

"He's a long way from home in Punakaiki." Dave commented. "3.5 kilograms, that's a good weight. He put Keanu into the box with a big juicy worm. At first Keanu was torn between trying to escape and eating the worm. Remembering how hungry he was, Keanu chose the worm. Keona didn't have a band, so she was given a full check.

"This is a female, 4.5 kilograms. They are both doing well here." Dave commented. Keona too was placed in the box after being tagged.

Keely and Kupe were then picked up. Keely joined her parents while Kupe was given his check and tagged.

"We have a male, about a year old." Dave said before reuniting him with his family. Dave and John carefully picked up the box and took it outside.

"What direction did you find the young one, Mike?" Dave asked.

"I found her over beyond the garden." Mike replied. Dave and John took the box into the forest, followed by the Gilmores.

When Keanu saw they were in the forest, he started scratching at the box. Very carefully, Dave and John put down the box and gently turned the box onto its side.

The family quickly emerged and disappeared into the forest. Dave turned on the transmitter receiver and heard steady clicks in the direction of the burrow.

Back at the burrow, the Kiwis received a warm welcome from Fern Fantail, who fussed over Keely, saying how happy she was that Keely was safely back.

In the burrow, the family checked each other – they all had matching bands. They listened to Keely's story of her adventure. Keanu was relieved. Big Kamoku the Kiwi was right, Kiwi are safe from humans now, after all.

CHAPTER FOUR

THE EARTHQUAKE

Keely Kiwi was helping her friend Holly Hedgehog put away some books in the school library at the back of the cave, when suddenly there was a rumbling sound and the ground began to shake!

"It's an earthquake!" Owen Owl exclaimed. "Children, come out of the cave as quickly as you can!"

All of the children escaped from the cave, except Keely and Holly, who found themselves trapped behind a wall of rubble when part of the roof fell down. It was very dusty and very dim, with only one small Glow worm to give the girls light.

"What are we going to do?" Holly asked. "I'm scared."

Secretly, Keely was scared too, but she tried not to show it. She could not hear anyone on the other side of the rubble, so it could be some time before they were rescued.

"We will be alright Holly," Keely tried to comfort her. "We will be rescued soon."

"Perhaps if we shout, someone will hear us and come?" Holly suggested.

"That's a good idea." Keely agreed.

"HELP! CAN YOU HEAR US?" they called out together at the top of their voices.

Their calls were met by silence.

"Are you hungry Holly?" Keely asked.

"Yes," replied Holly, "but what will we find here?"

"Well, the earthquake may have disturbed some beetles, so we could have a look while we are waiting to be rescued." Keely suggested hopefully.

"Yes, we don't know how long it will be before they come for us." Holly agreed, trying not to worry.

Together they did a search. Keely tapped the floor, finding two beetles and a nice juicy worm. Holly was searching near the back wall of the cave when she felt some fresh air rushing past her nose. She gave a big sniff, which brought Keely rushing over.

"What have you found?" Keely asked.

"Can you feel the air coming in?" Holly replied.

Keely put her bill to the spot where Holly had shown her and with delight and relief felt the life-giving air flooding her body.

"This may be another way out of here!" Keely said excitedly, and the two friends started to dig.

Outside the cave, Owen Owl gathered the pupils and counted everyone, in the dim starlight as the earthquake had dislodged the Glow worms from the roof.

Owen Owl took the roll call and found that both Holly and Keely were missing. Harry had advised him that he had seen Holly in the library and Kupe had confirmed that Keely was with her. Owen looked at the large pile of rubble which now blocked the library area and knew that a rescue mission had to be mounted. He just hoped that the girls weren't harmed.

By this time, all the parents had made their way to the school after they had felt the earthquake. Owen Owl spoke to each one as they arrived, telling them school was cancelled because the cave was damaged and they could take their child home, but nobody did, waiting to see that everyone was safe.

When they found out that Holly and Keely were missing, they crowded around Keely and Holly's parents to give comfort. Very carefully Keanu and Keona and Henry and Heather entered the cave to look at the mountain of rubble where the library had been.

"HOLLY! KEELY!" they called, but only silence answered them.

"How can we get to them?" Keanu asked.

"We will have to find a way to support the walls and roof before we start moving the rubble." Paddy Possum said, worried that more rubble would fall on them.

"Can we get some tree ferns?" Daphne Duck asked. "The Maori used them for their houses, so they should be strong enough."

"We need something strong to pull the ferns out and bring them here." Henry Hedgehog suggested. "Would flax be suitable?"

"Yes!" Owen Owl agreed. "I think we have a plan!"

Paddy and Pansy Possum sent Percy off with all the other parents and children to start looking for suitable tree ferns to use. The Possums when to the lake shore, where large bunches of flax grow. Putting their large teeth to good use, Paddy and Pansy soon had a large pile of flax leaves, which they brought back to the group.

The group had swollen to a large crowd after the duck family summoned all the other ducks from the lake. The Bat family summoned the remaining bats from their colony and the Pigeon family called all the other Pigeons in the lake area in to assist.

Up on the mountain top, the Deer family was woken by the earthquake. Shortly afterward they saw the ducks, bats and pigeons flying in toward the school.

"I think they need help at the school." Stan the Stag informed his family. "We should go and see if they need our help." Stan, Delphinium deer and their children, Denny, Donny and Dusty made their way down the mountain slopes.

While the Possums and Hedgehogs split the flax, Sam Stoat and his parents, Stubby and Scarlett, along with Wendy Weasel and her parents, Wally and Wanda tied the flax into long strong ropes.

The Bats and the Pigeons lifted the flax ropes up onto the tree ferns and soon the forest echoed to the sound of the ferns being felled. When the Deer family arrived their offers of assistance were gratefully accepted. They were used to drag the ferns to the cave.

The sun was high in the sky when the last of the tree ferns were placed into position to protect the walls and ceiling of the cave. The night animals were then sent off for a well-earned rest while the daytime animals prepared to start moving the rubble.

Holly and Keely's digging soon opened up a big space, which looked like a tunnel rising above them. It was very dark and the girls could not see what lay at the other end. The feel and sound of fresh air as it rushed down the tunnel to them encouraged the girls to see what lay there.

"I wish we had some light to take with us." Holly was anxious at having to explore the unknown space in the dark.

"Please," said a little voice above the girls. They looked up to see the Glow worm was talking to them. "I don't want to be left here alone. If you lift me down carefully, I can give you light untill you are safe. Maybe we will find some other Glow worms for me to live with."

Holly climbed up on Keely's back and very carefully lifted Gloria Glow worm down from her spot on the wall, and together the friends began to make their way up the passage. As they went, the roar of rushing water became very loud. At the other end of the passage lay a large and rocky cavern covered in moss. On the other side of the cavern, they could see another passage with a twinkle of light at the end of it. In the girls' path was a narrow but deep stream which flowed into a waterfall. Above them was a colony of Glow Worms, their dim blue lights twinkled like stars in the sky.

"Who is it, and why do you have all of your lights on?" one glow worm asked.

Gloria introduced herself and her friends, explaining how they came. Immediately the other Glow worms put on their lights, bathing the cavern in light.

The friends were now able to see some small branches, which had been swept into the cavern during a flood. They made a bridge across the stream by wedging the branches together between some rocks.

Very carefully, Holly led Keely across to the other side. The rocks were very slippery and Keely fell into the water. Keely was in danger of being swept away as she tried to cling to the slippery rock with her claws. Quickly Holly picked up a stick and held it out for Keely to grab. Very slowly, Keely was able to scramble out again.

Once the girls were safe on the other side of the cavern stream, Holly carefully lifted Gloria up to the wall so she could join the other Glow worms.

"If any of the other Glow worms were saved, could you tell them I am here?" Gloria asked.

"Of course we will." Holly promised.

Before they left the cave, the girls took one last look at the twinkling blue lights, happy that Gloria was safe among them.

Onward Keely and Holly went, towards the light to find themselves in another large cavern, which sloped up to an enormous hole where the roof had been and they could see the sky!

Near the opening was a colony of Bats who were very noisily still settling after their night's work. As Keely and Holly made their way up the fern covered slope, Belle Bat spotted the girls.

"KEELY! HOLLY!" she shouted. The colony quickly descended into silence.

"Holly, Keely, are you alright?"

"Yes," Keely replied, even though she felt bedraggle after her dip in the cold stream. "We managed to find a passage at the back of the school cave, which led us to this cave. Can we get out of here?"

"I think you will need help." Belle told them. "Find yourself a spot under the ferns for a rest. We will let your families know you are here and get some help."

Belle and Benny flew out of the cave warily. There were Falcons around this time of day, who would consider them an easy meal. Down to the school cave they flew to find Holly and Keely's parents about to leave.

"Mr and Mrs Hedgehog, Mr and Mrs Kiwi, please stop!" Benny panted. "Holly and Keely are safe! They found a passage at the back of the school that took them to our cave. They are having a rest now but will need some help to get out later."

Everyone was overjoyed to hear the news.

"Will we see everyone back here this evening?" Owen asked.

There was a big "Yes" from the crowd before they disappeared for a sleep.

As the sun was setting, a big crowd gathered at the school cave. Belle flew down to say the girls had slept well and had some breakfast. She then led the way up the hill to the cave entrance. At the entrance, the cave walls dropped straight down for a metre – too deep for the girls to climb out, before sloping away to the next cavern. At the top of the cavern slope sat Holly and Keely, their eyes sparkled to see their families and all the other animals there to help them. There was much discussion as to the best way to get the girls out, when the Deer family arrived.

Stan the Stag took one look and said "Excuse me, I think I can help."

He asked the girls to move to the side of the slope, which they quickly did. Stan then leaped in onto the slope with the girls. He then knelt down and asked the girls to climb onto his back and hold on tight. Keely climbed on first, clinging to Stan's neck as firmly as she could with her claws. Then Holly climbed on and clung to Keely as tightly as she could. Stan carefully stood up and walked a short way down the slope before he started his run up the slope and leapt out of the cave with a single bound, to cheers and applause from all the animals. Holly and Keely were quickly reunited with their families before everyone made the walk down the mountain to the school cave, where the day animals were finishing clearing the rock fall. Everyone then sat down to a feast to celebrate the safe return of the girls and to thank everyone for their hard work to repair the school and make it safe to use again.

CHAPTER FIVE

THE STORM

School had begun the last session before the school holidays, when Daisy duck limped in, looking very weary and with a bandaged foot.

"I'm sorry I'm late." Daisy apologised.

"What happened?" Owen Owl asked, looking at her foot.

"I've been helping Aunty Dorothy with her ducklings and was having a nap when an Eel came and bit off part of my foot!" Daisy replied tearfully.

"My goodness Daisy!" Owen exclaimed. "Did you tell your parents about it, and would you know if you saw that eel again?

"I haven't been able to tell my parents yet as they are visiting my other Aunt Dahlia at the Kaniere Pond, but I did get a good look at the eel. It had three spots on its tail."

"That is very good Daisy." Owen Owl replied. "Eels are not allowed to attack other animals in this lake, so we must find out who did it!"

Owen Owl set the other children some work, asking Pansy Possum to look after them, while he set off with Daisy for the lake.

Once the lesson was over, Pansy Possum waved the pupils goodbye, telling them to take of themselves and each other during the holidays.

Kupe Kiwi and Sam Stoat trotted off to sit at their favourite spot under the flax bushes by the water's edge of the lake. They were planning all the fun they would have, when they saw an eel in the water swimming towards them. There was a little splash as the eel raised his head out of the water. After hearing of Daisy Duck's misadventure, both Kupe and Sam were now wary of the creature.

"Hello, I'm Ernie. Will you come in for a swim with me?" the Eel asked.

"Hello Ernie," Sam replied. "This is Kupe and I'm Sam. Thank you for inviting us in, but we aren't allowed in yet while we are still learning to swim."

"I will meet you again when you have finished your lessons." Ernie promised. He was turning to swim away, when Sam called out.

"Ernie, do you know who bit off some of Daisy Duck's foot?"

Ernie turned to face the boys. "I heard it was done by an eel called Elton.

"He has to face our Council to see what punishment he will get. I will let you know what happens."

"Please do." Sam replied.

Relieved, Kupe and Sam watched Ernie swim out of sight to the deep centre of the bay. They wondered what they would have done if they had met Elton.

The next evening, Kupe, Sam, Percy Possum and Danny Duck were out playing in the long grass of the eastern bay, which stretches along the waterfront, known to humans as Hans Bay. Kupe gazed out at the two heavily wooded Islands in the bay that sat like dark jade jewels in the evening light.

"I wish I could swim." Kupe said wistfully. "I would love to go and explore those Islands."

"Why don't we make a raft and sail over?" Sam asked.

"What a great idea!" Percy and Danny exclaimed excitedly. "Maybe we could make two rafts and have a race around the Islands!"

The friends set off to make the rafts. The first stop was at the flax bushes for some leaves to make rope to bind the rafts together. Next the friends went into the forest to search for fallen tree branches and dragged them to the shore. Harry Hedgehog came along to help them lash the branches together to make two fine rafts.

The rafts floated perfectly when Danny Duck gave them a test float. The friends searched for small forked branches and wove flax between them to make some oars, which Danny tested by paddling the raft out from the shore and back again.

Dawn was breaking by the time the rafts and oars were ready. The friends found some moss to protect them under the flax bushes before going home for a rest.

The next evening the clouds scurried across the sky and the westerly breeze created a chop in the usually calm waters between the Islands and the bay.

"Hmm," Danny Duck said. "I think we should go the long way to the Island."

The friends set off, keeping close to the shoreline, paddling the deep sheltered waters of the bay, admiring the water lilies as they went.

As the friends approached the wide passage between the bay and the Islands, they saw to their dismay that the wind was blowing stronger and the water was choppier than before. Bravely they set out, paddling as fast as they could. Kupe and Sam were half way across when disaster struck! A huge wave came and nearly upset the raft. Kupe and Sam hung on grimly, but lost the paddles, leaving them at the mercy of the waves. Danny Duck and Percy Possum saw that Kupe and Sam needed help and paddled over.

"Throw me your rope." Percy called.

With all of his strength, Sam threw the rope, but the wind blew them further away and the rope was left trailing in the water. Kupe and Sam became scared of what would happen next, when Ernie Eel's head popped up in the darkness.

"Hello Kupe and Sam, what are you doing out here?" Ernie asked with concern.

"We are sailing to the Island, but the water is very rough and we have lost our paddles!" Kupe replied.

"I will help you." Ernie offered them. With his mouth, Ernie gathered the rope and steadily towed Kupe and Sam's raft to the sheltered side of the Island, waiting untill Sam, Kupe, Danny and Percy had clambered to the safety of the shore and secured their rafts.

"You need to find shelter soon. There is a storm coming." Ernie warned.

The friends turned to thank Ernie for his help, but he had slipped away into the darkness of the lake.

The friends looked around them. The ground was covered with ferns and bushes and the trunks of tall trees soaring into the darkness of the night. The branches creaked, and the wind howled as it swept through the canopy above.

"I will find some shelter for us." Kupe offered his friends.

"And we will find some food." Percy replied.

Kupe went straight to the largest tree he could find. He noticed a small hollow at the bottom of the trunk and started digging. Very soon he had created a dry comfortable den for everyone to shelter in. As Kupe dug, Sam, Danny and Percy searched in the bush, returning with a bounty of slugs, snails, beetles, berries and flowers. The friends settled into the cosy space, placing some branches and ferns over the opening for protection.

A loud roar signalled the arrival of the storm. A wall of water descended from the clouds to drench everything it touched. In the comfort of the den, Kupe, Sam, Danny and Percy enjoyed their feast, and then with the sound of rain ringing in their ears, made plans for the remainder of their holidays.

On the shore, Keanu was concerned, wondering where Kupe and his friends were. Kupe had mentioned having a ride on a raft they had made. The increasing wind in the forest was making all the animals nervous. They were now busy seeking safe shelter as they sensed the approaching storm. Paddy Possum came to the burrow looking for Percy.

"Have the boys come back from the lake yet?" Paddy asked.

"No," Keanu replied. "I'm getting worried about them."

Keanu and Paddy scurried down the shore where the flax bushes were being battered by the waves crashing onto the shore. There was no sign either on the shore or in the water of the boys. Keanu and Paddy called for the boys, but their voices were met with silence; then by their feet Ernie surfaced.

"Hello Mr. Kiwi and Mr. Possum. Are you looking for Kupe, Sam, Percy and Danny? Ernie asked.

"Yes, we are." Keanu replied.

"Don't worry, they are on the Island and will come back when it is safe." Ernie reassured them."

"Are you sure?" Keanu asked anxiously

"Yes." was Ernie's confident reply.

"Thank you." Keanu and Paddy replied, before turning to seek shelter.

Keanu and Paddy ran back to the burrow to find the Duck and Stoat families had also gathered to hear news of their sons. There was much relief as Keanu reassured the parents that all was well.

Keanu offered shelter in the burrow for the night, which was happily accepted by everyone and they all settled down for a good chat as the storm raged overhead.

Soon a very wet Pukeko family came seeking shelter. The little creek was now a raging torrent and had flooded their home in the bulrushes.

An alarm call by Tania Tui was heard above the din of the driving rain.

Her nest had been swept out the Kowhai tree onto the ground. Tania and Terry tui were frantically trying to protect their chicks from the rain.

Willing paws picked up the nest with Tania Tui and Terry following closely behind, and brought into the safety of the burrow. A quiet spot was found in a tunnel for the exhausted family, who soon settled down to sleep.

When morning came, the storm had gone. Kupe, Sam, Danny and Percy stirred as daylight came into their den. Pushing aside the branches and ferns, the friends tumbled outside to stretch their legs. Everything was very damp. Water was still dripping off the leaves, which glistened in the sunlight. The lake was now its calm self again.

"I'm hungry." Percy complained.

"We are ALL hungry," Kupe replied, "but we should try to go back. Our parents will be looking for us."

At the water's edge, they found only one raft. Looking around, they spotted the other raft lying deep on the floor of the lake.

"Will the raft take the four of us?" Percy asked.

"I can always swim with you." Danny offered.

Very carefully, Percy, Kupe and Sam sat on the raft. When Danny stepped on, one corner of the raft sunk under the water, so he quickly stepped off again. They collected the paddles, and with Danny following, set off for Hans Bay on the eastern shore. The friends were enjoying the paddle across the bay when Danny was startled by something brushing his feet. He looked down to see the tail of an eel, and then Ernie surfaced next to him.

"Hello Danny. How come you are swimming and not sailing on the raft with the others?" Ernie asked.

"We lost one raft in the storm and the other raft started to sink with us all on." Danny explained.

"Can I keep you company while you swim?" Ernie asked.

"Please do." Danny replied.

Percy spotted Ernie swimming and talking to Danny.

"Hi Ernie, how did you get on in the storm?" he asked.

"We are lucky the lake is deep enough for us to shelter in calm water. The community had to attend the Council meeting last night, so we didn't notice the storm much." Ernie replied.

"What happened to Elton?" Percy asked.

"He has been banished from the lake and is not allowed to return." Ernie advised them. "Some of our wardens are taking him away now."

"Where are they taking him?" Kupe wanted to know.

"Elton is being taken to Mahinapua Creek," Ernie replied. "There are many eels living there. Elton will find it much harder to live there."

"Isn't there an eel cannery there?" Percy asked.

"Yes, there is." Ernie said quietly. The friends were silent for a few minutes, thinking of the future waiting for Elton. "When are your next swimming lessons?" Ernie wanted to know.

"They will be next term." Kupe advised him. The friends' journey back to shore went quickly while they chatted. Back on shore the friends waved goodbye to Ernie and went to find their parents. Danny's parents weren't home; neither were Sam's or Percy's. They were becoming worried. Where was everyone? They went with Kupe to his burrow. Inside they found the tunnels were full of animals sound asleep, including their parents. The friends sneaked outside again.

"It may be a while before they wake up." Kupe said. "Let's find some breakfast and have it as a picnic down by the lake."

When Keanu, Paddy, Daffy and Stubby eventually came out to see where their boys were, they found them having a big feed down by the water's edge.

"Is there any left for us?" they asked, before sitting down to join in the feast and listening to the boys' adventures.

"Next time you go to the Island, we would like to go too." Keanu said.

"We will make sure there are no storms coming though." Paddy Possum warned.

"We will also make sure we have a proper boat that won't sink." Stubby Stoat added.

"And we will also make sure everyone can swim." Daffy Duck said finally.

Everyone laughed, and they made plans for their next trip over to the Island.

CHAPTER SIX

HOLLY HEDGEHOG'S BIRTHDAY

Keely Kiwi, Daisy Duck, Peony Pukeko and Petunia Possum had come to the old totara tree where the Hedgehog family lived, for Holly Hedgehog's Birthday.

Holly loved flowers, so Keely made a white Clematis necklace for Holly to wear. Daisy Duck made a pink water lily and fern hat for Holly's head. Peony Pukeko made a Daisy ring for Holly's paw and Petunia Possum made some Kowhai flower bracelets for Holly's wrists and ankles.

Heather Hedgehog had a surprise for the girls. They were going for a picnic at the waterfall; known to humans as Dorothy Falls. Heather tucked a large basket under her arm and, with Henry and Harry, led the girls to where a large boat was waiting on the shore of Lake Kaniere. Holly's second surprise was a boat ride up the lake to the picnic spot.

Following the boy's trip to the Island, the men had found a suitable fallen tree and made it into a boat during the long winter months. At the boat, the Kiwi, Possum, Duck, Pukeko and Stoat families were waiting for them. Everyone piled into the boat and set off for the waterfall with Keanu, Paddy, Daffy, Pongo, Stubby and Henry rowing.

Everyone enjoyed the view of the forest from the lake as they sailed to the stream that runs from the waterfall to the lake. Paddy and Stubby tied the boat to a large tree while Pongo, Daffy Keanu and Henry helped everyone out of the boat. They all then make their way upstream to the waterfall by walking along the river bank.

The first sight of the waterfall filled the children with wonder. At the top of a tall cliff, the waterfall emerged from the forest to flow down over the rock wall, before forming into a white glistening veil of water spilling into a deep pool at the bottom and tumbling down a rocky stream towards the lake. In the rocky stream were several shallow pools, just right for a swim.

Scarlett Stoat gave the children two woven balls to play with. The families watched with delight the sight and sounds of their children laughing and shouting as they tossed the balls to each other while swimming in the water.

When the picnic was ready, everyone found a spot to sit on the rocks surrounding the falls for the picnic. After the picnic, the children decided to explore the cliff next to the waterfall. The bank was covered in ferns, mossy rocks and small trees that had found a toehold on the steep slope. The boys led the way, clambering up through the rocks and ferns to a ledge high on the cliff wall.

The girls followed and were making their way up the slope when Holly found to her dismay that her foot was stuck fast between two rocks.

"Help!" Holly called. "I'm stuck!"

Holly tried to hang on, but the rocks were too slippery. Her leg twisted, causing her pain as she fell back. Keely was coming behind her, saw Holly was about to fall and moved up underneath to support her.

Everyone gathered round to help. Harry, Percy, Kupe and Sam tried very hard to move the rocks to free Holly, but the rocks would not budge.

By this time Paddy, Stubby and Henry had come to help, while Keanu, Pongo and Daffy had placed themselves underneath Keely in case the girls fell. With a big heave by both the children and the men, Holly's foot was finally freed. Holly's weight was now fully on Keely, who was starting to slip. As they tumbled down the slope, both Keely and Holly were relieved to be caught and carried down the slope to safety and the waiting arms of their mothers.

When Holly found she was unable to use her foot, Heather asked Daffy Duck if he could fetch Primula Pigeon. She would know what to do. Off Daffy flew to the Hinau tree, where Primula lived, and brought her back to the group.

Primula looked at Holly's foot with concern. The leg was sitting at a crooked angle, which Primula knew meant it was broken. Very gently, she asked Holly if she could open and close the paw on her sore foot. Holly shook her head, with tears in her eyes.

"I'm sorry, it hurts too much." Holly cried.

"Now Holly," Primula began, "To mend your leg, we need to get some special help for you from an animal doctor that humans call a "vet". The vet may put your leg in a firm bandage untill it heals. He may put you to sleep to do this, but he will wake you up again afterwards. Your leg will be very sore untill it begins to heal. You may also have to stay at the vet's for some weeks before you come back. You will need to be very brave. Can you do that?"

Holly nodded.

"How do we get Holly to the vet?" Heather asked.

"There is a lady on the western side of the lake (known to humans as Sunny Bight) who looks after sick and injured animals." Primula explained. "She took Tessie Tui to the vet when she hurt her leg."

117

After packing up the picnic, the group made their way to the boat. Paddy Possum gave Holly a ride on his back.

"It will be quicker if we go straight across the lake from here." Primula advised Keanu as they were getting into the boat. Luckily, the lake was calm as the boat made its way across the lake. The setting sun cast a golden glow on the hills and the water.

At Sunny Bight, they paddled along the shore till they came to a wooden jetty where Primula asked the men to bring the boat to shore. Paddy stepped out into the shore and gave Holly a ride up the path to the bach, which was lit very brightly by a light on the verandah.

He was followed by the Hedgehogs and the other families, who kept out of sight in the bushes. Henry and Harry gave Holly a big hug before Paddy made his way up the steps. Holly clung to his neck as hard as she could, with Heather following them up onto the verandah. Once Holly was safe, Paddy then sneaked off to rejoin his family in the bushes.

Heather was giving Holly a cuddle and telling her to be strong when the door opened. A man was looking at them! Oh dear! Where was the lady that Primula had mentioned?

Greg and Jane were settling down for the evening by the fire when they heard some noise out on the verandah. Greg went to see what the noise was and found a mother and young Hedgehog on the verandah.

"Jane, come and look. We have some hedgehogs. I wonder if they want a feed." Jane put down her book and came to see.

When Heather saw Jane appear, she nuzzled Holly telling her that everything would be alright; then moved away. Holly panicked and went to follow her mother, but found she could only limp one step. Jane spotted the problem straight away.

"Why, the young one is hurt! I think the mother has brought it to us!" Jane exclaimed. "I will look after it for you." Jane said to Heather, before picking up Holly and taking her inside. As Jane picked up Holly, she noticed the Clematis around her neck.

"This little one has flowers on! I bet it's a girl. Where did we put the box Greg?"

"Here it is." Greg replied, bringing it out of the storeroom.

Jane had a good look at Holly's foot.

"She needs the vet." Jane said quietly, as she put Holly into the box with a soft rug in the bottom.

"I will call the vet to see if they can treat her." Greg replied as he went to the phone.

The families watched as Greg and Jane came out the door with a big box and left in the car and returned some hours later without the box. Jane saw Heather sitting at the bottom of the stairs. Heather looked up at Jane as she came.

"Your little girl is at the vet's." Jane told her. They are taking good care of her. It will be some time before she comes home."

After hearing this, Heather sadly turned and ambled off into the garden to find Henry and Harry. It had been a long day. It had started so well with the picnic; she had no idea the day would end like this! After Jane and Greg had gone back inside their bach, the families crowded around Heather to hear what had happened to Holly.

"Where is Holly?" Harry asked.

"She is at the vet's." Heather replied. The lady said it would be some time before Holly comes home."

"We will stay here till she comes back." Henry decided. Heather agreed.

"I will come every day to see if there is any news." Primrose promised them.

"We will be back for you when Holly returns." Paddy added.

Heather, Henry and Harry waved everyone goodbye as they set off back to the eastern side of the lake, then started searching for some supper, for it was a long time since the picnic.

"I think there is a garden on the other side of the house." Henry advised Heather. "It is similar to the Gilmore's garden."

"Is it really?" Heather asked. She brightened at this news. The insects and worms at the Gilmore's were always bigger and better than those in the forest. The family happily foraged the garden before finding shelter under the bach.

Several weeks went by as Greg and Jane came and went without a sign of Holly, then one afternoon Jane came home with the box she had taken Holly away in. Jane smiled when she saw Heather sitting at the bottom of the stairs.

"Hello," Jane greeted her. "I have your little girl with me." She took Holly out of the box and put her next to Heather.

"Hello Mum!"

"Hello Holly love!" Heather replied, nuzzling Holly and checking if she was all right. "How is your leg?" Heather asked.

"It is sore, but I can use it if I am careful."

Henry and Harry came out from under the bush where they had been hiding and came to see Holly. The family slowly made their way to the garden. Holly had been fed some mince while she was away and was looking forward to some food from the garden. While they were feeding, Primula came for a visit.

"Oh! Holly is back!" Primula exclaimed. "Shall I call the others to come and collect you?"

"Yes please." Henry accepted Primula's offer. "We will be down by the jetty."

It was dark when the boat appeared across the water. Everyone was on board. The quiet swish of paddles was the only sound to be heard as they came near. There were many hugs as the family took their places in the boat. To Holly's joy, the girls gave her more flowers to replace the ones she lost at the picnic.

"Her last surprise is ready." Keona whispered to Heather. Heather smiled.

Back on shore, Holly was given another ride on Paddy's back as everyone made their way to the burrow. A meal was brought out to celebrate Holly's return. Holly had a big story to tell of her adventure at the vets.

It started as a bumpy ride in the noisy car before Holly was taken into a strange cave similar to the Gilmore's bach. The cave had bright lights and a hard table that Jane put Holly on while the vet looked at her leg. Another lady came into the room after Jane and Greg left and put a mask over Holly's head. When Holly woke up again, she found she was in a cage, in another cave with many strange animals in cages that were ill or injured.

Holly made friends with a white parrot called Charlie, who had learnt to talk in human language. He was at the vet's after escaping from his cage and broke his wing trying to fly through a window. Charlie promised that if he ever managed to escape again, he would come out to the lake to visit her.

Holly also made friends with another Hedgehog called Harvey, who lived in Hokitika, where there were plenty of gardens to explore and to find food. Harvey was recovering from being poisoned by some snail pellets someone had put in their garden. Harvey didn't like the medicine the vet gave him to stop the poison from harming him.

Harvey told Holly about the dangers of living in a town. Animals like Dogs and Cats which would chase and hurt you if they could. There were also cars and motorbikes that would run over and hurt you as well.

Harvey hoped to go home soon and offered Holly a safe place to sleep and a tour of the best gardens for food if she ever visited Hokitika again.

After Holly's welcome home meal was over, Heather brought out a surprise. It was a special cake filled with insects and worms, berries from the Totara and Rimu trees and flowers from the Rata tree, which Holly declared was the perfect end to her return home.

CHAPTER SEVEN

THE BOOK

One wet evening at school, Owen Owl asked the children to choose a book to read.

Kupe joined the other children in the library to look at the shelves. His eyes were drawn to a large old book on the top shelf and out of reach. It had the same markings as on the wall at home. Kupe gazed at the book with wonder. His instincts told him this was a special book. He just had to look at it! Kupe could reach it with a ladder, but it was too big to get down by him-self. Pansy Possum saw Kupe looking up at the books.

"Do you want some help?" she asked.

"Yes please." Kupe replied. "Can you get me that big book with the claw on the front?"

"Are you sure?" Pansy asked Kupe.

"Yes," Kupe insisted. "We have that symbol at home. I need to see it."

"Just a minute please, Kupe," Pansy replied. "I will check with Mr. Owl"

"Kupe has found *The Kiwi Kingdom Book*." Pansy said quietly to Owen Owl. "He insists on looking at it."

Owen Owl looked at Kupe's pleading eyes and knew Kupe's moment of destiny had come. Owen gave Pansy a little smile.

"You had better get it down for him then. Can you also fetch his parents? This is a special moment that will change his life. They should be here to support him."

Pansy fetched the ladder and very carefully removed the book from the shelf and brought it down to the floor where Owen Owl had laid a flax mat for Kupe to sit on.

"Kupe," Owen Owl said, "Before you open this book, I need to tell you about it. This is a very special book made by your ancestor Keoni for the next leader of the Kingdom. It tells the history of the Kiwi Kingdom and is the Law of the Kiwi Kingdom. When Kiwis ruled this area, the Kiwi Kingdom was a special place where all the animals lived in harmony with each other."

"But don't we do that now?" Kupe asked.

"Yes, we do here at the lake," Owen Owl replied. "But this is only a small area, the only place left in what used to be a large kingdom. If you leave this lake, Kupe, the world is a very different place to the one you know. In that world, animals do not usually get on with each other. Animals such as dogs, cats, possums, stoats and weasels fight Kiwi."

"Yes!" Kupe exclaimed. "I remember stories Mum and Dad told me of the animals that chased them when they came here from Punakaiki."

"You will need to beware of other Kiwis as well." Owen Owl warned. "These days they all have their own little territories that they defend with their lives if a stranger comes near."

"Are there any other places like this?" Kupe wanted to know.

"If there are, we don't know about them." Owen Owl replied.

While Owen Owl was talking to Kupe, Pansy Possum dashed through the rain to Keanu and Keona's burrow.

"Are you at home?" Pansy called as she reached the burrow. Keona quickly invited Pansy in.

"Can you both come to the school straight away?" Pansy asked.

"Of course we can. What has happened? Is Keely ill or has Kupe hurt himself again?" Keona asked.

"Neither," said Pansy with a smile. "Something very special has happened. We want you to share it, but before we go, do you have a symbol in your home of a claw?"

"Yes we do. Why?" Keona asked, puzzled, and turned to show Pansy the symbol still visible on the wall. Pansy went over to the claw and looked at it with reverence.

"Do you know what this means?" Pansy asked.

"We meant to ask Owen Owl, but forgot about it." Keona replied.

"It is the sign of the lost Kiwi Kingdom." Pansy told her. "Keanu's great grandfather Keoni was the leader before it was destroyed. He and Kaimani had to flee for their lives, but he left a book for the next leader before he left." With eyes shining bright with happiness, Pansy added, "Kupe has been chosen as the next leader!"

"What?" exclaimed Keanu, both proud and anxious at the same time. "How has it happened?"

"All will be explained at the school. Please come!" Pansy pleaded.

Keanu and Keona swiftly followed Pansy to the school and shook themselves off once they reached shelter. Some of the neighbours saw Keanu and Keona's dash to the school and decided to come and see what was happening.

At the school, the other animals abandoned their reading when they realised something special was happening for Kupe. When Keanu Keona and Pansy arrived, followed promptly by their neighbours, Kupe was sitting quietly at the front of the class with a large old book sitting in front of him.

Keanu and Keona immediately saw the same symbol Pansy had asked them about at home, was on the book. Keely and the other children watched with interest from the reading mats.

"Thank you for coming." Owen Owl beamed. "Did Pansy tell you about the Kiwi Kingdom?"

Keanu and Keona nodded, looking at Kupe who smiled to see Mum and Dad here. Kupe had a mature, serene look they had never seen before. Owen Owl waited for everyone to be settled before beginning his speech.

"You may be surprised to hear that Kupe has been chosen to be the next leader of the Kiwi Kingdom. The book Kupe has in front of him is a very special book. Only future leaders are drawn to read it. Only future leaders are allowed to read it. Kupe, are you ready?"

"I am." Kupe answered.

Owen Owl sat next to Kupe and opened the book. Inside the front cover was a large pouch with a parchment, which he drew out to read.

On the front page were five small pouches. Four were empty. The fifth had a length of fine twine trailing from it.

"Kupe Kiwi, you have been chosen as leader of the Kiwi Kingdom. Are you ready for the role?"

"I am."

"Do you, Kupe, promise to uphold the laws of the Kiwi Kingdom?"

"I do."

"Do you Kupe, promise to serve and protect all the animals of the Kiwi Kingdom?"

"I do."

"Do you, Kupe, promise to promote a kingdom where all animals live in harmony with each other?"

"I do."

"By the power invested in me, Owen Owl, Kupe Kiwi, you are now the leader of the Kiwi Kingdom.

Owen Owl pulled the twine from the pouch. Attached to the twine was an amulet made of nephrite Jade (Pounamu) known to humans as greenstone. Owen Owl carefully lifted the twine over Kupe's head.

"Kupe Kiwi, you now carry the mantle of leader of the Kiwi Kingdom. You are to wear this amulet at all times as long as you live. In times of extreme danger to you or the amulet, it is to be returned to the book."

"I will."

Cheers and applause erupted in the schoolroom, and everyone crowded around to congratulate Kupe. Pansy picked up the book and put it on Owen Owl's desk.

"You may come and read this book whenever you wish, Kupe." Owen informed him. "This book has all the information you need to be leader of your kingdom."

"Thank you." Kupe replied, excited at the prospect of reading the special book.

"Is Kupe allowed to take the book home?" Keanu asked, hoping he would get the chance to see it too.

"It will be safer for both Kupe and the book if it stays here." Owen Owl advised. Keanu agreed.

"The book looks very fragile and may not last long." Kupe observed. "While I am learning, could I make a new one?"

"That is an excellent idea." Owen Owl agreed. "I will arrange for the paper you need."

The school session was about to end.

"Can I read some of the book now?" Kupe asked.

"Yes, you may." Owen Owl replied with a smile.

"When you have finished, put the book in the bottom of my desk."

I will." Kupe promised and thanked him.

Kupe waved goodbye to his family, telling them he would be home in a little while after having a look at the book. As everyone left the cave, Percy Possum and Danny Duck came to Kupe.

"We know we can't read your book, but would you like some company while you read it? There are plenty of other books in the library for us to read." Danny asked.

"Oh, thank you!" Kupe replied with relief. "Being a leader will be very lonely if I have to do everything on my own."

"Remember, Kupe," Percy advised him, "We will always be your friends. You will only be alone or lonely if you choose to be."

"Thank you both." Kupe replied, giving them a hug. Little did he know how those words would comfort and sustain him in the future, when Kupe was both alone and lonely.

As they sat down on the mats to begin their reading, Sam Stoat, Harry Hedgehog, Pete Pukeko and Tony Tui came into the cave.

"We heard the news! "Sam was tearful. "Will you still be our friend now?"

"Of course I will." Kupe replied. He looked at them all. "Your friendship is more important to me now than it ever was before. Before we start reading, I want to do something. Let us form a circle and hold paws or (he looked at his own body) claws." Once the circle was formed, Kupe spoke the words that cemented their bond. "We will be friends forever."

"Friends forever!" his friends answered.

When Owen Owl came back later to see how Kupe was coping with his reading, he was surprised to see Kupe happily engrossed in the book. He was surrounded in a circle by his friends, who were equally engrossed in their own books.

Owen Owl tiptoed away from the boys. It was obvious he wasn't needed any longer, now that all Kupe's friends were here to support him.

While they were reading, Kupe became strangely aware they were not alone. He looked up to see the spirit of a Kiwi in front of him. He knew immediately this was his ancestor, Keoni, who had come to talk to him.

"Hello Kupe. Welcome to your Kingdom. You have many challenges ahead of you to restore your Kingdom. You are doing well to keep your friends near you. When you lack knowledge, follow your instincts. I will be watching over you."

As Keoni's image faded, Sam looked up.

"You look like you've seen a ghost, Kupe!"

"I have," Kupe smiled, "but it was a friendly one."

They all laughed and continued reading. When their session was finished, Kupe and his friends made their way to his burrow, where a feast had been prepared to celebrate the occasion. In a quiet moment, Keanu asked Kupe a question. "Do you want to take over this burrow and territory now?"

"No Dad. I'm enjoying my life here with you and Mum. When I'm ready to take a mate, I will decide where I want to be. Hopefully it's not too far away. I have no intention of moving you from your home."

"This is the leader's home." Keanu reminded Kupe, looking at the claw sign.

"Well, we can always share – in the spirit of the new Kingdom, of course!" Kupe twinkled up at him. This place is big enough and we can always expand it if we need to.

"You must have the tunnel with the symbol." Keanu insisted.

And so it was arranged. Kupe now slept where his parents used to sleep and they chose a tunnel that led near the stream. Keanu and Keona were now able to slip away to their own quarters or come and go by their own entrance if they wanted to.

"I always wanted a view of the water." Keona observed happily.

The new arrangements worked out very well in the coming weeks as animals from near and far from around the lake came to congratulate and pay homage to their new leader.

CHAPTER EIGHT

THE SNOW TRIP

Snow covered the mountains behind the hills at Lake Kaniere and the air was fresh as Kupe and Keely walked to school.

Owen Owl announced to the class that next week there would be an excursion to the Alps at Arthur's Pass to enjoy the snow. Harry was excited at the news. He had gone on the snow trip last winter and had a wonderful time.

The Kiwi children were given a list of items they would need for the trip, which they read with puzzlement.

Hat, Scarf, Mittens, Boots, Rope, Flax mat, Rug, Food.

When Keona saw the list, she took it to Heather hedgehog.

"Do you know where we can get these things for the school trip?" Keona asked.

"Yes," Heather replied. "I have them from last time when Harry went. I have to get some more supplies because Holly will be going this time as well. Come with me to see Wanda Weasel. She gives us all the woollens we need for these trips.

"What are woollens?" Keona asked. She had never heard of them.

"There is a farm at the far end of the lake." Heather advised her. "Wanda collects sheep's wool from the farm fences and makes the warm clothes and rugs we call woollens."

Heather took Keona to a small cave high on the hillside to see Wanda. The cave was a busy place. Keona watched as three young Weasels chased, rolled and pounced on a woven ball. In the back of the cave sat Wanda weaving a flax mat, and her daughter Wendy, was making a rug as they watched the little ones.

Big brown eyes twinkled at Heather and Keona as Wanda welcomed them to a rock seat. The walls behind them were piled high with garments of all shapes and sizes.

"Hello Heather. Tell me your news." Wanda greeted her.

"Hello Wanda and Wendy." Heather replied. "This is Keona. She has come from Punakaiki to live with us. Her children Kupe and Keely are at the school with Harry and Holly."

"How are Holly and Keely?" Wanda asked. "Have they recovered from their adventure in the cave?"

"Keely and Holly are fine, thank you." Keona reassured her. "They are going on the school trip next week and need some woollens."

"We need some for Kupe as well." Heather added.

Heather and Keona were given a large load of woollens to take home.

"Can I give you something or do something for you?" Keona asked. She had come from a community where everything had to be paid for in some way. Keona looked at the children while they played.

"Can I look after the children or you to give you a rest?"

"I would love that!" Wanda replied. "I will be busy this week making orders for the trip though."

"When the children return from the snow trip, I will come." Keona promised.

The day of the snow trip came, and everyone gathered at the School cave, where a number of Tahr were waiting for them with woven saddles strapped to their backs.

Kupe Percy and Harry were lifted onto Tim Tahr's back, followed by Sam, Danny and Pete Pukeko onto Tommy Tahr. Keely, Holly and Daisy took their place on Teeny Tahr, while Wendy Petunia and Peony sat on Tammy Tahr. The Tuis, Fantails, Pigeons, Black birds and Owls twittered and chattered with excitement as they settled on Tara Tahr. Owen, Keanu and Paddy took the lead with Heather, Keona, Pansy and Fern at the back.

They set off at a steady walk through the dense forest north-east of the lake, increasing to a gallop as the passed through open woodland near the upper Arahura River where the Tahr carefully waded through the icy water of the fast flowing stream. After the Taramakau River, the Tahr kept to the hillsides as they headed for Arthurs Pass.

Near Otira they came to the first snow that blanketed the steep mountain slopes, which soared around them. Everyone was glad for the scarves and rugs they had brought to put on in the cold alpine air.

The Tahr pick their way around narrow winding paths in the snow, steadily climbing high into the mountains overlooking the pass untill they came to a snowfield with rock formations at the top; that gave shelter from the wind.

Everyone put on their boots and hats and found a spot to sit on their mats on the crisp snow to open their food packs for a snack. While the group was eating, the Tahr went searching for their meal and found some tasty long grass to feed on by scraping away some of the snow.

Feeling satisfied after their snack, everyone eyed the snow covered slopes in front of them, but who was going to try it first?

"I will go!" Harry offered to be first, sitting on his flax mat. He held onto the handles on each side of the mat and launched himself down the hill to the cheers of everyone watching.

Soon there was much laughter, shouting and squealing as everyone had varying degrees of success in riding down the slopes. The noise they made rung around the surrounding mountains.

The school group did not know about a group of Kiwis who lived on the other side of the mountain. The Kiwis had heard and seen the group before, thinking how strange they were. This time it was different. Among the different voices they heard the familiar call of Kiwis.

Kanai was the leader of the local group. He was born at Totara Flat but had spent nearly all of his life in the Alps at Arthur's Pass. He listened to the calls. It sounded like a family and they were mixing with other animals!

Kanai made a call so loud, it echoed through the mountains and valleys. His own Kiwi community heard it and stopped to listen.

"Hello. This is Kanai. Who are you and what are you doing here?"

"This is Keanu. I am here with my family on a school trip to enjoy the snow with other animals from the school. We return home tomorrow. Are you alone here?"

"No." Kanai replied. "We have a community here."

"Will you join us for a meal?" Keona called.

"Yes, we will." Kanai replied.

Kanai called to his mate, Kalama, to collect the children. They had been invited to a meal with some visitors across the mountain. Kalama and their daughter Kalea collected some worms and beetles while Kanai found their son Kekoa.

Other Kiwis who had heard the calls also busied themselves collecting food from their stores and made their way to the snowfield where the group was playing on the slopes.

There was much commotion as Keely Daisy and Holly raced down the slopes on their mats against Peony, Wendy and Petunia. As they reached the bottom, a group of Kiwis stood watching the scene in front of them with amazement.

Kupe, Sam, Danny, Percy, Pete and Harry were yelling and laughing as they played tag with snowballs. The younger Kiwis wasted no time in introducing themselves and joining in the fun.

Keanu spotted the Kiwis as they appeared and called out to them.

"Hello! Please come and join us!"

Kanai, Kalama and the Alpine Kiwi parents made their way across the snow to the rocks where Keanu and Keona were waiting with other parents. After Introductions were made, everyone sat down to watch and enjoy the scene as the local Kiwi children played with the visiting animal children.

Soon a thick mist began to form. The children were beginning to have trouble seeing each other and their parents. They roped themselves together and made their way up the hill, to where their parents were.

"Mum! Where are you?" Keely called.

"We are here!" Keona replied. "Keep coming! Can you hear me?"

"Yes!" Keely answered.

Keona kept repeating, "We are here! Keep coming!" untill the children emerged from the mist, to all the parents relief.

"Have you found the shelter yet?" Kanai asked Keanu.

"No, we haven't seen it yet. Please show us." Keanu replied.

Kanai led the way to some large slabs of rock. He scratched at the snow to reveal some long mountain grass. Kanai pulled back the grass to reveal the entrance to a cave that went far underground.

Snow was beginning to fall as everyone climbed in and found a spot to sit with their new friends. They swapped stories of their lives in the Alps and at the lake, while enjoying their meal together. Outside the Tahr found shelter under the rock slabs and fed on the mountain grass.

Keona noticed Keely was talking to the young male Kiwi Kekapa for some time. The local Kiwis also noticed this with interest and concern, as Kekapa was already courting a local Kiwi named Kalasia. *Was this the beginning of a courtship between Keely and Kekapa?*

Keona wondered with some anxiety. Life here was very different and more difficult than the one Keely enjoyed at the lake.

Kupe was sitting with Kekoa, telling him about the adventures he had with friends at the lake, when Kekoa spotted the greenstone amulet Kupe wore around his neck.

"Where did you get the stone?" Kekoa asked.

"It was in a book called *The Kiwi Kingdom* that I read in our school library." Kupe replied quietly.

He was astonished at what happened next. Kekoa reached into the feathers near his neck and brought out a similar amulet. He bowed down before Kupe.

"I will serve you all the days of my life." Kekoa declared. "What can I do to serve you?"

"Thank you," Kupe replied. He had to think quickly. What had been the biggest influence in his life? "Do you go to school here?"

"No," Kekoa replied. "We are educated at home."

"If you get the chance, go to school with other animals and learn to live in harmony with them." Kupe advised him.

"Thank you," Kekoa replied. "You are very wise. Our Kingdom will soon rise again if everyone does as you ask."

"I don't expect *everyone* to do as I ask." Kupe said with amusement.

"No." Kekoa replied. "We will have to fight for our Kingdom."

"I am not starting a war!" Kupe exclaimed, starting to get nervous.

"No," Kekoa replied, "but there are some who will oppose any change and will try to stop you."

"I have never had to fight anyone in my whole life. I don't know where to begin." Kupe said anxiously.

"Ah!" Kekoa said with relish. "I shall teach you." He bowed to Kupe again.

"Thank you." Kupe replied, though he was not sure he was going to enjoy the experience.

Kanai and Keanu saw Kekoa bowing to Kupe.

"What are you doing?" Kanai asked Kekoa, with a frown.

"Kupe is the new leader of the Kiwi Kingdom!" Kekoa shouted, pulling Kupe's amulet out to show his father. At Kekoa's announcement silence came over the cavern as Kanai looked at the amulet with amazement. Kekoa's amulet, a family treasure from a past no one had expected to return, had been handed down over the generations. Slowly Kanai also bowed and pledged his service to Kupe, followed by all the other Alpine Kiwis.

Eventually, it was time to leave. The snow and mist had cleared, and it was time to say goodbye to their new friends. Keona asked Keely whether she wanted to stay.

"Not this time, Mum, but I would like to come for a visit in spring time." Keely replied. Keona nodded her agreement.

"Perhaps we can arrange for some of your Kiwis to visit us at the Lake?" Keanu asked Kanai.

"We will welcome that." Kanai replied. "Your invitation has given me an idea. Some of our Kiwis do not survive the extreme conditions here every winter, so our population is decreasing. Maybe it will help if we spend our winter at the lake, returning to the Alps for the summer?"

Keanu spoke to Owen Owl about the idea. "Are there any other unused burrows still at the lake?" Keanu asked.

"Why, yes there are." Owen replied. "We will look into it when we get back."

And so it was arranged. Those who were interested in visiting the lake for the winter would come the following week. Keanu and Owen would return with the Tahr to collect them. As they said goodbye, everyone looked forward to meeting again soon and strengthening the bonds of their friendship.

When the group returned to the lake, heavy rain had set in, but the wet did not dampen the excitement of the other animals when they heard of the coming visit of the Alpine Kiwis.

While preparing for the Kiwis' visit, Keona remembered her promise to look after Wanda's children. When Keely, Holly and Peony heard of Keona's visit to the Weasels, they asked if they could come too, to see Wendy and help look after the children.

Early one wet evening, Keona and the girls went to Wanda's home to find the three younger Weasels, Willie, Winnie and Willow already busy playing and making mischief.

Wanda welcomed Keona and the girls with relief because the children were unhappy with being kept inside for several days because of the heavy rain.

Wanda waved the children goodbye, promising to return before morning.

Keona and the girls had each brought a bag with them with something special inside, which they made the children guess.

Willow won first with a game of Pickup sticks, which Holly showed her how to play. This game kept the children busy for some time.

Willie won next with a game of Knuckle stones. Winnie won a slate and a piece of rock chalk for drawing. Keely spent some time showing the children how to draw simple pictures of animals and plants they liked.

Keona taught the children the game I Spy, and each child had a turn while everyone else guessed what the item was.

When Wanda came back, she was amazed to see the children sitting quietly and listening to a story Peony was telling about an animal legend. She was even more amazed to hear of all the new games and skills they had learnt that night.

"Thank you so much for looking after the children." Wanda said. "When the weather is better, would you like to come on a ramble in the forest with us?"

"We would love to do that." Keona replied. Keona and the girls waved goodbye as they left, happy that everyone had enjoyed their night.

CHAPTER NINE

KUPE'S VISION

Kupe splashed through puddles of water as he made his way to the school cave. The new book was nearly finished. He hoped to complete it tonight before the Alpine Kiwis came tomorrow.

Kupe felt unsettled. He had not slept well. His night had been full of vivid dreams he didn't understand.

Tanis Tui saw Kupe's weary expression. "Do you want to do this another time?" Tania asked gently. "You look like you have the world on your shoulders."

Kupe gave a wry smile. "In a way, I think I do." Kupe explained his poor night of sleep. "I'm determined to get this book finished today before they come tomorrow. We need a safe place for these books – for all the books!"

"What was in your dreams, Kupe? Why are you so troubled?" Tania asked anxiously sensing that trouble was coming to the community.

Kupe told Tania about some of his dreams – how the school library was destroyed. Tania could see pain and panic in Kupe's eyes.

"What else do you see?" she asked gently.

"Some of our Kiwis will be killed." Kupe whispered.

"Do you see who will do it?" Tania asked with concern.

"It is the Alpine Kiwis." Kupe replied with misery. "I know they have pledged to serve me, but my instincts are telling me they are coming to serve themselves." Kupe pulled himself up. "We must prepare." Kupe then pulled out his amulet.

"Have we, or can we get another amulet that looks like this? The real one needs to be kept safe with the book untill we are certain the Kiwi Kingdom is safe again."

"Are you sure?" Tania asked.

"I am very sure." Kupe replied with conviction.

Tania put the paper and feather pen in front of Kupe. "We have much to do and little time to do it, but prepare we will." Tania reassured Kupe. "How long will it take you to complete the book?"

"One or two hours, I think." Kupe made an estimate.

"Good. The school will become busy, but just concentrate on the book." Tania ordered him.

"I will." Kupe promised, feeling a little better now that he had shared his troubled feelings.

"I am going to consult the council and organise a plan." Tania advised Kupe. "I will be back for the books when you have finished."

Kupe concentrated on the book he was copying, losing himself in the words, trying to memorise them as he went. Kupe barely noticed the sound of a horn echoing through the forest or the patter of feet around him as most of the books were moved from the library.

Finally the book was finished. Kupe checked through the book. The new parchment was in its place. He turned to the front page where the small pouch was waiting for his amulet. Looking at the other four empty pockets, Kupe wondered, *If the first amulet was given to the alpine Kiwis, where were the other three?*

Kupe then remembered a mysterious rhyme from the book and knew it was the key to finding the other amulet holders, whom he needed to save his kingdom.

One is near
One is far
One is high
One is low
from south to north
you need to go.

Kupe went to remove the amulet, but Tania Tui, who had been standing behind him, stopped Kupe.

"Not yet," Tania said. "The community is here."

Wearily, Kupe turned around. Silently and gravely, the whole community was waiting for him.

"Thank you all for coming to rescue our books." Kupe began. "The loss of our books means the loss of knowledge, the foundation of our wonderful community. We cannot allow anyone to take that from us! I am also concerned an attempt will be made to replace me and use my amulet to force a way of living that will destroy our Kingdom forever."

"While I accept that my life may be short or long, we must also preserve the way for another leader to follow me. To make certain of this, I am returning my amulet to its rightful place."

There was an audible gasp from the crowd at this news.

"Mrs Tui," Kupe addressed her, as he turned to her and bowed his head so she could remove it easily. She struggled with tears in her eyes. Pansy Possum stepped forward to help her lift the twine over Kupe's head. Percy Possum stood with the new book open. Tania and Pansy carefully place the amulet back in its place, before Tania carefully dried her eyes.

"We have a little surprise for you. We have found another amulet for Kupe to wear untill the Kingdom is safe again."

Petunia Possum stepped forward with another Jade amulet, tied with twine. Kupe looked at it. The amulet was very similar to the original one.

"You have done well." Kupe smiled as he bowed his head while Tania and Pansy placed the new amulet over his head to applause from the crowd. When the clapping stopped, Kupe spoke to the crowd again.

"My biggest concern is for you, my community. I fear many of your lives will be lost if you remain here, especially those involved with the school. I advise you to seek shelter with family or friends outside the lake area. If you cannot leave, try to send some of your family to safety, so that when the time comes we can rebuild our community. I will not always be here to protect you, as I will have to leave the lake soon on a quest for help to save our Kingdom.

We have an hour for everyone to decide what to do. We will arrange for Donny and Denny Deer to be at the school to take your family members to safety. We will see you all here then."

As everyone dispersed to their homes, Kupe joined Keona and Keely, who were waiting with the Hedgehog family. They went back to the burrow. All were quiet with their thoughts.

Henry and Heather spoke to Holly and Harry. "We want you to go to Hokitika. It will be safer there."

"I will stay for now," Holly decided. "I will see how many of my friends are going."

"I won't go unless you come too." Harry said stubbornly to his parents.

Harry looked at Kupe. "We will miss you when you're gone."

"It won't be forever." Kupe reassured him.

Kupe looked at Keely with troubled eyes. "I wish there was somewhere safe for you to go."

Keona saw Kupe's troubled look and suddenly was filled with fear. Kupe knew Keely wasn't safe!

"I intend to visit my friend Kahi at Punakaiki. Come with me!" Keona pleaded.

Keely shook her head and smiled. "I have too much keeping me here."

Keona knew Keely meant Kekapa, who was coming in the morning.

In the Rata tree, Paddy and Percy were saying goodbye to Pansy and Petunia, who were going to Taramakau to stay with Perry and Prunella. Pansy made them promise to visit often.

In the bulrushes, Pongo and Pete were saying farewell to Poppy and Peony before they made their journey to stay with their Uncle Phil and Aunty Paeonia at Kokatahi. Pongo and Poppy were also looking for a new home. If the Alpine Kiwis took over Keanu and Kupe's burrow, they would be far too close to them for comfort.

Stubby and Scarlett decided to stay. They could match any Kiwi in a fight if they had to. They were worried about Sam though, as he had no experience in fighting. They would have to teach him in a hurry. Stubby asked Sam if he would like to stay with relatives at Lake Mahinapua.

"I'm not going anywhere without you." Sam said with determination. "I will miss Kupe terribly when he goes, but I have other friends still here. Besides, someone has to stay to keep the new Kiwis in line." Stubby and Scarlett laughed and gave him a hug.

Wally and Wanda Weasel were concerned the new Kiwis would take over their home, so they had a word with Billy and Bessie Bat.

"Is there room in the Bat cave for the family if needed?"

"You are welcome to come and share with us." The Bats agreed.

All the birds decided to stay. It was easy enough to fly away if there was a problem.

Everyone gathered again at the school to say goodbye to Pansy, Petunia, Poppy and Peony. After many hugs and reminders to keep in touch, the girls were finally on their way, leaving their families sad and lonely.

Kupe invited everyone back to the burrow for some rosehip syrup. "However, before we start on the syrup, we need to organise a welcome for our guests.

138

We know our visitors will be tired after their journey. Some fresh ferns and a basket of worms in their burrows should be welcome."

"Do you mean we don't have to welcome them in person?"

"No you don't." Kupe replied. There were smiles all round.

In no time everyone was back at the burrow, enjoying the rosehip syrup and talking about the good times they had together. It was agreed that everyone would stay close to home for a day or two to prevent the spread of the "flu" that was keeping everyone away from the welcome. When dawn came, everyone was sound asleep at the burrow.

"Wake up every one!" Kupe called. "It's time to go home. Now remember to stay home for a day or two." as he saw them out of the door.

When the Tahr stopped with their passengers at the school cave, only Kupe was present to meet them. Once everyone was dismounted, Kupe stood on a rock to address them, showing a confidence, maturity and firmness neither Keanu nor Owen had seen before.

"Hello and welcome to my Kingdom. My community could not join me to welcome you as there has been illness here and everyone is being kept at home untill we are sure everyone is well. I know you have had a long and tiring journey and will be ready for a rest. Your burrows have been made ready for you to use. This evening there will be classes here for those who are interested."

"We have a few rules here we expect you to live by while you are staying with us. You must respect all animals, regardless of who or what they are. You may not injure or kill any animal you meet while you are here. Anyone found doing so will be expelled, never to return. Unless there is an emergency, visitors are expected to be in their burrows during normal resting time in the day. We hope you will enjoy your time with us. Keanu, Owen and I will show you to your burrows. Please let us know if there is anything you need."

Kupe took Kanai and his family to their burrow.

"I hope you will be comfortable here." Kupe offered in welcome as he showed them the entrance. Kanai grunted as he pushed his way inside, followed by Kekoa.

"I'm sure we will be." Kalama thanked Kupe as she followed them inside.

Kupe admired Kalea, who had the palest grey fur he had ever seen and gave him an encouraging smile as she went past him into the burrow.

Once the visitors were settled into their burrows, Keanu, Owen and Kupe returned to the school cave.

"Are Keona and Keely alright?" Keanu asked, questioning their absence.

"Yes Dad," Kupe reassured him. "They have had a very busy night getting all the burrows ready and leaving a meal for the guests. They are very tired and were asleep when I left. How was your trip to the Alps?"

"It was cold!" Keanu complained.

"Have there been any special queries or requests from our guests?" Kupe asked.

Keanu looked at him sharply. "Why?"

"No special reason." Kupe replied, hoping he looked calmer than he felt. "Our guests do have a different way of life to us, so this will be a big change for them."

Kupe is full of surprises this morning! Keanu thought. This Insightful Kupe was new.

"Are you ready to go home?" Keanu asked.

"You go ahead, Dad," Kupe replied. "I want to talk to Owen about the book. I won't be long."

After Keanu had left, Owen looked at Kupe. "What has happened here? The whole community is absent. Most of the library is missing, including the book! And you, in a few days have grown beyond your years!"

"I've had a warning!" Kupe said, and told Owen about everything that happened while they were away.

Owen looked at Kupe with both pride and fear. "You are truly Keoni's grandson!"

Kupe was puzzled at his words.

"Keoni also had the gift of seeing the future."

CHAPTER TEN

A LUCKY ESCAPE

Keanu entered the burrow to find Keona and Keely sound asleep. He snuggled up to Keona for warmth. He still felt cold from the trip to Arthur's Pass, where there was more snow than the previous week, making it more difficult for both Tahr and Kiwis to move around.

Keona promptly woke up, happy that Keanu was safely home again. After hearing about his trip to the snowfield, she told him how busy they had been, getting ready for their guests.

"We were lucky there were plenty of worms in the Gilmore's garden to get everyone a good meal." (Keona did not worry Keanu with Kupe's vision and all the changes the community had made.) She then changed the subject. "We should have this burrow to ourselves again soon. Kupe is planning to take a trip away to restore the Kingdom, and if Keely's friendship with Kekapa develops, she will be gone as well."

"Are you ready for the patter of little feet again?" Keanu asked.

"It would be nice," Keona smiled. "This place is too big for just the two of us."

That evening Keely made her way to the school cave with mounting excitement. This was the first time she had seen Kekapa since the trip to the Alps. *Was it only a week ago?* Keely thought. It seemed like a lifetime ago. At the cave she saw a group of Kiwis gathered together, looking uncertain. Among them she spotted Kekapa.

"Hello everyone. Welcome to the school." She called, with a big smile. Keely tried to look at everyone, but her eyes went to Kekapa, who grinned back.

The school lesson began with Daphne Duck assisting Owen Owl while Pansy Possum was away visiting Perry and Prunella at Taramakau. As the lesson progressed, Keely could feel someone looking at her. She turned around to see one of the female Alpine Kiwis, Kalasia, looking at Kekapa with a mixture of anger, fear and Misery.

Surprised, Keely realised Kalasia also cared for Kekapa. Was she in a relationship with him? Keely noticed Kekapa was ignoring Kalasia. How could she find out?"

Keely said to Holly, "I like Kekapa, but there is something I need to find out." Holly nodded. She too had seen Kalasia's unhappiness as she looked at Kekapa.

"Shall I find out for you?" Holly offered.

"Would you?" Keely asked. "I don't want to come between Kalasia and Kekapa if they are already together."

At the end of the lesson, there was a short break. Holly went to the library and found a picture book, which she took and sat among the Alpine female Kiwis, who were sitting in a bunch together. Holly spent the remainder of the session with the Alpine Kiwis. At the session's end, Kalasia looked happier and gave Keely a little smile when she looked at her.

Holly rejoined Keely and Daisy as they made their way home. "You were right about Kalasia and Kekapa." Holly told Keely. "They were courting and were going to make their own burrow untill recently."

"You mean when I came on the snow trip?" Keely asked.

"Yes," Holly replied. "I have told Kalasia you don't want to come between them." Holly then added with a smile, "Kalasia also asked if you were interested in meeting her brother Kaori, who wants to meet you."

"I might do." Keely replied; feeling disappointed that Kekapa was not available to her.

During the school session, Owen gave Kupe an atlas and told him to study the maps of the land where they lived. Kupe was amazed at the size of the area the Kingdom used to cover. He found some paper and started to copy down all the lakes, rivers and mountains, so he could find his way when his quest began.

When the school session was over, Kupe was still studying the map and his friends read books with him. Kaori, an Alpine Kiwi came to see what Kupe was studying.

"Where are we on the map?" Kaori asked.

"We are here." Kupe replied, pointing out Lake Kaniere on the page. Kaori studied the map more intently.

"It all makes sense now." Kaori murmured to himself.

"What makes sense?" Kupe asked with interest.

"My great-grandfather was a follower of your grandfather. He was killed over a dispute for power and territory. That is how Kekoa now wears the amulet. One thing his family doesn't know, is a certain rhyme, and repeated in a whisper, "*One is near, One is far, One is high, One is low, from South to North...*"

"You need to go." Kupe finished for him.

Kaori nodded before adding, *"To find those who you seek, you should start near the Head to find Arthur's Three Sisters."* Kaori pointed out places on the map as he spoke. "That is where you will find the bearers of the other amulets." He said quietly.

"Why isn't that part of the rhyme in the book?" Kupe asked.

"Your great grandfather asked his followers to make up a rhyme only they and their families would know in case the book or any of the amulets came into the wrong hands. Speaking of sisters – your sister Keely isn't safe." Kaori said anxiously.

"I know!" Kupe replied with despair.

"She shouldn't be left alone while Kekoa and Kekapa are here. I Know Kekapa has dumped my sister Kalasia, for her."

"Is he after her because of me?"

"Yes," Kaori sighed. "We need to talk to her.

"Do you want some help?" Percy chipped in.

"We need all the help we can get." Kupe accepted Percy's offer grimly. Kaori and Kupe went with his friends in search of Keely.

Keely was quietly feeding in the forest when she heard Kiwi footsteps behind her. She looked up to find Kekapa and Kekoa were coming.

"Hello," Keely greeted them. "How did you find the lessons?"

"They were a bit boring." Kekapa replied. "We already know everything we need to know from our parents."

Keely didn't know how to answer this challenge without an argument, so she remained silent. Kekapa had started leaping and hopping around in front of Keely. She realised he was trying to court her.

"You can stop that!" Keely said firmly to Kekapa. "I only want to be a friend."

Kekapa stopped. "I know you want me. Are you trying to play hard to get?"

"No," Keely replied, starting to feel anxious now. "I know you have dropped your mate Kalasia for me. Is it because I'm Kupe's sister?"

143

"You are smarter than you look," Kekapa sneered and changed the subject. "Where is *The Kiwi Kingdom* Book?"

"I don't know."

"I don't believe you!"

Keely looked around in panic for a way to escape as Kekapa moved towards her.

"Stop! Leave her alone!" Kupe yelled.

Kekapa, Kekoa and Keely suddenly found that Kaori, Kupe and his friends had surrounded them.

"I was just joking." Kekapa blustered.

"We aren't!" Kupe growled. "You will not go near Keely ever again! And, speaking of taking things that aren't yours," Kupe's attention then switched to Kekoa. "That amulet you wear. If you are the rightful owner, you will know a rhyme that goes with it. Tell me what it is!" Kupe demanded.

With eyes full of confusion and anger, Kekoa admitted he didn't know. "I don't know anything about a rhyme. It was just given to me."

"I know!" Kupe replied. "Your ancestor killed the owner. It is time to give it back."

Reluctantly, Kekoa lowered his head so the amulet could be taken. Percy and Sam removed it and gave it to Kupe.

"Who does it belong to?" Kekoa asked.

"You already know!" Kaori replied angrily. "It's why you came after my sister Kalei."

"Is it true?" Kalasia asked, as she stepped out from behind a tree.

"You can't blame me for trying to gain the power of the Kingdom for our family," Kekoa muttered. "Anyone else would do the same."

Kalasia then looked at Kekapa. "You were doing the same with me too!" Weren't you?" Under her penetrating stare, he hung his head.

"It seems," she said to Keely with a sigh, "that 'I've had a lucky escape too!'"

After seeing Kekoa and Kekapa disappear into the forest, the friends went down to the lake and sat by the water's edge.

"Keely, are you alright?" Kupe asked.

"Yes. I'm lucky you came when you did though." Keely replied with relief. "I'm not sure I want to stay now. I will see when Mum is going up to Punakaiki." Keely turned to Kalasia. "What are you going to do now Kalasia?"

"I'm not sure," Kalasia replied. "I like it here at the lake, but it's not safe to stay while Kekoa and Kekapa are here. I don't want to return home either." She added.

"I was going to join Kupe when he starts his quest. Do you want to come with us?" Kaori offered her.

"I may, or I may join Keely and her mother when they go to Punakaiki." Kalasia said with a smile.

Kupe brought out the amulet. He was about to give it to Kaori when Danny Duck interrupted.

"I think we have trouble!"

Everyone looked around. Keanu and Kanai were coming with Kekoa and Kekapa. Quickly Kupe put the amulet over Danny's head.

"Go!" Kupe said urgently. "Find Tania Tui and put it in the book!"

Swiftly Danny took off over the water before heading to the forest. Kupe then turned and stood up. His friends stood up with him.

"Hello Dad. Hello Kanai. What brings you all here?" Kupe asked.

"Why did you take Kekoa's amulet?" Kanai was angry.

"Give it back!" Keanu demanded. Kupe looked at his father. He saw fear in his eyes. Kupe then knew his father had been threatened. Kupe had to be strong for both of them.

"No, Dad." Kupe said regretfully. "I can't give it back." Turning to Kanai, Kupe added, "The amulet was taken from Kekoa because he failed the ownership test."

Kupe then challenged Kanai. "The test was created in case the amulet came into the wrong hands. Do you know what the ownership test is?"

Kanai knew he was defeated.

"What is the test?" he muttered.

"There is a rhyme that only the true owner of the amulet knows." Kupe replied. "Do you know it?" Kupe asked again firmly.

"No, but it's a family heirloom." Kanai protested.

"It is only your family heirloom because your ancestor killed the owner and took it from them," Kupe replied. "It doesn't belong to your family."

"Where is it?" Kanai demanded.

"The amulet has been returned to where it belongs," Kupe replied calmly. "In the book."

Kanai grabbed at Kupe's amulet. "You have taken our amulet, now I will take yours!"

Kupe stayed calm. "It won't do you any good if you do."

Kanai looked closely at the amulet. "This isn't the one you were wearing when we met you!"

"No, it isn't." Kupe confirmed. "The real one is also safe in the book."

"Where is the book?" Kanai asked sullenly.

I can honestly say I don't know where it is," Kupe replied. "I asked my community to put it in a safe place. The members involved have been moved away for their own safety."

"You will live to regret this!" Kanai hissed at Kupe, turning to stomp off and forcing Keanu to go with him, followed by the other Kiwis. Just then, Danny Duck glided back across the water, minus the amulet.

"None of us are safe." Kupe said quietly in the silence after the Kiwis had left. "Everyone, gather your families and tell all the others. It is time to pay a visit to Poppy and Peony at Kokatahi. We will use the boat and meet the deer at the farm."

Kupe and Kaori took the girls back to Kupe's burrow before seeking out Owen Owl at the school cave. Danny Duck was already there with his family, pleading with Owen to come. Owen looked at Kupe with sad eyes.

"I cannot come." Owen said. "This school is my life. I know some of the visitors have enjoyed the lessons. I may be able to get them to change and get them to persuade the other Kiwis to change too."

"You may not survive if you stay."

146

"My mate Odelia is already teaching our children everything I know." Owen told Kupe. "The knowledge is safe."

Back at the burrow, Keely and Keona were trying to persuade Keanu to come too.

"I can't." Keanu said flatly. "They have promised to harm me and everyone else if I try to leave. Besides," Keanu sighed, "I invited them here. It would be an insult if I was to leave too."

Tearfully, the family said their goodbyes. As Kupe left the burrow, he turned to take one last look at his father. In that moment, they both knew it would be the last time they would see each other in this life.

As the family made their way to the boat, one of the Alpine Kiwis, Kane stopped Kupe.

"What is happening? Everyone seems to be leaving."

"We are a close community." Kupe told him. "We are going to visit some of our community who are staying in the next valley."

"Will you be coming back?" Kane asked.

"Maybe," Kupe replied noncommittally. "Some of your group have shown themselves to be hostile to us. We will not return untill it is safe to do so."

"Is there anything we can do?"

"Try to protect the members of our community that have stayed behind and live in peace during your time here."

As Kupe turned to lead his family to the boat, he did not see all the Kiwis who had come out to see them go. Many of the visiting Kiwis had troubled looks on their faces.

"We will have to do something!" one muttered.

CHAPTER ELEVEN

THE PICNIC

Kanai, Kekoa and Kekapa had come to the shore, watching in silence as the boat was loading. Everyone tried to ignore them as they took their seats. As the boat cast off, Kanai, Kekoa and Kekapa turned and disappeared into the forest. Kupe knew they were heading straight for Keanu's burrow.

There was a carnival atmosphere on the boat as it began to make its way along the eastern bay. Suddenly the water around the boat seemed to boil as all the Eels in the lake surrounded the boat. Among the eels Kupe spotted Ernie.

"Hello Kupe! Hello everyone! Where are you going?" Ernie asked.

"We are visiting Poppy and Peony Pukeko at Kokatahi." Kupe replied.

"I heard that you were leaving for good!" Ernie said tearfully.

"I am leaving for a while to restore the Kingdom, but I will be back." Kupe advised him firmly.

Elijah the leader of the Eels' council then spoke "We are pleased to hear you intend to return and wish you well in your quest for the Kingdom. To farewell you, we would lie to escort your boat up the lake."

"We are delighted you are going to join us." Kupe replied with a grin. The wriggling mass of Eels sorted themselves out to become a grey shadow that surrounded the boat as it made its way up the lake.

The sound of clicking announced the arrival of Benny Bat and his colony in a mass of black wings as they came swooping down from the mountaintop. Kaori and Kalasia cowered in fear.

"Don't be afraid." Kupe reassured them. "They are my friends Benny and his colony. "Hello Benny!" Kupe called, as everyone on the boat waved to them.

"Why are you leaving?" Benny called as the colony flew around above the boat.

"I'm going away to restore the Kingdom. I will be back though." Kupe told them. There was a big chorus of "Good Luck" before they returned to the mountain. The Deer saw the Bats leave the cave to visit the boat down on the lake. As the Bats flew overhead, Stan the stag asked what was happening.

148

After Benny had told him of their farewell to Kupe, Stan raised his head and gave an almighty roar. Word of Kupe's leaving quickly pass around the Deer. Soon the mountains surrounding the lake were echoing as the Stags roared their goodbyes.

The noise brought Greg and Jane out of their bach to the jetty. This wasn't the roaring season. What was going on? Greg brought out his binoculars. He missed the boat as it was hidden by the islands in Hans Bay, but he did spot the Bats as they returned to the Mountain.

Greg also saw a big flock of ducks, as they flew out of the forest surrounding Hans Bay before swooping on the bay behind the islands then emerging and flying in formation up the lake.

"I think something is happening among the animals over there." Greg said, before they retreated to the bach to wonder what was happening.

At Hans Bay, the Alpine Kiwis had quietly gathered on the edge of the forest and saw Kupe and the animals board the boat with Kanai Kekoa and Kekapa watching from the shore.

They watch with amazement as the Eels, Bats and Ducks visited the boat to say goodbye and were in awe of the roaring Stag's calls echoing around them. As the boat disappeared into the distance, the Alpine Kiwi Kane became concerned.

"Keanu is alone now. We should check that Kanai has not harmed him."

Kane led the Kiwis to Keanu's burrow. His calls were met by silence. He took the Kiwis inside to search the tunnels. They were met by empty spaces. Returning outside, Kane looked around. The forest was silent.

"I don't suppose any of the animals here saw where Keanu has gone." Kane said to himself.

"Excuse me," a little voice called. It came from the stream. Kane went over to the water. Fuchsia Frog leapt out by his feet. "If you are looking for Keanu, three of your Kiwis took him away, I think to the school. Please be quick. They were being very rough with him!"

Kane thanked her and swiftly led the Kiwis to the school.

Sally the sheep was grazing peacefully in the paddock by the lake when she noticed some Deer appear at the edge of the forest, looking out to the lake. Then a flock of Ducks flew in. They lined up on the bank, watching the water too. Soon a boat appeared. As it came to the shore, Sally was amazed to see the boat was full of animals. She saw Wanda Weasel among them.

"Hello Wanda!" Sally called. "Where are you going?"

"We are going for a picnic at Kokatahi." Wanda replied.

"I wish I could come too!" Sally said wistfully, knowing that she couldn't go anywhere, with the fence around her.

The Ducks said their goodbyes as everyone left the boat. Percy had spotted the deer and showed everyone where to go while Paddy, Daffy, Henry, Stubby, Pongo and Wally pulled the boat up on the shore and hid it among some bracken.

The Deer loaded and sped everyone through the forest to the Styx River, which flows through thick forested hills with the Southern Alps towering behind them. They made their way down the stream to Kokatahi, where Holly spotted a row of blue Hydrangeas in full bloom, nestled by the forest.

"Can we stop and pick one?" Holly asked.

"No," Heather replied. "But you may find some in Hokitika when we go there." With this to look forward to, Holly was happier to leave now.

In a marshy paddock next to the forest, they came across a large bunch of bulrushes. The arrival of the Deer with their family and friends brought Poppy and Peony Pukeko out of the shelter in a rush. After the family had been reunited, Poppy asked Pongo how long they had together.

"We are staying untill it is safe at the lake," Pongo told her, and added with some sadness, "This picnic is a farewell for everyone. Henry's family is going to Hokitika. Stubby and Wally's families are going to Lake Mahinapua. Paddy and Percy are off to Taramakau. Kupe and Kaori are heading south; Keona Keely and Kalasia may travel with them or go to Punakaiki."

"Where's Keanu?" Poppy wanted to know.

He insisted on staying behind," Pongo replied. "We are all worried about him." Pongo saw Keona and Keely huddled together with Kalasia and wondered about their future.

"I hope Keanu will be alright," Keona said fretfully, "I'm having a chick and I can't look after it without him." Keely and Kalasia were silent for a moment, as they realised Keona may have to try to hatch her egg alone.

"Don't worry Mum," Keely comforted her. "I will help you."

"And so will I!" Kalasia chipped in.

Keona looked at the two girls. "You can't possibly do it!" she protested.

"Yes, we can!" Keely replied with a grin. "We will think of it as practice for when we have our own children. Have you decided where we are going Mum?"

"I would have liked to go to Punakaiki," Keona replied, "but I need protection now that I'm having a chick, so we will go south with Kupe and Kaori."

"Maybe we can go to Punakaiki when the chick is old enough to travel." Keely suggested.

Once everyone had sat down with their picnic, they chattered about all the different places they were going to, and what they would find there.

Kupe was relaxing after the meal, when a vision of Keoni and Keanu appeared before him.

"I am at peace now." Keanu said to Kupe, before the two vanished.

Kupe went over to Daffy Duck, who was instantly alert to the troubled look on Kupe's face. Very quietly Kupe gave Daffy the news they were all dreading.

"I know they've taken my father's life from him," Kupe told Daffy. "Can you go and see what is happening? Make sure they don't catch and harm you!"

Without a word Daffy turned and flew towards the lake.

"What's happened?" Keona asked. She knew something serious was happening.

"I'm just getting Daffy to check whether it is safe to return to the lake." Kupe replied as calmly as he could.

Keona was not fooled. She had seen the stricken look in his eyes. She went over to Kupe.

"Tell me what's happened!" Keona demanded.

"I'm sorry Mum;" Kupe said gently, "Dad's gone." He looked her in the eye. "He is with Keoni. He is at peace now."

"How do you know?" Keona asked, not believing what Kupe was telling her.

"Their spirits came to me. Dad and Keoni were together. Dad told me he was at peace now."

Kupe turned to the community. The conversation had stopped while Kupe and Keona were talking.

"When Daffy comes back, we need to be ready to go."

Everyone gathered around to comfort Keona before quietly packing and waiting for Daffy's return.

"You are coming with us, Mum" It was a statement, not a question. "It will be safer." Kupe added.

Keona nodded. In her mind, she was screaming *Keanu! Where are you?"* Suddenly a strange calmness came over her and Keona knew Keanu's spirit was with her.

When Daffy winged his way back to the bulrushes, the subdued faces told him that everyone now knew the bad news.

"You were right," Daffy told Kupe. "Keanu has gone." He said to Keona "I'm sorry." She nodded in reply. "You will be pleased to know," Daffy added as he addressed everyone, "there has been a rebellion among the other Kiwis. Kanai, Kekoa and Kekapa have been expelled. Kane is now in charge. He has told all the others to live by the Kingdom rules Kupe set."

"Is Owen safe?" Kupe asked

"He has been injured, but he is still alive," Daffy replied. "They tried to destroy the school, but Kane and the other Kiwis stopped them."

"Where have Kanai, Kekoa and Kekapa gone?" Kupe asked.

"They are coming this way." Daffy advised him.

"Are they on foot?" Kupe asked.

"Yes." Daffy confirmed.

"Good! We have a head start." Kupe replied with some relief.

Wally and stubby decided to go to Lake Mahinapua, but only for a few days, before returning home. Henry's visit to Hokitika was for a week or so to check out all the gardens Holly had told them about. Paddy and Percy were off to Taramakau to collect Pansy and Petunia. Tania Tui and Daphne Duck would need some help while Owen was recovering. Pongo and Poppy Pukeko decided to spend a couple of days at Sunny Bight on the way home, inviting Uncle Phil and Aunty Paeonia to come with them.

After their goodbyes had been said, everyone went their separate ways, with only the Ducks, Tuis, Fantails and Pigeons heading for home.

"Are you sure this is the right way?" Kekoa asked, as they steadily made their way through the forest.

"The boat came this way, so it must be." Kanai replied grimly. The impact of his failed attempt to take over at the lake, followed by their expulsion by the Alpine Kiwis, and finally rejection by his mate and daughter Kalea were now starting to hit him.

Suddenly, the sound of hooves came thundering their way. Instinctively they shrunk behind a tree as a deer carrying Tuis and Fantails sped past. Kanai listened carefully in case any more were coming, but the forest remained silent.

CHAPTER TWELVE

MEETING AT MAHINAPUA.

After saying their final farewells to the Kiwis at Woodstock, the Stoats and Weasels made their way down from Arthur's Town to Mahinapua. As Dusty raced along Mahinapua creek in the soaking rain, Wanda Weasel was beginning to have doubts about this trip. She preferred to be in the dry comfort of their cave, but the thought of Kanai, Kekoa and Kekapa kept her clinging to Dusty's back.

When Dusty turned into the fern tunnel and slowed to a trot, they knew they were nearly at the lake. The fern tunnel opened out onto the big open grassed area of the camping ground, which was empty. They had the lake to themselves. Leaving them by the water's edge and promising to return in a couple of days, Dusty quickly returned to the protection of the forest.

Wanda and Wally saw a bach nestled in the bush high up on the hill, and with Scarlett and Stubby's help, the families scampered up the hillside to find shelter under the bach.

After Willie, Winnie and Willow had curled up in their dry grass nests, Sam and Wendy sat planning the fun they would have swimming in the lake and exploring the forest.

Wally and Wanda and Stubby and Scarlett sat looking out into the night. The forest surrounding the lake was now cloaked in darkness. They wondered where Keona and her family were now and hoped they would stay safe. Eventually, they too went to sleep, to the steady pitter patter of the rain on the roof.

Daylight saw Sam and Wendy lead Willie, Willow and Winnie down to the lake for a swim. The weed-covered floor made the water dark and difficult to see if anything was in the water. While the three younger Weasels splashed in the shallows with Wendy, Sam swam out into the middle of the natural pool, which had bulrushes and water lilies growing on a sandy ridge, separating it from the main lake.

Suddenly, Sam saw a dark shadow emerge from the rushes and quickly swam back to the Weasels.

"Get out! I think there is an Eel coming!" he called to them.

The Weasels quickly climbed out of the water and watched as the Eel followed Sam, who scrambled onto the water's edge. As the Eel turned away, Sam saw three spots on its tail. Sam splashed the water loudly with his paws.

"What are you doing?" Wendy was alarmed that Sam was trying to get the Eel's attention.

"I think I know him!" Sam answered. Sam splashed some more, and the Eel turned around. Sam called, "Elton, is that you?"

The Eel came right to the edge and stuck out his head. "How do you know my name?"

"I'm Sam. I know Ernie from Lake Kaniere. We are here for a visit. How do you like living here?"

"I love it." Elton replied. "There aren't any rules! I'm going back some day though."

"Are you going back to see your friends?" Sam asked innocently, knowing that Elton was banned from returning.

"I have some unfinished business there." Elton replied before turning away. The grim expression on Elton's face sent a chill down Sam's spine. He would have to warn the lake Eels of Elton's intentions.

While exploring the long grass of the camping area, they found a trail leading into the forest. As they followed the trail, they found some supple jack vines to play in. As they climbed, swung and slid among the vines, Sam felt they were being watched. Racing up the trunk of the Rata Tree, Sam found a young female Stoat gazing with wonder at the antics of the Weasels playing on the vines.

"Hello, I'm Sam." He said, startling her. "Would you like to join us?"

"I'm Silene." She introduced herself shyly. "Why are you with Weasels?"

"We go to school together and are here for a holiday."

"Where do you live?" Silene wanted to know.

"We live at Lake Kaniere. Do you know where it is?"

Silene shook her head.

"Do you have a tree that is taller than all the others?" Sam asked. "I will show you where we live.

As Sam and Silene came down from the Rata Tree, Wendy and the younger Weasels joined them.

"This is Silene," Sam introduced her. "I'm going to show her where we live."

Silene led Sam and the Weasels through the forest untill they reached the trunk of a white pine that reached far beyond the tree tops. Sam led the way, climbing to the canopy of the tree. As they negotiated the branches, Silene hesitated.

"Can you see anyone up there?" Silene called.

"Who would be up here?" Sam asked.

"Sometimes the Owl is here." Silene warned him anxiously.

Sam turned around. In front of him stood the largest Owl he had ever seen, and it was giving him a furious glare!

"Hello Mr Owl." Sam said with a smile. "I'm Sam. I'm sorry if we disturbed your sleep. We came to show Silene where we live."

Oscar was intrigued by this stoat. Most animals trembled in fear or fled for their lives in terror when he appeared, but this young stoat seemed relaxed and comfortable in his presence, as though he was used to talking to Owls.

"Hello Sam. I'm Oscar." The Owl replied. "Where do you live?"

Now it was obvious Sam was safe, the Weasels and Silene came to join him. Sam turned and pointed to Mount Graham. "That mountain is called Mount Graham. Beyond it is Lake Kaniere, where we live." Sam then looked around and spotted the ocean and gasped. "That must be the Tasman Sea. Look how big it is!"

"How do you know the names of the mountain, lake and sea?" Oscar was impressed.

"We learnt them at school."

"Who teaches you at school?"

"Tania Tui teaches us day animals and Owen Owl teaches the night animals." At the mention of Owen's name, Oscar instantly became more awake. He had met Owen and knew of the school Owen held for local animals. "How is Owen?" Oscar asked with a smile.

Sam became tearful, remembering the events of the past week. "I wish I knew!" he wailed. "We are all worried about him." As Sam told Oscar about the meeting with the Alpine Kiwis and the trouble they had brought with them since arriving at the lake, Oscar became concerned. When Sam told him Keanu had been killed and Owen had been injured, Oscar made up his mind.

"I will go and see Owen tonight." Oscar promised Sam.

"Will you?" Sam was relieved. "We are staying under the bach." Sam pointed to the tin roof that could be seen through the trees. Oscar nodded.

"I will come after I've seen Owen.

After thanking Oscar again, Sam led the Weasels back down the Tree to the forest floor, and Silene, still amazed they had survived the encounter with the owl, led them back to the bach. At the bach, Stubby and Scarlett and Wally and Wanda wondered where the children were and what they were doing. They were relieved and interested to see them return with a young female stoat.

After meeting Silene and hearing of their encounters with Elton Eel and Oscar Owl, Stubby and Wally decided to come along when Silene offered to show them the "safe beach" where the water was clear.

"The Eels can't sneak up on you there," Silene told them. "Also, there are plenty of trees there for shade."

The Stoats and Weasels had a wonderful carefree day climbing up and down the slope to the lake with the tree roots creating natural steps in the bank, before cooling off in the water.

As he went to sleep that night, Sam heard an Owl calling and wondered if it was Oscar. Just before dawn, they were woken by the sound of a large bird on the roof. Sam knew it was Oscar and scurried outside.

"Is that you, Oscar?" Sam called.

"Yes, it's me." Oscar answered.

"How is Owen?" Sam asked anxiously.

Oscar was silent for a moment. He had been shocked at how ill Owen looked and was surprised he was still alive.

"You were right," Oscar told Sam. "Owen has been badly hurt. I will visit every night untill he is better."

"Thank you." Stubby said as he came forward to comfort Sam. "Before Keanu Kiwi's family came home, Owen's family kept our community together.

We need them more than ever, now that Keanu's son Kupe has left to restore the Kingdom."

Oscar nodded before flying off to find his mate, Olivia, to tell her all the news. It was also time to think about an education for their children.

Daylight brought with it a stiff breeze that rippled across the water. It also brought some visitors. Silene had brought her parents, Slim and Sage to see them.

"Silene wants to go with you when you return home." Slim said with a smile, as he saw Silene join Sam.

"Did you want to come for a visit to see she is settled?" Scarlett asked, seeing Sage's anxious look.

"I would like that." Sage answered with a smile.

"Life's a bit different at our lake." Stubby warned.

"We are quite happy to fit in." Slim replied.

"Where is Dusty?" Stubby asked Dianthia when she came to take them home at night.

"He has gone down south with a message for Kupe."

"Do you know what the message was?"

Dianthia shook her head. Stubby couldn't help feeling uneasy with this news, but in the confusion of getting everyone together, forgot about it.

The trip back to Kokatahi and the lake was a leisurely affair. With the extra load on board, Dianthia could not travel very fast. This was helpful for a male Weasel named Woody, who had spotted Wendy at the lake. Woody had hoped for an opportunity to speak to her alone, but none had come, and he was now frantically trying to catch up with her.

Luckily the deer was walking slowly, and he could keep up. When Dianthia stopped for a rest in the bushland at Woodstock, Woody was also very tired, but he knew he had to try to see Wendy here or he might not see her at all. As he was peering around a tree, Scarlett saw him and called him over.

"Hello, are you one of the local Weasels?"

"Hello, he said shyly as he came out from behind the tree. "I'm Woody, from the lake."

"You have followed us all this way?"

"Yes," Woody grinned. "I was hoping to meet Wendy, but she was busy with the young ones all the time she was at the lake."

"Wendy is always busy with the young ones." Scarlett laughed, as she called Wendy over to meet him.

Wanda saw the meeting and her heart sank. She knew this moment would happen sometime, but had hoped it wouldn't happen for a little while longer. This meeting meant she had to make changes when she got home. Willie, Willow and Winnie's carefree days at home were now over as they would be off to school; a new home would need to be found for Wendy and her mate, and she may need to do all the woollens for the school herself or teach Winnie and Willow to help.

When Dianthia was ready to leave that night, she had an extra passenger. Across the Kaniere Bridge she strode as fast as she could to seek shelter in the bushes by the river as she made her way upstream to Kokatahi.

At old Nesses Creek Dianthia slipped into the thick Manuka bushland to take another rest stop.

The old creek once was a favourite spot where humans would picnic and swim, as the river meandered among the willow trees. Now, it is a silent lonely place, its waters stilled forever. The creek was now diverted to a new course. The stoats and weasels were thankful, though for the quiet sanctuary it gave them on their long trek home. When Dianthia reached the forest at the Styx River, a sense of excitement rose among the Weasels and Stoats. They were almost home.

As the lake finally came into view, they climbed down to stretch their legs. While Stubby and Wally thanked Dianthia for their safe return, Sam looked among the bracken for the boat and was happy to find it hadn't been touched.

Both Silene and Woody were amazed at the adventure their life had become since they had met the Kaniere Stoats and Weasels. Neither had ridden on a Deer before, and now they were going to ride on a very large lake in a boat. Once Wally and Stubby pushed the laden boat into the water, everyone who was big enough to row was given an oar. After much thrashing and wetting each other with water, and laughter they finally got underway.

As the boat made its way to Hans Bay, there was a splash as Ernie surfaced by the boat.

"Hello Sam," Ernie called. "How was your holiday?"

"We had a great time at Mahinapua." Sam told him. "I met my mate Silene, and guess who else I met there?"

Ernie looked at Sam's serious face.

"Was it Elton?"

"It was him, and I think he is looking for more trouble!" Sam warned Ernie. "Elton said he is coming back to this lake for some "Unfinished business."

"Thanks Sam. I will see you later." Ernie promised before disappearing into the depths of the lake to warn his community.

Percy and Danny were paddling in the water of Hans Bay when the boat came into view.

"Sam is home!" Danny cried, flying to the boat to welcome them home, while Percy raced into the forest to tell everyone of the Stoats' and Weasels' return.

CHAPTER THIRTEEN

HOLIDAY AT HOKITIKA

Heather looked around her with bewilderment. They had a long ride through the open farmland from Kokatahi to Kaniere, where they followed the river to the old tram track that took them to Hokitika. At the edge of Hokitika, Delphinia Deer left them before disappearing into the darkness of the bush track, promising to return for them in a week.

Heather wasn't so sure now, about this adventure. There were bright lights on tall poles, high fences everywhere, and hardly any trees to be seen; and where were the gardens Holly had talked about?

"I think I can see the vet's." Holly said as she recognized the building she had been taken to. "Harvey should be nearby."

As Holly led the way, Heather hoped they hadn't too far to go, as it was now raining and she couldn't see much shelter. A car went past with very bright lights, splashing them with water as it went. Holly led the family round a corner and called "Harvey! Harvey!"

At first there was no response. She called again. A nose appeared under a nearby gate.

"Harvey! Is that you? It's Holly. I have my family with me."

"Come in! Come in!" Harvey replied, inviting them in.

With effort, they all squeezed under the gate and followed Harvey. Once inside they found the tall wall completely sheltered them from the weather and a large garden bed with plenty of plants and shrubs to hide under.

They found some supper before snuggling down to sleep. Holly and Harvey sat and talked quietly for some time, catching up with each other since they had been in the vet's together. Holly told Harvey about the snow trip they had and how the visit of the Alpine Kiwis had brought such drastic change to their lives, and how her best friend, Keely was now gone.

"Will you go back to the lake with your family?" Harvey asked.

"I will see how I like it here first." Holly replied with a smile. "Have you seen Charlie at all since we were at the vet's?" she asked.

"Yes, he is back in his yard. I will show you where he is tomorrow." Harvey promised. "We will also visit some friends of mine at the horse racing track." When Holly asked if horses were there, Harvey's response was "No. They usually race when the weather is warmer."

"We have much to do tomorrow. We should get some rest." Harvey suggested with a smile, and together they settled to sleep.

When Heather, Henry and Harry woke, Holly and Harvey were still sleeping.

"They were talking for a long time." Harry told them.

"Was it about anything interesting?" Henry wanted to know.

"We will meet some friends of Harvey's at the horse racing track and see Charlie the Cockatoo, who Holly met at the vet's."

When Holly and Harvey finally woke, Henry Heather and Harry were exploring the garden and making friends. Heather had introduced herself to Bergenia Blackbird, and they were searching for food together. Henry startled Candy the household cat, who had been stalking Bergenia, by talking to him. The Hedgehogs usually curled up in a ball when he came near. They had a long talk about all the animals in the neighbourhood and how he got on with them.

Candy hadn't heard of a school for animals and liked the idea of a school where all the animals could meet and learn to get on with each other. Candy also said he would promise to stop chasing birds if other dogs and cats could be taught to stop chasing him.

Harry was talking to the neighbour's dog, Trixie the Terrier, through a small hole in the fence. Trixie was bored. Her owners were out, so she was glad to have someone to talk to. She was also intrigued a Hedgehog was talking to her. None of the others she met in the garden would.

When Harvey woke, he could hardly believe his eyes. Here was Henry talking to the cat, Heather was making friends with a blackbird, and Harry was talking to the neighbour's dog!

"This is how our community lives at home." Holly commented with a smile in response to Harvey's look of amazement. "It is normal to make friends with other animals."

Heather, Henry and Harry said goodbye to their new friends, promising to see them later, as Harvey took them up the street. Harvey led the family up a steep hill and then took them along a narrow track running behind backyards. Suddenly Holly stopped. There was Charlie, and he was calling out very loudly!

"There's Charlie!"

"Would you like to go and see him?" Harvey asked.

"Can we?" Holly looked doubtfully at the steep bank of long grass from the track to the yard.

"Just curl up in a ball and roll down after me." Harvey instructed her, before rolling down the bank. "Come on!" he called when he reached the bottom.

Holly's head was spinning when she reached him, but it was fun. Holly picked herself up and went over to Charlie's cage.

"Hello Charlie! How are you?" Holly asked.

Charlie stopped calling out and climbed down to the floor to talk to her.

"This is a lovely surprise. How long are you staying?" Charlie asked.

"I'm hoping to live here, so I will be able to visit you often." Holly replied. She introduced Harvey to Charlie before telling Charlie her news.

"Do come back soon!" Charlie pleaded. "I get lonely in this cage."

"We will be back, and we will get our friends to visit too." Harvey promised before they climbed back up the steep bank.

Meanwhile, Charlie's owner, Isabelle, was wondering why Charlie had suddenly stopped calling out. She had been at her wit's end. Ever since Charlie had returned from the vet's he had been restless and called out frequently. The neighbours were starting to complain about the noise he was making.

Isabelle went to the window and was astonished at what she saw. Charlie was down on the floor of his cage, and he seemed to be talking to two hedgehogs outside the cage. Isabelle watched as Charlie and the Hedgehogs talked to each other and noticed how frantic he became when they turned and walked into the long grass at the back of the garden. It then dawned on Isabelle; *Charlie was lonely!* She would have to get a mate for him. She went to find the number of the pet shop.

While they were waiting, Henry, Heather and Harry foraged in the long grass by the track and found some large snails to feast on. They had a nice feed ready for Holly and Harvey when they returned.

"I must say, you have plenty of food here." Henry was impressed.

"I was going to take you to a vegetable garden for a feed before visiting my friends at the track." Harvey told them. "We can go straight there instead."

"But we must take something!" Heather exclaimed. "Do you have any flax here?"

163

"What is flax?" Harvey asked with puzzlement.

It's a plant with long strong leaves and has long spikes of red Flowers." Holly informed him.

"I think there is one in the next street." Harvey said, leading the way. When they found the flax, Heather and Holly chewed at the base of a leaf untill it separated from the plant and stripped it into pieces, making it into a basket.

"Where's the vegetable garden, Harvey?" Heather asked a smile, seeing his amazed look at the basket.

"There are vegetable gardens all along here. We will go into this one because there aren't any dogs here." Harvey told her as he led the way into the garden.

The family took no time in filing up the basket with a load of goodies. It was so heavy Harry and Holly had to help her carry it.

Walking the streets, Holly saw some red roses with beautiful perfume.

"What are they?" Holly asked Harvey.

"I don't know." Harvey confessed.

I will have to look at a flower book." Holly resolved.

Harry saw a Tui in a Kowhai Tree and said "Hello." Toby Tui came down to a low branch to see who was talking to him.

"Hello, I'm Harry. Do you live here?" Harry asked.

"Yes, this is my home." Toby told him. "Where are you from?"

"We are visiting from Lake Kaniere. Our friends Tania and Terry Tui live there."

"Where is the lake?" Toby asked

"Can you see that mountain?" Harry asked as he pointed to Mount Graham. The lake is on the other side of it."

"I will go and visit them." Toby told him. "We don't have many Tuis here now that cats and other birds live here."

At the horse racing track, a row of fir trees stood. Bright red toadstools sprouted at their feet. Harvey led the way into the yard to a long wooden stable with many doors in a row. The viewers' stand towered in front of them.

Harvey squeezed open a door into a large room. The floor was covered with straw. When Heather saw the straw, she smiled at Henry.

"What does this remind you of?" she asked.

"The barn at Kaniere." Henry replied with a grin.

Inside the room Hector and Heidi Hedgehog and their children, Huey and Helena were waiting. As Heather brought in the basket, they gathered around it.

"Hello Harvey. What is the special occasion?" Hector asked, as the family tucked into the food that Heather had brought them.

"I've brought Holly and her family, Henry, Heather and Harry. They are visiting from Lake Kaniere."

Hector looked at Henry with a puzzled look on his face because he knew Hedgehogs didn't normally live at the lake.

"Have you always lived at the lake?" Hector wanted to know.

"No, Henry replied with a smile. "Heather and I moved to Kaniere when we were young."

"Are you Hori and Herby's children who went missing?"

"Yes, Hori and herby are our parents." Heather confirmed with a smile. "We didn't mean to leave. That was an accident!"

"What was the accident Mum? You didn't tell us about this!" Harry was astonished.

"Well, your father and I were neighbours, and one day he took me to the hay barn to see some newborn mice. There was a boat parked near the haystack that day, and after we saw the mice, we climbed on the boat for a look.

The next thing we knew, a car backed into the shed and we felt the boat moving. When we stopped, we were out at the lake. Mr Thomas, the boat owner, found us and put us in the vegetable garden at his bach.

While we were there, Primula Pigeon found us. When we told her that we were far from home and needed shelter, she showed us the Totara tree and introduced us to all the other families, who helped us to feel at home there."

"You don't want to go back to Kaniere?" Hector asked.

Heather thought for a moment.

"It would be nice to visit, but our home is at the lake now."

Heather noticed Helena was asking Harry lots of questions about his life at the lake.

"Are you saying that there aren't any other Hedgehogs at the lake?" Helena asked Harry. "Aren't you lonely?"

"Up to now, I haven't been." Harry beamed. "Among my best friends are a Kiwi, a Possum, a Duck, a Pukeko, a Stoat, and a Tui." To Huey and Helena's look of disbelief he added, "We go to school together and have had a wonderful time as we grew up together." Harry then spent some time telling them about the school and some of the adventures he had been on with his friends.

Hector noticed Helena's attention to Harry with concern. He had wanted her to mate with a male in Hokitika, whose family he wanted to be allied with. Up to now, she had shown no interest in the male for a mate.

All too soon, it was time to leave, and they promised to visit again soon.

Harvey led the family through the darkened streets till they came to a high cliff covered with bush. The sea could be heard as it tossed the forest timber, brought down by the flooded river, back onto the beach as driftwood.

Sneaking behind the bushes, he led them up a path, and there in front of them on the cliff was a colony of Glow Worms! Holly was delighted. She hadn't expected to see Glow Worms near the town. As dawn broke, they all settled down below the Glow Worms for a well-earned sleep.

Very early, while Henry, Heather and Harry were still sleeping, Harvey took Holly for a walk to a narrow steep road that led up the cliff. On both sides of the road lay a large border of blue Hydrangeas. Holly was so happy Harvey had brought her here. These were the flowers she had seen at Kokatahi.

At the top of the cliff was a big open area where Westland Hospital once stood. Here they could see the sea. Holly was amazed at how much bigger it was than the lake.

"Will you be my mate?" Harvey asked her.

"I would love to be." Holly replied, beginning a lifetime of happiness together.

CHAPTER FOURTEEN

THE RESCUE

Heather woke up in the evening light. Henry and Harry were still asleep, but Harvey and Holly were missing. *Where could they be?* She wondered. Hearing cars passing close by, she began to panic. *Have they been run over?* Then she saw them coming up the path. The happy look on their faces told Heather what she had suspected; Harvey and Holly were becoming a couple.

"Hello, I wondered where you were." Heather told them.

We went up on top of the cliff to see the sea, Mum. You should see how big it is!" Holly exclaimed.

At this Henry and Harry woke up.

"What's going on?" Harry yawned.

"We have some news for you," Harvey said with a smile. "Holly has agreed to be my mate."

"Congratulations! We hope you will be happy." Heather gave Holly a big hug.

"Welcome to the family." Henry smiled at Harvey.

"You have beaten me to it!" Harry said, grinning.

"You are interested in Helena?" Holly asked in amazement.

Harry nodded with a smile.

"You don't want to meet any other females?" Harvey asked him.

Harry shook his head. "I liked her as soon as I saw her."

"What if she is interested in someone else?" Harvey asked.

"Is she?" Harry was stricken with anxiety.

"No," Harvey smiled. "I was only joking. I will take you back to see her tomorrow. This evening though, I will take you to see the sea."

Harvey led Holly and her family out of the Glow Worm Dell to the road. All was quiet as they crossed the southern highway to the safety of bushes on the other side, and then made their way past a row of houses to the sand dunes at the beach.

"Oh, this is hard to walk through!" Holly exclaimed as her paws sunk into the soft sand.

Harry sniffed at the sea breeze blowing the salt laden air over the beach. "It smells different here than at the lake." Harry commented. Can you drink it or swim in it?" he asked, taking in the vast area of water before him.

"No, you can't drink the water," Harvey told him. "You can paddle on the edge if you are careful, but it is too dangerous for swimming."

On the beach in front of them, driftwood of all shapes and sizes were scattered all around. They found a large piece of driftwood for shelter, while they watched the sinking sun spread its golden glow across the horizon with its red and orange halo lighting the evening sky.

"Would you like a paddle?" Harvey asked, as the stars began to twinkle in the sky above them.

"I'll try anything once." Henry agreed with a grin.

Harvey took them down to the wet sand where the tide was coming in. "If we stand here," Harvey indicated a spot halfway to the water, "the water will come to us."

After a couple of waves, a larger one swept up the beach in a surge of white foam and swirled around their ankles.

"Oh, it's so cold!" Heather exclaimed, retreating to the dry sand.

Harvey, Henry, Harry and Holly paddled among the waves untill they too felt cold. Harvey then led them along the beach towards a bonfire some humans had lit. The humans had now gone; the hedgehogs happy to warm themselves near the remaining red embers of the fire.

"It's a pity we can't have one of these to sleep by." Harry sighed.

"Harvey sniffed the air. Although the stars were out, he sensed that rain would be here by the morning.

"We need to move on," Harvey told Holly. "I have a big garden to show you."

As the family walked through the streets, they passed neat wooden house, some of them with lights on outside their front porches. Beyond a large white church with a tall tower, they came to a large open space known to humans as Cass Square. On the outer edge were several large gardens, with shrubs and trees of all sizes for the family to explore.

In a garden, Heather met Millie, a field mouse, whose nest was under a large dense shrub.

She was getting some rest from her little ones, who had tired themselves out from exploring the garden.

"This is a large place you live in." Heather commented to Millie as she looked at the large running track surrounding the playing fields within it. "Do humans disturb you here?"

"We are lucky here. When humans run on the track or play with a ball on the field, they don't disturb us. Have you met Helga her family yet?"

"No," Heather replied. "This is our first visit here. Is Helga a mouse?"

"Helga is a Hedgehog like you. You should find her over in the next garden."

After saying farewell to Millie, Heather and Holly led Henry, Harry and Harvey over to the next garden, where they heard a rustle in the bushes.

"Is that Helga?" Heather called. "I'm Heather, and this is my family. Millie told me you may be here."

At that a large female Hedgehog with three young ones emerged from the bushes. "Hello Heather. Do come in. I'm just feeding my children. I won't be long."

"We will help you." Heather insisted. Holly and Harvey helped Hannah. Henry and Harry assisted Hayley while Helga and Heather took Harriet to search for food. Soon everyone returned with something delicious for a feast. They were sitting down to enjoy their meal when Helga's mate, Hayden came with three of his friends and their families to join in the party.

Some hours later, Harvey and the family were able to retreat and make their way to his garden, but only after promising to return for another visit.

By the time they returned to Harvey's garden, the stars were replaced by dark threatening clouds sweeping across the sky. As the first raindrops began to fall, the gate rattled and the wind battered the wall. Inside the family snuggled down to sleep, knowing they were protected from the storm.

It was raining steadily when Harry woke. Looking around, he could see that Henry, Heather, Holly and Harvey were still sleeping. He wanted to see Helena again, but knew he would have to wait for the family to come too.

Harry went over to the fence to see if Trixie was there, but Trixie was inside with her owners. With a sigh, he turned to wait for the others, but was surprised to find they were now waiting for him.

"We know you want to see Helena again." Harvey told Harry. "Is it alright for us to call in and see Charlie on the way?"

Harry nodded with a grin. Harvey had to keep Holly happy too.

When they saw Charlie's cage, they received a surprise. Not only was Charlie quiet, but he had a new companion.

"Hello Charlie!" Holly called when they reached his cage. "Who is your new mate?"

"Hello Holly. This is Crocus." Charlie introduced her with pride. "My owner brought her to me yesterday."

"I hope you are happy now." Holly told him.

"We are happy!" Crocus answered for him. Charlie could only grin.

After saying their goodbyes, the family made their way to the horse racing track. When they reached the stable, only Heidi was there. She seemed uncomfortable when she saw Harvey had brought the family to see her.

"Hello Heidi." Harvey greeted her. "Have the family left you on your own?"

"Hello Harvey." Heidi replied sadly. "Hector and Huey have escorted Helena over to Hugo."

"Has she agreed to be his mate?" Harvey asked, trying to hide his shock.

"No she hasn't!" Heidi couldn't hide her unhappiness.

"They can't force her to be with him!" Harry couldn't hold back his words.

"They will try." Heidi's reply was bleak.

Harry's mind was in turmoil. If he went after them he would be outnumbered. Besides, he had only met Helena once. There was no guarantee she would agree to be his mate after only one meeting. He realised there was nothing he could do but wait and hope. With an effort, Harry managed a smile.

"I came here today to see Helena with the hope of being accepted as her mate. However, as her father has a different plan for her, I can only wish for her happiness."

Heidi nodded, unable to speak. Heather gave her a hug before escorting the family outside. She turned to Harry.

"There is nothing we can do."

"I know, Mum. We can only wait."

Harry was now troubled by the feeling that Helena was in danger.

"Where is the river?" her asked Harvey. "We haven't seen that yet."

Down by the riverbank, Harvey and Harry found themselves some distance in front of Henry Heather and Holly, as they lingered over plants they had not seen at home. They were at the old customs house and looking at the rock wall that protected the riverbank when Harry spotted them. Helena was trying to run across the rocks, with Hector Huey and Hugo chasing her!

"There they are!" Harry whispered to Harvey. "We have to help her!"

Harry ran along the path as fast as he could, with Harvey running after him. Drawing close to them, Harry called to her.

"Helena! Helena! Come over here!"

Helena began to make her way over to the path but was barred by Hugo. Harry climbed on the rocks to reach her, but was barred by Hector and Huey.

"You are wasting your time." Hector said grimly. "Helena is now Hugo's mate."

"If she has accepted him, why is she running away?"

"Helena will do as she is told!" Hector growled. Harry ignored him.

"Helena, do you accept Hugo?" Harry asked.

"No I don't! She cried.

At this Hugo became angry. "If I can't have you, no-one will!" He pushed her towards the water.

"Harry, help me!" Helena screamed.

Harry scrambled to the edge. "I'm coming!" he called.

As Helena began to fall into the water, Harry jumped in too. When he came to the surface, Helena was struggling. She didn't know what to do and was gasping as she bobbed up and down in the water. Harry treaded water as Helena was swept towards him.

"I'm here!" he called, seeing panic in her eyes. "Hang on to my back." Harry ordered her as she reached him.

Taking her weight, Harry slowly swam across the current towards the bank as they were swept downstream. Harry hoped he would find a beach before they reached the bar, where the river met the sea.

After watching Helena and Harry drop into the water, Hugo, Hector and Huey climbed off the rocks. As they passed Harvey, Hector gave him a little shove.

"You can tell Henry and Heather they are too late."

Hector Huey and Hugo then disappeared into the laneways leading to the town. Harvey turned around to see Henry, Heather and Holly approach.

"I'm sorry," Harvey said with tears in his eyes. "It's too late!"

"What do you mean?"

"I saw Hugo push Helena into the water and Harry jumped in with her!"

"Did he hit his head or get injured?" Heather asked.

"I couldn't see from the path, but Hector said it was too late!"

"Harvey, Harry can swim!"

Harvey's eyes widened with amazement as Heather's words. They all rushed over to the edge of the rock wall. Looking down into the water below them, nothing could be seen.

"There they are!" Henry yelled, pointing towards the mouth of the river. Two little heads were seen heading towards the beach.

Harry was exhausted. He had swum harder than he had ever done at the lake. He had to fight the river current all the way as it tried to force them out into the middle of the river and into the sea. They were nearly at the beach when Harry felt he could go no further.

"I'm sorry, Helena. I can't go any further."

"Put your feet down! I think we are there." she said with a smile.

Harry allowed his feet to sink. Relief filled his body as his feet touched the sand. Carefully Helena moved from his back to his side to cuddle him. She saw Harry's family and Harvey crossing the beach towards them.

"We are safe now."

After Harry and Helena had been helped onto the beach, they sat down to recover.

"Harry, there is something I need to tell you." Helena said. A look of pain came over her face.

"You may be having Hugo's children?" he asked. Helena nodded.

"If you do, I will bring them up as my own. We will give them a lifetime of love and care they would never have known with Hugo."

"You don't want any of your own?" Helena asked.

"Of course I do." Harry replied with a twinkle in his eye. "We will have them only when you are ready. We have the rest of our lives to think about it." He gave her a hug.

Helena smiled her gratitude as she snuggled into him, but found she couldn't stop shivering. Harry looked at her with concern, realising she was going into shock.

"We need to get some shelter." Harry looked at Harvey. "Where can we go that is safe?"

"There is another big garden on the way to Charlie's. We will try there."

Past Cass Square they went. In the distance Harry could see some tall gum trees in a section of thick bush.

"Is that the garden?" Harry asked. Harvey nodded.

After squeezing under the wire fence surrounding the property, Harvey led them through thick bushes to a tree which towered over all the other trees.

It took some time to calm Helena, who was reacting to the horror of her father forcing her to mate with Hugo and then trying to drown her! She was also mourning the fact that she didn't expect to see her mother again.

"We know it is a terrible thing that has happened to you," Henry said gently, as Harry cuddled her. "But they didn't succeed and you are now safe with us. You are part of our family now."

As Harry and Helena and Henry and Heather found a comfortable spot to sleep, Holly sent Harvey off to see Helga. When he returned some hours later, he gave her a nod and a grin before they too settled for a rest.

The late afternoon sun sent shafts of light among the trees as Harry pulled aside the long strip of bark from the gum tree and looked around. Next to him Helena was still sleeping. Harry heard the flutter of wings and looked up. It was a pigeon. He looked at her in amazement. "Is that you, Primrose?" Harry called.

"Yes," she called. "How is your holiday? I've come to see when you will be ready to go home."

By now Heather and Henry had emerged to join him. "Can you get Delphinia and Dianella to take us to Kaniere?" Henry asked. "We want to see our family on the way home. Also Harry and Holly have partners to bring with them."

With a smile of delight, Primrose sped from the tree towards the lake, eager to share her news of the new members of the Hedgehog family.

Under the cover of darkness, the family quietly made their way to the spot where Delphinia had left them. Helena could hardly believe her eyes when she saw Helga and her mother Heidi waiting for them.

"Mum!" she cried as she rushed into Heidi's arms.

When the sound of hooves announced the arrival of Delphinia and Dianella, Heidi gave her a final hug. "Have a good life, my love."

Happy she now knew her daughter was safe, Heidi slipped away to Helga, who had been keeping watch in case Hector had tried to follow them. Heidi was going to miss Helena terribly, but she would now have the comfort of helping Helga bring up her three girls.

CHAPTER FIFTEEN

FLIGHT TO OKARITO

As Denny Deer crossed the farmland at Kokatahi, Keona was still struggling with the shock that her mate was gone, and she could not yet think of her life without him. She was glad that riding on the Deer's back gave her an excuse to cuddle her children. Looking backwards, she could see Donny Deer, who was carrying Kaori and Kalasia, was close behind, with the Stoats and Weasels on Dusty. The Hedgehogs were following behind them in the distance on Delphinia.

When they came to the river to cross to Woodstock on the south side, the river was swollen from a flood and too dangerous to swim across.

"We can't cross here," Denny advised them. "We will have to risk the bridge."

Denny Donny and Dusty then turned to follow the river to Kaniere. Swiftly they crossed the bridge. Bats chasing insects in the street lights were the only witnesses to their flight before they blended into the woodland at Woodstock.

The Kiwis then said their final goodbyes to the Stoats and Weasels, who left them to travel down Arthur's Town to Mahinapua.

"Don't fall down any mine shafts." Denny warned Dusty.

"Watch Elton doesn't nip your toes!" Kupe warned the Stoats and Weasels.

The Kiwis then travelled the bush trails at Woodstock to reach the lightning track, a steep but short path up the hillside to Rimu. At the top they stopped briefly to look at the lights of Woodstock twinkling up at them from below. Mount Graham rose beyond the velvety darkness of the countryside in front of them. A gust of wind and some drops of rain came as a reminder that it was time to move on.

As the deer made their way through the forest east of Lake Mahinapua, Denny saw a hunter crouching and pointing a gun at him! Denny sprang to shelter behind a tree. The whistle of the bullet as it flew past his ear followed by the bang of the gunfire echoing through the forest, sent the deer fleeing for safety and the Kiwis hanging on grimly for their lives.

On Denny and Donny raced through the forest. They didn't pause untill they reached the Ross Road. When they reached the outskirts of Ross, a goldmining town nestled by bush-clad hills, the deer negotiated the bush near the settlement very carefully, alert now for any unexpected encounters. Thankfully, none came.

Through the wet and windy night they pressed on; untill daybreak, when they reached the dense forest at Lake Ianthe. Here the rain and wind gave way to a grey mist that descended to surround the lake and forest. The Kiwis huddled together in the burrow Kupe and Kaori had made for them.

Kupe woke to the sound of raindrops on the ferns surrounding the burrow. He noticed how closely Keely and Kalasia were curled up to Keona. Suddenly he had a vision of Keona, Keely and Kalasia looking after a newborn Kiwi and knew he now had another sister to protect.

Quietly Kupe slipped out of the burrow and began feeding. He was soon joined by Kaori, who was feeling anxious. He knew they had made good progress on their journey, but was worried that Kanai, Kekoa and Kekapa would find a way to follow and find them.

At the Styx River, Kanai Kekoa and Kekapa were silently feeding in the shelter of the forest near the river when Kekoa spotted two deer grazing nearby. He went over to talk to them.

"What are you doing?" Kanai asked, seeing Kekoa move towards the deer.

"If we are to catch up with them," Kekoa answered, "We need a ride."

Dusty and Dianthia Deer were quietly feeding when they saw a Kiwi was coming. It was one of the Arthur's Pass Kiwis.

"Hello, I'm Kekoa. Can you give us a ride?" he asked as Kanai and Kekapa joined him.

"Where do you want to go?" Dusty asked.

"We have to find Kupe to give him a message. Can you take us to him?"

Dusty knew that Denny and Donny had taken Kupe's family south and was sorry he couldn't go too. This was his chance to join them.

"Yes, I will take you." Dusty agreed. He turned to Dianthia. "Can you pick up the Stoats and Weasels from Mahinapua for me?" She nodded. He then knelt down so the Kiwis could mount. Kanai climbed on first with Kekoa and Kekapa behind him. Crossing the Styx River and keeping to the forest east of Kowhitirangi, Dusty started to make his way south.

When Keona Keely and Kalasia emerged from the burrow, the rain had cleared. The rising moon was creating a silver path across the lake.

"What a pity we can't walk on it." Keona mused on seeing the moon's pathway.

Kedar the Rowi Kiwi was fossicking for food at the water's edge of Okarito Lagoon, when he was startled by the noise of some large animals moving through the forest. He quickly hid behind a bush and was astonished to see two deer emerge from the trees, then knelt down and allowed five grey Kiwis to climb down from their backs. One of the Kiwis spoke quietly to the deer before they rose and disappeared back into the forest. Kedar decided it was time to see what they were up to on his territory.

"Who are you and why are you here?" Kedar called.

"I am Kupe, leader of the Kiwi Kingdom at Kaniere, and this is my family. We come in peace. We are here to find an old friend."

Kedar came out from behind the bush. It was the Kaniere Kiwis turn to be surprised. In front of them stood a Kiwi, but it had long brown feathers. Kupe recognised it from books in the school library. It was a Southern Brown Kiwi, a different species.

"Hello, I'm Kedar. Welcome to Okarito. We have some Kiwis like you not far from here. I think you may find your friend there."

"Thank you," Kupe answered him. "Can you tell us where to find them?"

"They are inland from here. I can take you to them, though it may take some time." Kedar offered.

"Would it help if the Deer take us?" Kupe offered.

Kedar looked doubtful, as he had never been on a Deer before, but he was persuaded to ride with Kupe. Before he left, Kedar found his mate Kerry, to tell her where he was going.

"Don't be gone too long." She warned him. "We will have some little ones to care for soon."

"When can we expect them? "Kedar asked her.

"They will be here when the next moon comes."

Kerry wasn't the only Kiwi to watch Kedar and the Kiwis leave. Kalan Kiwi had seen the Kiwis cross the river on the deer and had followed them, curious to see why they were here. When he heard that Kupe was from the Kiwi Kingdom, his ears pricked up. He had relatives from further south whose ancestors had been part of the Kingdom. As Kupe and Kedar headed inland, Kalan decided it was time to pay his relatives a visit.

Kedar soon began to enjoy the view from the Deer's back. They were near the mountains when Kedar called a halt and asked them to dismount.

As Kedar led them through the forest, Kedar asked Kupe about the Kingdom at Kaniere.

The Kingdom we have at Kaniere was spread throughout Westland by the supporters of my great grandfather Keoni, who was the leader then.

Kedar stopped in his tracks and looked at Kupe with incredulous eyes.

"Are you here to bring the Kingdom back?"

"With my friends' help, I hope to." Kupe replied. "How do you know about the Kingdom?"

"We were part of the Kingdom too!" Kedar replied with pride. "The end of the Kingdom at Kaniere was a great loss to us all here."

"Would your Kiwis be part of this new Kingdom?" Kupe enquired.

"I know they would." Kedar replied with conviction. Kupe saw Kedar's gaze on his amulet.

"Do any of your Kiwis wear one of these amulets?" Kupe asked.

With a little smile, Kedar plucked at his breast feathers and brought out an amulet. It was tied with the same twine as Kupe and Kaori's amulets.

"There is a rhyme." Kaori intervened.

Kedar looked at Kaori and Kupe with a questioning look.

"Kaori is from Arthur's Pass in the mountains. His family is the owner of one of the amulets. He and his sister, Kalasia are supporting me on my quest to find the other amulet holders. Can you tell me what the rhyme is?" Kupe asked gently.

Kupe suddenly became aware they were being watched. Kedar whispered the familiar words in his ear. He too could feel they were being watched. Kupe turned to Kaori with a smile.

"Kedar has passed the test! He is a true supporter of Kiwi Kingdom." Kupe announced to them all.

"Where is Kaori's amulet?" Kedar wanted to know.

"His great grandfather was killed. The amulet was held by another family untill recently. Kaori's amulet is now stored safely in the book untill it is safe to return it to him.

Kupe saw Kedar's look of concern.

"I fear we are being followed by the Kiwis who took the amulet from his family and wish to destroy us and everything we stand for. I can only hope we are not bringing trouble to your community."

"We can look after ourselves," Kedar replied. "Can't we Keio?" he called to the bushes. At this, Kupe and his family were surrounded by a group of grey Kiwis.

"We can!" Keio replied. "How many of your enemies can we expect?"

"There are three of them." Kupe advised him. "They are Kanai, his son Kekoa and a friend of Kekoa's, Kekapa."

Kedar looked around the group of Grey Kiwis. Where is Keka?"

"He is visiting Katoa at the ice river. Why do you want him?" Keio asked.

"Kupe and Kaori are here to see him." Kedar replied. "I can take them to Keka, but it would be safer for Kupe's mother and their sisters to stay here.

Keio had already noticed the three females Kupe and Kaori had brought with them, in particular the larger female. He was struck by the stricken look on her face and wondered what had happened to cause such sorrow.

"If you females are willing to stay with us, we will keep them safe till you return." Keio promised.

Keona was feeling tired. They were far from home, facing an uncertain future, and now it seemed Kupe was to leave them. She looked at Keio and saw kindness and concern in eyes.

Keona looked at the two girls. "I think we will be safe here." They both nodded. Keona then turned to Keio. "We will be happy to stay, thank you."

"Kupe and Kaori, you must rest here before you go further." Keio insisted. "There is a storm coming. The ice river is a dangerous place to be near when storms come."

Kupe sent Denny and Donny off for some shelter, telling them to return when the weather had cleared.

Keona was surprised to find Keio's burrow similar to her own at Kaniere. *"I could feel at home her."* She thought with a little smile.

Keio saw Keona's smile as she looked around the burrow and was encouraged. He had been alone since his mate left him for another Kiwi, two winters ago. There were no children to ease his loneliness.

"Your mate couldn't make the trip with you?" Keio asked. He needed to know why she was on her own.

""No," Keona answered quietly. The pain had returned to her eyes. "We did try to persuade him to come, but he chose to stay. Now they have killed him."

"Are you sure?"

"Yes. One of the ducks in our community flew back there and was able to see everything that happened."

"I'm sorry," Keio offered his sympathy. "I know it is far too soon to think about, but you may be able to start a new life some day."

"I don't know." Keona's face was bleak. "I am expecting a chick. There aren't many males who will accept another male's child. Keely and Kalasia have offered to help me raise it."

Keio tried to stop himself from smiling. Here he had an available female, with a family for him as well!"

"I insist you all stay as long as you like, and I would like to help you with the little one when it comes." Keio offered.

"You don't have a mate either?" Keona asked. She sensed his happiness.

"No, she left me for another male two winters ago."

"Do they have children?"

"No, they don't."

In the forest Denny and Donny were resting quietly. The wind could be heard whistling in the trees above them. Suddenly, they heard the footsteps of another deer coming their way.

Denny and Donny hid behind a large tree in case it was a local Deer coming to defend its territory. To their amazement, they saw it was Dusty and he had three Kiwis on his back!

"Dusty! What are you doing here?" Denny called.

Dusty slowed and turned around as he heard his brother's call.

Kanai could hardly believe his luck. If these Deer had brought Kupe and his family here, they couldn't be far away.

CHAPTER SIXTEEN

THE CHASE

Keely and Kalasia were the first to wake up. They slipped out of the burrow for a feed and to explore their new home. Keio woke as they were leaving and smiled. He decided to join them and show them the best feeding spots.

"This is just like home!" Keely exclaimed as they waded through a patch of ferns, tall pongees forming a green roof above them. Beyond the ferns, lay a large log covered in silvery fungus and green moss. With her bill, Keely tested the log for any insects that may be hiding. Kalasia decided to climb on the log to see what lay on the other side.

Kalasia's scream pierced the night air. Instinctively Keely crouched down as she saw Kalasia turn to jump off and run for the burrow. To Keely's horror, she saw Kekapa in hot pursuit! Keely looked around for somewhere to hide. As she moved away from the log, she felt a claw in her neck.

"It's time you joined your father!" At Kekoa's words, anger rose inside her. With a ferocity she didn't know she possessed; Keely turned on him.

Kalasia's scream woke everyone in the burrow. Searching the burrow, they found Keely Kalasia and Keio were missing. They were about to go out to investigate when Kalasia came rushing in, distraught and shaking.

"They are here!" she cried in anguish.

"Where is Keely?" Kupe asked urgently.

"She is by the big log." Kalasia replied, as Keona came to comfort her.

Kupe Kaori and Kedar charged out of the burrow to find Keio and his neighbours, who had come running at Kalasia's scream, had surrounded Kekapa and were pushing him into the forest. Kupe looked beyond them and saw movement by the big log. They raced down to the log and were stunned to find Keely leaning over the limp body of Kekoa.

"Keely! Are you alright?" Kupe called.

Keely looked at them with a blank look on her face that Kaori recognised as shock. She looked back a Kekoa again, and her expression crumbled.

"I tried to hide when Kalasia was being chased, then I felt a claw in my neck." Kupe could see a little trickle of blood running from Keely's neck. "He told me it was time I joined Dad. I don't know what came over me!" Keely wailed, beginning to cry.

Kaori rushed forward to comfort her. "It's alright now, Keely. He can't hurt you anymore."

Kupe scanned the surrounding bush and listened for any sign of Kanai, but there was none, before they carefully withdrew to the burrow.

In the forest, Kanai had woken to find both Kekoa and Kekapa were missing. Denny Donny and Dusty were grazing nearby. He was annoyed at their disappearance because he had told them both to stay close by, so they wouldn't be detected.

Then Kanai heard Kalasia's scream.

Kanai waited in vain for Kekoa and Kekapa to return. When he spotted a shadow watching him from behind a tree, Kanai realised that both Kekoa and Kekapa had been caught and now he was a target.

Kanai called to Dusty. "It is time to move on."

"You aren't waiting for the other two?" Dusty asked.

"No, I don't have time." Kanai advised him. "I will return for them on my way back.

As Kanai began his journey, Denny and Donny went to see if Kupe and Kaori were ready to leave as well.

Kedar quickly returned to the burrow to tell Kupe that Kanai was heading south to a Deer he called Dusty and that Dusty had been grazing with Donny and Denny.

Kupe frowned. "We have a few questions we need to ask Denny and Donny when they come."

"At least there is only one of them we need to worry about now." Kedar commented. Kupe nodded his agreement.

Kupe suddenly had a vision of Kanai chasing him on the ice. "Have any of you been on a glacier?" Kupe asked.

"What is a glacier?" Kedar asked.

"It is an ice river." Kupe explained.

They shook their heads. Kedar thought for a moment. "Katoa at the glacier might have."

"I need to see Katoa as well as Keka when we get there." Kupe told him.

Kupe Kaori and Kedar said goodbye to Keona and the girls. "Take care," Keona told Kupe. "We don't want to lose you as well."

Outside, Kupe could see Denny and Donny walking in the forest. "Denny! Kupe called, "We are here!"

"Are you ready to go?" Denny asked.

"Yes, Kupe replied, "but there are a few things we need to ask you about. Denny, did either of you know Dusty was bringing Kanai down to us?"

"No," Denny replied. "It was a complete surprise to us when they went past us in the forest. Did you get the message?"

"What message?"

Denny looked troubled. "When Dusty came back from taking the Stoats and Weasels to Lake Mahinapua, he was approached by Kekoa to take him, Kanai and Kekapa to you, as they had a message for you."

Kupe sighed. "Dusty has been deceived." Kupe told them. "Their aim was to come here and kill us all!"

Denny and Donny now looked distressed.

"Kekoa and Kekapa are no longer a danger, but Kanai has gone ahead, we think to lie in wait for us. We will have to be careful."

Denny agreed.

Kupe mounted Denny while Kaori and Kedar rode Donny. Steadily they made their way through the forest towards the glacier.

"It's been snowing." Kedar commented.

"How do you know?" Kaori asked. Having lived in the Alps, he also knew the signs.

"Can't you feel that extra chill in the air and the low cloud?" Kedar asked. Kaori nodded with a smile.

"I'm worried about Kupe. He hasn't much knowledge or experience with Alpine weather."

"Yes, Kedar agreed. "He's going to need all his intuition to keep alive up there."

When they came to the Waiho River, Kupe stopped. "Does Katoa live on this side or south of the glacier?" Kupe asked Kedar.

"We head upstream now." Kedar replied, taking the lead. They were starting to climb when they saw Dusty coming down. He was alone.

"Dusty," Denny called quietly when he came nearer.

"Where's Kanai?" Kupe asked.

"There is deep snow up ahead." Dusty told them. "Kanai tried to make me go through it, but I refused." Kupe nodded.

"It's time we walked as well." Kupe decided. "Go home and rest now." He told the Deer. "Return to Okarito in three months when the new moon appears."

Onwards the Kiwis climbed, Kedar leading the way. In the alpine forest, the trees and bushes hugged the rocky slopes. Ahead of them a thick mist was descending.

"Shouldn't we have a rope?" Kupe asked Kedar?"

"What do we need a rope for?" Kedar was puzzled.

"In case we get separated in that mist." Kupe explained.

"It's not a bad idea." Kaori agreed, remembering how grateful he felt when the lake children produced ropes to lead everyone to safety, when the mist caught them in the snow.

"There's some tussock over there." Kupe pointed to the clumps growing next to the mountain stream.

"What will we cut it with?" Kedar asked doubtfully.

"We will cut it with one of these." Kupe held up a sharp rock with his claw.

Kedar and Kaori watched with amazement as Kupe pulled over a blade of the tussock and rubbed the rock against it. When Kupe held up the cut tussock, they also looked for rocks to use. By the time the rope was ready, a swirling white curtain of mist and snowflakes had surrounded them.

The trickling stream meandering down the mountainside was the only sound in a now silent world. Carefully, the followed the stream uphill, their feet crunching in the snow, sometimes slipping and sliding on icy rocks, untill Kedar showed them how to keep a grip by digging their claws into the ice.

When they came to a towering rock wall, Kedar led them around it to another steeper slope. As they started to climb, Kupe thought he heard footsteps behind him. He stopped and tugged on the rope.

"I think I heard something." Kupe whispered.

They stopped and listened, but heard nothing. Onward and upward they climbed.

After hearing more footsteps, Kupe became convinced Kanai was following them. He had to find a way to lure him away from the others.

They came to a lonely windswept tree, where Kedar dug in the snow, till he revealed a tussock. Pulling it aside, there was an entrance to a burrow.

Kedar and Kaori disappeared inside. Kupe threw his rope inside before quickly covering the tussock with snow again.

"Is it the wrong one?" Kupe called out loudly before moving on up the slope. When Kupe heard the footsteps pause at the tree, he stomped his feet loudly and pretended to grumble.

"You didn't tell us it was this steep!"

As Kupe made his way upward, he smiled to himself. His trick had worked. The footsteps were following him. Kupe knew from the maps the glacier was somewhere to his right, and he headed in that direction.

In the burrow, Katoa, his mate Kalauni and Keka were sheltering from the snowstorm, when they heard someone scratching at the snow outside, then in burst Kedar and another male Kiwi.

"Hello Kedar. What brings you here?" Katoa asked.

"I've brought Kaori from Arthur's Pass and Kupe from Kaniere to see you."

Kaori looked behind him to find Kupe was not there. "Where is Kupe?" Kaori said in panic.

They heard the snow being replaced and Kupe say loudly, "Is it the wrong one?" Kupe's footsteps then faded away into the distance.

Katoa and Keka looked at Kedar and Kaori's troubled faces, when Kedar whispered, "That was Kupe, Keoni's great grandson!" As Keka's eyes widened, "He is trying to protect us!"

"Who is he protecting you from?" Katoa asked.

Before Kedar could reply, more footsteps approached the burrow. Kedar and Kaori positioned themselves to attack whoever came in.

The footsteps paused then also faded away.

"You know what Kupe's done," Kaori asked Kedar, "don't you?" Kaori looked at Kedar's puzzled face. "He is luring Kanai to the ice river!

Katoa looked alarmed. "They both will probably die there, or if Kupe survives, we will have to help him to get off the ice again."

Katoa looked at the rope. What is that you have brought with you?"

"It is a rope we made from tussock when the mist came down," Kaori told him. "We used it to stay together in the mist and snow."

Katoa tested the rope's strength. "We will need it out on the ice."

He then began to prepare for their journey to the ice river.

CHAPTER SEVENTEEN

THE GLACIER

When Kupe came over the ridge, he saw the mist lifting, and there in front of him lay the dazzling white and blue ice river. The roughness of the ice and the depth of the crevasses made him shiver.

Hearing footsteps approaching, Kupe quickly raced down the slope to the glacier, not stopping to look around untill he reached the ice. He looked up the slope to see Kanai coming after him.

Carefully, Kupe stepped on the ice. It was very cold and very slippery. Remembering to dig his claws in, Kupe made his way into the glacier, quickly losing sight of Kanai in the steep terrain.

As Kupe climbed further into the glacier, he faced a difficult decision. In front of him lay two different paths. The more secure one led into the centre of the glacier where there were many crevasses and no easy way out.

The other path led to safety, but a flimsy ice bridge over a large deep crevasse lay in his path. Kupe wasn't sure the bridge would hold his weight. Kupe took a chance and headed for the ice bridge. He was half way across the bridge when Kupe felt movement behind him and knew Kanai was on the bridge too.

Quickly, Kupe crossed to the other side with the bridge shaking and the sound of ice cracking beneath them.

As Kupe reached up and anchored a claw in the bank, he felt Kanai's claw cling to his back claw.

With an enormous bang the bridge gave way, taking Kanai with it. Kupe could feel himself being pulled down. Desperately, he wriggled his foot to free himself from Kanai's grip.

Kupe felt pain, then realised he was free. With his remaining strength, Kupe pulled himself up onto the bank. He found a spot out of the wind and curled up in a ball.

Kupe was exhausted and in pain. His front claw was missing and his foot was bleeding. He pressed his foot against the ice to help stop the pain. He realised he needed he needed help, but no-one knew where he was. Kupe had never felt more alone or lonely, then he remembered Percy's words. *"We will always be your friends. You will only be alone or lonely if you choose to be."*

As Kupe drifted into unconsciousness; Percy's words gave him comfort.

Meantime, while Kupe lay on the ice, Percy was at the school. Suddenly, Percy felt afraid and knew his friend was in trouble. He went to find Danny, Pete and Sam.

"Kupe is badly hurt, and he needs our help."

Forming a circle and joining paws, they silently supported Kupe with their thoughts.

With a grass mat strapped to his back, Katoa led Keka, Kedar and Kaori out of the burrow. The snow had stopped and the mist was lifting.

In the tree next to the burrow was Kallen the Kea, who visited the tree regularly to eat the seeds when the tree finished flowering.

"Hello Kallen," Katoa called to him. "We have two Kiwis on the ice river. Can you find them for us?"

Kallen ran down the slope, his wings outstretched to catch the wind, and soared into the sky. Up and down the glacier Kallen flew, looking for movement. He found none. Then he spotted a grey ball curled up on the ice with a trail of blood leading to the crevasse. Kallen flew back to Katoa.

"I've found one of them, but he isn't moving and he is injured."

Katoa quickened his steps as he climbed the slope towards the glacier. If they didn't get Kupe off the ice quickly, it would be too late. As Katoa approached the glacier, Kallen flew down to stand guard over Kupe. A large brown Kite had also spotted Kupe and was circling overhead.

When Katoa and the Kiwis reached Kupe, he was still breathing but didn't respond when they spoke to him or shook him. They saw the injured claw, which had stopped bleeding. Carefully, they slid Kupe onto the mat.

Kaori saw the trail of blood over the ridge and decided to investigate. There before him lay a wide, deep and dark crevasse. At the bottom Kaori saw large chunks of broken ice. Kallen also looked at the crevasse.

"The other Kiwi is down there in the ice."

"Is he moving?" Kaori asked.

"No. His neck is broken. His spirit has left him."

Once off the ice, the Kiwis had difficulty pulling Kupe up the steep slope. Kaori saw a Tahr watching them.

"Maybe that Tahr can help us!"

Kedar Katoa and Keka watched in amazement as Kaori approached the Tahr.

"Hello," Kaori called to the Tahr. "I'm Kaori. Can you help us?"

"I'm Theo," The Tahr replied. "How can I help you?"

"My friend is badly injured. Can you help pull him up the slope and back to our burrow?" Kaori asked.

"Yes, I will help." Theo agreed. "Who is your friend?"

"He is Kupe of Kiwi Kingdom at Kaniere."

"I have heard of him from our cousins at Kaniere.

Theo gave a bark and his mate, Torena appeared.

"Kupe Kiwi is hurt. Help me get him back to their burrow."

Using the rope, Kupe's mat was made into a stretcher and carried between the Tahr. Gently and steadily they made their way up the slope. Katoa and Keka led the way, with Kedar and Kaori following. Kallen circled and kept watch overhead.

Back at the burrow, Kupe was still very cold and barely breathing. Kalauni wrapped Kupe in some sheep's wool rugs. When she saw Kupe's injured claw, she frowned.

"I need some herbs." She told Katoa and went outside to find the Tahr waiting to hear news of how Kupe was. "He is very ill. It is too soon to know if he will recover."

"Can we help?" Theo asked, seeing Kalauni making her way down the hill.

"I'm looking for some herbs for Kupe's wound." She told him.

"I will give you a ride." Theo offered, kneeling down beside her.

Kalauni climbed on and held on tight as Theo stood up. She was alarmed at first at being so high off the ground, but then she began to enjoy it. Kalauni showed Theo where the manuka bushes were, and in no time, they were back at the burrow with an armload of manuka leaves.

"Thank you, Theo." Kalauni said as she dismounted. "Please let me know if we can help you with anything."

Inside, Kalauni rubbed the manuka between two rocks untill it produced some oil. Carefully she dabbed the oil on Kupe's wound.

She noted that Kupe was warmer and his breathing was stronger. Kalauni went out to tell the Tahr.

"Kupe is looking better. If his wound heals, he should recover."

"Is he awake yet?"

"No. Not yet."

"I will come back tomorrow." Theo promised. The mist was reforming again.

"Take care." Kalauni called as the Tahr galloped back into the mountains.

In the burrow, Kaori and Kedar cuddled up to Kupe to help keep him warm because he had begun to shiver.

"It's alright Kupe. You are safe now." Kaori murmured to him.

Although he still shivered, Kupe seemed to be calm and settled to a deep sleep. While Kupe was sleeping, Kaori told his new friends of his life at Arthur's Pass, the meeting with the Kaniere Kiwis and all the events since.

Kupe stirred. He was in a dark place and it was warm, which was strange because he thought he was still on the ice river. Kupe breathed heavily as he remembered trying to escape from Kanai's grip and being pulled into the crevasse.

"Kupe, wake up! It's alright. You are safe now." Kaori reassured him.

Kupe opened his eyes. He was in a burrow, and Kaori and Kedar were bending over him.

"Yes Kupe. You are safe now." Kedar told him. He introduced Katoa, Kalauni and Keka.

"Thank you all for saving me. Where is Kanai?" Kupe asked.

"He is in the ice river. His neck was broken when he fell." Kaori reassured him.

Kupe took a deep breath and let it out with a sigh, as he realised he really was safe now. When Kalauni produced a basket of worms, he also realised he was starving!

"Thank you for looking after me." Kupe said, expressing his gratitude.

Kupe attempted to sit up, using his injured claw. He lifted it up to look at it. The injury was still raw. Strangely, it hurt as though the claw was still there; even though he could see the claw was missing. Kalauni noticed Kupe was looking at his injured claw.

"You will be staying untill it is healed." Kupe looked at Kalauni and Katoa in surprise. Her tone allowed for no argument.

Katoa looked at Kupe with a twinkle in his eye. "She has spoken. There will be no escape untill Kalauni is happy you are healed."

With a happy sigh, Kupe settled himself back into the wool rug. He decided not to argue, when they had made him so comfortable. During the night, they spent many hours discussing the Kingdom and how they could restore it among their communities.

"It won't be easy," Kupe warned them. "You will have to work hard to change attitudes of those who like their lives as they are. Making friends with all the different animals in the area where you live will be needed, as well as starting a school for everyone to attend, so they learn to get on with each other. If you need help to get your schools started, send someone to our school at Kaniere and Owen Owl and his helpers will help you."

When Theo returned the next day, it was snowing heavily, but Kupe insisted on making a brief appearance outside the door to show Theo that he truly was moving and on his feet.

"I want to thank you." Kupe thanked him. "You helped to save my life. I will be forever grateful to you. Go now and seek some shelter."

Theo happily scampered off to spread the news.

The following day Tommy Tahr came down from the mountain to the school where Percy Danny Pete and Sam had been keeping a vigil, till they received a sign that Kupe was better.

"I have some good news for you." Tommy told them. "One of my cousins, Theo who helped rescue Kupe, has come. Theo saw him yesterday. Kupe was well enough to come to the opening.

"Kupe has an injury?" Percy asked.

"Yes. He lost a claw. Kupe will be resting there untill he is healed."

"There were three Kiwis chasing him!" Percy was worried.

"Only one of them was at the ice river." Tommy told him. "Kupe is completely safe now. None of them can harm him anymore." Tommy added with a smile.

"This is wonderful news. We will have to celebrate! Thank you, Tommy. We can look forward to Kupe's return now."

Kane the Alpine Kiwi, who had been leading the community while Kupe was away, saw Tommy talking to Percy before leaving for the mountain.

"Are you leaving us Percy?" Kane asked.

"No." Percy replied. "Are Kanai's mate Kalama and his daughter Kalea still here?"

"They have gone north to visit family in Punakaiki. Why?" Kane asked.

"I've had word that Kanai Kekoa and Kekapa will not be returning." Seeing Kane's questioning look, Percy added, "They will not be able to hurt anyone ever again."

Kane gave a sigh of relief and then looked at Percy with concern. "What about Kupe?" Kane knew Kupe's friends had been keeping a vigil for him.

"Kupe has been injured, but he will return when he has recovered. We are planning a small celebration to celebrate the new beginning for the Kingdom. Will you join us?"

"Yes, we all will." Kane replied with a smile and rushed off into the forest to spread the good news.

CHAPTER EIGHTEEN

NEW LIFE AT OKARITO

Keona left the burrow for some fresh grass to make a nest. Keely and Kalasia were feeding nearby. Keona looked up into the night sky. The new moon was just visible as a bright yellow crescent, in the star-filled sky. A sense of urgency came over her, and she knew it was time to deliver Keanu's legacy. Scooping up some grass, Keona returned to the burrow.

At the lagoon, Kerry also looked at the new crescent and wondered where Kedar was. She also knew her time had come to deliver. With a sigh she also returned to her burrow.

Keely and Kalasia were about to follow Keona into the burrow when the sound of Tahr approaching stopped them. In the dim night light, Theo and Torena emerged from the forest with Kupe, Kaori, Keka and Kedar.

"Kupe, Kaori! You are back!" Keely cried.

Theo and Torena sat down to allow Kupe Kaori and Keka to dismount.

"I will see you again soon." Kedar called as the Tahr stood up. He waved goodbye before disappearing towards the lagoon.

In Keio's burrow there was much celebrating as everyone reunited. Keely struggled with her feelings. She had missed Kaori more than she had realised.

While Kupe and Kaori retold their adventures at the glacier, Keona slipped into her tunnel. This baby would wait no longer. Keely saw her mother leave and followed her. She found her mother crouched and straining to expel her egg.

"It's your time, isn't it Mum?" Keely asked.

Keona could only nod as she concentrated on bringing the new life into the world. Slowly the egg emerged. With a final push, the egg lay on the fresh grass Keona had gathered and laid ready for this moment.

With a sigh Keona settled on the egg and closed her eyes. Now she was very hungry, but would have to ignore her hunger untill later when she would get a break.

"Don't go to sleep yet, Mum. I will get you something to eat." Keely said gently.

Keona opened her eyes and smiled her gratitude.

When Keely emerged, all eyes were on her. "Mum has delivered her egg."

"Is she alright?" Keio asked anxiously.

"Yes, but she is tired and hungry. I'm going to get her something to eat." Keely said, heading for the entrance.

"No," Keio said firmly but kindly. "You stay with her to make sure she is alright and I will get her a feed." He slipped out of the burrow.

At the lagoon, Kerry was also settling down for a rest. Beneath her was a white egg she had laboured hard to produce. She had been fretting about Kedar, but tiredness came over her. She decided not to worry anymore untill it was time for a break.

She was closing her eyes when a rustle at the entrance brought her back to full alertness. To Kerry's relief Kedar's familiar frame padded in. He immediately spotted the egg she was sitting on. He gave Kerry a cuddle.

"I will take over now dear." Kedar told her.

Tired as she was, Kerry took the opportunity to feed while she could. She had another egg to deliver in the next few weeks. There would be plenty of time to catch up later.

"Thank you, love." She murmured before making her way out into the night.

Kalasia joined Keely in watching over Keona untill Keio returned. The tenderness Keio displayed towards Keona when he fed her worms and the way he cuddled up to her afterwards, left Keona and the girls in no doubt about his feelings. Keona gave a deep and happy sigh, and with a smile on her face she snuggled into him.

Keely and Kalasia tiptoed away. Keely with tears in her eyes, realised she would never have to worry about her mother's welfare ever again. Kupe saw the tears when she emerged from Keona's tunnel.

"What's the matter Keely?" Kupe asked anxiously. "Why are you upset?"

"I'm not upset. They are tears of happiness," Keely answered with a smile. She looked Kupe in the eye. "Mum's found her soul mate."

Kupe looked astonished. "You mean he looks after Mum better than Dad did?" Keely nodded.

Kalasia said wistfully to Keely, "We can only hope we find someone like him."

"Yes," Keely agreed. "Males like him are few and are hard to find." She then changed the subject. "I don't know about you, but I'm starving!"

"Yes," Kalasia replied. "Let's see what food we can find. This calls for a celebration!" They made their way out of the burrow.

After the girls left, Kupe looked at Kaori with a big grin. He knew Kaori wanted Keely for his mate and was waiting for the right moment to approach her.

"It looks like you will have to do something extra special to win her now."

Kaori nodded glumly. He followed Kupe outside for a feed, wondering what he could do; maybe Keio would have some ideas.

Once outside, Kaori shook his feathers and revelled in the forest smell. After travelling from the glacier, it was good to be away from the cold and snow. At that moment, he realised he didn't want to return to the Alps at Arthur's Pass again, although he knew he must; even if it was only for a visit to his parents and his sister Kalei. He also had to consider what he would do about his future. Now that Kanai was gone, the Kiwis at Arthur's Pass would look to him to lead them.

Kaori turned his attention to Kupe. "What about you, Kupe? Have you met anyone you would like to have as your mate?"

Now, it was Kupe's turn to look miserable. "I have, but I'm not sure she will be available for me.

She may have someone else by the time I get back."

"I can only wish you luck." Kaori offered, with sympathy in his eyes. "When will we be heading back up north?" Kaori asked. There were a couple more months of winter before they could look forward to the warmth of spring again.

"I'm not in a hurry to move on." Kupe was thoughtful. "There will be two or three months before Keona and Kerry's little ones are here, and I want to see my new sister."

Kaori was pleased at this news. It meant he had more time to develop his relationship with Keely.

One fine morning Keely was feeding in the forest, the sound of rushing water could be heard nearby as the river flowed through the forest. Keely stopped her feed to listen to Bonnie the Bellbird sing. Hearing a rustle behind her, Keely turned to find Kaori emerge from the trees.

"Did you hear Bonnie?" Keely asked with a smile.

Kaori nodded. He too had heard her melody ringing in the forest. Together they wandered towards the river, exploring the depths of an old hollow log as they went.

As Keely pulled aside some ferns to look at the river, she stopped in her tracks. In front of them on the riverbank was a Dog, and it was looking right at them! Memories of the last time she met a dog came back in a flash.

"There's a Dog!" Keely wailed.

In a panic, Keely turned and ran towards the log, with Kaori following close behind her.

Rex the Retriever had escaped from the yard of his home in Whataroa and was enjoying his freedom, running along the river and exploring all the sights sounds and smells he came across.

Rex loved the sound of the river as it flowed past him on its way to the sea, although he didn't like how cold it was when he put a paw in the water to have a drink.

Rex did, however, like Bonnie the Bellbird's song when he heard it, but didn't enjoy her screaming and pecking at him when he tried to climb the tree to see how her chicks were growing. Rex smelt a strong earth smell and wondered what it was. He spotted two feathered animals looking at him from the ferns in the forest. They quickly disappeared as soon as he saw them. Was this someone for him to play with? Charging into the ferns, he barked and called to them. "Wait for me!"

Rex liked playing Chasey with Penny and Jack in the yard at Home, but these two were much faster than them. Now they had gone. Were they playing Hide and Seek with him? This was another game he loved to play with Penny and Jack. Carefully he followed their scent to the hollow log. He knew they were here somewhere, but where?

Round the log Rex went, exploring and sniffing till he found the opening. Their smell was very strong here too! Rex could see one of them looking at him. It had quite long claws on its feet too! He gave a little bark.

"I've found you! Are you coming out now?" Rex gave a little whimper when there was no response. "Come on! I want to play!"

Realising that they weren't coming out while he sat there, Rex moved away from the log but lay down in a spot where he could see them come out. In the log, Kaori could feel Keely trembling as they heard the Dog pacing and sniffing around the log. Kaori positioned himself ready to strike, should the dog try to come in after them.

When the dog found them, it gave them a little bark and then it gave a whimper before settling down away from the log. Keely remembered the whimper Lady gave when she was trying to help her and realised that this dog was trying to be friends.

"I don't think this dog will hurt us." Keely whispered to Kaori.

"How do you know?" he asked doubtfully.

When I was little, a dog found me. It called its owner, who took me home for a check. That's how i have these bands on my legs. While I was at their house, the dog tried to help me. It made the same noise this one did. Let me try to talk to it."

"Be careful then. I couldn't bear to lose you!" Kaori advised her.

"I couldn't stand it if anything happened to you either!" Kaori and Keely looked at each other and smiled, realising they both cared for each other.

"We will go together." Kaori decided.

Rex saw Kaori and Keely come to the entrance of the log. He panted and wagged his tail.

"Hello. What is your name?" Keely called out to him.

"I'm Rex. What sort of animal are you? Have you come out to play?"

"I'm Keely and this is Kaori. We are Kiwis. We would like to play, but we are night animals and it is nearly our bedtime. Do you come here often?"

"No," Rex sighed. "I live in a small yard but managed to escape. I will have to go back soon or the humans will be looking for me."

"Don't they look after you very well?" Keely asked with concern.

"Yes, they do look after me. I get plenty of food and water every day. Their children play games with me and take me for walks, but it isn't the same as being able to run free."

Kaori and Keely nodded. They remembered Sally the Sheep at the lake farm who was kept behind a fence and was unable to join them for the picnic.

"Before we go, we will play a game." Keely decided. "We will close our eyes while you go and hide."

With an excited bark, Rex scrambled off to find a hiding place. As soon as it was quiet, they opened their eyes.

"Did you hear which way he went?" Keely asked Kaori.

"He's over behind the big tree, among the bracken." Kaori grinned.

Keely and Kaori took their time to search, leaving the big tree till last, and pretended to be surprised when they found him.

"There you are!" Keely called as she spotted him. "That was fun, but we must go now. Our family will be wondering where we are soon."

After saying their goodbyes, Kaori and Keely watched Rex disappear towards the river. They were sad they may not see their new friend again.

Back at the burrow, there was rejoicing. Keona's egg had hatched. Keely found a little girl snuggled up at her mother's feet. Keio was hovering nearby with a big grin on his face.

"What are you calling her Mum?" Keely asked.

"We are calling her Keilana."

The white Heron flew into the Okarito lagoon and landed in her nest in a tree above the water's edge. Also busy at their nest were Kedar and Kerry, who had welcomed Kahil into the world, and now were waiting impatiently for his sister Kohia to be hatched.

CHAPTER NINTEEN

KUPE'S RETURN

Kedar and Kahil were showing Kohia how to find a worm when Kalan appeared. He had a group of Kiwis with him. Looking at the grim expression on their faces, Kedar could tell us this was not a friendly visit.

"Go to your mother." Kedar told Kahil and Kohia, watching them head for the burrow before turning to face Kalan.

"Where is Kupe of Kiwi Kingdom?" Kalan asked. "These are relatives of mine. Their ancestors were part of the Kiwi Kingdom too."

"Do they want to join the new Kiwi Kingdom?" Kedar enquired.

"Of course they do."

"I can fetch him to see you, although it may take a couple of days."

"Can't you take us to him?" Kalan asked which made Kedar suspicious.

"He is staying beyond our territory. We can't just go to him without permission." Kedar advised Kalan. He then looked at the visitors directly. "Did Kalan tell you Kupe is a grey Kiwi?"

Shaking his head, their leader, Kona frowned. Kedar was about to ask what his problem was when the sound of galloping Deer hooves were heard approaching. Kalan and his relatives rushed to cower in the bushes.

"Ah," Kedar said with a smile. "I think that may be him now."

"KUPE, IS THAT YOU?" Kedar called loudly. At his call the approaching deer slowed to a walk.

"It's me." Kupe answered. "Where are you Kedar?"

"I'm over here." Kedar called as the deer emerged from the forest with Kupe, Keely Kaori and Kalasia on their backs.

"We are here to see your family before we move on." Kupe smiled down at Kedar.

"There are some visitors here to see you!" Kedar advised him, seeing that Kupe was preparing to dismount. Hearing the warning tone in Kedar's voice, Kupe kept smiling but stayed where he was.

At Kedar's words, Kalan and his relatives came out from the bushes.

"This is Kalan and his relatives. Their ancestors were part of the Kingdom too." Kedar introduced them to him.

"You are from the south." Kupe said, pointing towards Haast and Fiordland.

"How do you know?" Kona asked. "Have you been there?"

"No," Kupe replied, "but I know what all the different types of Kiwis in this land look like."

"When are you coming to take over our territories?" Kona demanded.

"I'm not taking over anyone's territory!" Kupe retorted. "If you choose to be part of my kingdom, there are a few simple rules to follow."

"What are your rules?" Kona was curious.

"You must respect all animals, regardless of who or what they are. You may not injure or kill any animals you meet while in the Kingdom and establish a school for your Kiwis and other animals to learn to live in harmony together."

"Why are you involving other animals?" Kona was puzzled. "Shouldn't the kingdom only be for Kiwis?"

"In my great-grandfather Keoni's time, other animals were included. This land and all the animals in it have changed since then. If we want a safe future, we have to find a way to live with them and each other."

"You have a school with other animals in your kingdom?"

"Yes," Kupe smiled. "Some of my best friends are Stoats, Weasels, Possums and Hedgehogs, along with Pukekos, Ducks, Pigeons, Bats and Eels, not to mention Deer and Tahr. The teachers at our school are Owls and Tuis."

Kona shook his in amazement.

"Aren't there any dangerous animals in your kingdom?"

Kupe stopped smiling. "The most dangerous ones I've met have been my own kind!"

"How do we join your kingdom?" Kona asked thoughtfully.

"If your neighbours and other Kiwis in your territories agree, live by these rules and send someone to our school so we can show you how to start your own."

Kerry was heard calling Kedar in the distance. Kona gave a little smile. His mate was far to the south in Fiordland, and he was missing her already.

"It has been a pleasure to meet you." Kona gave a little nod to Kupe. "We won't keep you from your family." Kona said in farewell to Kedar before leading Kalan and the group towards Kalan's territory.

The early morning sun was rising over the lake hills when Danny, Pete, Harry Helena and Harvey emerged from the water at Han's Bay. They had been teaching Harvey and Helena how to swim. After seeing Harry successfully save Helena from drowning in the Hokitika River, Harvey and Helena were determined to learn how to swim too. Percy and Sam came to join them when the sound of galloping Deer made everyone look up.

"Kupe, you have come back at last!"

Percy raced towards the approaching deer, followed by the others. Primula Pigeon saw the deer from the nearby Totara Tree and flew off to the forest to spread the good news. As Kupe Kaori Keely and Kalasia dismounted from Denny and Donny; there was a small commotion as Kane led the community out of the forest to welcome them home.

"Welcome home!" Kane called. They were quickly surrounded by a sea of familiar faces and a few new ones.

"Thanks," Kupe grinned back at him. "How has the community been here?"

It was Kane's turn to smile. "Once everyone settled in, it has been very peaceful. We have enjoyed it so much that some are refusing to return to the Alps when we return." Looking down at the two newborn Kiwis at their mother's feet, he added, "We have also been busy producing some new young ones for your community."

"When you return home, Keely and I will be coming too."

At Kane's enquiring look, Kupe added, "Keely is Kaori's mate now." This statement brought a chorus of cheers and congratulations from the crowd. "I will be coming too because my quest isn't finished yet. I have another amulet holder to find in the north."

"Who will look after the community while you away?" Kane asked.

Kupe looked at Owen Owl with a smile. "This community managed without us for many years. I'm sure it will be fine untill we get back."

"Where is Keona?" Heather asked. Although Holly and Helena were good company, she missed Keona a great deal and was glad that some of the Alpine Kiwi females staying on were starting friendships with her.

"Keona is well." Kupe told her. "She has found a new mate, Keio at Okarito. She is very happy with him. He is helping her to raise her little girl, Keilana."

Kane looked at Kaori, who was gazing at the lake with a contented look on his face.

"You are going to miss this, aren't you?" he said quietly.

Kaori looked at Kane with a look of determination. "I'm only leaving to hand over the leadership role to my family and help Kupe finish his quest before I return."

Kane was surprised. He now knew Kaori was intending to hand the mantle of leadership to his sister, Kalei. The Alpine Kiwis had not had a female leader before. Would they tolerate her?"

After the welcome, Kupe Keely Kaori and Kalasia went to Kupe's burrow. Kupe approached his burrow with some anxiety. Everything outside seemed to be the same. Fern Fantail was chattering in her tree, tending to her latest brood of chicks. Pongo and Poppy had returned to their nest in the bulrushes. He smiled at the sight and sound of the brook gently flowing through the forest. Kupe hesitated. The last time he had been in the burrow, his father had been there. Would he feel his spirit there? Could he live there again?"

Keely saw his hesitation and rushed to comfort him.

"It's alright Kupe. We will go inside together."

Carefully Keely pulled back the bush guarding the entrance and led Kupe in. Inside, Kupe absorbed the feel and sight of the familiar dark tunnels before him. To his relief, it seemed to be welcoming him. He gave a sniff and released it with a sigh. Turning to Keely with a smile he was able to reassure her with his words. "Heather has been in. I can smell the fresh grass." He turned to pull back the bush with a smile to Kaori and Kalasia.

"Come in. Welcome back to my home!"

Later in the afternoon, Kupe made his way to the school. He was hoping to see Owen Owl before the school session started. Near the cave entrance, he saw a mound of earth, with some small ferns taking hold and knew this was where his father lay. He put his claw on the mound.

"Mum and Keilana are safe and happy now."

Walking into the cave, all was quiet. The pongees lining the walls and roof gave the space a snug feel. New flax mats covered the floor and all the books were back in the library, which had been expanded. *Where did they get them?* He wondered.

Hearing a noise behind him, Kupe turned to see Owen fly in. Kupe could see a frailness caused by injury.

"Hello Owen." Kupe smiled. "Have you recovered from your injuries?"

"I have." Owen replied, remembering the incident.

Seeing Keanu set upon by Kanai Kekoa and Kekapa, Owen had rushed in to defend him. When Kane and his followers burst onto the scene, Owen lay next to the lifeless body of Keanu while Kanai was in the school, trying to wreck the library.

Koana Kiwi ran to the tree where Owen's nesting hole was and began to shout. "Mrs Owl! Mrs Owl! Can you hear me?"

Odelia poked her head out of the hole to see who was making so much noise.

"Mrs Owl!" Koana called. "Can you please come to the school quickly? Mr Owl has been badly hurt!"

Seeing the young Kiwi was upset, Odelia told Ollie and Orchid to follow her and flew off to the school. She arrived to find Kane's followers holding back Kanai Kekoa and Kekapa, with Kane bending over Keanu and Owen.

"I'm sorry," Kane apologised as Odelia landed beside him. "Kanai tried to take control here, but we have stopped him. You may have him punished as you see fit."

"Any punishment you give needs to be by the Kiwi Kingdom rules that Kupe set out."

Kane nodded in agreement with Odelia's wishes. He was pleased no more blood was to be shed in this peaceful place.

"Keanu is beyond our help," Odelia said, seeing that his spirit had left him, "but we need to get Owen to shelter."

Ollie and Orchid landed next to their mother.

"Will Dad be alright?" Ollie asked. His beak quivered when he saw his father's injuries.

"I hope so," Odelia answered. "Can you and Orchid bring a mat out?"

As Ollie and Orchid rushed to obey, some of the Alpine Kiwis came to help. Willing claws gently cupped to lift Owen onto the mat. They pulled the mat into the cave with their bills. Odelia Ollie and Orchid gathered around close to Owen to keep a vigil. "We will be staying here untill Dad is well enough to fly." Odelia told Ollie and Orchid. "We will take turns to find our food while we are here."

Kane asked, "What would you like to eat?"

"Some insects will be welcome, if you can find some." Odelia replied and thanked him.

During that long night, Owen gradually regained consciousness. When he woke to find his family around him, he gave a little smile and accepted an insect from Odelia before returning to sleep. Ollie and Orchid looked at their mother with a questioning look.

"Yes," she reassured them with a smile. "Dad will recover. We can get some rest now."

The next evening Oscar and Olivia flew into the cave. They had brought some mice as a gift.

"I heard from Sam the young Stoat that you were injured." Oscar told Owen. "He was very worried about you."

Through his pain, Owen managed to smile and tried to reassure them. "I will be alright." Everyone present could see though, that it would be some time before he would recover.

While new feathers covered the scars of his physical wounds, Owen's smile hid the fact he only recently had the confidence to return to his duties. "What about you?" Owen enquired of Kupe. "I see you have a permanent reminder of your battle too." Kupe lifted up his foot with the missing claw and looked at the scar where the claw had been.

"Yes, Kanai took it with him to the bottom of the glacier."

They smiled at each other, both knowing how close the other came to losing their lives.

"How are Kalama and Kalea coping?" Kupe asked. "It must be hard for them to accept everything that has happened."

Owen was silent for moment before he answered. "We may never know. They have gone to relatives who live in the north."

Kupe nodded his agreement before changing the subject. He asked how the Alpine Kiwis were progressing with their lessons, but inside, Kupe was in turmoil. The disappointment at finding Kalea had moved and agony of not knowing where she was overwhelmed him. Making his excuses to Owen, Kupe slipped away for some solitude. Owen watched him leave with concern. Kupe had been unable to disguise the look of despair in his eyes.

Up the rugged slopes of Mount Tuhua Kupe climbed. Higher and higher he went untill he found a rocky ledge to sit on near the summit. From his perch Kupe was able to see all of the lake and the mountains surrounding it.

The Islands of Hans Bay reached out like a green finger from the arm of the bay into the dark waters of the lake. Beyond the lake hills, the white tips of the Southern Alps marched into the distance to Mount Cook and Tasman in the south. Hokitika and the Tasman Sea stretched out to the west.

The vast beauty of the scene before him calmed Kupe's spirit, and as he watched the sun disappear into the ocean beyond the lake hills.

Kupe made a promise to himself. *I will not return untill I have found her!*

With renewed determination, Kupe scrambled down the mountainside. At the school, he found everyone waiting for him. The *Kiwi Kingdom Book* and the amulets were on display. Looking at his amulet, Kupe knew it was too soon to reclaim it. He had a vision of conflict yet to come.

"Thank you all for coming here this evening," Kupe addressed the crowd. "While it is too soon for me to reclaim my amulet, it is my pleasure to return Kaori's to him and his family." To much cheering and clapping, Kaori stepped forward to reclaim his amulet.

Kupe saw Owen look at him with a questioning look and gave him a wry smile. Owen knew immediately that Kupe had had one of his visions which meant there was more trouble ahead.

CHAPTER TWENTY

THE NORTHERN QUEST

Keely could hardly believe her eyes as the Tahr made their way up the mountain slope under the cover of the Alpine forest. Before her lay beauty she had not expected. Last time Keely was here, everything was covered in a thick carpet of snow. Now she was surrounded in a mass of red. The southern Rata was in bloom.

"Are you sure you want to leave this?" Keely asked Kaori.

"I'm sure." he replied quietly but firmly.

Near the edge of the tree line, they dismounted. Keely looked up at the slopes where only tussock will grow to the sheer rocky peaks, some still clothed in snow. Kaori led the way to the family burrow. Inside him, tension was mounting.

"Kaori, Kalasia, you are home!"

Their sister Kalei rushed to meet them, followed closely by their parents. After they had greeted each other, Kaori noticed a male waiting in the background. He had a young male chick at his feet.

"Kaori, Kalasia, this is my mate Karua, and our son Kawaka."

Seeing the happy look on her face, Kaori could tell she had found happiness at last.

"You have been busy since we last saw you!" Kalasia exclaimed to Kalei, smiling with delight at her new nephew.

"You haven't been the only one who has been busy." Kaori grinned at Kalei. "I have brought along Kupe and his sister, Keely. She is my mate now."

Kalei was surprised at this news.

"Are you with Kekapa again?" Kalei asked Kalasia.

"No, we had a lucky escape there, didn't we, Keely?" Keely nodded with a smile. Kaori answered for them.

"Kanai Kekoa and Kekapa will not returning. They will not harm anyone ever again!"

Kalei knew something drastic had happened, and then she spotted the amulet around Kaori's neck.

She pulled it out to look at it. The last time she had seen it, it had been around Kekoa's neck.

"You have a great deal to tell us." Kalei said as she sat down next to Karua and Kawaka.

Kupe saw Karua frown when Kalei looked at Kaori's amulet. Karua's reaction to the amulet created questions that needed to be answered.

"Are you going to stay to be our leader now?" Kalei asked when they had finished.

"No," Kaori replied. "I love my life at the lake, and when Kupe's quest is over, I intend to live there permanently. This amulet is our family heritage and responsibility. The main reason I have come back is to ask you to be our leader for the Kiwi Kingdom."

"What if the local Kiwis won't accept me?" Kalei was nervous about the responsibility that now lay on her shoulders. She looked anxiously at Karua. Kaori saw her discomfort.

"Kane will be a suitable leader if you cannot or will not. He took on the role at the lake while we were away." Kaori reassured her.

Kalei smiled with relief. "We must ask him."

"Karua, I noticed you weren't happy when you first saw the amulet. Are you against the Kiwi Kingdom?" Kupe asked quietly.

"No," Karua replied with a smile. "I think your kingdom will be a wonderful place if we can persuade enough Kiwis and animals to be part of it. The reason I was unhappy is that I come from the mountains over by the sea." Karua pointed in the direction of the Paparoa Range "I was forced out of my territory by a Kiwi who was wearing one of those amulets."

Kupe was shocked. "What is his name?"

"Kakate."

"Do you want your territory back?"

"No, my home is here now. I suppose I should be grateful to him. If he hadn't forced me out, I wouldn't have met Kalei and have my son."

"Do you think you can show us where he is?" Kupe asked, as he began drawing a map of the island on the floor with a stick. "We are here." Kupe put a dot on Arthur's Pass.

Karua looked at the map intently. Carefully Karua scratched in the path he had travelled with his claw.

"He is here." Karua pointed at the Three Sisters Mountain. (The Three Sisters Mountain has been renamed on maps, but is still known locally as the Three Sisters Mountain.)

"Is he on the side facing the ocean or the valley?"

"You can see the ocean."

"Is he near the summit or the base of the mountain?"

"With my territory, Kakate now controls the whole side of the mountain facing the sea."

Kupe nodded. Persuading Kakate to either change his ways or give up his amulet was going to be a big challenge.

"I am going to see Kane." Kaori said as he stood up.

"Tell Kane I want to see him." Kupe advised Kaori. "If he agrees, he will have to take the pledge."

Kaori nodded as he made his way out of the burrow.

"Kane, are you there?" Kaori asked as he approached Kane's burrow. Kane put his head out. "I'm sorry to bother you when you've just got home, but Kupe wants to see you."

"Does he want me to be the next leader here?" Kane asked. He had wondered who would take the role if Kalei would not.

Kaori nodded. "You already have experience in the role. We want you to do it."

Kane nodded.

"You will do it?"

"Yes." Kane agreed, smiling.

"Bring your family." Kaori told him. "This is a special occasion that they should share."

The news that Kanai's family was not returning had spread like a wild fire.

Everyone now wondered who the next leader would be. Those who remembered Kaori's family in the role expected them to regain the leadership. When word passed around that Kaori was leading Kane and his family and his family to his burrow, they were followed untill a large group was present.

Back at the burrow, Kaori put his head inside.

"Kane has agreed to be the leader. Nearly everyone has come to see it."

With a smile, Kupe led the family outside into the bright moonlit night where the leadership of the Alpine Kiwis passed onto a new family.

When it was time for Kupe Keely Kaori and Kalasia to say goodbye, Kalasia looked around her, trying to keep a vision of her old home in her memory. Kalasia had no idea if she would return to see her family again, which made her sad, but she was also happy as she felt her future awaited her somewhere in the north.

Through the mountains Kaori led them untill they came to the Taramakau River. Kupe remembered it from the journey to the Alps. There was no playing or relaxing in these waters as they crossed. They could feel the cold snow water right through to their bones.

From there, Kupe took the lead, heading through the forest towards the northwest. At Lake Brunner they rested for a couple of days before they continued their journey to the Grey Valley, with the peaks of the Paparoa Range looming in front of them.

Charlotte the Chamois and her sister Charmaine were grazing in the forest by the Grey River when they saw four grey Kiwis quietly walk by. They had seen and heard Kiwis before near their home in the Paparoa Range, but not in this area.

Charlotte and Charmaine were even more surprised when one of the Kiwis spotted them and led the other Kiwis over to speak to them. None of the local Kiwis had spoken to them before.

"Hello, I'm Kupe from Kiwi Kingdom with my sister Keely, her mate Kaori, and his sister Kalasia. Do you live in this forest?"

"Hello Kupe." Charlotte replied. "I'm Charlotte, and this is Charmaine my sister. We are visiting here from our home in the north, in those mountains." She turned to look at the northern Paparoa Range.

"We are visiting some Kiwis near your home. Could you give us a ride?"

Charlotte was astonished. She had not heard or seen anything like this done before. Have you had rides from Chamois before?"

"No, but in my Kingdom, Deer and Tahr are part of our community. They happily give us a ride when we need to travel long distances or climb into the mountains."

"Do you have any other animals in your Kingdom?"

"Yes. Some of my best friends are Possums, Stoats, Weasels, Ducks, Pukekos, hedgehogs, Bats and Eels. We are happy to fit in with you." Kupe reassured her.

After agreeing to take the Kiwis, the Chamois spent happy hours ambling through the forest, learning about their lives at the lake and the Alps and the Kingdom.

"If you start a community where we live, we would like to be part of it." Charmaine commented.

"Of course we will include you." Kalasia replied, happy to have met new friends.

Kakate was patrolling his territory when he heard a noise in the bushes. He was about to challenge the intruder when the bushes parted and he was confronted by two young Kiwi strangers. There was another rustle and he found himself surrounded by all the male Kiwis in the area.

"Are you Kakate?" one asked.

"How do you know my name? Kakate asked. "Who are you?"

"Karua told me. You took his territory. Fortunately, he doesn't want it back, but there are some other Kiwis here, who do want their territory returned to them."

Kakate was about to say "You will have to fight for the territory." When Kupe added, "I am Kupe of the Kiwi Kingdom at Kaniere. My great-grandfather founded it many years ago. This area is part of it. I have come to restore the Kingdom to this area. Will you join your neighbours?"

Kakate remained silent.

Kupe held up his amulet for Kakate and all the other Kiwis to see.

"As ruler of the Kingdom, I wear this amulet. My great-grand father also gave his closest supporters amulets to show that they and their families represented the Kingdom in their area. I see, Kakate that you are wearing one. Was your amulet given to your great-grandfather? If it was, you will know a rhyme that only the true owner will know. Do you know it?"

Kakate knew his reign her was over. The amulet he wore was one of the trophies he had gained in his quest for power and territory.

Kakate suddenly lunged forward to strike Kupe in the chest.

As Kupe staggered back from the force of the blow, the Kiwis behind Kakate pounced on him and held him down. Kupe ignored the pain and blood than now coated his front and stepped forward.

"You took the owner's life to get this, didn't you?" Kupe asked as he lifted the amulet from Kakate's neck. "It doesn't belong to you."

"I'm going to destroy you!" Kakate threatened Kupe, struggling to free himself.

"You may take my life, but you will not destroy the Kingdom!" Kupe retorted with a smile.

"You are being expelled from these mountains and those to the east." Kupe pointed to the Southern Alps. "There is a large river to the north called the Buller Gorge. You are to live beyond it."

Kakate's bill dropped. "We've already been forced out of that territory."

Kupe was firm. "You will have to make peace with them and live by their rules. Do you have family here?

"I have my mate and our son."

Kupe addressed the crowd. "Kakate's mate may choose whether to go with him or stay. If she chooses to stay, she is not to be harmed or harassed. Everyone else can reclaim their territories."

"What about Karua's territory?"

"If someone needs a new home, they may claim his burrow, but the territory is to be free for anyone to walk through and feed on." Kupe ordered, before turning towards the nearby stream, followed closely by Kaori.

Immersing himself in the stream, Kupe allowed the cold water to wash away the grime of the battle.

Kupe was tempted to let the stream sweep him away. As Kupe relaxed further into the water, Kaori's claw gripped his shoulder.

"Kupe wake up!"

With a little sigh, Kupe opened his eyes and stood up.

"Kakate's mate is here."

Turning towards the riverbank, Kupe faced a young grey Kiwi named Kalani. The large dark grey form of his mother Kura stood by him. The local Kiwis gathered behind them. Kalani's bright accusing eyes watched every move that Kupe made.

"Why are you sending my Dad away?"

Kupe felt sorry for Kalani, who now had to grow up in a hurry. "Your Dad took things that didn't belong to him and wouldn't give them back. Your Dad also killed a Kiwi." Kupe told him as gently as he could. "The old ways of killing and taking what you want are over."

"Why?" Kalani asked. "Is it wrong to kill?"

"Yes. Your Dad tried to kill me because he didn't want to live under my rules. I am Kupe, the leader of Kiwi Kingdom. In my Kingdom you are not allowed to kill or harm Kiwis or any other animals. You must respect each other and the things that belong to them."

"Have you decided what you will do?" Kupe asked Kura.

"We will move with Kakate." She replied. "The territory we have left is difficult to live on when it is cold."

Turning, Kura walked away. The Kiwis of Three Sisters Mountain parted to allow her to join Kakate and lead Kalani to an uncertain future.

"Is Kakate's territory to be free too?"

"Yes. Do you know who your leader was before Kakate took over?" Kupe asked. It was time to choose a new leader.

"Kapali's father was our leader. We want Kapali to lead us."

Kapali stepped forward.

"Kapali, do you agree to take on the role of leader and uphold the laws of Kiwi Kingdom?"

"I do."

The end of Kakate's reign was cause for celebration at Three Sisters Mountain. No longer did they have to fear for their lives or homes. When Kakate's territory was checked, it was found to have a large cave, the perfect place for a school. Keely and Kalasia set it up. Kalasia became the teacher for the night animals, while Charlotte Chamois became the teacher for the day time students.

CHAPTER TWENTY ONE

PUNAKAIKI

Kupe was sleeping one day, when he had a vivid dream. Kalea was trapped under a house, and he had to rescue her!" Kupe instantly awoke. He now knew where she was. He had to go to Punakaiki where his parents came from.

When it was time to say goodbye, Kalasia stayed behind. Kapali had asked her to be his mate, so she now had another reason to stay.

"So, you're keeping the leadership in the family after all." Kaori commented with a grin.

Kapali had not been told about Kalasia's family history yet. He looked at her with puzzlement. "What does Kaori mean about keeping the leadership in the family?"

Kalasia looked at Kapali with a smile and replied. "Our great-grandfather was one of Keoni's supporters and was given an amulet, but was killed. The amulet was held by another family untill recently. When Kupe returned it to us, we didn't want the responsibility, so it was given to a family we know will serve the Kingdom well."

As Charlotte and Charmaine approached Punakaiki, Charlotte became nervous.

"There is danger here!" she exclaimed.

"I know." Kupe replied. "That is why I came. I need to rescue someone."

"Who is it?" asked Keely, also feeling tension in the air.

"I'm looking for Kalea. I know she is here somewhere!"

The desperation they heard in Kupe's voice revealed his feelings for her. Kupe looked at homes he could see through the palms, untill he saw one, sitting on the hillside. He knew that was where he had to go.

"We will walk from here." Kupe decided and thanked the Chamois for bringing them there. After watching the Chamois disappear into the forest, Kupe Keely and Kaori started making their way up the hill. As they walked, there was a distant rumbling and the ground trembled under their feet.

"It's an earthquake!" Keely said in panic, remembering being trapped in the library in the school.

"It's alright," Kupe comforted her. "You are safe here."

On the hillside another rumble was heard as a slip developed. They heard the loud cracking and crash as part of the house collapsed onto the slip. As Kupe came nearer, he saw two humans scramble out of the wreckage.

Racing to the house, Kupe peered underneath at the jumble of timber by the bank and called. "Kalea! Kalea, are you there?"

There was silence, so he called again.

"Kalea, its Kupe! Are you there?"

Kupe heard a muffled "Is that you, Kupe?"

"Yes, it's me! I'm here to help you!"

Kupe called Kaori and Keely over to help and without regard for their personal safety, began digging under the rubble. Kalea saw a small opening had appeared in the wall before her. She dug too and quickly scrambled out to join Kupe Keely and Kaori.

"Are you alone?" Kupe asked.

"Yes, there was just me here." Kalea replied, as Kupe led them to safety. Having led the Kiwis clear of the house, Kupe and Kalea stopped to take one last look at the place where Keanu and Keona used to live. As they watched, another shockwave rippled under their feet. The slip widened, sending the remainder of the house and burrow down the hill.

"Do you want to find your mother to see she is alright?" Kupe asked Kalea.

"No," Kalea replied. "Kamoku is her mate now. He looks after her well. They wanted me to mate with Kamoku's son, Kanoa. When I refused, I was sent to live in this burrow alone."

Kalea led them down to the Pancake Rocks to experience the wonder of this wild place. As they stood looking out to sea, with the sea spray splashing over them; Kupe felt deeply contented and could tell his parents had been here before him. Kupe turned to Kalea.

"Will you be my mate, Kalea?"

"Yes, my love."

They watched the sun setting in the western sky. As they turned to leave, they were confronted by a young angry male Kiwi.

"Kalea, I thought you were dead! Who is this you are with?"

215

"This is Kanoa." Kalea introduced Kamoku's son to Kupe.

"This is Kupe," she told Kanoa. "He is the leader of the Kiwi Kingdom. He came to rescue me."

"Kalea has agreed to be my mate." Kupe added.

Kanoa nodded sadly, realising he never had a chance at being Kalea's mate, because she had been waiting for Kupe to come.

"We had heard the Kingdom was coming here soon," Kanoa told Kupe, "but Dad said you would have to fight him for this area."

"I have no intention of fighting your father," Kupe told Kanoa. "Because you will be the next leader of this area, I am telling you that you and your Kiwis will only become part of the Kingdom, if you want to, and if you all agree to live by the rules of the Kingdom."

Kanoa was impressed. No one had acknowledged his future role or given him choices before.

"Can I come to visit your Kingdom some time?" Kanoa asked.

"Would you like to come with us?" Kupe invited him. "We are on our way home now."

"Thank you. I would love to come."

Seeing Kaori and Keely waiting for them, Kanoa went to join them. Kupe and Kalea took one last look at the sun as it disappeared below the ocean waves before they began their trek home.

As they left the Pancake Rocks and headed south, a large grey female Kiwi emerged from the bushes. It was Kahi, Keanu and Keona's neighbour, who had been keeping a friendly watch over Kalea.

She was shocked to see the land where Kalea's burrow had been and the house that stood over it now in ruins down the hill and had rushed to fetch Kamoku and Kalama. Their calls had been met with silence, and the worst was feared.

"Kanoa, Kalea! Where are you going? Your parents are frantic. We saw the house and thought you both were dead! They will be so pleased you were able to save her. Aren't you going to see them and let them know you are safe?"

"I didn't save her though. They can thank Kupe for that. Kupe is the leader of Kiwi Kingdom."

Kahi looked at Kupe and Keely. They seemed to have a familiar look about them.

"Should I know you?" Kahi was puzzled.

"No." Kupe replied with a smile. "You may know our parents though. They lived next to you before they moved to Lake Kaniere."

Kahi was amazed when she heard this news. "You are Keanu and Keona's children? How are they? When are they coming back for a visit?"

"Dad died some time ago and Mum has a new mate down at Okarito. They are bringing up our sister, Keilana. They are happy there, so it unlikely they will return again."

"Kanoa said you are the leader of the Kiwi Kingdom. Aren't you going to see Kamoku? He is the local leader here."

"I know Kamoku is against the new Kingdom and I have no intention of fighting him for this area." Kupe told Kahi. "Kanoa will be the next leader here. It is for him to decide whether to join the Kingdom. The Kiwi population here will have to agree as well. We are on our way home now. Kanoa is coming with us for a visit to see the Kingdom."

"You can tell them that we are safe." Kanoa told Kahi. "I will return home when I am ready."

Kahi looked at Kalea. "You aren't coming back?"

"No." Kalea replied with a smile. "I have agreed to be Kupe's mate."

Kahi watched them leave with some anxiety. She wasn't sure Kamoku or Kalama would be happy to hear this news. Should she tell them?

There was much rejoicing when Kupe Kalea Kaori Keely and Kanoa arrived at the lake.

"Can I bring it out now?" Owen asked.

Kupe nodded with a smile. With Kalea by his side and the lake Community gathered around him, Kupe finally received the mantle of his Kingdom. As the amulet was laid around his neck, Keoni and Keanu stood before him with big smiles on their faces.

"Welcome back to your Kingdom." Keoni declared.

As the community celebrated, Kupe and Kalea slipped quietly away to begin their life together. Kupe's quest was now complete.

KUPE

KIWI'S

KINGDOM

CHAPTER ONE

THE VOWS

Kupe and Kalea Kiwi sat on the water's edge as their son Kamaka splashed in the shallows of Hans Bay at Lake Kaniere.

"He will have to have some swimming lessons soon." Kupe commented as they watched him.

"Yes," Kalea agreed. "I will see if Peony Pukeko can take him in her class." The breeze rippling across the water was light and the water was becoming warmer as summer approached.

"It won't be long before the school carnival." Kupe said with a smile He will want to be part of it.

"Will you be going in it?" Kalea asked. Keely had asked if they were taking part, but until now Kupe had not decided if he was going to compete.

"No," Kupe replied, "I am expecting that I will have a visitor here. Word has come that Kehi the leader of the Kiwis in the Buller is coming to see me. I will be busy entertaining him so you will have to compete for us."

Kalea nodded; pleased she would be expected to join the other mothers who were taking part. Kupe gave a happy sigh of contentment. As he sat by the lake shore, Kupe thought of all the places he had been and vowed that he would never again leave his kingdom.

In the far north Kalani Kiwi stood in thick bushland in a bay that faced the Tasman Sea. His mood matched that of the storm. Dark threatening clouds hung low over a now angry sea. Lightning flashed and thunder rumbled overhead. White caps whipped up on the turbulent water to form large waves that rolled in to smash onto the shore, sea spray drenched the foliage of the dense forest above. As Kalani stood looking out to sea, the storm raging about him, he also was making a vow – for revenge!

After Kupe expelled his father Kakate and sent his family into exile from the Three Sisters Mountain, the family set out on their journey. They took their time, for there was no hurry to arrive at a place where Kakate and Kura knew they were going to be parted. As they slowly made their way through the Paparoa Range, word was already being sent ahead of them.

Keo kiwi fossicked in the forest above the Buller River. A soft call heralded the arrival of his son Kuna from the Three Sisters community.

"Have you seen them yet?" Kuna asked.

"Who are you talking about?" Keo asked. "There hasn't been anyone cross the bridge for some weeks."

"Kakate and his family have been expelled." Kuna replied triumphantly. "They have been ordered to live north of this river!"

"Who expelled them?" Keo was both surprised and delighted at this news.

"Kupe, he's Keoni's great grandson." Kuna said with glee. "He has brought back the Kiwi Kingdom."

"Who is leader of the Three Sisters community now?" Keo wanted to know.

"Kapali has agreed to take over."

A large beam of joy spread over Keo's face. Kapali's father had been a close friend of his. Grieving, he had fled to safety after Kakate had taken his friend's life in order to control the area.

"There is justice after all." Keo said quietly. A thought made him frown.

"Does Kupe know Kakate was thrown out of the north?"

"Yes." Kuna grinned. "Kupe has also ordered him to live by their rules!"

"I wouldn't mind being a fly on a fern over there." Keo replied as he raised his head and called out loudly.

"IS ANYONE OVER THERE?" In the distance there came a reply.

"Is that you Keo?"

"Yes, I have some news for you!"

Presently a northern kiwi appeared on the opposite bank.

"What's up Keo?"

"Tell your leader that Kakate and his family are coming back."

"They aren't welcome here!" was the hostile reply.

"They have been expelled and have been ordered to live on your side of the river, under your rules!" There was silence at this news before the next question.

"Who ordered it?" the northern kiwi wanted to know

"Kupe did. He is Keoni's great grandson. He is restoring the kingdom."

"We will be ready for Kakate when he gets here!" was the final retort before the northern kiwi disappeared into the forest. The northern kiwis put on a watch at all the crossings to make sure the family didn't slip in unseen.

As the family approached the bridge Kakate and Kura stopped to look at each other.

"Any regrets?" Kakate asked Kura.

"None." She said firmly and with a smile. They turned to look at Kalani.

"We may be separated soon." Kakate told his son. "Look after your mother."

"Will we see you again?" Kalani asked anxiously

"I doubt it." Kakate replied as he gave Kura and Kalani a final cuddle.

With purpose Kakate then led his family across the bridge. They could feel eyes watching them as they crossed. They had barely reached the shelter of the forest when a challenge rang out.

"Who comes there?"

"It is Kakate and my family."

"If you want a place here, you will have to fight for it."

Without pausing or looking back, Kakate rushed into the forest to confront the challenger. A lone kiwi stood waiting for him. As Kakate reached the kiwi and put up his claw to strike, they were surrounded by other kiwis which closed in to hold him. Kakate did not see the blow that ended his life.

A short time later Kura and Kalani heard footsteps approach from the forest where Kakate had disappeared. Kura hadn't heard him call, so she expected the worst – which was that Kakate would never return to her. She drew herself up with all the dignity she could muster. When Kalani saw what she was doing, he did the same, to confront the large group of kiwis emerging from the trees.

There was silence for a moment as they assessed each other.

The local kiwis were surprised at how big she was, and that she was fertile too, taking in the young child at her side.

Kura tried to guess what this group's intentions were – were they going to send her to Kakate or was she to begin a new life? Looking at their faces, Kura realised they weren't hostile, only curious. Inside she relaxed a little.

"I'm Kura." She said into the silence. "And this is my son Kalani."

"You are Kakate's mate?"

"Yes."

"He won't be returning to you. We have a male who needs a mate. Are you prepared to accept him?"

Kura knew that their lives depended on her answer. She pretended to think about it for a moment.

"What if the male doesn't accept Kalani? He isn't old enough to be completely independent yet."

The leader Kehi had already noticed Kalani's watchful and distrusting eyes and knew he would have to keep a close eye on him.

"He will come to me for a short while."

"Mum!" Kalani cried out, his distress was plain to see.

"Be strong!" Kura told him firmly.

"But I'm going to lose both of you!"

"No," Kehi intervened. "Your mother needs time to adjust to her new partner and life here. You can see her tomorrow."

Kura gave Kalani a hug before standing up to look the leader in the eye.

"I'm ready." She said. Kehi nodded before turning to introduce her new partner to her. She noticed with relief that her new partner looked completely different to Kakate. She wouldn't be reminded of what she had lost when she looked at him.

As Kakate watched his mother being led away rage rose within him. One day he would seek revenge. A vision of Kupe appeared in his mind.

During the following months and years Kakate was careful to keep his feelings hidden, pretending to settle in and enjoy his new home. As Kalani stood looking at the bay, he knew it was nearly time to meet his destiny.

He was now old enough and big enough to take care of himself in a fight – he always won in the fights he had.

Soon Kalani would also be old enough to take a mate, though he had no intention of staying and having a family here as his mother had done. He couldn't tell her what he was intending to do in case she tried to stop him or let the community know his plans and prevent him from leaving.

"What are you up to?" a voice behind him interrupted his thoughts. Inwardly Kalani cursed and wiped the scowl off his face as he turned to Kehi who was still keeping a close eye on him.

"I'm just enjoying the storm." Kalani lied.

"I saw anger in your face. What are you planning?" Kehi demanded.

"I have some unfinished business." Kalani said with a sigh, taking a step back in case he had to defend himself.

"You are talking about your father?" Kehi asked quizzically. Kalani nodded.

"When are you going?"

"I haven't decided yet, but it will be soon."

Can we expect you to return?"

"No."

"What about your mother?"

"It's best she doesn't know. She will only make a fuss."

Kehi nodded with relief. He knew this kiwi was trouble from the day he came and soon he would be leaving.

"I am heading south to visit some allies shortly. I will see you when I get back."

Kalani could only nod his agreement. He knew that his every move would be monitored while Kehi was away. He couldn't go untill the leader was ready to let him go.

As Kehi walked away he was troubled. He now knew that Kalani was planning to harm Kupe. He would have to warn him! He planned to start an alliance with Kupe, but if Kalani was successful what would become of the kingdom?

CHAPTER TWO

PENE PUKEKO

It was early morning. The sun had yet to touch the peaks around Lake Kaniere as Peony and Piera Pukeko gathered their large group for a swimming lesson. Peony's daughter Pearl and Peira"s son Peka paddled in the shallows with Kamaka and Ketara Kiwi, Hyacinth, Hebe and Hone Hedgehog, Wisteria and Winkie Weasel, Slinky and Shimmy Stoat and Daffodil and Dudley Duck.

Their mothers Kalea and Keely Kiwi, Helena Hedgehog, Wendy weasel and Silene Stoat were gathered on the beach to give encouragement. Daisy Duck was also there to assist Peony and Piera and to keep an eye that her children obeyed Peony's instructions.

The bush and lake were a hive of activity as many of the animals were up early to prepare for the carnival. Keely noticed the eels were racing each other up and down the bay. Flora fantail was practicing her flying skills. Her children practiced with her for the junior competition. Sam Stoat was also racing Percy and Petunia possum up and down the nearby totara tree.

Suddenly, there was the sound of a car approaching on the nearby road. This made everyone stop what they were doing. Humans weren't usually around at this time of the morning. The screech of the car's brakes had everyone racing towards the road, for it could only mean that someone was in danger.

Kalea, Keely and Peony peered around the flax to see a battered pukeko emerge from under the car to stagger towards the water. It was Peony Pukeko's partner Pene. With a cry of alarm Peony went racing towards Pene, but as she approached the car she was forced to jump into the bushes as the car door opened and a man got out and started to chase Pene.

Eighteen year old Aleck was driving out to Hans Bay early to pick up his mate Bruce for work. Bruce's car was in the workshop for a service and wouldn't be ready until later in the day. As he approached Hans Bay a pukeko ran in front of his car. Aleck braked hard to avoid the bird but he heard the car strike the pukeko. After he stopped he saw the injured pukeko stagger out and decided to go after it. Aleck doubted the pukeko would live for long. It would make a tasty change for tea tonight.

As Aleck reached down to pick up the pukeko he received a shock. A growl from behind him made Aleck stop and look around. Aleck found he was being confronted by a large bundle of brown fur in the form of a possum that bowled in to rake his hand with long sharp claws; before quickly retreating out of reach.

Stunned at this turn of events Aleck looked from his now bleeding hand to the hostile gaze of the possum. As the pukeko was now out of sight, safely hidden in the bushes and flax by the lake, Aleck beat a retreat to the car and drove off to see Bruce. After they had washed and dressed Aleck's hand they drove carefully back to the spot where he had hit the pukeko – blue and black feathers remained on the road, but there was no sign of either the pukeko or possum.

"PENE, Where are you!" Peony called as soon as the car drove away. She saw Percy possum plunge into the bushes by the lakeside and quickly followed him, to find Pene crouching and shaking in fear.

"We have to get you home," Percy told Pene urgently. "Before the human comes back again. Can you move?"

Pene managed to nod, before slowly and carefully limping back over the road with his friends to melt into the safely of the forest. Once in the forest Pene had to stop as his battered and bruised body wouldn't go any further. Percy and Petunia, Silene and Sam, Kalea and Keely and Peony all gathered around him to give him warmth and support while wondering what to do next. The sound of the car driving slowly past could be heard nearby.

"Shouldn't we try to get help for him as we did for Holly Hedgehog when she hurt her leg?" Peony asked; she was becoming more worried as her partner slumped on the ground.

"I will ask Primrose Pigeon," Tessie Tui called from her perch in the tree above them. "She will know what to do." Tessie flew off to find her, calling as she went.

Primrose took one look at Pene's drawn face and knew they had to get him to shelter quickly. Dark clouds were now gathering in the west. It wouldn't help Pene if he got wet as well.

"I'm going to fetch a mat." Primrose advised them; "Can someone find some moss to lie on it?"

While Primrose pigeon flew to the school cave to fetch a woven flax mat for Pene to lie on, Sam and Silene rushed off to find some sphagnum moss to spread on the mat. Kupe and Ollie were in the school cave discussing the program for the carnival when Primrose arrived.

"Quick," Primrose called urgently. "Pene has been hit by a car and is injured. I need a mat for him to lie on."

"I will help you." Ollie offered as he and Kupe grabbed a mat to pull it outside.

Primrose and Ollie then grabbed a side of the mat with their claws and flew into the forest, with Kupe running close behind them. Sam and Silene arrived back with the moss as Primrose and Ollie appeared with the mat. The moss was quickly laid on the mat and Pene helped to lie on it. With a grateful sigh Pene snuggled down and laid his head on the moss.

"We should take him back to the cave." Ollie suggested, remembering the care that his father needed after he had been injured. "He needs to stay dry and warm untill he recovers."

But as everyone looked at Pene's ashen face they wondered if he would recover, for they could see he was in shock, a condition that can kill both animals and humans too.

"What about the carnival?" Peony asked pensively.

"That can wait untill he is safe." Ollie decided.

Carefully and slowly the possums, stoats and weasels lifted the mat and carried Pene to the school cave where Primrose pigeon and Tessie Tui were waiting.

"We need some more moss," Primrose ordered. "To protect the mat from any draughts that may come into the cave." The stoats and weasels rushed off to do her bidding. Soon there was a high wall built around the mat. Peony pukeko and Percy and Petunia possum positioned themselves around Pene again to keep him warm as he was shivering again.

The stoats and weasels joined Kalea and Keely to find some food for everyone who was staying for the vigil while Kupe and Kaori went to find Peony's brother, Pete Pukeko who rushed to Pene's side. For Pene had been a close friend of Pete's ever since they were young.

Normal school lessons were suspended for the day.

Tessie Tui allowed the children to read quietly from the library or go home. As it was now raining steadily outside nearly everyone elected to stay to read – and see how Pene recovered.

Pene's shivering eventually stopped and he fell into a deep sleep for the remainder of the morning. The kiwis and possums cuddled up in a dark corner near the library to cat-nap. They weren't going anywhere while Pene was so ill. They were encouraged when Pene woke briefly to say he felt a little better. It was nearly nightfall before Pene woke up properly wondering if they had anything for him to eat. By now the cave was crowded with both day and night animals, all waiting to see him.

"You will be ready for the carnival tomorrow!" Percy joked when he saw Pene was well enough to eat.

"He won't be ready till next week!" Peony retorted while Pene gave a wan smile.

Fortunately Pene had no broken bones, but he had been badly shaken after being tumbled on the road by the car. He would be much more careful when crossing the road in future. The accident also made him wonder whether they should move to a safer place where there were no roads nearby. Peony said she had an aunt in the next valley near the forest where there were large fields to fossick in. After the carnival was over he would suggest a visit.

The next day Pene was back on his feet but didn't stray from the cave, having frequent rests on his mat and watching the school lessons with interest. It had been some time since he had been to class.

The following morning Peony stirred wondering if Pene was awake yet to find he had left the cave. She looked up to see Tessie Tui smiling at her.

"I think our patient has recovered. You will find Pene down at the stream." With a big beam on her face Peony ran out to join her partner.

CHAPTER THREE

KEHI'S VISIT

Kehi Kiwi arrived at the junction at Lake Kaniere and gazed at the water before him. It had taken him some weeks to make the long journey here. He hoped Kupe or one of his followers was nearby as he was both hungry and tired from travelling all night. He was amazed when a voice in a nearby tree called him.

"Hello, are you Kehi Kiwi?"

Kehi looked up to see a large native pigeon beaming down at him."

"I am. Who are you?"

"I'm Primrose, one of the community members here. Kupe is expecting you. I will go and fetch him." Primrose then flew off towards Hans Bay, leaving Kehi to marvel at the sort of community he was coming to. The Kiwi Kingdom had been famous in the land for including other animals, but he hadn't expected to meet them so soon.

Kupe and Kalea were asleep when an urgent voice woke them.

"Kupe, wake up! Your visitor is here!"

Kupe and Kalea instantly awoke and bolted out of the burrow to find Primrose waiting for them.

"Kupe, Kehi has arrived. He is at the junction."

Kupe turned to Kalea. "Can you find some food for him?" She nodded before leaving to search for a meal.

Primrose flew off towards the junction with Kupe following swiftly on foot.

Tessie Tui saw Kupe and Kalea get up and went to find Kaori.

"Kaori wake up!" she called.

Kaori put his head out of his burrow to see who was calling.

"Kaori, Kupe's visitor is here! Kupe and Primrose are heading for the junction."

"Thanks Tessie." Kaori called. He briefly returned to the burrow to tell Keely before following Kupe to the junction.

When Kupe reached the junction, he found a large grey Great Spotted Kiwi, who was a similar size to him gazing at the lake. Kupe was surprised the kiwi was alone. The kiwi turned around at Kupe's approach. There was a brief moment as they sized each other up before smiles broke out. Kehi saw Kupe wore an amulet and wondered what it meant.

"Hello Kehi. Welcome to my kingdom."

"How big is this kingdom of yours?" Kehi wanted to know.

"The lake and all the forest you can see around it." Kupe replied. "We have communities at Okarito, Arthurs Pass and in the Paparoa ranges south of where you live as well."

Kehi nodded thoughtfully. He had never heard of these other places. This kingdom was more widespread than he thought.

"If something happened to you, the kingdom wouldn't end?" Kupe could see Kehi had both fear and sadness in his eyes.

"No." Kupe reassured him. "This kingdom is a way of life that our community has kept since Keoni's time. You can see my future?"

Kehi nodded miserably.

"I think we should let the future take care of itself!" Kupe said firmly before changing the subject, leaving Kehi to marvel at the courage of this Kiwi who was allowing fate to dictate his future.

"You must be tired and hungry?" Kehi nodded. "Kalea is getting a meal ready for you before you have a rest." He turned to lead Kehi to Hans Bay when Kaori came running to join them.

"This is Kaori, one of my supporters." Kupe introduced him with a big smile. His family supported Keoni in his kingdom. They are from the Alps, but he chooses to live here."

"You didn't bring any of your supporters?" Kaori asked. He was also puzzled that Kehi came alone.

"No," Kehi answered with a smile. "I wanted to see your kingdom for myself without any influence from my men."

Kupe grinned and nodded. "There are some things you have to do alone. You have come at the right time." Kaori changed the subject. "We have our carnival in a couple of days' time." Kehi looked at Kupe enquiringly.

"It will be a treat for you to remember when you go home." Kupe replied with a smile. "You will get to meet most of the animals in our community."

Kehi was glad of the meal of worms and the tunnel Kupe gave him to sleep in for his stay. There was fresh grass to lie on too. The welcome he had received had already made his long journey worthwhile.

The burrow was empty when Kehi awoke that evening. He went exploring and was confronted by the claw symbol in Kupe's tunnel. As he stood gazing at it, Kupe's voice made him jump.

"Keoni made that as a symbol of the kingdom. It's still very powerful today." Kehi could only nod his agreement. He was feeling very humble, an emotion he wasn't used to.

Would you like to see the school? Kupe asked. The night classes will be starting soon."

"What is a school?" Kehi was mystified.

"It's a place where animals (and people) go to learn things." Kupe replied as he led Kehi out of the tunnels.

"Didn't your parents teach you what you need to know?"

"Yes," Kupe replied. "I know that is kiwi tradition, but there is a whole world of things to learn about that tradition doesn't teach us."

Intrigued Kehi allowed himself to be led to the school cave.

There Kehi was mesmirised by the glow worms who were turning on their lights ready for the class. He looked around him at the pongees lining the wall and the ceiling, making the cave a "cosy" space. Woven flax mats were scattered over the floor. Kupe lead Kehi to the back of the cave and took a book off a Pongee shelf. Kehi was spellbound by the pictures of animals and flowers he had never seen before.

He also brought out a book about all the Kiwi species in New Zealand.

"This book is all about us!" Kupe said as he showed him all the different species. Next Kupe took out an atlas and showed Kehi a map of the New Zealand Islands.

"We are here." Kupe pointed to the lake on the map. "You live here." Kupe Showed Kehi the area above the Buller River."

"We are surrounded by water!" Kehi was shocked at the vast body of water around the Islands.

"Yes," Kupe agreed. This planet we live on is called the water planet."

A movement behind them made Kupe smile.

"Hello Ollie." He called. "Meet Kehi. Kehi, this is Ollie the night teacher and also the guardian of the kingdom."

Kehi turned to see a morepork owl glide into the cave and land next to them.

"Hello Kupe," Ollie greeted Kupe with affection. "Hello Kehi and welcome to our Kingdom." His greeting to Kehi was more formal.

"Hello Ollie." Kehi returned the greeting. "I'm interested to know what your role is as the guardian."

"When we are here, he is the master of ceremony for any events. While we are away he runs the community and makes sure the kingdom rules are kept." Kupe answered for him.

Kehi looked idly at the shelves but stopped when he saw The Kiwi Kingdom book. Kupe saw his gaze on the book and smiled.

"That book is the history and is the law of our kingdom that Keoni laid down. Only the leader is allowed to read it."

"How did you get these books and how are you able to read them?" Kehi wanted to know.

"A human called Emily came to live here during Keoni's reign. She made many of the books and left them behind when she left. Orion Owl was a close friend of Keoni's during his reign. He saw Emily teaching her children the human language and sat in on her classes. Orion learnt to read and write the language which he passed on to his family and the animals in the community. The owl family has been teaching the animals here the kingdom rules and the human language ever since."

"Have any of the other communities learnt about this?" Kehi asked amazed.

"Yes, Kupe replied with some satisfaction. "All the communities with our supporters now have schools which teach the human language and promote the kingdom rules along with the local community laws.

Kona kiwi, a southern brown kiwi is the leader of his group down Fiordland. He has become allied with the kingdom and has sent a member of his community to our school to learn the knowledge to take back and become part of the kingdom."

"But," Kehi was puzzled. "Aren't the southern Brown Kiwis a completely different species to us?"

"Yes." Kupe agreed." Southern Brown Kiwis were part of Keoni's kingdom and they still are in it today."

"What do we have to do to become allied with the kingdom?" Kehi was still suspicious

"You don't have to do anything." Kupe reassured him. "We have a few simple rules for the community to live by.

If your community agrees to them, you then become part of the kingdom. Are you interested in hearing about them?" he asked finally. Kehi nodded.

Respect and help all animals regarding of who or what they are.

You may not injure or kill any animal you meet in the kingdom.

Establish a school for your kiwis and other animals to learn to live in harmony together.

"Now I understand why you expelled Kakate instead of eliminating him."

"How did he settle back into your territory?" Kupe wanted to know

"He submitted to the local law." Kehi's reply was cryptic.

The day of the carnival arrived with a clear blue sky. It had been decided everyone to gather than at Hans Bay. All the night animals went over to the bay before dawn, to find a suitable place to rest untill the start of the carnival in the late afternoon. Kehi helped Kupe to dig out a temporary burrow that they squeezed into with Kalea and Kamaka.

"It's a bit cosy in here." Kehi complained good-naturedly

"At least we can't lose each other." Kupe quipped back.

There was much excitement as the eels opened the carnival with their races across the bay to the creek. Elijah and two of the guardians watched at the finish line to make sure there was no cheating or foul play as the contestants crossed the line. Ernie was happy to come second in his race.

The fantails impressed the crowd with their acrobatic twirls, loops and dives. Flora had to be content with third place but she was very proud that her daughter Freesia won first place in her competition.

The children's race was next, starting with a sprint across the picnic area; then a swim back along the shore to the stream. Peka Pukeko came first in the sprint while Slinky Stoat won the swim across the bay.

As the Adult kiwis and pukekos lined up for their race, a small bowl was placed next to each competitor. Kalea and Keely looked at each other puzzled, before Percy and Petunia Possum appeared at the opposite end of the field with a large bowl of worms each.

"You only pick up one worm at a time to place in your bowl. The one with the most worms wins. The first three get to eat them!" Percy instructed as he and Petunia poured their bowls of worms in a line.

"Get set Go!" by Ollie was lost in the stampede for the worms before they slivered to the safety of the nearby forest. Kaori won the event with five worms, which he kindly shared with Keely and Kalea.

The hedgehogs were split into two teams for a tug of war! A long flax rope was brought out for the two teams to pull on; a short length of flax was tied to the middle. Two stones were placed a metre apart at the middle. To the encouragement of the entire crowd, the two teams started to pull. Harry Hedgehog's team nearly had the centre of the rope over their rock when Harvey Hedgehog's team put in an extra strong effort to bring the centre of the rope back over their stone to win!

The Pigeons Tui's and Owls then competed in the bombing competition. Tessie Tui won the event by being the first to get her Cabbage tree berry into the small bowl in the bombing area.

The bats that had been waiting patiently in the trees surrounding the picnic area flew out and began to form a tunnel which swirled this way and that. The junior bats took turns to fly through the bat tunnel which became smaller and smaller untill Begonia Bat was declared the winner.

The stoats and weasels ran a relay race, using woven balls to pass to the next runner. The stoat's team won the competition by a "head."

Coloured ribbons had been wound round the upper branches of the trees surrounding the picnic area ready for the possums' tree climbing competition. Percy and Petunia were half way down after collecting their first ribbon when Orchid Owl who had been acting as a lookout gave a warning hoot. Everyone froze.

"Quickly everyone," Orchid called. "Hide or flee for humans are coming!" As she spoke the sound of a Ute with its lights on could be heard and seen coming along the bay.

The bats, pigeons, tuis and fantails rose and flew to safety. Everyone else ran quickly for cover in the forest surrounding the picnic area. They hid just in time as the Ute swept into the picnic area.

A large bright spot light was swept around the trees. Most animals ducked down and hid their eyes but Percy poked his head around a branch to see what was going on. He was instantly blinded by the light in his face.

Petunia quickly pulled Percy's head back behind the trunk. As she pulled Percy felt a sting in his ear, followed by the loud bang of a gun.

"OW!" Percy yelled. "Something has hurt my ear!"

"Hush!" Petunia implored him. "Keep still! They are trying to shoot you!"

Realising the danger he was in, Percy curled himself in behind the tree trunk as much as he could.

"What do we do if the humans come into the forest?" a terrified Kehi asked Kupe.

"We will all run for our lives!" Kupe replied with a grin. "We are having more excitement this evening than we were expecting."

Bruce had invited Aleck out to his bach for the weekend. After a couple of drinks they decided to go out spotlighting. Aleck swept the spot light under the tree where Percy and Petunia were now trapped. There was no sign of the possum.

"I'm sure I hit the possum." Aleck said to Bruce. "It must still be up the tree."

Getting out of the Ute Aleck started to walk towards the tree, his gun trained on the spot where he had shot at the possum. Behind them a vehicle could be heard racing down the road towards the picnic area. Frowning Aleck turned around to see who it could be. A van roared into the picnic area and screeched to a halt next to Bruce's Ute.

"STOP, Put down your rifle! This is the ranger." Aleck was commanded by the ranger with his microphone. Aleck noticed that two men in the van had rifles trained on both him and Bruce. Bruce and Aleck didn't know it, but the ranger just happened to be visiting his mate who lived on the Sunny Bight Road. As Lake Kaniere is a scenic reserve where shooting is forbidden, the sound of the gun shot had the ranger, his mate and his neighbour reaching for their guns as they came to see what was happening.

Very slowly Aleck put down his gun and put up his hands before the ranger came forward to take the gun.

"Shooting is prohibited here!" the ranger admonished Aleck. "What were you shooting at?"

"We're sorry ranger." Aleck apologised. "It was only a possum."

"Did you get it?" The ranger asked, "And, do you have a licence to hunt possums?" Aleck shook his head.

"Just as well then," The ranger continued as he made the gun safe and handed it to his mate before pulling out his notebook. "You have just lost your gun. Do you have any other guns with you?"

"I don't." Aleck was able to answer, wondering how his father was going to react when he found out his gun which was his pride and joy, was confiscated. After searching Bruce's Ute and confiscating his rifle as well, they were then free to leave. Very sheepishly and sedately they returned to Bruce's bach to sit out on the veranda and console them-selves with another drink.

Once the humans had left and Sunny Bight was quiet again Kupe led everyone out of the forest to the picnic area.

"Thank you Orchid, for the warning. Did anyone get hurt when the human used his gun?" Kupe asked with concern.

"Percy has a sore ear, but he is fine." Petunia reassured Kupe.

"Is everyone ready to go home?" Kupe asked.

"What about the possums' competition?" several voices asked.

"Ollie, will you start them please?" Kupe asked with a big grin as he and the audience sat down again to enjoy the final competition.

Percy contented himself with second place. His sore ear kept distracting him as he brushed it against the tree branches. The bullet wound healed to leave a small hole in Percy's ear which he wore as a badge of honour for the rest of his life.

Before Kehi departed for home he made an offer to Kupe.

"If humans try to destroy your community or anything should happen to you, Kalea and any of your supporters will be welcome to come and live with us."

235

Kehi took his time to return to his territory. He took a detour to Kane's community in the Alps and also called in on Kapali and Kalasia at the Three Sisters Mountain. He would love to bring it to his own community too, but would they accept it.

His answer came as he approached the bridge to cross the Buller River. Several kiwis from his community were waiting for him with big smiles, which he did not trust.

"Welcome back Kehi, how was your trip?" they asked. Kehi knew his life and that of his family depended on his reply.

"The Kingdom is a wonderful place, BUT it isn't for us. Kupe's mate Kalea may come to us when Kalani has finished with him. Where is He by the way?"

"He is impatiently waiting for your return and what are you going to do with her?" the kiwis wanted to know.

"She will have to be eliminated of course!"

As the kiwis parted to allow Kehi to lead them across the bridge they didn't see Keo who had quietly positioned himself nearby to witness the meeting. To his horror he realised that Kupe was now in danger from Kalani and Kalea was being invited into a trap, but what could he do? If he took on Kalani and lost, he wouldn't be able to help anyone. The only thing he could do was to wait here and try to divert Kalea if she came this way.

Shortly afterwards Kalani made his way across the bridge. As Keo watched Kalani's vengeful form pass by, he grimly began his long and anxious wait.

In his burrow Kehi cuddled his mate Kiyo and son Koro with relief. No kingdom was worth losing your life and your family for.

"How was your trip Dad?" Koro asked with excitement. "Did you meet any of the animals?"

"It was a wonderful trip, and I saw lots of the animals there. How have things been here?"

"It has been peaceful and we have missed you!" Kiyo replied with a smile as they turned their conversation to mundane matters.

Koro was disappointed Kehi didn't tell him a story of his travels, but both Kiyo and Kehi knew it wasn't yet safe. There would be plenty of time later when the listening ears became bored and left them in peace.

CHAPTER FOUR

THE AVALANCHE

The day of the annual school snow trip arrived with sunshine over the lake but dark clouds hung over the Alps. Slinky and Shimmy Stoat and Wisteria and Winkie Weasel followed Wendy Weasel to the school to join Kamaka and Ketara Kiwi who were playing Chasey with Pearl Pukeko and Hyacinth, Hebe and Hone hedgehog.

Flora Fantail herded her children Freesia, Foxglove, and Frangipani to a nearby tree where they twittered excitedly as this was their first trip away. Primrose Pigeon came with her children, Protea and Pahia who sat quietly near Freesia while waiting for their ride to the Alps. Petunia Possum brought her children Pinky and Peaches, who joined in the game of Chasey. She left them with strict instructions to obey the adults while on the snow trip.

Pete Pukeko, Ollie Owl and Kalea and Keely Kiwi gathered as Tommy and Tammy Tahr lead Tara and Timmy out of the forest. Wendy Weasel and Primrose pigeon organised the children to be ready for their journey, making sure they had brought everything.

"It is snowing up the tops." Tommy advised them, "So you definitely will need your woollens this trip."

"Did you hear that?" Hyacinth asked the other children. "It's snowing!"

There were smiles and beams all round at this news. It didn't take long to load everyone onto the saddles on the Tahr's backs. Kupe came along to wave them off. Little did he know that it would be the last time he would see his son.

As the tahr approached Arthurs Pass, the air became much cooler. Grey clouds hung low, hiding the mountains. The tahr had to pick carefully through the deep snow which carpeted the ground.

Gentle snowflakes floated down to settle on the group and everything around them. The children laughed and put out their paws and claws to feel the flakes as they fell. Kalea, Keely, Wendy and Flora pulled their woollens closer with big smiles. It was going to be nice soft snow for the children to play in.

The tahr took the group to Kane's community where they were reunited with old friends and some new ones. Kaori's nephew Kawaka was now old enough to come and could not wait to join in the games on the slopes.

Kane and his community came along to join in the activities. They showed the group where the safe slopes were. They had to be careful where they played as the new snow had made some slopes unstable.

After everyone had tired themselves out with rides down the slopes, having snowball fights and making snow burrows to play in, they all retreated back to the big cave where the Alpine and lake kiwis had first met for a well-earned feed.

While the adults talked and the children played, Kamaka and Ketara and Kawaka became restless and sneaked outside to play in the snow again. The light was fading in the evening sky as Kamaka Ketara and Kawaka played hide and seek amongst the rocks and the snow burrows they had made earlier.

When it was Kamaka and Ketara's turn to hide from Kawaka, Kamaka found a rock which overhung a steep slope below it.

"They won't think to look for me here!" Kamaka thought with a smile as he snuck down below the rock. When Kamaka crouched under the rock he received a shock. He was standing on a giant snow drift which was beginning to move under his feet! Frantically he tried to climb back up to solid ground but found himself being swept away as the avalanche gathered speed. As Kamaka began to tumble down the slope, he curled himself into a ball as tightly as he could. The sound of snow roared in his ears as it crashed down the slope with him.

When Kamaka finally stopped, it was pitch dark. He had no idea what way was up or down. Kamaka also found he could not move. He tried to call out for help, but his voice was very quiet, even to his own ears. *It is nice and cosy in here. I'll have a little nap while I'm waiting for everyone to find me.* Kamaka thought as he allowed himself to drift off to sleep.

On the slopes above him Kawaka had found Ketara and they were now calling him.

"KAMAKA, you can come out now!" Kawaka and Ketara called, but there was no answer. As they called they heard the avalanche. Kawaka looked over to the slope beyond the rock and frowned. He started to walk over to the rock, studying the snow as he walked, with Ketara following him.

"What are you looking at?" Ketara asked curiously.

"I'm looking at these footprints." Kawaka said. "I think Kamaka may be in trouble."

"What do you mean?" Ketara asked alarmed.

"I think Kamaka may be buried under the avalanche we just heard!" Kamaka replied as he reached the rock and saw the footprints disappear into the snow where the avalanche had swept the giant snow drift away. He called out to Kamaka, but still no answer.

"Come on," Kawaka said to Ketara. "We have to get some help."

In the cave the conversation paused as the roar of the avalanche could be heard outside. All the parents checked to see where their children were before continuing their conversation. Kalea and Keely and Kalei all started to look frantically for their children when they couldn't see them.

"Kamaka, are you there?" Kalea called.

"Ketara, where are you?" Keely called.

"Kawaka, come out NOW if you are hiding!" Kalei called, but there was no answer. They were about to go outside to search for them when a distressed Kawaka and Ketara came bursting into the cave, which stopped all conversation.

"Mum!" Kawaka wailed, "I think Kamaka may be under the avalanche!" His face crumpled as he tried not to cry.

"Why, what happened?" she asked, casting a quick look at Kalea's shocked face.

"We were playing Hide and Seek. I found Ketara but we can't find Kamaka. I think they are his footprints walking to where the avalanche has been." Kawaka said. His distress obvious.

Kawaka ran into his mother's big body for comfort.

"Can you show us where you think he is?" Kawaka's father Karua asked as he led the way out. Kawaka managed to nod as he left the comfort of his mother to join his father outside where darkness now reigned under the golden light of the moon.

After Kawaka had led the searchers to the rock, Karua, Kane and Wendy took a look over the edge while Ollie took off to swoop down over the slope to listen for any signs of life in the snow. They were all dismayed to see the massive pile of snow now covering the lower slope.

"If Kamaka has survived the fall, it will be difficult to dig him out." Ollie reported gloomily. "I didn't hear him trying to call out as I passed over the snow down there."

As they stood on the edge of the slope, they could hear the creaking sound of unstable snow.

"It's too dangerous to go down there now." Kane decided. "We will have to wait untill daylight to see what it is like then." There were sad nods of agreement as they realised that Kamaka probably wouldn't survive untill then, before turning and taking the bad news back to the cave.

As Kamaka began his struggle on the slopes, Kupe felt Kamaka's fear. He immediately stopped feeding and looked up towards the shadows cast by the moon in the forest. Knowing that Kamaka was in danger, Kupe turned and made his way to the water's edge where he kept a vigil. Ernie Eel saw Kupe's troubled face staring out over the water and came over to see him.

"Hello Kupe," Ernie called, "Are you alright?" At first Kupe didn't answer him, which troubled Ernie even more.

"KUPE," Ernie shouted, "What's wrong?"

"Kamaka's in danger and there is nothing I can do to help him!" Kupe cried in anguish.

Ernie immediately swam to find Danny Duck who was resting further down the bay.

"Danny, wake up!" Ernie called as he beached himself near his friend. Danny was immediately wide awake. Ernie didn't usually wake animals up at night, so it had to be serious.

"Kupe's over there on a vigil. He says that Kamaka's in danger!"

Danny immediately flew off to find Kaori, very noisily calling "Kaori where are you?"

This woke everyone else up too. Soon everyone who had stayed behind gathered with Kupe on the shore to keep him company.

Kamaka had no idea what time it was when he woke up, it felt very stuffy in here. He wanted some air. Kamaka tried to move and realised where he was. Then he thought he heard some footsteps. He gave a call, as loud as he could.

"Help, Can you hear me?"

The footsteps came nearer.

"HELP, Can you help me?" Kamaka managed to call louder.

To Kamaka's relief a voice answered him.

"I can hear you. What are you doing in there?"

"I was playing hide and seek under a rock when the snow gave way and sent me down here. Please help me. I can't move and I need some air!"

Teeny Tahr (Who was no longer tiny) was on his way to his home in the Deep South after visiting some friends, when he thought he heard an animal calling in the snow. He came over to the noise and was shocked to find that there was a little kiwi calling and he was in deep too!

Teeny started digging furiously. If the kiwi needed air, he didn't have much time to reach him before the air pocket ran out of air. After much digging, Teeny broke through to him. Kamaka took big gulps of freezing air which hurt his lungs to begin with, but it felt so good he didn't complain.

"Are you one of the local kiwis?" Teeny wanted to know.

"No. My group live at the lake." Kamaka replied. "We came on a snow trip (he looked around him and couldn't hear or see anyone) but they've all gone."

"Would you like to come on an adventure?" Teeny asked.

"Yes please." Kamaka liked adventures.

Teeny knelt down for Kamaka to climb onto his back. Kamaka hung on tightly to his long woolly coat as Teeny stood back up and continued on his way among the Alps.

At the lake there were several minutes when Kupe also felt short of air then started gasping, which alarmed everyone greatly. They were all relieved when he gave a sigh of relief and breathed normally again before announcing to the crowd.

"He's safe! Kamaka is safe. We can all get some rest now. Thank you for staying with me."

When daylight finally dawned, a weary group emerged from the cave to find a large deep hole had been dug in the snow at the bottom of the slope. Ollie Owl and Primrose Pigeon immediately flew down to examine the animal footprints they could see in the snow near the hole.

"These are Tahr tracks." Ollie called to Primrose.

"There are small kiwi prints here." Primrose called back. "Kamaka's alive!"

They flew back to give the good news to Kalea, who had been prepared for the fact that Kamaka would be lost in the snow forever.

"Kamaka has been rescued by a Tahr." Ollie advised her. We don't know where they are going, but at least we know he is alive."

Kalea nodded at the wisdom of Ollie's words, that she should be grateful that Kamaka was alive, but she could not help being forlorn. Kamaka was too young to know how to get home. Would they ever see him again and how would Kupe take it when they came home without his son?

When the group finally arrived home Kupe and the community was anxiously waiting for them.

"Where is Kamaka?" Kupe asked when he couldn't see him with the other children. Kalea's stricken face told him something extra had happened. He rushed over to her and cuddled her.

"I knew something had happened to him." He reassured her. Kupe's next words made her look at him in amazement. "I could feel Kamaka's fear and later in the night there were a few minutes when I had trouble breathing and was gasping for breath before I could breathe normally again. I knew then that he was okay. How come he didn't come home?

"Kamaka was caught in an avalanche." Ollie spoke for Kalea as she was still too upset. "It was too dangerous to search for him when it happened, so we had to wait till daylight when we found a Tahr had dug him out and taken Kamaka with him. It is just as well the Tahr came along because he was in too deep for us to dig him out."

"You don't know where the Tahr went?" Kupe asked hopefully.

"The tracks were heading south."

"We can only hope Kamaka is enjoying his new life, wherever it is leading him." Kupe tried to be philosophical before he led Kalea away to their burrow to grieve.

In the meantime Kamaka was having a wonderful time. As Teeny negotiated the ridge of the mountain top, the cloud had cleared to reveal a wonderland of peaks which were covered in white velvety snow in the moonlight. It was the first time he could see how vast the country was. The Tahr's long coat kept Kamaka warm during the long night when the temperature dropped below freezing.

By morning Teeny had reached the Alpine forest where they both searched for a meal before having a rest. The sun was still high in the sky when they moved on again.

Kamaka was happy to doze as Teeny continued his journey through the Alps. When Teeny stopped again to rest that evening Kamaka enjoyed the freedom to feed and explore the local area. In the early morning when Teeny was ready to move on again Kamaka was ready to be rocked to sleep again on his back.

As Teeny reached his home territory Kamaka was sorry the journey was over, but he was also excited to be starting a new adventure of his own and wondered what animals he would meet here.

After saying goodbye to Teeny Kamaka started exploring the local area to feed and find a suitable spot for a burrow. He didn't have long to find out. As Kamaka was examining the base of a large tree a voice behind him challenged him.

"Who are you and what are you doing here?"

Kamaka swung round to find a large male southern brown kiwi standing over him.

Kona, a southern brown kiwi and leader of the group in Fiordland heard someone moving around and feeding on his territory and wondered who was being so bold, for no-one in the local group would dare do it.

As he sneaked up on the intruder he was surprised to find a young grey Great Spotted Kiwi who was making itself at home. Given this young kiwi was a very long way from home Kona needed to find out how he got here.

"Hello." Kamaka smiled. "I'm Kamaka. I was visiting the Alps on a snow trip with my school friends. While we were there we were playing Hide and Seek, then the ground gave way and buried me in some snow. When Teeny the Tahr rescued me, my family and friends had gone so he brought me here on an adventure."

"Who is your father?" Kona wanted to know.

"He is Kupe."

"Is that Kupe the leader at Lake Kaniere?"

"Yes. Do you know him?'

"We have met." Kona smiled, remembering the confidence the young Kupe had when he met him. "You will be heading home now?"

"Don't you want me to visit your territory?" Kamaka asked suspiciously.

"I don't mind you visiting us," Kona replied in a mild tone, "but your parents will be worried about you."

"I can look after myself now!" Kamaka drew himself up assertively.

"I'm sure you can." Kona was amused now, but tried not to show it. "You are to attend our school while you are here." He had no intention of allowing Kamaka to roam around unsupervised.

"You have one?"

"Of course we do." Kona allowed himself a smile. "I will take you along this evening. Now, it's time we found you a spot to sleep." Kona decided to keep Kamaka on his territory so he could keep a good eye on him.

As Kamaka drifted off to sleep he had little idea of the challenges his new life was going to lead him.

CHAPTER FIVE

KAMAKA'S CHALLENGES

Kamaka woke with a start. *Where was he?* Then he remembered he was now on his new adventure. It was time to explore his new home. A fantail fluttered nearby, looking for insects.

"Hello Fantail," Kamaka said quietly. "I'm Kamaka."

"Are you talking to me?" the Fantail asked astonished. None of the local kiwis had spoken to her before. This one was quite different!

"Yes" Kamaka replied. "We have Fantails like you at home who are part of our community, along with all the other animals who live there."

"I'm Flossie." She introduced herself. "What other animals do you have?" Flossie wanted to know.

"We have Owls, Tuis, Pigeons, Pukekos, Possums, Stoats, Weasels, Hedgehogs, Ducks, Bats, Deer and Eels." Kamaka reeled them all off.

"You have Possums, Stoats and Weasels in your world?" she asked amazed.

"Yes, we are all good friends."

"What about your eggs and chicks?" Flossie asked, for in her world she and all the other birds had to be forever vigilant against having their eggs or young snatched for a meal.

"They aren't allowed to touch them. If an animal harms another, they are expelled from our territory."

"I wish we had a community like yours here." Flossie said wistfully.

"It should be like ours," Kamaka replied with a frown. "This area is allied with our kingdom. Animals are not supposed to harm each other and are supposed to respect and give each other help."

In the distance they could hear scuffling noises and cries as though someone was in battle. Kamaka looked at Flossie enquiringly.

"What is happening over there?" Flossie looked at Kamaka with sad eyes.

"Can you fight well?" she asked. Kamaka looked at her in horror.

"I have never had to fight before!"

"Watch your back!" Flossie warned him before fluttering back into the tree. The sound of footsteps heralded Kona's arrival.

"There you are! Are you ready?"

"I am." Kamaka replied as cheerfully as he could, but inwardly he was dreading his new "class". Under a giant tree covered in moss and lichen, was a group of southern brown kiwis of all different ages who were taking turns to fight each other. Kamaka looked at Kona with a frown. Kona saw Kamaka's look and smiled.

"I know it is Kingdom rules not to harm, but outside your kingdom some animals do harm us, so we teach our young to defend themselves."

Kamaka knew he could not argue with such logic. By now all eyes were on him and he knew he had to try to prove himself.

"This is Kamaka, the next leader of the Kiwi Kingdom." Kona introduced him. "He is here for a visit."

Kona thrust Kamaka into the middle of the group where an older male was waiting. Kamaka managed to get a leg up to defend himself before the blows rained on him. Kamaka earned their grudging admiration for not one word of complaint or pain did he utter during the bout as he silently absorbed the blows, before he managed to strike a blow back – into the male's eye, which quickly closed up so he could not see on that side. Kamaka then took advantage and gave a few blows to his body, as hard as he could. The male stepped back, admitting defeat. Kamaka also stepped back out of the group. He started to look around, listening for any water nearly. He wanted to soak his battered body.

"What are you looking for?" Kona asked, wondering if Kamaka was looking to escape.

"I want a swim. Do you have any lakes or streams nearby?"

"We have a waterfall." His opponent spoke up. "Do you want to see it?" Kamaka allowed himself to smile and nodded.

"We have one at home too!"

As they negotiated the thick undergrowth of ferns and fallen logs, Kamaka noticed that Kona was also bringing all the other kiwis along too. Kamaka could also hear the sound of rushing water nearby. Suddenly they emerged from a small opening in the forest to stand on a large rock where a wide stream swept over the cliff to plunge into a pool in the river below.

"Is it deep?" Kamaka asked.

246

"It's very deep!" the kiwi replied.

Before he could warn Kamaka about the eels, Kamaka launched into the air to land in the water next to the waterfall, to gasps from the assembled kiwis on the rock. Kona was silently cursing that he hadn't stopped this excursion to the waterfall. He knew that they would be lucky to see Kamaka again after this.

Under the water Kamaka was being soothed by the cool fluid as it penetrated his feathers. Then he noticed some familiar shapes swimming up from the deep dark pool below him. Kamaka turned and swam towards them, giving them a wave as he swam.

Eli the eel leader both heard and felt the splash as Kamaka plunged into the water. This usually meant an animal had fallen in and was desperately trying to get out again, giving them an opportunity for a snack. As Eli led his group to the surface, they were surprised to find a young grey kiwi swimming down to them and it appeared to be signalling to them! To Eli's astonishment this kiwi was happy to have the eels surround him and was gently stroking them as they came near. When the kiwi signalled he was returning to the surface, his new friends swam with him.

On the rock Kona and the southern kiwis were getting worried. Kamaka had been under the water a long time. Had the eels taken him? To their relief Kamaka broke the surface with a big grin, but he was surrounded by the eels. "It's lovely in here!' Kamaka called. "Aren't you coming in?"

"Watch out!" Kona called, "You have eels all around you."

"I know." Kamaka grinned. "I have made friends with them. This is Eli." Kamaka introduced him as he stroked his new friend's body.

"It's time you got out!" Kona called, but Eli had other ideas. It was rare for a land animal to be friendly to them.

"Would you like a ride?" Eli asked Kamaka.

"Yes please."

Kamaka felt Eli's strong firm body swim underneath for him to cling to. Kamaka barely had time to yell back to Kona "They are taking me for a ride." before he was swept down the river on the ride of his life.

Above the waterfall the young kiwis looked at Kona's grim face.

"Do you think we will see him again?" one asked hopefully. Kamaka was obviously someone special. To defeat the older male the way he did, then be able to swim and make friends with the eels!

"Maybe" Kona replied doubtfully. "He's off on another of his adventures. Now, it's time for your lessons!' Kona commanded them as he shepherded them back to their school.

Kamaka gasped as he was taken through some white water rapids. He could feel the power of the water as it tumbled over the rocks below. When they were back in calm water, Kamaka started to shiver, for he was soaking wet. Eli could feel him shaking and took Kamaka over to the bank.

"Thank you for the ride." Kamaka called out once he was safely ashore.

"We will see you again." Eli called back before leading his group back up the river.

Kamaka went searching for his next meal. All the activity had given him an appetite. He was also happy he was completely free again to roam and explore this new territory to meet new friends.

CHAPTER SIX

THE HEDGEHOGS ADVENTURE

Helena was grateful for Harry's comforting cuddle as they waved goodbye to her children Hyacinth Hebe and Hone with mixed feelings. They were sad that the children were leaving to start a new life in Hokitika, not knowing whether they would return to the lake for a visit; but Helena and Harry were also happy that they could now start the family they had patiently waited for.

Through the forest to Kaniere Delphinia Deer galloped as she took the young hedgehogs to their new home. She didn't know how long her family could stay either. Stan the Stag had heard of deer being taken from valleys nearby, never to return. They had learnt to avoid hunters who stalked them in the forest, but now there was a new threat, from the sky which was much harder to hide from.

As Delphinia reached the township, she slowed down to walk, keeping to the shelter of the pine forest. Suddenly she heard the sound of an animal bounding towards her. A large dog was charging at her!

Delphinia knew she couldn't run away so she faced the animal and rose up on her back legs to flail the dog with her front legs as it came near. The three hedgehogs hung on tight as Delphinia turned to protect herself, but when she reared up the hedgehogs were unable to stay on and quickly rolled up into balls as they slid off her back to tumble onto the soft floor of pine needles.

The dog didn't like how much bigger the deer suddenly became and it didn't want to tangle with those flying hooves either, so it quickly retreated. After the dog had gone Delphinia came over to the hedgehogs.

"Are you alright?" she called to them. "You are safe now."

"Yes" Hone replied as he and his sisters came out from hiding. "Go back to the forest." He urged her. "It isn't safe for you here. We will find our way from here."

"Are you sure?" Delphinia asked, though secretly she was relieved she wouldn't have to go any further into human territory.

"Yes, we are certain." Hyacinth and Hebe joined in firmly.

They too were happy to explore in Kaniere before they headed to Hokitika.

After Delphinia had disappeared back in to the darkness, Hyacinth had a snuffle around.

"There isn't much food around here." She complained in disappointment. Although she had fed before they left the lake, she was ready for a snack now.

"Come this way." Hone called to them. He had been exploring and had seen some street lights and houses. Helena had taught him that gardens and food was there too.

To the hedgehogs surprise and delight there was much more food in these gardens than at the lake. By sunrise the three hedgehogs were very happily tucked under some leaves in a garden compost heap. However their sleep was disturbed by Mr Marsh who came out later in the morning to turn over the compost heap with his gardening fork.

As he moved the leaves he spotted Hyacinth. With his hand Mr Marsh removed the rest of the leaves to find Hone and Hebe. Very carefully he picked them up and moved them under a bush in the flower bed.

Each night they found a different garden to dine in and a place to sleep during the day. During their stay in Kaniere they also met some of their cousins who showed them the best spots to eat and shelter.

One wet and windy morning they were taken to Mr Thomas's barn to shelter. Hone had a big grin on his face as he snuggled into the hay. A boat was parked near the door.

"What are you grinning at?" Hyacinth asked puzzled.

"This is the barn where Grandad and Nanna came to see some baby mice, and that is the boat that took them to live at Lake Kaniere!"

"Well, we will be staying out of the boat. I'm not ready to go back to the lake just yet!" she replied firmly.

"Nor me!" added Hebe.

"Of course not!" Hone replied, though he was missing his parents and the lake already. *Maybe I will find someone who would like to live out there* were his thoughts as he drifted off to sleep.

The night finally came when they reached the outskirts of Hokitika. Hone looked up at the tall buildings of the milk powder factory as they passed, knowing there wouldn't be any food or shelter for them there. He was happy to see rows and rows of houses and gardens as far as he could see. They wouldn't have to worry about food or shelter here.

"Where would you like to go?" Hone asked Hyacinth and Hebe. "Do you want to explore this street or do you want to find the park where Helga lives?

"Let's explore this street? Hyacinth replied. We need to find our way around before we look for anyone we know."

Every night Hyacinth Hebe and Hone would find a new street to explore and feed in, meeting new friends as they went; then one night Hyacinth explored a new garden. She thought Hebe and Hone had followed her, but they had lingered behind. When she realised she was completely alone, she became frightened and began to cry.

"What's the matter?" called a voice from the next bush.

Hyacinth looked over to see a male hedgehog peering at her with concern.

"I'm Hyacinth; I've lost my brother and sister."

"I'm Hiren." He introduced himself. Don't worry; I will help you find them. What garden do you live in?"

"I'm not sure, we are visiting."

"Where do you live?" Hiren was curious. "We hadn't heard of any hedgehogs visiting the town. Who are you visiting?" His father Hugo had become the leader of the Hokitika Hedgehogs and through his friends he knew nearly everything that was happening.

"We are just visiting the town. Our mother used to live here. Who is your father?"

"My father Hugo is the leader here."

Hyacinth suddenly felt very nervous. She tried not to look alarmed, but Hiren sensed something was wrong.

"What's the matter?" Hiren asked suspiciously.

"Nothing!" she replied, but thought better of it. "No, everything's wrong!" Hyacinth drew herself up as much as her small frame would allow.

"Do you know about Helena?" she asked boldly, staring Hiren in the eye. Hiren frowned at this question.

"I've heard about her, but she died."

"No, she didn't." Hyacinth replied with much satisfaction, "She is my mother. Hugo is our father, which makes you our brother!"

Hiren was both disappointed and alarmed at this news. He was disappointed she was his sister. He liked her spirit and would have liked her for his mate. He was also alarmed to hear he had a brother, who would be competition for him to be the next leader.

"Is Helena here too?" Hiren asked.

No, she didn't want to put herself in danger, besides she is happy where she is."

"Of course you won't say where you live?"

"No." Hyacinth replied firmly. In the distance they could hear Hone's voice calling her.

"Hyacinth, where are you?"

"I'm here." She called back. "I have to go." She added to Hiren and fled towards Hone's voice as fast as her legs would carry her.

Hiren didn't try to follow her. He had so much to think about. *So the rumours were true! Helena had survived after all and he had a brother who was older than him. Would he challenge for the leadership?* To Hugo's disappointment, He had only one son, all the other children had been girls. Behind him a voice broke Hiren's thoughts.

"Why are you looking so glum and who is that female you were talking to?"

Hiren had to smile. It was his sister Heni. He had not realised she was in the garden too.

"That was Hyacinth, our half-sister. I've just found out we have two older sisters and a brother."

"How can that be?" Heni was puzzled. She hadn't heard about Helena and Hugo.

"Before dad mated with mum, he also mated with a female called Helena. When she rejected him for someone else, dad pushed her into the river." Hiren nodded at Heni's shocked expression. "Everyone thought she had died, but she hadn't. Our two sisters and brother are visiting. It looks like I may have to fight for the leadership now."

"Have you met him?" Heni asked

"Not yet." Hiren admitted.

252

"Come on!" Heni urged him. "It's time we met our new family members." And set off after Hyacinth.

"There you are!" Hone exclaimed as Hyacinth returned to them. "I thought we had lost you."

"I've just been having a chat to our brother Hiren!" Hyacinth replied breathlessly. "He didn't know that mum had survived. Apparently Hugo is the leader here now. Hiren wanted to know where we live, but of course I didn't tell him."

"We don't want to cause any trouble here." Hone frowned. "I think we may have to find somewhere quiet for a while." Hone turned to lead Hebe and Hyacinth out of the town but was stopped by the arrival of Heni and Hiren.

"Hello." Heni greeted them with a smile. "I'm Heni and this is Hiren. He tells me you are our brother and sisters! Where are you heading off to?"

"Hello Heni." Hyacinth smiled back. "I'm Hyacinth and this is Hebe and Hone our brother. We were just looking for somewhere quiet to feed and shelter."

"We aren't here to cause any trouble." Hone added with a worried frown. Hiren knew then he could make friends with his new brother.

"Allow us to show you the best feeding and shelter spots in town." Hiren offered with a big grin as he led the way with Hone while Heni followed with Hyacinth and Hebe.

This meeting began a new chapter in their lives where they were welcomed into a new family and made Hokitika their new home.

CHAPTER SEVEN

THE DEER FARM

Dianella Deer became frightened as the blades of the helicopter whirred noisily overhead. She cuddled up to Dianthia as the machine hovered closer and closer over the forest canopy. When she felt the down draught from the blades blowing down on her, she panicked.

"I can't stay here!" Dianella tried to say, her words drowned in the noise of the helicopter.

Breaking free, Dianella began to race down the slopes of the mountain to escape from the monster above them. Dianthia felt she had no choice but to follow and somehow try to protect her.

"There's one, no, there's two!" Alistair said as he pointed to the fleeing deer below them. With a smile the pilot began his pursuit.

As they raced down into the open woodland at the Styx River Dianthia became worried the monster was keeping up with them. Suddenly they felt a large net drop onto them. Dianella and Dianthia tumbled over as they found themselves hopelessly tangled in the net.

Alistair ducked out of the helicopter as it landed and grabbed two long straps which were attached to the net. He looped them together before dragging the straps to attach them to the helicopter before climbing back inside.

Dianella and Dianthia found themselves being lifted high into the air above the treetops and carried across the countryside. Roads, rivers, fields, homes and another lake (Lake Mahinapua) passed beneath them till they were set down again in a wide open field. Through the net Dianella could see it was surrounded by a high fence. The fence was too high to jump over to escape! A human called Fred was waiting in the field came over to help Alistair to unhook the straps from the helicopter.

"What are they going to do with us?" Dianella asked. She trembled with fright as the helicopter pilot revved the helicopter's engine for take-off.

"I don't know," Dianthia replied, "but I think we are on a deer place. I can see other deer through the fence."

After the helicopter clattered away into the sky, Alistair and Fred came over to the net, carefully untangling and unwrapping the net from the deer. Dianella started to struggle, tangling herself further.

"Keep still," Dianthia told her, "they are setting us free."

Dianella didn't like the humans to be so near to her. She snorted at them but did as she was told. When Dianella and Dianthia were finally free from the net they quickly rose and bounded towards the fence where the other deer were watching.

"Where are you from and what is this place?" Dianthia asked.

"We are from the forest to the south." One answered. "This is a deer farm."

Dianella knew what a farm was – a place where humans kept animals. She had studied the animals on the farm on the southern shore of Lake Kaniere. She also knew that she and Dianthia would be here for the rest of their lives.

"The human will come to see if you are carrying any young. If not, you will be put in with the stag."

"What if we don't breed?" Dianthia asked with concern.

"You will be sent away."

Dianella and Dianthia grew to hate their life on the farm. There was no shelter in the fields from sun rain or wind, with only grass to eat. After they had been examined, Dianella and Dianthia were placed in the field with the stag.

"What is your name?" Dianella asked after they had introduced themselves.

"What do you mean by a name?" the stag asked confused.

"Didn't your parents give you a name?" Dianella asked.

"I never met my father and I was taken away from my mother as soon as I could eat grass." The stag replied sadly.

"You have spent all of your life on this farm?" Dianella was amazed. She couldn't imagine a whole life lived within fences.

"Yes," the stag replied. "Where have you been before you came here?"

"Can you see those mountains over there?" The stag followed her gaze to the lake hills. "All of our lives we have run free, in the forests there. There is plenty of shade and shelter from the sun wind or rain when it comes. Dianella noticed there was a gate from this field to a field next to a house. The fence around that field was very low – easy to jump over!

"Has anyone ever escaped from here?" Dianella asked.

255

"No." The stag replied. "Where would we go?"

Dianella felt sad to hear his words, that he had no idea of how to live life outside of the fence.

"It is a completely different world out there," Dianella replied "and we miss it."

She vowed silently that if she was given the chance to escape, she would take it. Weeks became months after they were placed in the paddock with the other females who were carrying young.

When their time came, the other mothers gathered around to protect and encourage them as Dianella and Dianthia delivered their young. Dianella named her daughter Dahlia while Dianthia named her son Dusty. Dianthia knew he wouldn't have a long life, like his cousin who was still free.

The day came when Dusty was taken to a separate field.

"Mum!" Dusty cried as he was herded away.

They are taking you to a field with other young males. You will be alright." Dianthia tried to reassure him.

She knew she would be placed with the stag again soon. So both Dianella and Dianthia were shocked late one afternoon when Dianthia was moved to a separate field.

"Take care of your-self" Dianthia nuzzled Dianella as it became obvious that they were being separated.

This field held several older mothers or females who had failed to breed. She knew that they would be taken away soon. Dianthia studied her surroundings. This field was next to a sand dune. The noise and smell of the sea was much closer here. She moved closer to the fence which was sitting high on the steep bank of the sand dune. She was more sheltered here from both the sun and the wind. As she gazed, Dianthia noticed there was a slight gap in the fence above them, however Fred the farmer was still watching her, so Dianthia sat herself down on the ground and pretended to doze. Eventually Fred left the field to return to the farmhouse. Once Fred was out of sight Dianthia went over to the fence and started to dig. Shortly there was a big pile of sand on the paddock.

"What are you doing?" the other females wanted to know as they crowded around to see what Dianthia was doing.

"I'm getting out of here!" was Dianthia's curt reply.

"We can't get out of here, it's too high!" one scoffed.

Dianthia didn't answer, but kept digging. As she brought more of the bank down, the gap in the fence widened untill she could squeeze her body through the gap. With a final push and grunt she scrambled up the steep bank to freedom. Two other hinds quickly followed her. A third hind became stuck at the fence.

"Help, I can't get through!" she called to Dianthia.

"Go back and dig some more sand out." Dianthia instructed here.

The hind did as she was told and soon she too was enjoying her freedom. The night was still young as Dianthia led her new friends along the beach.

"To stay safe, we will have to travel all night and find shelter to rest in the day."

"Where will we shelter?" asked Dorothea who had been brought up on the farm.

"There are big forests to the south where there is plenty of food and shelter and few humans go there."

Dulcie and Dehlia were happy to regain their freedom after being trapped and flown to the farm as Dianthia had done. By the time the first rays of light had crept over the horizon Dianthia and her new friends were safely hidden in the forest near Fergusons Bush.

"If we hear any helicopters, we must keep still; otherwise they will see us moving and capture us again." Dianthia warned them.

"It is so hard to keep still when those noisy and windy machines are so close to us." Dulcie protested.

"Yes, but it is the only way we will survive." Dianthia reminded her.

In their new upside down life of resting in the day and travelling at night, Dianthia and her friends steadily made their way down the island, untill they came to an area where there were no roads.

"I think we are safe now." Dianthia said as they began their new life in Fiordland.

CHAPTER EIGHT

REVENGE

Kupe Kiwi woke with a start and looked about him. He was relieved to see he was safe in his burrow with Kalea, for Kupe had just been visited in a nightmare by the one who would end his life.

Kalea stirred at his movement then settled back to sleep again as Kupe gazed at his mate with a loving smile. His heart ached to know their life together would soon end. He worried too for the future of the new life that she carried. *Would her new father accept and protect her?* Kupe fretted. Kalea sensed Kupe's anxiety and soon was wide awake. His smile could not disguise the grief he was feeling.

"What is it?" Kalea asked. "Have you had one of your dreams? Kupe could only nod miserably.

"We will go for a walk." Kalea said with resolve, leading the way out of the burrow. They both blinked at the bright daylight from the sun directly overhead. In the distance a dozer could be heard clearing land for the new housing that would soon be built in the bay.

Flora the fantail saw them leave the burrow and head towards the lake. She was about to ask what they were doing up at this hour, but the grim looks on the kiwis' faces stopped her. Flora went to find Tessie Tui who woke Kaori and Keely with an alarm call at the entrance of their burrow.

"What is it Tessie?" Keely yawned.

"Come quickly, Kupe and Kalea are up at their sleep time. Something is wrong!"

"Where are they?" Keely was now fully awake.

"They've gone to the bay." Tessie replied before flying off to warn everyone.

The sunlight danced and shimmered on the waters of the bay. Kupe had never seen it look as beautiful as he quietly stood and cuddled Kalea by the shore. The flutter of wings in the trees above and the rustle of bushes in the forest behind them told Kupe and Kalea that they were no longer alone. Ernie's anxious face also surfaced near the shore after being warned by a young eel that had spotted Kupe and Kalea by the shore.

"I'm sorry we've disturbed everyone....." Kupe began.

"We all know it's serious, so please tell us!" Kaori interrupted him.

258

Kupe looked around at everyone before he began, stopping at the concerned eyes of Ollie Owl.

"You've had one of your dreams haven't you?" Ollie asked quietly. Kupe nodded his agreement.

"It is time for the kiwi community to leave again." Kupe began. "Humans are coming to live here. They are bringing animals that will make it impossible for us to stay here."

"What about the Kingdom?" Ernie asked.

"I expect that the animals that stay will continue to live by the kingdom rules." Kupe smiled.

"What about the book?" Ollie asked.

"One copy will stay here. The other one will be sent to safely." Kupe said as he clutched the amulet around his neck. "Tomorrow evening we will have a meeting of all the animals before we depart." Kupe declared; "Now it's time we had some more rest." With Kalea he turned to lead the kiwis back to their burrows.

"Where will we go?" Kalea asked when they were snuggled up in their burrow. "I don't fancy returning to Punakaiki."

"We won't be." Kupe replied. "I'm sending you and the book up to the north." Kalea was silent for a moment as she digested this news.

"Why aren't you coming?"

"Do you remember Kakate the kiwi I expelled from The Three Sisters Mountain?"

"Yes I do, why?"

"His son is coming to take his revenge.

"Where will you go?" Kalea sobbed.

"I'm staying here!" Kupe was firm.

"I'm staying with you!" Kalea was equally firm.

"No." Kupe sighed as he gave her a hug and patted her tummy. "I need you to be safe – to keep our daughter safe. Kehi Kiwi knew about Kalani's plan when he came to visit me and tried to warn me, though I wasn't ready to listen." Kupe added with a wry smile. "Kehi offered to take care of you and any of my supporters should anything happen to me or the kingdom."

The next evening there was a carnival atmosphere as everyone gathered in the bay. The bats flew in to roost in the tree branches. The ducks were already waiting on the gravel shore to welcome everyone as the Kiwis Pukekos Hedgehogs Possums Stoats and Weasel families arrived. The children splashed in the shallows with the younger eels in a game of tag. Stan the Stag and Delphinia arrived and were quickly in demand for rides from the children in the forest nearby. The Pigeons Tuis Fantails and Owls all gathered in the branches with the bats to chat before joining the other animals on the gravel.

Elijah Erigon and Ernie wriggled onto the gravel to Kupe.

"We will miss you." Ernie said simply.

"We will miss you too." Kupe replied, watching his friend slip back into the water. Kupe then bent down to Elijah and whispered in his ear.

"I won't say goodbye because I'm staying."

"Just like your father did!" Kupe nodded with a little smile.

"Who's coming for you?"

"Kalani" Kupe whispered. Elijah nodded and wriggled over to Percy Possum.

"When it's all over, bring Kalani to us!" was his cryptic message before Elijah returned to the depths of the lake.

Percy looked at Elijah's retreating form with astonishment and worry. *What did he mean? - When it's over; and who was Kalani?* As Percy watched his friend greeting and chatting to everyone, a distant memory slowly came to his mind. *Was Kalani the son coming for revenge?* The more he thought about it, Percy knew he was right. He spoke to Ollie Owl and Primrose Pigeon.

"We have to keep a lookout for Kupe. He's in danger!" They both nodded.

Keely was sitting with Kalea while Kaori was with Kupe.

"Why are you looking so stricken? You have the warm northern beaches to look forward to! You remind me of Mum when she lost Dad!" Kalea managed a smile *If only you knew!* She thought.

"We've had such a wonderful time here; I can't bear to leave." Kalea managed to say. "Are you looking forward to the Alps?" Kalea asked, trying to change the subject.

"Yes" Keely's eyes were shining. "I've been there in summer and winter and loved it both times. Kaori is looking forward to seeing his family again too."

"Are you sure this is the right thing to do?" Kaori asked Kupe.

"Yes" Kupe replied. "The humans will be here all the time, so will their animals. It's for the best."

Kaori nodded his agreement, but he was feeling miserable. He had never expected to leave here, but Keely was keen to try life in the Alps.

"We could always come back for a holiday." Kaori commented.

"Be very careful if you do." Kupe advised him.

Too soon the time came to say their goodbyes. Kaori and Keely led a group south to the Styx River and the Browning Pass. Another group was going with them, on their way to Okarito. A group was also heading north to The Three Sisters Mountain.

Delphinia followed Kupe Kalea Ollie and Percy to the school cave. The Kiwi Kingdom Books were brought out to Kupe. He lifted his amulet over his head and placed it into the old book. Percy then carefully placed the new book into the woven saddle on Delphinia's back. Kupe and Kalea gave them a hug before mounting Delphinia. Kupe looked at the mound where his father lay. *I will be joining you soon.* He thought.

Delphinia strode steadily through the forest to the Arahura River. When they reached the river bank they dismounted and had a long hug before they parted.

"Take care, my love." Kalea managed to say. She was glad there was no moon so he couldn't see the pain she felt or the tears she was waiting to shed. She didn't look back as Delphinia crossed the river to head north.

Kupe quietly searched for a feed as he made his way back to the lake. He thought he hadn't been seen, but he was wrong. Orchid had silently been following Delphinia on her journey.

When she saw Kupe separate from Kalea, Orchid flew back with the news.

"Ollie, Kupe is coming back. He has sent Kalea away on her own!"

Ollie was worried to hear this news. Percy was right. It could only mean trouble was coming their way. He flew to find Percy.

"Percy, Kupe is coming back, look out for him!"

Orchid wasn't the only animal to spot Kupe. Kalani was about to cross the Arahura River when he saw a deer appear on the south bank. To his astonishment he saw two kiwis on the deer's back. He knew instinctively it had to be Kupe. He waited untill the deer had crossed the river with Kalea before striking out after Kupe.

As Kupe moved through the forest, he felt someone was following him. When he looked around no-one was to be seen. However the feeling of being followed remained strong. Kupe had almost reached the school cave when he felt someone jump onto his back, a claw slashed across his neck as he went down. Kupe struggled to remove the weight but failed as he tried to catch his breath. As he lost consciousness he had the grim satisfaction of knowing his friends were here to help.

Both Percy and Ollie were screaming Kupe's name as they clawed at Kalani to pull him off. Orchid flew to find Tessie Tui, but it was too late. Kupe's spirit had left him. When Kalani was held securely with some twine, Ollie wondered what they were going to do with him. Percy read his thoughts.

"Elijah knew this would happen. Last night he told me that when it's all over, to bring Kalani to them."

Kalani saw all the animals look at him with pity and for the first time he became afraid.

"Who's Elijah?" he asked. No one answered.

By dawn the mound where Keanu lay had been made into a larger one, with Kupe now lying with his father. Kalani was dragged to the shore of the lake, where Percy slapped the water as hard as he could. Kalani saw an eel raise its head near the shore. Shortly afterwards the water became a seething mass of grey bodies as the eels came to claim him.

As Kalea rode during that long night, Kupe's spirit came to her.

"It's all over." Kupe said. "I'm with Dad and Keoni now." She drew comfort that he was watching over her on her long journey to an uncertain future.

CHAPTER NINE

NEW LIFE AT THREE SISTERS MOUNTAIN

The Paparoa Ranges now lay to the south as Kalea Kiwi and Delphinia Deer came to a deep wide river with sheer cliffs down to the water. This had to be the Buller River that they had to cross. They followed the river in the dense forest untill Delphinia spotted a bridge.

"It's time for a rest." Kalea decided.

Delphinia was happy to let Kalea off for a break as it would soon be daylight and she was ready for a feed too. There was no rush to cross the river now that they were here, for they needed to see when it was safe to cross. They watched as a truck negotiated the bridge, its lights lit up the bridge and forest. As Kalea dismounted from Delphinia, a rustle in the bushes startled her.

"Who is there?" Kalea called softly.

A dark grey kiwi emerged and twinkled at her. "I'm Keo. Where might you be going on that large beast?" Kalea couldn't help smiling back.

"I'm Kalea from Kaniere. I was Kupe's mate."

"What happened to him?"

"Kalani killed him." She said simply.

"You mean Kakate's son?"

"Yes." Keo shook his head at this news.

"They were a bad bunch. I suppose this is the end of the Kingdom?"

"No" Kalea replied. "I'm carrying Kupe's child and The Kingdom Book is with me. Some time ago Kupe met Kehi the leader of the northern kiwis." Kalea looked across the river as she spoke. "He promised to look after the family and the kingdom if anything happened to Kupe."

Keo shook his head again at this news.

"I'm glad I stopped you. I saw the kiwis meet Kehi when he came back. They would destroy the book if they could. You and your child aren't safe with them either. "

Kalea was shocked at this news, her mind in turmoil at the lucky escape she just had.

"I will go to the Three Sisters Mountain. I will be safe there."

"I will show you the way." Keo offered.

Kalea called to Delphinia who was feeding nearby to tell her of the change of plan.

"Are you able to travel some more?" Kalea asked hopefully. She just wanted this long journey to be over now.

"If it means you will be safe, of course I can."

Delphinia was also relieved they were heading south as she knelt down for Kalea and Keo to climb on. As they turned away from the river they didn't see a lone kiwi that had spotted them from the northern bank. Quietly and stealthily he crossed the bridge and followed them.

Kalasia and Kapali were preparing for sleep when a neighbour came rushing in.

"Kapali, Keo is riding in on a deer. He has a female with him!" Kalasia ran out with Kapali and could hardly believe her eyes.

"Kalea, what brings you here? Where is Kupe?" She also noticed Kalea was pregnant, ready to deliver her egg at any time.

Now that she was safe, Kalea allowed her grief to show, tears welling in her eyes. Kalasia rushed to give her a cuddle and sat her down. Gradually Kalea told them of Kupe's dream and how he had disbanded the community and sent her up north for safety. Kalasia looked at Kapali and he nodded.

"Kalea, you are to stay with us. We will welcome the others when they come." Kalea sighed with relief. Keo then came forward.

"I will head back, in case anyone else tries to cross the river and send them here."

"Can I help?" said a voice behind him. Everyone turned round to see a male kiwi with a look of concern on his face. "I'm Koro, Kehi's son. When dad got back from his visit to Kupe, he knew that Kalea would be in danger if she came to us, but he had no way to let her know, so he sent me to the river to make sure she didn't cross. I saw Kalea on the deer and knew it had to be her. I followed her here to make sure she was going to safety."

"Thank you Koro." Kalea smiled. She could see by the earnest look on his face he was being genuine.

"We need to find out what has happened and what Kalani is doing now." Kapali said with a worried frown. He went outside to the cabbage tree where Pippi Pigeon was feeding on some berries.

"Pippi" Kapali called, "You have relatives at Lake Kaniere don't you?"

"Yes" Pippi replied. "Has something happened at the lake?"

"Yes. Kalea Kiwi has come and told us that Kupe has been killed by Kalani Kiwi. We need to know what happened and where Kalani Kiwi is now."

Pippi immediately launched into the air towards the coast. As Pippi flew south, she took with her the news of Kupe's death. When Kanoa heard the news, he dared to hope he would see Kalea again. It didn't matter that she was his step sister, he would always love her. Kamoku had tried in vain to mate him with other females, but failed. When Pippi returned, Kalasia and Kapali were relieved to hear that Kalani was no longer a threat to the kingdom.

"The lake is a busy place." Pippi told them. "Animals are coming from all over the land to say goodbye to him."

"When Kalea has hatched her egg, I will go." Kalasia decided.

"I will go and see Kaori." Kapali decided, but that evening Kane, Kaori and Keely surprised them by their arrival.

"We were going to go to the lake, but we heard Kalea had gone north and guessed she was with you."

Keely would stay with Kalasia and Kalea while Kane, Kaori and Kapali set out for the lake. They would fetch Kedar and Keka if they hadn't already arrived. In the excitement of meeting, they didn't realise that Kalea had disappeared. When Kalasia went looking for her, she found Kalea asleep with a new white egg tucked snugly beneath her. After Kapali Kane and Kaori set off on Delphinia, (They had Left Koro to protect their mates), Kalasia and Keely took turns to sit on the egg while Kalea fed and rested. Early one evening Kalea heard tapping on the egg. She swiftly rose in time to see a tiny bill emerge through the gap it had made. Kalea called to Keely and Kalasia.

"Come quickly, she is here!" As they gathered around, the chick emerged from her shell. Kalea's daughter had her fair colour, but her father's eyes shone at her audience.

"What will you call her?" Keely and Kalasia asked.

"She will be Kohana."

CHAPTER TEN

KAMOKU'S VISIT

Kohana Kiwi squealed with delight as she was sprayed by sea water from the blowholes. Kalea, Keely, Kalasia and Koro smiled as they watched her explore the pancake rocks. They were at Punakaiki, on their way to Lake Kaniere. Keo Kiwi was in charge at The Three Sisters Mountain while they were away. Charmaine and Charlotte Chamois were waiting patiently in the thick bush nearby then Kalea heard her name being called.

"Kalea, is that you?" Kanoa Kiwi hardly noticed the other three adult kiwis standing with her.

She turned around to find Kanoa hurrying towards her and gave him a smile.

She is still the same. He thought as he smiled back.

"I'm sorry to hear about Kupe. What brings you here?"

"Kupe sent me away for safety before he was killed. I've been staying with Kalasia untill Kohana was born and able to travel. We are heading back for the farewell. I have Keely and Koro with me. Koro is from the north."

She gave Koro a gentle smile as she introduced him. It was too early to commit to a new relationship, but she knew that it would come. Kanoa saw her smile and knew his last opportunity with her had already gone.

"I would like to come with you. Is there room for me?" Kanoa asked turning to look at Charmaine and Charlotte who were hovering nearby in the bushes. Kalea nodded.

"I will just tell dad where I'm going. I won't be long." Kanoa said as he sped off towards the hills behind the rocks.

There had been much shouting and threats from Kamoku after Kanoa returned from his last trip to the lake. Kanoa had listened patiently as his father ranted at his disobedience.

"Tell me dad," Kanoa cut in. "Did you do everything that your dad told you?'

This question made Kamoku stop and smile.

"You take after me after all!" There had been a new respect for Kanoa from his father after that. Kamoku knew then that Kanoa would tread his own path despite any intervention on his part.

"Dad, where are you?" Kanoa called urgently.

"What is the matter?" Kamoku asked, hearing the urgency in Kanoa's tone.

"I've just seen Kalea. I'm going down to the lake with them. Do you want to come?"

"Why would I want to come? "Kamoku asked irritably. He didn't want anything to do with a kingdom he didn't believe in.

"Kupe is family! You should at least pay your respects."

Kamoku shook his head. Kanoa gave him a look of disgust and turned to leave.

"Wait, I will come!"

Quickly Kanoa led him back to the pancake rocks where Kamoku received his first taste of the power of the kingdom. Kalea saw with surprise Kamoku's familiar frame following Kanoa, who had a big beam on his face.

"Is there room for dad too?" Kanoa asked.

"I'm sure we can find space for him." Kalea replied as she turned towards the chamois.

"Charlotte, Charmaine," she called. "We are ready to leave now."

Kamoku jumped as the two chamois emerged from the dense bushes and knelt down on the ground. Keely Kalasia Kalea and Kohana jumped on charlotte while Koro and Kanoa jumped onto Charmaine.

"Come on dad!" Kanoa called as they waited for him to mount.

Gingerly Kamoku climbed on, and clung on tightly to Charmaine's fur.

"Are these animals part of the kingdom?" Kamoku asked as the chamois steadily moved through the Paparoa range towards the Grey valley.

"Yes," Keely replied. "Kupe made friends with them on his trip up north.

As Charlotte and Charmaine journeyed south, the animals at the bay were becoming anxious. Two Youths, Ricky and Arthur had come to live at the lake. Every day they would wander the forest at Hans Bay to explore. One evening as the light was fading they found the entrance to the school cave.

"Look," said Arthur. "There's a cave. Shall we have a look?"

"It's getting dark," Ricky replied as he gave the mound a kick, moving some of the soil covering Kupe. "Let's come back tomorrow."

Tessie Tui and Ollie Owl watched from a nearby tree with alarm.

"What will we do if they damage or take the books?" Tessie asked.

"It would be a terrible loss." Ollie replied "but it won't stop the classes. We have enough knowledge to carry on without them. What worries me is that they have disturbed Kupe and Keanu's resting place. We need to find somewhere they won't be disturbed."

To Tessie and Ollie's relief steady rain set in the next day, with no sign of the boys to be seen.

"I will see if Wendy Weasel can make some baskets." Tessie offered as they watched the rain wash away more of the disturbed mound.

"That's a good idea." Ollie replied. "We only have to find a safe place for them."

As night fell Ollie flew down to the bay and sat on the log. He was so deep in thought wondering where the safest place would be, he barely noticed the splash of an eel at the edge of the water.

"Hello Ollie, what's the matter?"

"Hello Ernie. I'm worried about Keanu and Kupe. Humans have disturbed their resting place. I'm trying to find a safe place for them."

"I will talk to Elijah." Ernie replied and promptly disappeared into the darkness of the lake.

Kamoku was deeply humbled by his visit to the kingdom. As the chamois strode through the forest near Lake Kaniere a pigeon greeted them.

Keely! Kalea! Kanoa! You are back! I must tell everyone!" Keely smiled at Kalea as the pigeon sped off.

"There is no chance of us sneaking in. Primrose will see to that!"

When the chamois stopped in a small clearing, waiting for them was a large group of kiwis. Some of them were brown, a completely different species to them, Kamoku noticed. As he looked around he saw a stag and his hind waiting in the background along with a number of tahr. With the kiwis stood families of Pukekos, Stoats, Weasels, Possums and Hedgehogs. In the trees around them numbers of Fantails, Tuis, Pigeons and Owls sat, chattering to each other and to the animals below. One owl stood with the kiwis.

Carefully the chamois sat down to let the kiwis off before joining the deer and tahr. Keely and Kalasia quickly joined Kaori and Kapali who were waiting with Kane, Kedar and Keka. Kohana was overwhelmed by all the animals that were here and huddled by her mother. Koro, Kanoa and Kamoku remained by Kalea's side. Ollie Owl introduced the visitors as everyone lined up to speak to her, which took some time. Kamoku was struck by the friendship between all the animals and the friendliness they showed towards him as a stranger.

When all the introductions were complete Ollie signalled to Stan the stag and Delphinia Deer who came forward to kneel by the cave entrance. Kane Kapali Keka and Kedar came forward to drag two baskets from the cave. Percy Possum and Sam Stoat came forward to tie the baskets to the deer with long woven ropes. Gently and carefully they stood up and lead the procession to the shore of Hans Bay.

As everyone found a place to sit, Kamoku was startled to hear clicking followed by a black cloud of bats that descended from Mt Tuhua to join the birds in the surrounding trees. Kamoku noticed some eels' heads bobbing in the bay but was distracted by the ducks flying towards them in formation, to land on the shore and join the crowd.

Kane Kapali Keka and Kedar then came forward to pick up the woven ropes with their bills and dragged them to the water's edge. As they dropped the ropes the water became a sea of grey as all the lake eels came to the lakeside. Kamoku was alarmed to see two huge eels wriggle out of the water towards Kalea who stepped forward towards them.

"Hello Elijah and Erigon." Kalea greeted the eels. "We leave Kupe and Keanu in your care now."

"We will take good care of them." Erigon reassured her. "In our sanctuary they will never be disturbed again."

As Elijah and Erigon returned to the water, the guardians of the lake came forward and took the ropes into their mouths to pull the baskets into the water. They were then surrounded by the lake eels on their journey to the safety of the eels' sanctuary.

Before the baskets submerged a grey feather escaped from Kupe's basket to be lifted high on the breeze towards the islands in the bay. Kohana stunned everyone by running forward and calling out. "Daddy!"

What Kohana could see was Kupe's spirit. Even though she had never seen her father, she knew it was him! Kupe's spirit was soaring in the sky, playing with the feather, batting and flicking and kicking it with his claws untill the feather and his spirit descended into the forest on the island.

Kamoku saw her follow the feather's flight towards the island and wondered whether Kupe's spirit was here. When Kalea heard Kohana call to her father, she knew Kupe had returned and drew comfort from his presence.

Afterwards everyone returned to the school cave where Kanoa showed Kamoku the library.

"You mean you can understand and read human language?" Kamoku asked with amazement. Kanoa nodded.

"Their books show us a completely different world of plants, animals and places and help us understand our world better too." Kanoa held up a book about kiwis as he spoke. "This book is about us." Looking at Kamoku's astonished face. "Yes," Kanoa added. "We are protected now."

"So that is why we aren't hunted anymore."

All of the children had gathered on the reading mats to chat and play games. At first Kohana clung shyly to Kalea but the twins, Hoya and Hini Hedgehog who were only a couple of weeks older than Kohana persuaded her to join them. On the long ride down to the lake Keely had told Kohana of the wonderful time she had playing with her friends at the lake, and now to her delight it was happening for her.

Kanoa saw the tenderness between Kalea and Koro when they spoke to each other and sighed. Koana Kiwi, one of the alpine kiwis that had come back for the farewell heard his sigh.

"Why are you so glum?" Koana asked. "Your sister will be well looked after by Koro."

Kanoa turned to look at the vibrant female who was demanding his attention and despite himself was drawn to her.

"Probably, because I'm jealous!" Kanoa admitted sheepishly.

"Do you have snow at home?" Koana wanted to know

"Hardly ever, in fact I can't remember the last time we had any." Kanoa grinned back at her.

Kamoku saw the banter between Kanoa and Koana and realised his wish for Kanoa to find a mate would happen at last. Despite being happy with Kalea's mother Kalama, Kamoku had recently been feeling old and tired at how life had turned out. Losing his first mate Keteri to another male and the death of his first son (Kamoku) in a fight had been a bitter blow to him.

He was happy Kanoa would finally settle and maybe produce a family to carry on the leadership in their area. He smiled to himself, and to think he nearly didn't come!

Outside the cave, the deer tahr and chamois were getting restless. Delphinia deer put her head in the cave and called to Ollie owl to come out to them.

"Ollie, we are heading up the mountain. It is more secure there. Send someone when you want us."

"Thank you, all of you for your help. Have a good rest now." Ollie responded. As he watched Delphinia lead the way up the slopes he wondered how long it would be before they too would have to leave the kingdom.

As Delphinia the deer hind led the way up Mt Tuhua she warned the Chamois and Tahr not to eat anything except grass or leaves on the trees. Humans had been dropping poison in the area and if a noisy aircraft flew low over the forest, to find a big tree to hide under and not keep running. She had lost two sisters who had been caught and taken to a deer farm. The tahr nodded. They had seen deer chased and caught in nets to be flown away and never seen again.

Before dawn Protea Pigeon flew up to the mountain. The visitors would be ready to go home later that day. The deer tahr and chamois rested and dosed during the day before making their way back to the cave early in the evening.

Kamoku and Kanoa took Koana kiwi back to Punakaiki on Charlotte Chamois, while Kapali and Kalasia took Kalea Kohana and Koro back to Three Sisters Mountain on Charmaine. Kohana was tearful at leaving her new friends, but Kalea reassured her she would see them again one day and she would make some new ones at home.

Keely and Kaori Kiwi took an extra passenger when they returned to Arthurs Pass. Keely's sister Keilana was visiting the Alps. Now that Keona and Keio were busy with a new family, she wanted to get to know her sister better and visit new places.

When Keka Kiwi who came with Kedar and his children Kahil and Kohia, were ready to return to Okarito, Stan the stag and Delphinia deer offered them a lift, for they were on their way to Fiordland. It wasn't safe for them to live near the lake any longer. They would seek a new life down south, in the safety of Fiordland.

CHAPTER ELEVEN

THE QUEST

Amy sighed as she looked at the pages of "Homes for Sale" on her computer. She listened as the house timbers creaked in the southerly gale that swept in from Cook Strait to buffet her home on the hillside and to the rain as it pelted on the window pane behind the thick drapes.

Terry her husband was late home from work again. Both of them were so busy with their jobs – Terry worked long hours at the bank and she worked shifts as a nurse at the hospital. They didn't have time for the life they had hoped for.

Amy glanced up at her favourite painting which had been handed down from her great- great grandmother Alice. A white timber house was nestled in Fir trees; Alice played Chasey on the lawn with her brother Tom. Their father Jimmy sat smiling on the veranda, a large pram was parked next to him with their baby sister Carrie, their dog Toby laid at Jimmy's feet. Amy wished they could find somewhere like it for themselves. As Amy clicked on the next page she gasped, for there in front of her was the house. It was listed for sale!

Terry's voice made her jump. She had been so engrossed by the house she hadn't heard him come in.

"What's up?" Terry asked as he leaned over to see the screen.

Amy turned to him with shining eyes.

"It's my great grandmother's house. It's up for sale! How would you like to move there? You would be able to write the book you always wanted."

Stunned, Terry was silent as he looked at the house on the screen. A small frown crept into his face. He had abandoned his ambition to write once he had started on the corporate ladder at the bank.

Amy saw the frown and knew he wouldn't be joining her in her new life, for she knew with all her being that she had to buy this house!

"Don't worry," she reassured him, "I know it's a shock. Maybe we could buy it as a holiday home?"

"I don't think so." Terry's frown deepened. "I would be looking for a villa in the sun; somewhere like the Seychelles or the Mediterranean." Amy nodded realising just how far apart they had grown.

"How was work today?" Amy asked as she closed down the computer. Her house would wait till tomorrow. Terry brightened at the change of subject.

"I have some news too, though it's not official yet." He couldn't contain his excitement. "The manager is looking for someone to transfer to head office in Auckland. He asked me to think about it. What do you think? You could get a job at one of the Auckland Hospitals." Terry added hopefully. Amy hesitated for a moment before replying with a bright smile.

"That's wonderful news. You will do well up there."

Terry was immediately serious.

"You aren't coming?"

"No." Amy shook her head sadly. "I've just realised we want completely different things from our lives. I've had enough of a career that comes first in my life. With my shifts and your long hours at the office, we hardly see each other anymore." Amy took a deep breath before continuing. "At some point I want to have children. I don't want to be a working mother whose children are brought up by someone else or have to leave them for long hours in day care."

"So it's over for us." Terry said flatly before turning to walk back out of the door and out of her life.

Three months later Amy eased her car into the long drive to her new home; the furniture removal van followed behind her. She couldn't help smiling as she felt a sense of coming home. All the trials of the separation of their relationship; of selling the Wellington house; securing a new job that now awaited her at Greymouth hospital and the buying of her new home were now behind her.

Safely tucked into the boot of the car was an old chest Amy had found while cleaning out the attic at the Wellington house. In the chest was a journal her great-great grandmother Alice had written of her life.

Amy was fascinated to read about the family's early years living in a tent on the gold fields and out at Lake Kaniere. The lessons they had in a cave which had glow worms and an owl who would fly in to sit and watch their activities; the wonderful picture books their mother Emily had made and left in the cave after their father had his accident and lost his leg when a tree fell on him.

Her happy memories of the day when they moved into the family home, where they would climb the trees in the orchard for fruit for their mother Emily, who made preserves from the fruit at the end of summer. They also helped their father Jimmy in the vegetable garden. There was a daily hunt to find and collect the eggs from the chicken run and spent long hours playing in the hay in the barn and having rides on Hector the horse.

A favourite pastime was to climb the fir trees behind the house to look at the bushland around them, and the Hokitika River as it swiftly flowed to the sea. Her happiest time though was helping her father to look after her little sister Carrie while their mother was at work as a tutor.

As Alice grew older the responsibilities of running the family home – cleaning washing and cooking was placed on her shoulders to help her mother as she had more pupils to teach.

A trip into town for shopping was a treat she looked forward to along with the dances at the hall that were put on each week, where she met her husband Joe who worked on the family farm out at Kokatahi. Long days helping with the farm animals, tending the vegetable garden, running the home and caring for her own family left Alice no time to think about the heritage left behind in the cave. Picnics under the shade of the willows at Nesses' Creek or baking a batch of biscuits and cakes on the range before a visit to neighbours for afternoon tea on the weekend were now the highlight of her week.

Each night Amy would read pages from Alice's diary, marvelling at the busy life she had led, but her mind kept returning to the stories of Alice's early years. After she had read about the cave and the books there, she knew she now had a quest – to find the books that Emily had left behind; but where to start?

As Amy wondered about the missing books, she received a call from her neighbour Claire who lived on Kaniere Road. Claire was a widow who had two girls, Linda and Megan to care for. Claire worked at the local rest home while the girls were at school.

"Hi Amy, are you off on the weekend?" Claire asked.

"Yes, where are we going?" Amy replied. She was getting used to being included on outings that Claire was organising. So far they had been on a trip to Lake Mahinapua for a picnic; a visit to the turquoise waters of the Hokitika Gorge for a walk across the swing bridge and a barbecue down by the riverside.

I'm taking the girls out to the family bach at Lake Kaniere for the weekend. Would you like to come?"

Amy realised this was her chance to begin her quest.

"I would love to!"

When Amy came home from work on Friday afternoon it was pouring with rain. Some board games were added to her overnight bag just in case their weekend was spent indoors.

Out at the lake low cloud obscured Mount Tahua which lay behind their bach. All the bushland was soaked and the tree fern fronds hung low under the weight of the rain. As Amy splashed through the puddles of the path from the carport to the bach in her gumboots and umbrella she couldn't help smiling. She hadn't done this since she was a child.

While Amy pulled out the board games for the girls which they fell upon with glee, Claire prepared the sandwiches to toast in the waffle iron over the fire which Amy had lit. Amy also had another surprise for the girls in her bag – some marshmallows which were toasted over the hot coals of the fire. As Amy helped the girls to toast the marshmallows a knock came at the door. It was Brett from the neighbouring bach.

"Hi Claire, I saw your light on and came to see how you all are."

"Come in." Claire beamed at him. "This is Amy my neighbour."

Amy looked around at the tall stranger whose cheery grin seemed to lighten the room.

"Hello," Amy greeted him with a smile. "Do you like toasted marshmallows?"

"I will try anything once!" Brett replied as he settled himself down on the floor by the girls.

"Here, try this!" Megan offered him the marshmallow on her stick.

"Yum! Are there any more?" Brett asked.

Amy passed him a marshmallow on a stick to toast.

"Would you like a spin in the boat?" Brett asked as he toasted his marshmallow. "It is supposed to clear up tomorrow."

"Yes Please!" Linda and Megan chorused.

"We would love to!" Claire added for her and Amy. Amy nodded her agreement.

Several hours and a game of Monopoly later everyone retired to their beds. Although Amy slept well at home, she felt this was her best sleep since her marriage ended. *It must be the country air!*

When Amy woke Claire and the girls were still sound asleep, so she left them a note.

I've gone for a walk, will be back for breakfast.

Although the sky was still overcast, the cloud had lifted to reveal the bush clad slopes of Mount Tuhua nearby. Down the hill the lake was inviting her to explore there too, but Emily's legacy was still waiting to be found. Amy turned towards Mount Tuhua, wondering where to start her search.

As she walked up the road Amy heard footsteps behind her.

"You are up early." Brett called as he came up to meet her.

"Yes." Amy smiled. "I'm usually up early for work. I must still be on work time. Are there any caves around here?" she added.

"Are you feeling adventurous or is there a special reason?" Brett asked curiously.

"My great grandmother lived out here many years ago when she was young. The family lived in a tent but she and her brother had lessons in a cave. She talked about an owl that used to visit as they had their lessons. Their mother made some books which were left behind when their father had an accident...."

"You think they may still be here?"

Amy nodded, her eyes shining.

"Ever since I read her journal I've had a strong feeling they are here, waiting to be found."

Brett looked at the bushland in front of them thoughtfully. He had been coming here since he was a child so he thought he knew it all well, but he obviously had missed this cave. It must be well hidden. There was only one place it could be. *My walk this morning is going to be more interesting than I thought.*

"Come on in." Brett invited Amy into the forest.

As Brett led Amy through the bush she fell under its spell. Long tendrils of moss trailed from the tree branches; lichen covered a fallen log like a silver blanket. Ferns sprouted up a moss covered tree trunk, forming an aerial garden. Then she spotted some tiny toadstools, they were a brilliant blue.

"Oh, what are these? They are beautiful!"

"They are Hochstetter toadstools. They are nice aren't they?"

"I feel like I'm in fairyland!"

A fantail was chatting furiously at them. Amy and Brett didn't know it but Flora the fantail was asking them who they were and what they were doing here. She was alarmed that these humans seemed to be heading towards the school cave where a class was being held. The clearing could be seen nearby. Flora flew off to the cave.

"Quickly hide everyone!" Flora called out as she flew into the cave. Her own daughters Freesia, Fox Glove and Frangipani were among the pupils. "Humans are coming."

Tessie Tui lead all the birds out of the cave, to shelter in the surrounding trees, while Pearl and Peka Pukeko raced out of the cave with the stoats and weasels following close behind.

The stoats and weasels joined the birds in the trees while the pukekos ran to the nearby stream to shelter amongst the ferns.

Both Brett and Amy heard Flora's alarm call and saw the flurry of activity as birds and animals emerged from the cliff face which was covered in bushes ferns and vines. Brett looked at Amy with a smile.

"I think we may have found your cave."

Meanwhile Tessie Tui asked Flora Fantail to keep an eye on the children while she went to wake Ollie Owl.

As Brett and Amy crossed the clearing to examine the cliff, she could feel the eyes of the animals upon her. She looked up and was astonished to see the variety of birds and animals all clustered together, peering down anxiously at them. They were all silent. Amy realised then that she also had a community of animals to consider in her quest.

"Amy! I've found it." Brett called out to her.

Amy joined Brett at the entrance of the cave and was amazed at what she saw. Inside, the cave had been turned into a room. Pongees lined the walls and the ceiling. Woven mats covered the floor, several books lay open on the mats. In the dim light at the back of the cave shelves held a number of books.

Carefully Amy and Brett entered the cave. She loved the pictures of animals in the reading books Emily had made for her children. They moved to the library at the back of the room. Beautifully bound books caught her eye. Amy pulled one out to look at and was stunned by the colour and detail of the scenes from Emily's visit to Africa.

"Look at this." Amy couldn't contain her excitement.

"You realise it is worth a small fortune?" Brett asked her.

"I would NEVER sell them!" Amy replied firmly, "They are my family heirloom." She started to pull out the remaining bound books from the shelves. Brett nodded his agreement.

Amy and Brett were so engrossed with the books they didn't hear the arrival of Ollie Owl and Percy Possum. The sound of scratching from behind alerted them that they were no longer alone. Amy and Brett turned round to be confronted by the steely gaze of a Morepork Owl and a fierce looking possum. The Owl was using chalk to write something on a slate with his claw.

"Take it over to them." Ollie instructed Percy when he had finished.

Percy picked up the slate & chalk and laid them in front of Amy and Brett before retreating next to Ollie. Very clearly on the slate were written the following words.

Who are you?

What are you doing with our books?

Amy picked up the slate, rubbed out the questions and wrote her reply.

I am Amy. Emily my great grandmother left these books here. I have come to collect them.

Amy put the slate and chalk back down on the floor for the possum to collect. When Amy saw the alarmed and despondent faces of the animals as they read her words, she held her hand for the slate and added another sentence.

I will make a copy of the books for you to keep.

"Get out the chest." Ollie ordered Percy.

Amy was amazed when the possum started to drag an old chest out from a corner of the cave and started to stack the books on the floor into it.

"They are giving us the books!" Amy cried in delight.

Amy and Brett gathered the bound books and added them to the chest. They looked at the other books on the shelves and came across The Kiwi Kingdom Book. Brett was about to open it when Percy's growl stopped him. Brett quickly put the book down on the floor. Percy bounded over to pick up the book before retreating back to Ollie.

"We should let them copy it too." Ollie instructed Percy

"Are you sure?" Percy asked. Ollie nodded and added the book to the others in the chest.

Before Amy and Brett left the cave with the now heavy chest she wrote on the slate.

We will take good care of them.

After Amy and Brett left the cave and disappeared into the forest, all the animals descended from the trees to the cave where Ollie and Percy were waiting for them.

"That was Amy, the great granddaughter of Emily." Ollie told them. "She has taken the books that Emily left us but she is going to copy them so we can have the books too."

"We are getting our books back?"

"Yes."

Back at the bach there was much excitement from the girls who gathered around Amy and Brett when they appeared with the chest.

"What have you got there?" Claire asked as she paused from cooking the eggs and bacon for breakfast.

"It's a long lost family heirloom!" Amy replied with delight. Claire stared at Amy with amazement at this news.

"Where did you find it?" Claire wanted to know.

"In a cave; my great grandmother Emily lived out here many years ago and left the chest behind when her husband had an accident. It has been here ever since waiting to be found."

"How did you know it was here?" Linda wanted to know.

"Emily's daughter Alice wrote a journal of her life which I found when I was clearing out the attic in the Wellington house. She mentioned the lessons she and her brother had in the cave here and the beautiful books her mother had made. I knew I had to try to find them.

I was lucky (Amy smiled up at Brett as she spoke) that Brett happened to be out for his walk and knew where to look, otherwise I would still be out there looking."

"Can we have a look at them?" Megan a keen bookworm asked.

"After breakfast you can." Claire insisted as she served up the breakfast. This was usually a leisurely meal, but this morning it was bolted down in a hurry as Amy, Brett and the girls wanted to explore the contents of the chest.

As Claire cleared up the breakfast dishes there was many comments from the other room such as "Oh, look at this!" or "Isn't that beautiful?"

Heavy showers of rain now beat upon the roof, but Brett was oblivious to them as he was drawn into the world of The Kiwi Kingdom.

CHAPTER TWELVE

NEW BEGINNINGS

Delphinia Deer grazed in the remote wooded valley in Fiordland. Stan, Dianthia, Dorothea, Dulcie and Dehlia were nearby. She still could not believe that Dianthia had managed to escape the deer farm and bring her new friends with her. Then a voice called to her.

"Delphinia, is that you?"

Delphinia looked up to find a vision of Kupe Kiwi looking at her. She moved closer to Stan who had also heard Kamaka's call, but kept grazing.

"Stan, is that Kamaka?" Delphinia spoke quietly."

"It probably is," Stan replied, "but keep eating. Our life in the Kingdom is finished now." Slowly he led the deer away from Kamaka.

Reluctantly Delphinia did as she was told, but she was disappointed she would not hear of Kamaka's adventures since they last saw him before the snow trip. Kamaka was also disappointed. He had been sure he recognised some of the deer he had just seen.

As Kamaka strode through the forest towards Hans Bay he became excited at meeting everyone again. His adventure had lasted four long but happy years as he explored the forests of Fiordland, meeting and making friends with many new animals. Kamaka had become famous as the friendly grey Kiwi, but now he was an adult and ready to find a mate.

As he came to the open space at the bay, Kamaka noticed a big change. The long grass where he had played and hid was now short and smooth as a lawn. There was no-where to hide here now. As he looked around in the moonlight he noticed there were more buildings here too, some had lights on – had humans come to live here? Kamaka began to wonder how many changes he would find when he got home. He didn't have long to find out.

A new road cut through the forest towards Mount Tahua and he could see some new homes built in the bush. As Kamaka walked through the forest he had the feeling he was being stalked! Kamaka turned around to find a large ginger cat stealthily creeping towards him! Rather than fleeing, Kamaka turned and charged at the cat, which tried to put up a fight, but Kamaka's claws soon put him to flight back to his owners' home.

As Kamaka came to his parents burrow, the forest seemed too quiet. Where was everyone? They would usually be out feeding by now. He slipped down into the familiar tunnels, but they were empty too.

Kamaka checked down by the stream, even the Pukekos were gone from their home in the bulrushes. There was no sign of the day birds in their nests either. Kamaka decided to put out a call.

MUM, DAD, WHERE ARE YOU?

Amy and Brett heard his call and wondered what kind of bird it was. They were now married with two children, Lucy and Michael, and were out at the lake for the weekend. Ollie Owl also heard his call from the new school in the bat's cave. He asked Orchid to watch the pupils while they continued with their reading and flew down to find out who was here.

"Who's calling for Mum and Dad?" Ollie called as he flew over the bushland.

"It's me." Kamaka answered him. "Is that you Ollie?"

Ollie flew down to find a vision of Kupe waiting for him.

"Kamaka?" Ollie asked tentatively.

"Of course, who else would I be?" Kamaka smiled back.

"You look just like your father, but he is..." Ollie broke off his words.

"But he is what?" Kamaka asked, now becoming worried, "What has happened, where is everybody?"

Ollie gave a little sigh.

"There is no easy way to tell you, but your father died some time ago. He and your grandfather are now resting peacefully in the eels' sanctuary at the bottom of the lake."

"What happened? Did he get sick? Why are they in the lake and where has everyone gone?"

"No, He didn't get sick. I'm afraid your father was killed. After your father expelled a bad leader called Kakate from the kingdom, his son Kalani came to get his revenge. Some humans came to the cave and disturbed your father's grave, so the eels gave your father a place where he will never be disturbed again. Before your father died he sent everyone away because he knew humans were coming to live here. He also knew that Kalani was coming for him."

"Where is Kalani?" Kamaka's face was grim.

"The eels took him."

"Where is Mum?"

"She is living up at Three Sisters Mountain now. You have a sister called Kohana and your mother has a new mate from the far north called Koro. He is the leader Kehi's son."

"Is the far north in the kingdom now?" Kamaka wanted to know.

"No." Ollie replied. "The kiwis up there are hostile to the kingdom. Kehi was lucky to survive when he got home. He sent Koro to make sure that your mother stayed safe when Kupe sent her north for safety."

"Is there anyone left here now?"

"Come and see them." Ollie smiled as he turned to lead Kamaka up Mount Tahua. "We have moved the school up the hill to the bats' cave. The humans don't come near that part of the mountain."

After a long hard climb, Ollie led Kamaka down some pongee steps into a dark space. Out of the corner of his eye he saw some lights. The glow worms had moved here too. In a deep corner of the cave a new room of pongees had been built. He could see Pinky and Peaches Possum, but who were the two hedgehogs? Where were Hebe Hyacinth and Hone?

"Come and meet Hiki and Hoya Hedgehog, they are Holly and Harvey's children." Ollie led Kamaka down to the school room. Reading Kamaka's thoughts Ollie added "Hebe Hyacinth and Hone have gone to Hokitika to live."

"I noticed the Pukekos had gone from the creek. Where are they now?

"They left when Kupe disbanded the community." Ollie replied sadly.

"They went to Kokatahi to live but it was too dangerous to stay there as a farmer started to shoot the Pukekos, so they have moved back to the other side of the lake, away from the humans.

The Ducks, Fantails, Pigeons, Tuis, Possums, Stoats and Weasels are still here, you will see them in the morning, but the deer have gone. Dianella and Dianthia were caught and taken to a deer farm. Stan the stag and Delphinia have gone down to Fiordland."

Kamaka was disappointed to hear this news. He had been hoping for a ride up to Three Sisters Mountain. He also knew the deer he saw in Fiordland had been Stan, Delphinia and Dianthia. Kamaka then noticed there were mostly new books in the library.

"What happened to our old books? Kamaka asked sadly. He had loved all the beautiful pictures they held from faraway places.

"They've been renewed." Ollie replied with a big smile. "Emily's great Grand-daughter Amy came to visit and collected her books. She made a copy and gave them to us. She has also given us some other new books. Would you like to see them?"

Ollie led Kamaka over to the library. The Kiwi Kingdom Book was displayed prominently on a shelf. Kamaka ignored The Kiwi Kingdom Book and started looking at the new books Amy had left them. Kamaka did not know it, but he had just been tested. He was not to be the next leader of the kingdom after all. It seemed they had another long wait for the future.

After meeting everyone and revisiting all his old favourite places, Kamaka set out for his new home. He didn't really mind the long walk. He had more time to enjoy the places he passed through on the way.

As Kamaka was leaving another visitor was sneaking in, but this visitor was here to stay. Through the Browning Pass he had come. Skirting the farm on the southern shore he saw a trail that led to Sunny Bight and hoped that people would not come to live here.

He stood on the gnarled roots of an old tree to look up the lake, its branches reached out over the water. Mount Tuhua's dome was shrouded in cloud. The islands hid Hans Bay from view. He would love to return to the bay, but knew it was too dangerous to go there now. A footstep behind him made him swing round.

"Kaori!" a familiar voice exclaimed, "What are you doing here, where is Keely?"

Kaori had to smile. Peony and Pene Pukeko and their daughter Pearl were here.

"I came home." Kaori said simply. "Keely is staying in the Alps for now. She may come for a visit when the snow comes. Are you enjoying living on this side of the lake?"

"Yes," Pene smiled. "We tried living with our relatives on farmland in Kokatahi, but the farmer brought his gun out and started to shoot us, so we came back here."

"We will see you later." Pene said as they parted. They were pleased they weren't alone in making their home on this side of the lake. Kaori was also happy he wasn't completely alone here.

Slowly and steadily Kaori made his way up Conical Hill, exploring the slopes as he climbed, finding plenty of old burrows to shelter in.

They were cramped by his standards, but could easily be made more comfortable. With a happy sigh Kaori settled into his new home. Here he had a view of the whole lake and the place where his best friend now rested. He was even happier when he woke in the evening to explore the western side of the mountain to enjoy his first sunset and wished Keely was here to enjoy it with him. As Kaori fed that night some of the bats from the school cave flew over and spotted him.

Kaori, is that you? What are you doing up here?"

Kaori knew his quiet life was now over.

"I've come back to live here."

"Is Keely with you?"

"No. She may come later. She is still enjoying the Alps."

"We will see you later." The bats promised as they flew on towards the lights in Woodstock and Rimu.

In the next few days Ollie Owl, Tessie Tui, Flora Fantail and Primrose Pigeon all came to try to persuade Kaori to return to Mount Tahua.

"I may come for a visit, but I'm staying here." Kaori was firm. "I'm happy here." They all promised to visit regularly now that they knew he was here.

Kaori was enjoying the pre-dawn light down by the shore one morning, when Ernie called out to him.

"Kaori, we heard you were back. How long are you staying?"

"I'm here to stay. I hated it in the Alps."

"Welcome home!" Ernie said before disappearing to tell the other eels.

One evening Kaori descended from the hill, on his way to see Peony and Pete Pukeko. To his joy, Keely was there and she had brought Ketara and Keilana and their mates with her.

"Is it snowing in the Alps?" Kaori asked, thinking it had come early.

"No," Keely replied with a big smile. "We missed you!"

"How long are you staying?" he asked, expecting her to return in the spring.

"We are staying for good." Keely replied. "Ketara has come back because she missed the lake and Keilana wanted to spend some time here too. I like the Alps, but my home is with you."

Kiwi Family Tree

Roroa
Kamoku & Kailee – Kamoku, Kaimi, Keoni
Kamoku (Paparoa range) & (1) Keteri - Kanoa & Koana - Kamoku
       (2) Kalama

Kaimi & Kekona to Arthurs Pass - Kaori & Keely – Ketara
            - Kalasia & Kapali
           -Kalei & Karua – Kawaka
Keoni & Kaimani to Paparoa range - Keanu (1) & Keona – Kupe, Keely,
                  Keilana
            Keio (2) & Keona
Kahika to Okarito – Keka

Kaipo to Three Sisters Mountain → Kapali & Kalasia

Kale & Kuri - Kaimani, Kaliyah. Kale & Kuri to North Buller

Arthurs Pass - Kanai & Kalama – Kekoa, Kalea
      - Kane

Lake Kaniere - Kupe (1) & Kalea – Kamaka, Kohana
Three Sisters - Koro (2) & Kalea
North Buller - Koha & Kamora – Kiyo & Kehi – Koro

Rowi
Kahui to Okarito - Kedar & Kerry – Kahill, Kohia

Kahill & Kiori,
Kaga to Fiordland - Kona

The Owl Family
Lake Kaniere
Odette – Mother of Orion,
Orion - The first Guardian of the Kiwi Kingdom
Olivia - Orion's Sister
Ogilvie - Orion's brother

Owen (Guardian) & Odelia – Ollie, Orchid
Ollie (Guardian) & Odina – Oriel, Odelle
Orchid & Oswin   – Ophira, Owena, Odessa
Oriel (Guardian) & Odele

Lake Mahinapua
Oscar & Olivia – Odin. Odin & Ocena - Orlando

Three Sisters Mountain
Odion (leader) & Oana

About the Author

Rosemary Thomas was born in 1951 and lived in Hokitika on New Zealand's West Coast. Educated at Westland High School, she moved to Perth Australia where she married and had two children. Thomas worked as a registered Nurse. In retirement, writing and making craft to raise funds for charity keep her busy.

Contact at <u>rosemarythomas19@hotmail.com</u>